MIA

A Matthew Paine Mystery

MIA

A Matthew Paine Mystery

Lee Clark

Cypress
River
Media
LLC

Burlington, NC

Cypress River Media, LLC
Burlington, NC 27215
CypressRiverMedia.com

First Edition: April 2022

The publisher is not responsible for websites (or their content) that are not owned by the publisher.

Clark, Lee.
    MIA / Lee Clark. – First edition.
        Pages ; cm. – (A Matthew Paine mystery)
        ISBN 978-1-7368422-8-7 (hardcover) – ISBN 978-1-7368422-7-0 (paperback) – ISBN 978-1-7368422-6-3 (ebook) 1. Paine, Matthew (Fictitious character)

Matthew Paine Classic Mystery series
In order

Pre Kill (prequel short story)

Dead Spots

Prefer Death

MIA

Christmas Punch

Iced

Forbidden Relics (coming soon)

In loving memory of Austin Brett Guthrie (September 30, 1998 - April 20, 2022), a beautiful soul who left this earth too soon. Austin saw the world through the lens of an artist, creating beauty from his unique perspective that gave life to his phenomenal artwork. He showed us the world we see, but don't fully see, in new ways. Austin battled a substance use disorder that ultimately claimed his life. This book is dedicated to Austin and to the brave family he left behind who choose to share his story and the resources that are available in the hope of saving the lives of others.

The opioid problem isn't just in Miami where this book takes place, it's everywhere, it's prevalent, and it's lethal. This book is a work of fiction, but it purposefully provides accurate information about obtaining and administering naloxone, a medication that rapidly reverses an opioid overdose. My wish is to educate everyone about this procedure. You could save a life.

To locate treatment or resources for substance use disorders for yourself or someone you love, wherever you are, see the SAMHSA website: https://findtreatment.samhsa.gov/.

Contents

1 ~ Missing in Miami

It was a hot and sticky Tuesday evening in mid-June. Matthew Paine was laughing and talking over dinner with friends in the informal kitchen of the historic Lingle Plantation. They were discussing whether or not the old historic home was actually haunted, as most of the residents of Peak, North Carolina, the small town outside of Raleigh, North Carolina, where they all lived, thought it to be. In the midst of this haunting conversation, a loud banging made them all jump in their ladder-backed chairs, startled, and glance around the table at each other.

"It's just the front door," said practical, stoic, Homicide Detective Warren Danbury with a chuckle. "I'll get it."

Matthew had become friends with the siblings Leo and Penn Lingle when he'd helped Danbury solve the murder case of their brother, Allan Lingle, the month before. Gathered around the old wooden table in Lingle Plantation, as the locals called Penn and Leo's historic ancestral home that had been in their family for many generations, were Matthew, Danbury, Penn, Leo, and Malcolm. Penn and Leo's brother Allan had been brilliant but autistic, and Malcolm had been his care-giver, ensuring that his basic needs were met and that Allan didn't eat peanut butter and jelly sandwiches all day every day.

Matthew, a young physician at a family practice in Peak, North Carolina, silently cheered as he watched Danbury and Penn becoming an item romantically. Matthew had gotten to know the stoic Danbury two months prior when he'd been pulled inextricably into a murder investigation by an intriguing and alluring patient who visited his office exactly once. Danbury, who looked like a misplaced fabled Viking with his tall solid frame and Nordic good looks, was gaining notoriety for his ability to find murderers and motives. A man of few words, he had long been known for his short staccato questions and responses.

There was a commotion after Danbury opened the door as Dr. Rob, one of the senior partners and Matthew's mentor in the Peak Family Practice, rushed into the kitchen ahead of Danbury. At forty-two, Dr. Rob was trim, fit, and could have been confused with Matthew from behind, though he was slightly over a decade older. Both had broad shoulders over narrow hips and both were over six feet tall, though Dr. Rob missed Matthew's six-foot-three frame by about an inch. Both had wavy brown hair, but Matthew's was slightly darker.

His face ashen, Dr. Rob was clearly panicked. Looking from Matthew to Danbury and back again, he said, "I need your help! My daughter Ariel is missing!" As they all looked on in concern, he added, "I don't know what to do."

Matthew had just had a conversation with Dr. Rob in the hallway of their office before joining Danbury and the Lingles for dinner, which is how Dr. Rob knew where to find both him and Danbury.

"What do you mean, 'missing'?" asked Matthew.

"She's missing from the group that she traveled to Miami with. A group from her school flew down together about three weeks ago, after she finished her spring semester."

Malcolm made his apologies about not wanting to intrude on this personal matter and needing to study for an upcoming exam and slipped quietly from the room.

"OK," said Danbury, calmly. "Tell us what happened. As much as you know. From the beginning."

Dr. Richard Roberts, lovingly called "Dr. Rob" by pretty much everyone in the Peak community, took a deep breath and struggled to speak calmly. "Ariel wants to join the Peace Corps when she graduates, so she is pursuing a degree in health and wellness at UNC-Asheville. She's focused on the Hispanic Latino culture and improving access to and knowledge about healthcare for that population. Ariel volunteered and then raised the money to travel with a group from her school down to a suburb of Miami to work for a month in a cultural enrichment program with the Cuban population there."

As he said this, Matthew thought it sounded rehearsed and Dr. Rob had probably been sufficiently coached to give this "elevator pitch" by his daughter about her program and aspirations.

"When was the last time you heard from her?" asked Danbury.

"Night-before-last," answered Dr. Rob. "She was FaceTiming with me most evenings. She'd send occasional text messages and pictures during the day, mostly about her work there and her friends. But she didn't FaceTime last night, so I texted her this morning. I thought maybe she was just busy, but I didn't get a response. It's unlike her not to respond at all, even if it's just an emoji, but I was trying not to be an overprotective Dad and start worrying."

"How do you know she's MIA? Since when?" asked Danbury.

"Her best friend, Lanie, who's down there with her called just now to say that she didn't come in last night. And Lanie hasn't heard from her either. She's worried because those two are inseparable and have been for years. Lanie is like a second daughter, like the sister that Ariel biologically doesn't have. She was as much at my house when the girls were growing up as her own." Then he added miserably, "If Lanie doesn't know where Ariel is, she really is missing."

"Where is she staying? Where was she last seen? When? And by whom?" asked Danbury in his no-nonsense detective voice.

"They're staying at an old hotel that was partially renovated by this ministry, just outside of the city of Hialeah where they're working. It's one of the suburbs of Miami with a population that's heavily Cuban. Ariel, Lanie, and Ariel's boyfriend Gavin are in a suite with another student from their school. The suite has four bedrooms adjoining a common area. I've only seen the brochures. Her best friend, Lanie, said that Ariel and Gavin left to pick up a pizza last night sometime after 8:30 and neither has been seen since. Lanie has texted and tried to call Ariel but hasn't gotten a response and she's panicked now, so she called me."

"Has her mother heard from her?" asked Matthew.

"No. I called her to confirm that while I was walking over here after

Lanie called me. But Jules doesn't sound worried. She seems to think that she'll turn up. Which is hardly surprising."

"Why isn't that surprising?" asked Matthew.

"Ariel had to grow up early because her mother was still so immature. It's as if the roles reversed. Ariel took care of Jules when she was with her, instead of the other way around. I think it's why Ariel went to school where she did. To be close to her mother in case Jules needed her," answered Dr. Rob with a grimace.

"Have they called the local police?" asked Danbury. "Reported her missing?"

"No. I told Lanie to do that but she said that their group leader, a graduate student who's the fourth member of their suite, blew her off and said that Ariel and Gavin were probably just out exploring and it was too soon to report her missing anyway because the police wouldn't look for her until she'd been gone forty-eight hours. Is that true?"

"Not necessarily, no," said Danbury. "We need to file that report."

"That's what I told her, that she needed to report Ariel as missing," said Dr. Rob in a shaky voice. "I was hoping you could tell me how to proceed, what to do next."

"First, we call the Miami-Dade Police Department. I worked with them recently. Last month." And then Danbury added, as he thumbed through his phone, "I found the contact. I'll call for you. If that's OK with you?"

"Do whatever you need to do to find my daughter," replied Dr. Rob, emphatically. "I'll do whatever we need to do. This is not like her at all. She's so focused on why she's there. She's been preparing for it for months now, so she wouldn't just leave. And definitely not without telling Lanie."

"Detective Warren Danbury here," he said into his phone. "Out of Raleigh, North Carolina. Can I speak with Sergeant Nelson?" After a momentary pause, he added, "Yeah, I'll hold."

"Have you got pen and paper?" Danbury asked Penn, who was sitting quietly at the table listening.

"Sure," she said, as she got up and pulled a small legal pad and pen from a kitchen drawer, handing it to him. "Here."

"Dr. Rob, write down all vital information. Everything about your daughter. Full name. Age. Physical description. Approximate height and weight. Any identifying marks. Preferences. Anything that might be helpful. And text me recent pictures. Matthew can give you the number."

Then, into the phone, Danbury said, "Yeah, I'm still here. OK, I can do that. What's the number?" He motioned for the notepad and pen, which Dr. Rob slid across the table to him, and jotted down a phone number. "Yep, I got it. Thanks."

Matthew poked his phone and shared Danbury's contact information with Dr. Rob. Danbury tore off the sheet of paper with the phone number and handed the pad and pen back to Dr. Rob as the latter sat down at the table to write and Matthew put a hand on his shoulder.

"Katherine Ariel Roberts," muttered Dr. Rob as he jotted information on the pad.

"Ah. I thought you'd called her Katherine earlier. But then, I thought it was just my bad memory for names."

"No, she has gone by Katherine most of her life," said Dr. Rob, looking up from the pad. "When she was little, she loved her middle name because she was a redhead and very into the little mermaid. But then she started school and kids teased her about it so she wanted to go by her first name, Katherine. Then, when she got to college, she decided to go by her middle name because she hates being called Katy or Kathy instead of Katherine. She says, despite the association with a mermaid, Ariel can't be easily shortened to anything else."

"I'm trying to respect her wishes and call her by her middle name now, but I still slip up sometimes," added Dr. Rob before going back to writing and muttering. "Born – August seventh, 2000. Age – nineteen. Height – five feet four inches. Weight – a hundred pounds, maybe? Her eyes are blue, and her hair red, or auburn maybe is better. It's coppery colored. What else did he ask for?"

Behind them, Matthew caught a peripheral glimpse of Danbury poking his phone and then heard him mumbling into it as he went back down the hallway out of earshot.

"Any distinguishing marks like tattoos, piercings, birthmarks, or scars. Anything that would enable a police officer or concerned citizen to see a young woman matching her description and be able to say, 'Yep, that's her' with more certainty."

"Oh, um. She has one of those rod piercings in the top of her ear but you don't see it unless her hair is pulled back. And tiny moon phases tattooed on the insole of her right foot. She said that reminds her of the continuity of it. It's still there no matter how much of it you can actually see. I'm not sure how to describe the piercing."

"A rod cartilage piercing, maybe?" offered Matthew, uncertainly.

"I think it's called an industrial piercing," provided Penn helpfully. "One of my employees in Denver has one." Penn Lingle was in the process of replicating and opening a gym and spa in the Peak area of North Carolina that was patterned after one that she'd opened and was in the process of franchising in Denver. Originally from Peak, Penn had decided to move back home from Denver.

"Which ear?" asked Matthew.

"Oh, left ear," said Dr. Rob as he jotted down this information. "She and Lanie got them together. And I guess she still has her birthmark, though that would only be helpful if," and he choked and couldn't continue.

"Tell me what and where," said Matthew, taking over the writing pad.

"High on her left buttocks, it's heart shaped. Or, at least it was when she was little. If it's important, I guess I could ask Lanie if it's still there. She would probably know."

"OK," said Matthew, adding this information to the list. "And the pictures. Do you have any current ones of her on your phone? And of Gavin?"

"Yeah, a few from a couple of weeks ago when she was home between the end of her spring semester and this trip to Florida," said Dr. Rob as he pulled his phone back out and started poking at it. "How's this one?" he asked as Matthew hovered over his shoulder.

The picture was of a lovely young woman sitting on a brick wall in front of a fountain, leaning slightly on one arm, head tilted slightly, and smiling broadly at whoever was behind the camera. She had sparkling big blue eyes, a bright smile with straight white teeth, and a sprinkling of freckles across her pert little nose. Her most striking feature though, thought Matthew, was her thick long wavy hair that hung over one shoulder. It shone in the filtered sunlight and looked like polished copper.

"Wow, she's really grown up since I met her a couple of years ago," said Matthew. "She's a very pretty young woman," he added, handing the phone back.

"Inside and out," choked out Dr. Rob as he opened a text window on his phone and sent the picture, with a couple of others he'd selected, to both Danbury and Matthew. Poking around on his phone a bit more he added, "Here's one Ariel sent in a text a couple of days ago that includes Gavin. I'm cropping it down to just the two of them to cut out the rest of the group. I'll send it along too."

Danbury returned to the room, reached for the notepad, and started reading off the information into the phone. "What's the address? Where she's staying?" he asked, after having relayed all of the pertinent information from the notepad. "And the name and number of her friend?"

"Lanie James," said Dr. Rob and he gave Danbury the number. Poking through his phone some more, he said, "I'll look up the address." After a moment, Dr. Rob added, "Here it is." He rattled off a street address in Hialeah, the suburb of Miami. "The name of the group she's with is Ministerios de Conexiones Saludables."

"Healthy Connections Ministries," supplied Penn, her brow crinkled in concern.

"Exactly," said Dr. Rob. "It's a very reputable group that has locations around the US and a couple of healthcare facilities that rotate volunteer staff, globally. I checked it out pretty thoroughly. So did Ariel. She was hoping to be able to work at one of their global healthcare facilities next summer."

"OK, thanks," said Danbury into the phone after relaying the information. Turning back to face the others in the kitchen, he asked, "Dr. Rob, can you catch a flight out to Miami tonight?"

"I can throw a few things in a bag and be ready in under an hour."

"Good. Doc, are you free for a few days?" he asked Matthew.

Matthew and Dr. Rob looked at each other. The patient load had been inordinately heavy for the past few months, though it was neither cold and flu season nor back to school immunization and sports physical season. Their most senior partner, Dr. Steven Garner, had concluded that the influx of patients was due to the exponential growth of the little town of Peak over the past couple of years and proposed hiring a Physician's Assistant, a female, to round out their team. They'd made an offer and along with the PA was coming a Resident that she'd had in training at her office in Michigan.

"Our new PA isn't due to start for another week," said Dr. Rob. "She just moved here from Muskegon over the past weekend and I don't think she's settled in yet. But she's got plenty of experience so I wonder if she'd agree to start earlier? I'll call Steven and ask."

"Can I help in any way?" asked Penn, who still donned a sling on her arm after an injury the month before. "I can't do any heavy lifting, but I could maybe schedule your airline tickets, or hotel, a rental car?"

"That would be great," answered Danbury. "You'll need our information. We'll work on the hotel after flights. See if you can get flights out tonight. On whatever airline has them. Out of RDU. And I'll jot down my KTN. The Known Travel Number to add. When you book the airline ticket. So we can skip the long security lines. Here," he added, pulling a piece of paper off of the legal pad they'd been using and scribbling a string of numbers and letters on it.

"Here's mine too, in case I'm actually going," said Matthew, taking the pen and pad from Danbury and jotting on it. "I just got my KTN, but I applied for Global Entry instead of the TSA Precheck clearance thinking that I was going to fly to London to see Cici when my condo restoration work is finished. I wanted to speed up the customs process on the return trip and skip the security lines."

Cici had been Matthew's serious girlfriend for nearly five years before breaking up a year prior. Initially parting ways due to irreconcilable differences in their lifestyle choices, namely that Matthew wanted children and a quiet home life and Cici professed never to want children, they'd only reconnected two months previously. Before agreeing to go to London for a year to work with an important client, Cici had been heavily invested in the social scene in Raleigh where she worked at a high-profile law firm. Since they'd reconnected, though, Cici seemed to be coming around to the idea of having a family. Much to Matthew's surprise, she'd recently said that she might eventually consider it.

"I haven't gotten a KTN," said Dr. Rob, glumly. "I haven't flown anywhere in a couple of years. Not since the last big conference that Steven and I attended in California."

"I can make a copy of your driver's licenses, if you're all OK with that?" asked Penn. "And jot down the email address you want your ticketing information sent to," she added as she handed the pad and pen around.

"If they trust you, I trust you," said Dr. Rob, looking from Matthew to Danbury. Both nodded and Dr. Rob retrieved his license and handed it over before jotting down an email address and handing the note pad back. Then he began poking his phone as he slipped into the next room. Likewise, Matthew pulled his license from his wallet, handed it over to Penn, and jotted his email address on the notepad.

Danbury handed his driver's license to Penn, along with his detective badge. "See if this helps," he said. "With discounts or anything. And use my personal email address."

Penn disappeared down the side hallway with the collection of identifications and Matthew stood staring off into space thinking about what all of this would mean for the next couple of days.

"Why would I need to go?" Matthew quietly asked Danbury.

"Because Dr. Rob's daughter isn't the first," Danbury replied equally as quietly. "She's the third. The third young woman matching that description. At least the third one reported missing in Miami. In a two-week timeframe. She was likely targeted. That isn't good. Either way you look at it. The Miami Dade Police are stretched thin. Finding her quickly is key. Before the trail is cold. Chances of finding her are better, the more people looking."

"Oh," said Matthew, sliding down into a kitchen chair.

"Anything I can do?" asked Leo, looking up at Danbury.

"Probably," said Danbury. "Stay tuned," and he poked some more buttons on his phone and turned his back, walking slowly out of the room, to have what sounded to Matthew like a discussion with his superior at the Raleigh precinct.

"If Dr. Rob can get the new PA in this week instead of next week, then the only issue I have with leaving quickly is my cat. I just uprooted Max a month ago when my house was firebombed and it's not ready for me to move back into yet. He's at Cici's where I've been staying, but I'm not sure she'd be OK with anyone else having codes to get in there while she's in London, so I'm not sure how to handle that."

"You could bring him here. I'll take care of him," offered Leo, brightening at the idea.

"You like cats?"

"I've always wanted a cat or a dog, or maybe both. Our parents wouldn't let us have one, growing up. Our Mom thought that they were messy and wouldn't allow one in the house. Our Dad said pretty much the same thing about the yard. And I haven't settled down in one place long enough since then. Until now."

"Hmm," said Matthew, with one eyebrow raised as his foot tapped and knee jumped under the table in concentration while he pondered what the best plan would be for Max. "He seems to have adjusted well to the move to Cici's house last month. But I was with him there. Thanks for the offer, Leo. I might just take you up on that if Penn's OK with it too."

"If I'm OK with what?" asked Penn, entering the kitchen and handing Matthew his driver's license. She placed the others on the sideboard behind the table.

"Dr. Paine is worried about leaving his cat if he goes to Miami," said Leo. "I told him I'd take care of him here."

Picking up a tablet, Penn answered, "That's sweet, Leo. You always did want a cat or a dog."

"And you wanted a pony. But neither of us ever got them," added Leo with a smirk.

"Yeah, it might be too late for the pony," smiled Penn. "But you're welcome to bring your cat, Matthew. We'll be happy to take care of him. Max, right?"

"That's right. I think he hid when you were at my house, but he's a good big guy. He won't be any trouble, though you might have to put him in a smaller space with his litter box and food bowls until he settles in. He's not used to a place this big."

"Yeah, me neither, these days," echoed Leo. "He can stay in my room until he's happy in the house."

"He likes to snuggle up around my head at night," added Matthew. "If he does that, you know you're in with him. But you end up with 'hair by Max' in the morning, which isn't exactly attractive."

Leo chuckled, "He'll be fine, Dr. Paine. Don't worry about Max."

"Thanks, Leo. And please, just call me Matthew."

"Oh yeah, I keep forgetting that."

They heard rushed footsteps and Dr. Rob abruptly reappeared. "I called Lanie and the birthmark is still there. I told her that the Miami Dade police will want to talk to her, as will we as soon as we arrive. I told her I'll text her to let her know when we'll get in."

"I'm working on that now," said Penn, as she poked the tablet.

"I called Steven. He's going to talk to Megan and see if she's willing to come in early. If so, then he'll call Trina, our office manager, to set something up for either this evening or first thing tomorrow morning to expedite all of the paperwork. But either way, he said, 'go' and he'd hold down the fort here, one way or another."

"Megan?" asked Penn, curiously.

"She's the Physician's Assistant we're hiring," supplied Matthew as he rose, readying himself to go pack. "Megan Sims." Then he added to Dr. Rob, "What about Sadie Peterson, the Resident who's coming with Megan? Is she already here too? She's a second year, right? She could be helpful if she is already here too." As worried as he was for Ariel Roberts, he was also concerned about his patients and he knew that Dr. Rob was as well.

"Yeah, she is. I think the two women got apartments in the same complex until they can get a feel for the area. I think Sadie was hopeful we'd need another PA by the time she's finished. That and the cold weather chased her down here with Megan."

Danbury reentered the room from the hallway and all heads turned to him.

"What do we do now?" asked Dr. Rob as he paced the room running his fingers anxiously through his hair, unable to be still. His hazel eyes weren't twinkling as they usually did, and the boyish smile was also noticeably absent. Instead, creases that Matthew hadn't noticed before furrowed between his eyebrows and above his brow line.

"Now we pack. Quickly. And catch the first flight out. Penn, you'll need a credit card. I'm officially off the clock now. So, I'll give you mine," Danbury said, reaching for his wallet.

"I've got this," said Dr. Rob, holding up a hand. "Put that away," he added, reaching for his wallet and retrieving a credit card from it. "Here," he said, handing Penn a gold card with what looked to Matthew to be a ship's sail and helm emblem. Dr. Rob loved sailing in his spare time and he had gotten a larger sailboat the year before.

"You can fly into multiple airports," said Penn. "FLL, Fort Lauderdale looks to be cheaper but it's farther north. Or MIA, Miami International Airport, looks to be just south of Hialeah."

"MIA," answered Danbury, decisively. "If you can get us in there tonight. It's the closest. Though that doesn't mean much. In Miami traffic. Pick the fastest you can. And a couple of rental cars. An SUV, if you can get it. Big enough for us. And our gear. And maybe a sedan? We'll need hotel rooms, too. We won't likely be there much. Just to catch a few hours' sleep. That's about it, realistically. But book us in Hialeah. Or as near as you can. Please," he added to Penn.

Then, Danbury leaned over, kissed Penn on the top of her head, and said something very uncharacteristic for Danbury, something that Matthew had never heard him say before, "I'm sorry, Penn. I didn't mean to bark orders at you. Or treat you like an assistant."

"It's OK," she smiled up at him. "I volunteered, remember?"

To Matthew, Danbury said, "Bring your concealed carry permit. It's valid in Florida. You have handguns, right? Do you have a lock box?"

Matthew nodded.

"What sort of handguns?"

"I have a Glock 19 and a Colt 1911, with holsters and a lock box for both." The 1911, Matthew had bought as soon as he was old enough to get his concealed carry permit, but it was as much a nod to the history of the pistol as to the function of it, though he had researched that as well before making the purchase. He had gotten Colt's version of it, though the patent had expired and other manufacturers had been making the weapon since before he was born. It was as close as he could get to what Browning originally designed back in 1911, or at least that was his rationale.

"That Glock holds sixteen rounds. Nine-millimeter. But the 1911 magazine holds only eight. Of forty-five ACP, right?"

Matthew nodded, "Yeah, that's right."

"What's the difference between the nine-millimeter and the forty-five ACP?" asked Leo, innocently.

"In size, the nine mil is narrower than the forty-five and the tip is more pointed on the nine mil," replied Matthew. "If you're asking which is better, that's a big debate and people who are really into guns argue that heatedly. What Danbury is asking is mostly about how many rounds the magazines can hold because that can be modified, but mine aren't. As in, how many shots you can fire before you have to change out the magazine or reload one if you don't have another one preloaded. I have two magazines for each gun because I need to drop and reload for shooting competitions. I'd guess probably most people have at least two. A spare is always a good idea."

After a moment's contemplation, Danbury answered, "Box both. And the ammunition. But pack it separately. In the original packaging. Not in the magazines. Pack those empty. You can carry up to eleven pounds of ammunition. Pack what you have. And your holsters. Be sure to pack those. Put it all in a bag to check. We can't fly commercial with weapons in carry-on luggage. That has to be in checked, locked baggage. But that covers us for having them. If we need them later. You OK with that?"

"Yeah, I can do that," answered Matthew a bit reluctantly. Having fired the two handguns only on shooting ranges and in shooting competitions, Matthew sincerely hoped never to have to use either of them for any other purpose. He figured he was a decent shot but that was with nobody firing back; he never wanted to know what that would be like, ever.

"Hope for the best. Prepare for the worst," said Danbury to Matthew's reluctance. Then, turning to Dr. Rob, he asked, "Do you have one?"

Dr. Rob shook his head, "I don't. I've never owned weapons, guns or anything else."

"You both have laptops, right?"

"I do," said Matthew as Dr. Rob was simultaneously answering, "Yes, but I use my tablet more."

"OK, bring those," said Danbury. "And do you have identification? Identifying you as physicians? Like my badge? Anything like that?"

"We have badges from our office, with a shrunken laminated copy of our board certification on a plastic card behind them," answered Matthew. "They have our pictures on them, but it's nothing as official as your badge. Just for patients to see that we are who we say that we are. Mine is clipped to my lab coat in my office, but I can go get it." He was pretty sure Dr. Rob's was on a lanyard that usually hung around his neck, but he didn't offer that information.

"Yeah, grab those. And Leo," he said turning. "If we send you a couple of pictures, can you print them for us? Three copies each of Ariel and Gavin?"

"Yeah, happy to," said Leo. "Does the paper matter?"

"Whatever you have handy. We'll get them after we pack. Meet back here in…" Danbury checked his watch. "Say, forty-five minutes?" he said to Matthew and Dr. Rob.

"That works," said Matthew. "I can't meet you at the airport anyway, because I need to go pack Max, too, and then bring him back here before I can leave."

"Good," said Dr. Rob. "I'm in Cedar Creek, the opposite direction from the airport. So here is good. That gives me fifteen minutes to get there, fifteen to pack, and fifteen minutes back," he said, glancing at his watch. "I have no idea what to pack, but I'll check the weather down there. Thank you," he said to the room at large. "Thank you all."

Reaching behind her and retrieving the drivers' licenses, Penn handed Dr. Rob his license and credit card before he wandered out of the front door distractedly, without closing it behind him.

Matthew quietly asked if there were any leads on the other missing women in Miami.

"Not that I know of," answered Danbury. "They're only just now seeing the pattern. And putting it together. Three young women missing. All redheads. Two might have been a coincidence. But three? In such a short time span? I'm not banking on it. Neither are they. Maybe they'll have more when we get there."

"I hope so. I can't imagine how Dr. Rob feels right now," Matthew added. "Not that I have my own children yet to know, but I can imagine how I'd feel if anything happened to my niece Angel." Angel, his older sister Monica's four-year-old daughter, was his parents' only grandchild. She had chosen Matthew as "her person" from infancy and he adored her.

Penn handed Danbury his drivers' license and badge as he headed out the back door to his big black SUV that was parked in the back driveway behind the house. Matthew heard Danbury driving away from the back as he went out the front door, closing it behind him. As he walked briskly down the long front driveway that ran into the curve of Chapel Street, where his office was located, Matthew felt a slight breeze. He saw it stirring in the ancient oak and maple trees overhead and wondered if an evening storm was imminent. He slipped through the side door into his office to retrieve his ID, and then back out into the parking lot where he slid into his black Corvette. Firing it up, he headed quickly west out of town toward Cici's house in Quarry.

On the way, he called his neighbor, Mrs. Drewer, to tell her he'd be away for a few days and ask if she could check in on the work crew at his condo, which was on the other end of the unit from hers. She readily agreed and, after he explained the situation, she clicked her tongue and told him to let her know if there was anything else she could do to help. Matthew had initially thought she was the nosiest neighbor ever and he'd never have told her anything about his personal life, but they'd gotten to be friends, and he trusted her completely to keep an eye on things while he was away.

Next, he called his sister Monica and told her what was happening and that he'd be out of town. He wasn't telling his parents, just yet, because he knew his mother worried about him. But he also knew that she prayed at least as much as she worried, so he figured he'd eventually call her too when he knew more.

2 ~ PLANNING THE WORK

The three men reconvened at the Lingle Plantation and tossed their bags into Danbury's big SUV. Leo handed off a set of pictures in large manila envelopes to each of them, one of Ariel blown up and printed in color, and one of Gavin that wasn't quite as large or as clear but Matthew noted that you could see his basic facial features pretty well. Leo had also laminated the pictures for them, Matthew realized.

"Nice work," said Danbury.

"I figured in the humidity, they wouldn't hold up long, just on plain paper, so I printed them on card stock," said Leo. "And I've just gotten a new toy, a laminating machine, to protect some charts I'll need to reference a lot for business school. So, I thought I'd try it out."

"That's grand. Thanks so much!" said Dr. Rob, choking a little at the helpfulness of a new acquaintance.

Matthew left his Honda Element that he'd driven back from Cici's house at the Lingles' residence and left the keys for Penn and Leo. Having both only recently decided to move back to Peak, neither of them had bought a car yet and Penn was planning to return her rental as soon as she'd found a car to purchase.

After setting Max up, Matthew provided Leo with all of the relevant information about feeding and caring for his furry friend. Checking to ensure that Leo had his cell number programmed into a new phone to contact him with any questions, Matthew climbed into the SUV for the trip to the RDU airport.

"Penn got us on the last flight from RDU to MIA tonight. It was full. She also got us upgraded to first class. Using my badge. Without extra charge," added Danbury, as they headed quickly out of Peak. "We need to discuss logistics. How to handle this situation tactically. Dr. Rob, some of this won't be easy to hear. Let's start with what we know so far."

Taking a deep breath, Dr. Rob replied from the back seat, "I'm as ready as I'll ever be. It's OK, don't sugar coat it. I am completely willing to do whatever we need to do to find my daughter."

"First of all, her description. Your daughter's. It matches two others reported missing. In the past two weeks. That implies a pattern. Same general height and weight. All three redheads. Your daughter, though, is the only real one. The other two have hair dyed red. The other two are slightly older. Both in their twenties. One twenty-three. The other twenty-five."

"OK," said Dr. Rob, slowly. "What does that mean?"

"Maybe nothing," said Danbury. "There are lots of people reported as missing. Daily. Particularly in an area the size of Miami. And all of its little burgs. But these three share a general description. Ariel's description caught their attention. The officers down there. And they are just beginning to put it together. The Miami-Dade police compared locations. Where the missing women were last seen. The other two were last seen near a popular bar. In a hip area of Miami. It's on the water. On a river just inland from the coast. Off of a busy waterway channel. Did you ever hear your daughter mention Brickell? It's one of the suburbs of Miami. It's where the other two women live."

"Brickell," repeated Dr. Rob. "Is it near Hialeah?"

"Maybe nine miles. As the crow flies. But that could take an hour. Easily. 'Near' is a relative term in Miami. Or so I gather," replied Danbury. "One place can be two miles from another. And it could still take a half hour to get to. Depending on the time of day. And the direction you're trying to travel. You said they were picking up a pizza, right? She and her boyfriend. And it was what time, exactly? And do you know where?"

"Not exactly. Lanie was guessing they left some time after 8:30 but she didn't look to see. I can text and ask her about the location while we travel."

"Yeah, for our knowledge. The local Miami-Dade guys are probably talking to her. Or already have. They were headed that way earlier. When I spoke to Sergeant Nelson."

"OK, hang on," said Dr. Rob, as he poked at his phone.

The car got quiet for a few moments and then Dr. Rob said, quietly, after reading from his phone, "Their favorite pizza oven is in downtown Miami, just north of the place you were asking about, Brickell. It was after eight-thirty, nearly nine, when they left the group by Rydz, that service you can use an app to get rides with." He held his phone up, reading, and then said, "Even with traffic and delays, Lanie says she didn't start worrying until about eleven because Gavin was with Ariel. But then she woke up their group leader, Shawn Rawls, who blew her off saying that they were just out having a good time and he told Lanie to go to bed."

"They went into downtown Miami?" clarified Danbury. "Why would they go that far? And by Rydz. Just to get pizza?"

"They did," answered Dr. Rob. "And I have no idea why they'd go pick it up themselves instead of having it delivered, particularly that far away. But placing them in that area, what does that mean?"

Danbury took a deep breath before answering, "It could mean Ariel was targeted. Someone was targeting pretty young redheads. In that area."

"For what?" asked Dr. Rob in alarm.

"It could be just a coincidence," said Danbury, which brought Matthew's head around sharply to stare at him. Matthew knew that neither he nor Danbury believed in coincidence, but probably for very different reasons.

"I don't believe in coincidence," said Dr. Rob bleakly from the back seat. "So why would someone target redheads?"

"It's rare. Very rare these days," said Danbury, half to himself.

"What is?"

"That women are snatched. Not usually in the US. Not anymore. Not these days. It's too hard to detain them. Or to move them. Not after nine-eleven."

"Snatched? You mean abducted?" asked Dr. Rob in alarm as Danbury just nodded. Then, after a moment's pause, Dr. Rob added softly, "But I guess that's better than the alternative in terms of finding her. Maybe it is."

"It is," agreed Danbury and all three of them knew that the alternative Dr. Rob hadn't mentioned aloud was murder by a crazed serial killer with a fetish for or vendetta against redheaded women.

"The good news," said Danbury, "is that neither of the other two has turned up. No…remains. All three women are just missing."

"So far," added Dr. Rob, saying what Danbury hadn't, "she can't be dead. I know this sounds crazy, but I just don't think she's been killed. I am worried that she's in serious danger, though. Tell me more about this 'snatched' scenario. Abducted to where? By whom? For what purpose?"

"That's what I wanted to explain. The dynamics of all of that. There's more to it than I know. But I'll share what I do know. From some earlier training. Abducting and shipping girls and women IN to the country. That's more prevalent now. Far less prevalent is shipping them out. It all tightened down after nine-eleven."

"That's good news, I guess," said Dr. Rob. "Are they taken and somehow detained INSIDE the US?"

"I'm not sure. It would be difficult. With technology these days. Very hard to hold American women. Against their will, anyway. But I can tell you how it works. In general terms."

"OK," said Dr. Rob from the back seat. "The more I understand, the better I can help to find her."

"There's a buyer and a seller," Danbury explained. "And many layers of people in between. And more layers between the snatcher and seller. Snatchers are the first point of contact. For the girls and women. They're usually handsome guys. Very charming. They are provided with a general description. Of whatever the buyer wants. If that's what this is, probably young redheads in this case. The snatchers usually prey on girls in rough situations, though. Girls who have an unhappy homelife. Or an abusive one. Maybe they dream of stardom. As a singer. Or an actress."

Danbury steered onto I-40, hit the gas pedal hard, and continued, "Anyway, the snatcher quickly builds a relationship. Maybe it starts online. Or maybe in a library. Or a coffee shop. Somewhere public that seems safe enough. He tells them the things they want to hear. That they're pretty. Or that he loves them. That they can be a star. Whatever their insecurity, he learns it quickly. And uses it. He manipulates his target into trusting him. And then he snatches her. But none of that fits with Ariel. Obviously."

Nobody had to tell Danbury to hurry up because both Matthew and Dr. Rob were hanging onto their seats and the hand holds above them, as it was.

"The snatcher hands her off to the next person," Danbury continued. "The next link in the chain. At a prearranged time and location. The hand off spot. He gets paid, usually in cash. Or sometimes electronically. And he returns to his snatching. He knows nothing of the seller. Or the buyer. Just the next person in the chain who picks her up. And maybe picks up several others. And takes them to the next location. He gets paid. And then awaits instructions. For his next pick-up and delivery. And the women are moved on. Likely to multiple locations. By multiple people in the chain. To make it harder to track them. Eventually, the women are collected. Usually in a central location."

"They're likely drugged. To capture them to begin with. And to keep them quiet. While they're moved around. To keep them calm. Fentanyl, maybe. It's a synthetic opioid. But you know that," Danbury added, acknowledging the profession of both Matthew and Dr. Rob. "The point is that it's easily and readily available. Nothing addictive like heroin. Because they have to be made presentable for the buyer. At some point they get dressed up, made up. And they're put in front of a camera. They're filmed for the buyer. And the buyer gets to choose. From the videos."

"That's," began Dr. Rob and he hesitated, "that's sick!"

Matthew could hear him choke on those last words.

"It is, but it's better. Better than the serial killer that you alluded to. Because it buys us time. The whole process could take a couple of months."

"A couple of months, where?" asked Dr. Rob.

"That's what we need to find out," said Danbury, as he took the first airport exit and zipped through the slower zones to park in the parking deck. "If Ariel has been snatched. That's exactly what we're going to find out."

Danbury found a spot beside a column on the second level of the airport long-term parking lot and they all jumped out, grabbing their bags. Danbury clicked to lock the SUV remotely, and they trooped across the walkway and into the top departure level of the RDU airport.

Each of them had downloaded the Delta App on their phones. Dr. Rob had only a duffle bag of clothing and necessities as a carry-on. Matthew and Danbury each had carry-on bags with computers and they were able to quickly check their baggage containing the munitions, scan their phones, get their boarding passes, and get in the line for security. Danbury and Matthew looked at each other and then back at Dr. Rob.

"Mind if we meet you on the other side?" asked Danbury.

"Be my guest," said Dr. Rob. "I would, too, if I could."

Matthew felt bad for Dr. Rob as he stood in the line preparing to remove his shoes and go through the body scanner. Meanwhile, Matthew and Danbury walked straight through the nonexistent precheck line, through a metal detector, shoes and all, and out the other side.

Finally reconvening on the other side of the security line, Dr. Rob was shaking his head as he put his shoes back on and stuffed his belongings in his pockets. They headed for gate D6, from which their flight was due to leave in a mere twenty-five minutes.

"Boarding will start any time now," said Danbury. "Let's talk for a minute. About what we need to do. When we hit the ground."

As they arrived at the gate, Matthew and Dr. Rob slid into chairs on either side of Danbury and Dr. Rob tucked his carry-on bag under his feet. Matthew and Dr. Rob were leaning in to hear what he had to say above the repeated overhead announcements for final boarding calls and gates closing.

"We don't have a command center," said Danbury. "We're on our own without the police databases. But we're going to need to create a repository. To contain the information that we gather. Because we're going to need to split up. To cover more ground. As fast as we can. Maybe an online set of documents. In a location where we can all add information. And all access what's there."

"I can set that up," said Matthew. "And send you each a link to it, so we can access the information from our laptops, tablets, or our phones on the go."

"Good. We'll have two rental cars waiting for us when we land. I'll take one and head to the police station. To get their latest update and hear what they've learned. You two take the other. Go to where Ariel is staying. Go through her room. The police already did by now. But," he said, indicating Dr. Rob. "You might see something they missed. Something they wouldn't know to look for. Of importance to your daughter. Ask anyone who's still up about where she'd gone. Since she's been down here. Everywhere she's been. See if anybody knows why she'd go so far away. Particularly that late on a week night. Just to pick up a pizza."

"OK," said Matthew as Dr. Rob nodded agreement.

"Our next step will be canvassing the area where she went. To the pizza place and surrounding area. Unless you learn something new. Or unless the police did. We also need to canvass the hospitals. With pictures of both of them. Ariel and Gavin. In case they showed up there without ID. It's always possible. The police have probably already sent descriptions. But pictures are better. And shown in person is best. Directly to the Emergency Department staff. If they've seen or admitted anyone without ID, anyone who matches the pictures, the ED staff will know. We'll ask for staff from the last twenty-four hours."

"We'll arrive at the gate at 11:05," added Matthew, checking his watch. "According to the flight information, it's almost a two-hour flight."

"Yeah, it would have been a twelve-hour drive, and that's without stopping," said Dr. Rob looking around at the crowded waiting area. "So, I'm glad Penn got us on this flight. And thank you both for coming with me. I have no idea what to do in this situation and I'm not thinking clearly anyway."

Danbury and Matthew just nodded sympathetically at that and Danbury continued, "What we need in the documents, the ones we'll share. Pictures for us to access. The information we already have. We add any information we learn. As we learn it. Who told us, what, and when. It's not the police database. But it'll work."

"OK, I can create the documents on the plane, "said Matthew. "With everything we know so far. And then I'll upload them to a site and share it with you when we land."

"I'll help with whatever I can think of," said Dr. Rob.

"Good. You two sit together in the double seats. I'll take the one across the aisle. This plane is only four across. Two and two. Except in first class. Where it's one and two. I've downloaded some case files. Some that Nelson sent me. About the other two missing women. I'll review those on the plane. And let you know if anything pops."

As they were nodding in agreement about what would happen next, Dr. Rob's phone chimed. Looking down at it, he said, "It's Gayle, Gavin's mom, returning my call. I need to take this."

"Hi Gayle," he said and paused. "Yes, that's what Lanie said. When was the last time you heard from Gavin? Oh," he said in disappointment. "I was hoping you'd heard from him since yesterday. We're about to board a plane now to fly down there and start searching. I'll be in airplane mode for the next couple of hours, but if you hear anything new, text me? I'll check my phone as soon as we land."

After another pause, he said, "You are?" He put his hand over the phone and asked Danbury if another person would be helpful.

"If she's willing. To come down and get in the thick of it. She can be our command center operator. Tell her to bring a computer. If she has one. And is willing to do that."

Dr. Rob relayed the information just as the boarding call for first class was announced. He ended the call and scooped up his carryon bag as Matthew and Danbury stood up, stretched, and approached the counter to board the plane.

"She'll be flying down in the morning, with a laptop computer," Dr.

Rob reported.

"It's going to be a long night," said Danbury as he scanned his ticket and started down the ramp. "Maybe we can catch a few winks on the plane. After we finish with our files."

"I don't think I can sleep," said Dr. Rob, following suit. "Not even a few winks."

"I'll try," said Matthew, as he followed the others down the ramp to the plane.

"I can sleep on a rock," said Danbury. "Any time I get the chance. You learn to do that. To sleep when you can. And eat when you can. In my line of work. You never know when you might do either one again."

"Duly noted," said Dr. Rob. "I can try."

After they stowed Dr. Rob's carry-on bag, they took their seats and buckled in for takeoff. As soon as the plane was in the air and they were told that they could do so, they pulled out their electronic devices and set to work. Dr. Rob and Matthew had their heads together over Matthew's laptop computer on one side of the aisle, and Danbury was lost in thought as he read through the files he'd downloaded onto his laptop on the other.

Part way through the trip, they swapped seats and Danbury fed the information he'd gleaned from the files to Matthew, who copied in the relevant bits to their document collection. He named the folder *Locate A Roberts* and promised to share it with the others as soon as they were on the ground and he could get a connection to upload it to the cloud.

None of them managed to sleep during the flight and they were all wide awake when they began to see the lights on the shoreline getting closer as the plane veered in from its ocean path toward the coastline of Miami Beach. From his window seat, Matthew could see lights from tall buildings along the coastline and their reflection in the surrounding waters.

As the plane descended, Matthew peered out to see streets and more streets beneath him laid out neatly in grid patterns, with some veering off at odd angles. Then he realized that some of what he thought had been streets were actually canals and waterways because, unlike the streets that he was seeing, they sparkled with light reflecting off the water. Houses and buildings lined either side of those, as they did the streets, and Matthew realized that the preferred mode of transportation in Miami might be more varied than at home in Peak.

As he took it all in, Matthew wondered, idly, if people down here traveled as much by water as by road. He'd heard that driving in Miami was nightmarish in the best of conditions so maybe that was a viable option.

Overhead, they heard the announcement that all electronic devices should be off, tray tables stowed, and the like, but they had already finished with electronic devices and all three men were ready to get on the ground and get to work. Dr. Rob fidgeted in his seat and Matthew figured he was having the same adrenaline spike that he, himself, was experiencing. Then they heard the landing gear drop.

Watching through the window, Matthew could see that the plane dipped lower and banked slightly. Then, as it dipped more drastically, he began to see what looked like acres of pavement beneath that were crisscrossed in all direction with rows of blue and green lights. Occasionally, those were interspersed with blocks of yellow lights and smaller red ones. One more turn and they were approaching for final descent. As the wheels touched down a few minutes later, Matthew could see a fringe of palm trees in the distance on one side that were silhouetted against low light-colored buildings, which were lit from above and below. He could see similar groups of buildings farther away on the other side of the runway.

They taxied and waited, intermittently, and Matthew thought that he couldn't remember waiting in a queue to get into an airport, though he'd waited in many to take off from them. As soon as they were at the gate and the fasten seatbelt sign was turned off, all three of them jumped to their feet, with Dr. Rob sliding forward slightly to allow Matthew to stand up too. They formed an imposing wall through which it would have been difficult to see from behind them.

Each of them pulled out phones and switched them out of airplane mode and checked for incoming messages.

"Change of plan," said Danbury as he poked at his phone. "Sergeant Nelson is meeting us in Hialeah. At Ariel's suite. He had the same idea. To see if Dr. Rob can tell us anything new. We'll get both vehicles. Then drive them there together."

"Gayle Blevins is flying in on the first flight in the morning, arriving at 9:30 here," announced Dr. Rob. "She wants to know if we can pick her up or if she needs to get transportation. I'm assuming she needs her own."

"She does," said Danbury. "If she's comfortable driving down here. Another rental car would be ideal."

"I'll tell her," responded Dr. Rob, poking his phone.

Sensing the tension and wanting to add some levity to dispel it, Matthew glanced at his phone and said, "Max says hello."

"Who?" asked Dr. Rob, looking up seriously.

"My cat," said Matthew. "Just trying to lighten the mood," he added as Danbury grimaced at him.

"Nice try, anyway," said Dr. Rob, going back to poking at his phone.

Just then, the doors were opened and they were the first to exit the plane. They made their way up the ramp and then through the airport, following the signs to baggage claim. Matthew's and Danbury's small hard-sided bags, each of which were cable-tied closed due to the locked steel boxes containing the firearms and munitions inside, arrived surprisingly quickly on the conveyor belt.

Following the signs to ground transport, they ended up at a desk that seemed to handle rentals for multiple companies late at night. A single frazzled-looking clerk was manning the counter and attempting to gather their information, but he seemed to process what they were asking for very slowly.

"Two cars?" he repeated. "Going to Hialeah?"

"Yes. One sedan and one larger. Preferably an SUV," answered Danbury, reiterating what he had previously requested twice.

"Oh, OK," answered the clerk with a furrowed brow as he looked at a screen and clicked the computer keys. "Did you want the insurance on those?"

Danbury turned to Dr. Rob, on whose credit card it was all going and he nodded. "Both cars need us all listed. Right? To enable any of us to drive either of them?"

"Yeah, but that'll cost you extra," said the clerk, less than helpfully.

"How much extra?" asked Danbury.

The clerk stared, perplexed, at the computer screen. "Never mind," said Dr. Rob, impatiently. "Just put us all on there. Both cars. And insure them both."

"I need to see your identification," said the clerk.

They all handed over their driver's licenses and just when Matthew was beginning to think that it'd be the next day before they got out of the airport, the clerk finally handed them all back with two sets of keys and a wad of paperwork. "The shuttle is right outside. Just take it to lot F and the cars will be there about half way down on row five. Then, follow the signs out that say North LeJeune, Hialeah," he added, helpfully.

"Thanks," said Danbury tersely and a bit crossly, and they trooped out to the curb to catch the shuttle. A blast of moist warm air hit them like a physical blow as they stepped through the glass doors that opened automatically for them. Matthew realized that the temperature usually was hotter in Miami than it currently was, though it was still at least eighty degrees this late at night.

He was glad that he'd opted for his dry-fit collared shirt with khaki pants, and he wished he'd left off the collar. In that moment, he was also thankful that he'd packed shorts because he knew from the forecast that it was going to be over ninety degrees the next day. If the forecast was right, the next few days promised to be scorchers. June in Miami, he decided, must be more like August back home in Peak with little variability between night and day temperatures, and all of it scorching hot and humid.

"That took five times longer than it should have," groused Danbury as they walked away. Matthew hadn't heard much in the way of complaint from Danbury, ever, that he could recall.

"I was beginning to think I was going to have to climb over the counter and go enter the information myself," Matthew chimed in, also a bit the worse for wear, feeling both the late hour and the humidity.

Dr. Rob didn't respond. If he had negative thoughts on the experience, he'd chosen not to share them, realized Matthew. And that was probably wise. "There it is," Dr. Rob said, pointing to a shuttle that had just pulled away from the curb and headed away from them down the street. "I guess another will be along shortly," he added. "At least I hope so."

After another twenty minutes had passed and they were all feeling anxious with the wasted time, Matthew was just about to step back inside to ask the clerk about the next shuttle, and if there was another one coming, when one appeared amidst the thinning traffic from around the corner. As the door swooshed opened in front of them, a welcome blast of cool dry air hit them and they clambered aboard. The driver asked which lot and which row. Danbury looked down to check the paperwork and Matthew quickly replied, "Lot F, Row five," and took a seat.

"Ariel had already told me that nothing, neither traffic nor anything else, moves particularly quickly in Miami," said Dr. Rob as he plopped down next to Matthew. "I had no idea she meant that quite so literally."

"Frustrating, but true," added Danbury as he took the seat across from them.

"It's probably the heat and humidity," added Matthew. "Who would feel like moving at all, much less fast, in this climate?"

"We get the cars," said Danbury. "Put in the address. Meet up in Hialeah. Nelson will meet us there. Then, we probably go to the restaurant." Checking his watch, he added, "It's nearly midnight now. I wonder how late things are open here?"

"And on a Tuesday night," added Matthew. "Are we checking into the hotel at all tonight?"

"Yeah. I guess we should," answered Danbury. "We do need some sleep. At some point. We might manage a couple of hours. After the downtown trip, maybe. At least, that's my guess. Unless Nelson and his crew have it covered. It's doubtful. But maybe they have."

3 ~ LAY OF THE LAND

The car lot was well lit as they trooped off of the shuttle bus carrying and rolling their meager luggage. "There's the SUV," pointed Danbury. "And the white sedan. What is that? A Hyundai?"

"Yeah, it's a Sonata," replied Matthew as he pulled the key fob from his pocket and popped the trunk. He and Dr. Rob tossed in their bags and climbed in, adjusting mirrors and seats as they went. Matthew had offered to drive, given Dr. Rob's current emotional state of worry for his daughter, and the older doctor had readily agreed. Dr. Rob had pulled a charging cord from his bag before tossing the bag in the trunk, and he plugged his phone in and punched the address into it, having opted for navigating over driving.

"OK, we're going to go north on 953 just ahead here. Then left onto Okeechobee Road, which is Highway 27. It goes right by Hialeah and we'll get off there before we get into Hialeah proper. It's not far from the airport at all. Less than ten minutes at this time of night with no traffic."

"Is that how you pronounce that? I saw it on the map but I wasn't going to attempt it."

"What, Highway 27?" asked Dr. Rob, trying to make a joke, but the smile never made it to his eyes as he glanced over at Matthew. "That's how Ariel was pronouncing it anyway. She and her friends were joking about it, using it as an affirmative response to everything. Like 'okey-dokey,' I guess. Just being goofy, but they apparently thought their banter about it was hilarious. She said it was a location joke, like a bad dad joke, and that I'd have to be here to appreciate it. I'm here, but I still don't," he added, bleakly.

"Okeechobee," responded Matthew, with a slight smile.

"Yeah, something like that," said Dr. Rob.

"Hialeah. What does that mean in Spanish?"

"I don't think it's Spanish. From what Ariel told me, I think it's attributed to native American Indians. And it's something to do with a prairie. Pretty prairie, or high prairie maybe. Something like that."

"A prairie in south Florida?" asked Matthew.

"Yeah, between Biscayne Bay and the Everglades, I believe."

They rode the rest of the way in silence, except for Dr. Rob pointing out the turns, until they pulled up in front of a three-story building that looked older but had been partially restored. The building, as a whole, was well lit as was the parking lot. Matthew could see that the bottom two floors appeared to have new stucco and paint applied and the outdoor walkways were lined with lighting, though the top floor was dark.

"It's an old hotel for the racetrack here," said Dr. Rob.

"A racetrack?"

"Yeah, horse racing. It was built back in the 1920s, I think. I guess maybe we pull around over there to park," Dr. Rob added, pointing.

"Got it," said Matthew as he blinked from the headlights in the rearview mirror and realized that Danbury was still directly behind him. "I'll just pull in here. There's a police car on the other side of that stairwell so we're probably in the right place."

An old outdoor metal and cement staircase rose to the second and third floors and continued as a walkway along an outside corridor with doors along it on both floors. The suites were obviously accessed from the outside, noted Matthew, not from an inside hallway unless there was more than one entrance to each one. It looked like every fourth of the original doors was still a door. He could see where the texture of three door-sized spaces was different in between each remaining door, though it looked like someone had worked hard to blend it all in. On the third floor, which was unrenovated, he confirmed that suspicion when he noticed that there were three extra doors between each of those on the second floor. That must be how they made the suites from old hotel rooms, he thought to himself.

As they climbed out of the car and paused for Danbury to join them before ascending the stairway quickly to the second floor, Dr. Rob confirmed Matthew's assumptions. "Second floor, Suite 208. I don't think that top floor has been finished yet. From what Ariel described, I think it's just the first two floors that are in use. The first floor has offices and rooms where they teach classes, host some events, and work with clients. The second floor houses the volunteer workers," he added as they climbed.

When they reached the top, they saw light spilling from an open doorway and a uniformed police officer stepped out onto the walkway. Danbury went forward and made the introductions. "Sergeant Nelson? I'm Detective Warren Danbury. This is Dr. Matthew Paine. And Dr. Richard Roberts," he said indicating each in turn and they shook hands all around. "Thanks for meeting us here. And for all of your help."

"No problem," said the stout but sturdy man who looked to be in his early fifties with greying dark hair that was receding above the temples on either side of his forehead. "It comes with the job. Happy to help. I just wish I had more information and encouragement for you. My team didn't find anything helpful in the room here," he said, waving at the door he'd just come out of. "But maybe you'll have more luck, since you know the young woman well."

"I do," said Dr. Rob. "And I certainly hope so. We need something to go on, don't we, to know where to look? Could anyone here tell you why she'd have gone to a pizza oven so far away that late at night? That doesn't sound like her. She's fun-loving, but practical and hardworking to a fault. Late night pizza isn't unusual for her. It's the distance that's odd."

"Not yet. And there are pizza menus from more local places in their suite, so that is odd. One of the regular volunteers here said that they'd all gone down to that area one evening as part of a tour to show the new workers the lay of the land. They went to a bar down there. Well really, it's a whole event center, not just a bar. Dock Side. It's on the waterfront down there on the river. Some of them ordered from the pizza oven vendor truck and liked the pizza. So, they had been there before. Right after they arrived."

Sergeant Nelson hesitated as he flipped open a notepad and checked his notes. "Almost three weeks ago. They arrived on the second of June, and they went downtown on the tour on the evening of Tuesday the fourth. But why Ms. Roberts and Mr. Blevins would go all the way back down there when there are so many pizza places so much closer? That, nobody seemed to know."

"Was the pizza picked up?" asked Danbury.

"Pardon?" asked Nelson.

"They ordered a pizza. Then went to pick it up. Did they get that far? Did they pick up the pizza?"

Nelson flipped through his notepad, looking puzzled. "I don't know," he finally replied. "I don't have that information in my notes. I'll check on that. We're also trying to track down the Rydz driver to see if he or she can tell us anything. Like, did the driver just drop them? Wait for them? Take them somewhere else afterward?"

"Good. That's a good start. Have you talked to Ariel's friend? Lanie James. Does she know why Ariel might have gone down there? That far away, during the week. There had to have been a reason."

"Ah, no. We didn't think it was odd that they went down there because it's a hot spot for the younger set. Just that the stated reason was for the pizza. That's what we thought was odd."

"OK, let's start there," said Danbury. "Where's Lanie?"

Nelson stepped aside and pointed to the door he'd exited as they came up the steps, "Just inside there."

Dr. Rob walked through the door first and Matthew followed behind, but he stepped back quickly as a young woman jumped up from a sofa in the sitting area and launched herself, sobbing, at Dr. Rob. "I'm so sorry! I'm so sorry!" she kept repeating as she clung to him.

"Lanie, it's not your fault that she's missing," Dr. Rob said soothingly, as he pulled her back, brushed strands of mottled and streaked blond hair out of her face, and wiped a tear from her reddened cheek. "It's not your fault. And you're likely the best person to help us find her."

"But I always know where she is! And I should have gone with her.

Or called the police last night, like I wanted to," she shot an angry glare at a gangly youth who was sprawled on the other end of the sofa as she spoke. At that, he got up, sulkily, and went through the door farthest to the right, presumably his bedroom, and shut the door firmly behind him.

"OK, let's start from the beginning," said Dr. Rob, pulling Lanie over to the sofa and sitting down beside her. "Oh, and this is Detective Warren Danbury and my associate, Dr. Matthew Paine," he gestured to each in turn.

Lanie nodded shyly at the other two men and asked quietly, "What do you need to know? How can I help you find her?"

"Tell me whatever you can remember. About last night. Before they left," said Danbury, stepping forward. "Was anything different? Out of the ordinary?" He perched on the sofa on the other side of Lanie. When Lanie looked confused by the questions, Danbury clarified, "Were Ariel and Gavin arguing, for example?"

"Oh. No. Nothing like that. She wanted to go get pizza from that one specific place that we'd been to before. Gavin wasn't excited about going all the way down there to get it, but they didn't argue about it. She wanted to go, so he went with her."

"Do you know why? Why she wanted to go there? Instead of someplace closer?" asked Danbury. When Lanie hesitated, pondering, Danbury continued, "Is the pizza that much better down there?"

"I didn't think so," replied Lanie. "Neither did Gavin. He said so. But he really does love her, so when she insisted, he agreed."

"Did they order the pizza before they left?"

"Yeah, they called and ordered it."

"And then they got a ride down there?"

"Right, they used the Rydz app and left. I wasn't worried at first. I knew it would take them at least twenty minutes to get down there, even at that time of night without the awful traffic. But it's still downtown Miami, so it would take a while. And then that long back. So, an hour wasn't ridiculous, but when it had been two hours, I started to worry. They wouldn't have hung out down there. Not for any reason I can think of."

"And you wanted to call the police? To report her missing. Last night," prompted Danbury when Lanie hesitated and paused.

"Yeah, I did. But Shawn said they couldn't do anything anyway until she'd been missing for at least twenty-four hours, and maybe more like forty-eight."

"Then what did you do?"

"I kept texting and trying to call her. Shawn told me they'd come back eventually and just to go to bed because we had a group coming in first thing this morning. I was supposed to be doing a puppet show about getting shots for the children. So, I tried but I couldn't sleep. I kept texting and then I started calling her. The first time I called, it just rang. After that, her phone was sending me straight to voicemail."

"That's what I've been getting too," said Dr. Rob. "And her location won't display."

"We've checked into that," said Nelson from the doorway. "The phone for the number that Ms. James gave us is either turned off or not operational. We can't ping it. We're working on a last known location, but we haven't gotten that back yet."

"Did you try to reach Gavin?" Danbury asked Lanie.

"Yeah, when I couldn't get her, I did. Same thing. Straight to voicemail," replied Lanie miserably. "I didn't sleep much at all and then I kept trying to call her all day. I just knew something was wrong, so I told Marianna that she'd been gone since last night and then I called you. If I hadn't, Marianna was going to," she said to Dr. Rob.

"Marianna?" asked Danbury.

"Marianna Martinez. She's the Site Director of Ministerios de Conexiones Saludables here. She floats between this location and one over in Little Havana, but we're not allowed to go there. She says it's too dangerous. She sleeps here, but she's over there a lot too, during daytime hours."

"Where is she now?" asked Danbury, over Dr. Rob's shoulder.

"She was just here. I think she went back to her apartment. It's the last door on the end of the hallway to the right."

Turning back to Lanie, Dr. Rob asked again, "And you have no idea why Ariel would want to go all the way into downtown Miami for a pizza?"

Lanie chewed her bottom lip as she pondered the question. "Ariel has always had a mind of her own," she said, slowly. "Ever since we were little. I'm used to that so I didn't really think about it much."

"And now?" asked Danbury. "Now that you're thinking about it? Is there any reason you can think of? Even if it seems unimportant. Some little thing might be helpful."

"I just don't know," said Lanie, miserably. "I should know. She's my best friend. I should always know. I should have asked. I should have stopped her from going all the way down there," and she started sobbing as Dr. Rob put his arms around her and tried to calm her down. The anguish on his face was apparent as her sobbing continued with deeper and deeper shuddering breaths.

"I'll go talk to Marianna," said Danbury as he stood to slip away from the scene.

"We have a statement from her," said Nelson, stepping aside to let Danbury pass. "But she couldn't tell us anything. She said she wasn't here until later last night and she hadn't seen Ms. Roberts since earlier in the afternoon when they were finishing up with their clients for the day."

"It's OK, Lanie," soothed Dr. Rob. "It's going to be OK. We'll find her. We'll keep looking until we do," and he continued with the soothing reassurances, rubbing her back gently, until her breathing finally slowed. Matthew wondered if the reassurances were as much for Dr. Rob as they were for Lanie and, as he caught a glimpse of the anguish on the older doctor's face, he wondered if he believed any of what he'd just said or if it was all for Lanie's benefit. Dr. Rob did manage to calm her, just as he calmed and reassured the panicked children that he treated at their family medical practice back in Peak. The man had a true gift, thought Matthew, and he'd always admired Dr. Rob's ability to reassure their young patients.

"Could you look through her things in her room?" asked Matthew of Lanie and Dr. Rob. "Sergeant Nelson says the police went through them, but Danbury had wanted you to look too. Does she keep a journal or anything like that?"

"She isn't into journaling that I know of," said Dr. Rob. "Lanie?"

"No, she isn't. I had a diary when we were little but I don't think Ariel ever did."

Lanie rose and led Dr. Rob off to the left, "Her room is in here," she added. "The girls are on the left, the boys are on the right, with two bathrooms in between so we don't have to share one with the boys." In Matthew's experience, having grown up with an older sister, it was more likely the boys who didn't want to share the space, between all of the female paraphernalia cluttering every surface and the continual fight to gain access at all against the extended time spent primping in there. But he'd never have voiced that thought aloud.

Danbury returned, bringing with him a large woman with dark hair that was pulled back severely and tied at the nape of her neck. Matthew guessed her to be somewhere in her early forties, maybe, and she did not look happy. She side-stepped carefully by Sergeant Nelson as she entered the room and continued to glance nervously about at the other occupants of it.

"I don't think I can tell you anything helpful," she said as if she was continuing the conversation with Danbury. "I really don't. But if you think our young volunteer is in danger, I'm happy to try to help."

"We do," said Matthew, introducing himself. "What can you tell us about the place they went, Dock Side? Sergeant Nelson says that it's more of an event center than a bar."

"It's more known as a bar, but they do have large seating areas and food trucks, many of them like this pizza truck, regulars, I think. I haven't been down there in a while, though."

"We need to go ask around and show her picture to the staff there. Danbury wants to know if Ariel and Gavin picked up the pizza. If they did, maybe they said something that the staff overheard, anything about where they were going next or anything that could help us figure out where they were after they left there."

"Good luck to hearing anything in that place," said Nelson, who still hovered near the doorway. "It's always crowded and noisy with music blaring. One of our officers was there earlier, but they were very busy. He said the staff there just glanced at the picture he showed from his phone and went on about their business, very unconcerned. I'm sure they've seen it all down there," he added.

"It's crowded on a Tuesday night?" asked Matthew, incredulously. Nelson and Martinez just nodded.

"I agree that we need to go to the pizza truck next," added Danbury, checking his watch. "Even if it's only to get the lay of the land. And go back tomorrow morning. But maybe somebody can help us tonight. If it's still open."

"It should be. For at least another hour or so, maybe longer," said Nelson. "Dock Side has customers all night. The food vendors might shut down at some point on weeknights, though."

"Dock Side stays open. Even on weeknights?" asked Danbury.

"Oh yeah," said Nelson. "All week long."

"Because of the bar? What time does the bar close?"

"Close?" asked Sergeant Nelson, obviously confused by the question.

"The bar. You know, last call. No more drinks served."

Nelson stared, uncomprehendingly, back at Danbury, as if he had no answer.

"In North Carolina," began Danbury, taking a breath and trying again. "It's two AM. There's a last call. No more drinks are served. The bars close an hour later."

"Oh!" said Nelson. "No, the bars don't close here."

"At all?"

Nelson just shook his head and shrugged. "No, not in Miami. They're open all night, or at least they have the option to be."

"That's why I wasn't worried at first," said Martinez. "It's been known to happen before, the volunteers staying out all night. It's not that unusual."

Dr. Rob and Lanie reappeared from Ariel's room just then and, overhearing her comment, he introduced himself as Ariel's father. "My daughter is one of the most responsible young women I know. She can be goofy at times, and she's lots of fun, but she's very serious about her purpose for being here. She planned for months to make this trip and worked hard to earn the money to make that happen. She wouldn't just disappear and shirk responsibility like that."

"She wouldn't," agreed Lanie. "She was the one who wanted to come. She talked Gavin and me into coming too. But working down here this summer was all her idea."

"She has been a hard worker," agreed Martinez. "She helps out wherever she's needed and her Spanish is excellent. She's been working on a few dialect improvements, but she's one of the most fluent volunteers we've had who isn't a native Spanish speaker. I didn't know her well enough to be alarmed. We've had student volunteers disappear overnight before. We don't require them to check in by a certain time, and as long as they are respectful and professional and get the work done, we don't kick them out for keeping odd hours. I'm glad Lanie knew to be worried," she confessed.

"Did you find anything helpful?" asked Danbury. "In her room," he clarified.

"Some receipts, some scribbled notes on slips of paper, some names but no contact information or anything. Lanie thinks they're names of clients she was working with. Mostly 'to do' lists, which she is always making. Nothing earth shattering," said Dr. Rob. "At least nothing that looks to be helpful in figuring out why the pizza so far away or where she is now. What's next?"

"The pizza vendor," answered Danbury. "Nelson says it might still be open. Let's go see if anyone there remembers them from last night."

"Yeah, they're probably still open. Bars close at two AM in other places in Florida," added Nelson. "But not in Miami. And there are multiple bars at Dock Side. At least the main bar is open all night. So are some of the food vendors down there."

That explained why a pizza place would still be open at nearly one in the morning, thought Matthew, but he couldn't imagine who would literally spend the night in a bar. He realized, though, that he was about to find out.

4 ~ Working the Plan

"Let's roll," said Danbury. "Can you come too?" he asked Lanie, who nodded in response. "We can drop you back here. Let's take the SUV. And pick up the car when we come back. But let's hit it while it's hot," he added and stepped out onto the walkway into the thick humid night air.

Everyone else followed and Lanie clicked to lock the door, checked her pocket for the key, and closed the door soundly behind her. Lanie followed Dr. Rob down the stairs behind the others as Marianna Martinez, who had given Danbury her cell number, said her good-byes and headed back down the walkway to her apartment.

"Send her contact information to me and I can add that to our documents as soon as I get a few minutes and a wi-fi connection to share them," said Matthew as he followed Danbury to the SUV. "I'll get a satellite connection for my tablet as soon as I can tomorrow," he added. They all climbed in, Matthew in front with Danbury, and Dr. Rob and Lanie in the back seat.

"I'll navigate," said Matthew, as he pulled up the navigation app on his phone, found Dock Side, and expanded out the resulting view. "Lugar Italiano. Is that the one?" he asked Lanie.

"Yeah, I think that's right. I didn't remember the name, just that it's off to the right with the other food vendors in that huge place on the river."

"Dock Side," said Matthew.

"Yeah, that place is pretty big. It takes up more than a block, and it's all lit up. You can't miss it."

Matthew poked his phone and then laid it on the console in the middle as they heard the automated voice helpfully telling them to take a slight left in a half a mile.

"Isn't Lugar Italiano Spanish?" asked Matthew. "And not Italian?"

"Yeah, I think it's something like 'Italian Place' but it's in Spanish," answered Lanie. "It's weird, I guess, but I'm getting used to English as a second language down here. If you don't speak Spanish, you need to rehearse the standard reply."

"What's that?" asked Matthew, turning to look at Lanie.

"No hablo Español," answered Lanie. "And sometimes, as soon as you say that, they start talking in Spanish anyway, just because you did."

Matthew might have chuckled at that statement, but the situation was far too serious. Instead, he just nodded in acknowledgement and turned back to face front, picking up his cell phone to help navigate. As they made their way south and east, conversation in the vehicle had come to a halt. Each of the occupants seemed to be absorbed in thought.

As they made their way across highway bridges that seemed to be coming and going, overlapping, in all directions, they missed a right turn and Danbury swore quietly under his breath as they were rerouted, crossing one-way streets that went the wrong way in the downtown area.

"If the navigation system even hiccups, we miss things," said Matthew. "Roads are veering off and coming and going in all directions before the navigation app tells you that they're there."

"Yeah, I noticed," grumbled Danbury.

Matthew wondered why Danbury was grumpier on this trip than he'd seen him in the past few months that he'd known him, though he did not ask. Their friendship was short in duration, but they'd worked closely together on two murder investigations and Matthew had signed on as a "medical consultant" to the Raleigh Police department after the first one. Because he had gone above and beyond that role on both cases, they'd spent considerable concentrated hours together and

Matthew thought that he knew Danbury pretty well. As they arrived in downtown Miami, the first issue soon became where to park.

"There's a parking lot for Dock Side on the other side of the bridges," said Lanie. "We weren't able to park there when the shuttle bus brought us in because the lot was full. Maybe this time of night there are some spots. I think you have to pay to park all around here, but there's an app that you can set up and use to do that."

As they drove under the bridges, circling back around to see the bright lights all around Dock Side, directly in front of them they also saw tarps, blankets, and carts as well as a few people still milling about underneath the bridges as they passed under them.

"Wow," said Matthew. "This looks like a city under the bridges."

"Yeah," said Lanie. "We saw that too, the night we were down here. The people were all out in the streets and they're not shy about asking for money or food or a drink, whatever you might have. There are party buses that you can tour downtown Miami in and those come and go from down closer to Dock Side. They blare music and a couple of the guys from under one bridge were out in the street dancing to it. Some of the people on the bus were throwing coins out to them. Or at them. I'm not sure which, really. They looked like a bunch of drunk coeds that night."

"Noted," said Danbury, as he followed Matthew's new directions to take a right in front of Dock Side as SW 2nd Street formed a T intersection into it. As they made the turn, there were tall buildings on their right and one of the bridges crossing the river on their left had been blocked off.

They passed a gated parking deck underneath an upscale-looking building and Matthew said, "We take the next right, just past that alleyway there, and then there's a parking lot down on the right."

Danbury made the right turns and they found themselves in a parking lot that was beneath a row of multiple bridges. There were no vagrants in sight and it was well lit with iron fencing surrounding it. As they pulled into a spot, Matthew noted that a couple, holding hands, came through what must have been a gate on the street they'd just turned off of in the corner on the left, which was the direction they wanted to go.

Following the directions on the signs that were posted around the parking lot, Matthew quickly searched for the PayByPark parking app on his phone, loaded it, set up the payment method, and entered the information for the rental SUV. He added the code on the sign for the area they were parked in. As he climbed out to get the license plate number and take a picture of the SUV, he heard Lanie say, "I'm going to walk out to the street. Being under all of these bridges gives me the creeps."

"OK, let's go," said Dr. Rob, who obviously wasn't willing to let Lanie get even 20 yards away in this area without him.

The app flashed multiple messages informing Matthew that parking was $2.50 per hour, that he would get a reminder as the end of the time he selected approached, and that he could add time remotely from the app without having to return to the car. What Miami missed in affordability it made up for in convenience, at least when it came to their parking, he thought.

Danbury locked up and he and Matthew followed Lanie and Dr. Rob through the iron gate and turned left back down the street, looking around as they went. The street that they'd just walked down, and off of which they'd parked, ended at the river. They turned left on the sidewalk opposite the waterfront. Ahead, they could see the lights of Dock Side. Both it and the surrounding area were well lit, but the event center blindingly lit up everything around it.

As they approached, Matthew noticed a sign in a graveled pull-out area along the waterfront just after the bridge. Under any other circumstances, he would have loved to linger, read the sign, and taken in his surroundings. Too curious to ignore it, he jogged over, pulled out his phone, and snapped a picture before rejoining the group.

"Couldn't resist, huh?" asked Dr. Rob, seeming to be amused despite the grim circumstances of their trip.

"Yeah, I was curious. I took a picture so I'll read it later. It's about the history of the waterway, including this bridge and the future plans for rebuilding it and this area around it," Matthew shrugged a bit sheepishly. He was a self-confessed history buff, as well as a music enthusiast and motor head, so he couldn't argue about his inability to resist even if he'd wanted to.

In addition to learning and remembering historical trivia about places and events, particularly about empires and wars, he could play nearly any instrument he could get his hands on. Matthew had his own collection, including guitars, a mandolin, ukulele, drum set, and keyboards. He also kept up with current cars, particularly those built for speed, their specs by generation, and any upcoming changes.

They approached a high slat board fence that was contained within a chain link fence which rose just above their eye level. The board fence continued along the sidewalk, though lower as they got closer to the entrance, and they could see the tops of vendor food trucks, massive fans, and lights strung up poles crisscrossing above the outdoor venue. At least on this end, the area was open air and they could smell the wares of the food vendors wafting over the fence line, but there were roof lines ahead. It must not all be open air, thought Matthew, which made sense to him given Miami's reputation for afternoon showers that would spring up without warning.

Dr. Rob took a deep breath as they approached what seemed to be the main entranceway. It was midway along the fence line, to their right. They walked in under a roof. The cement sidewalk turned to wooden decking under their feet. A walk-through opening in white slat board fencing was directly ahead. On the other side of the slat board wall ahead of them, Matthew glimpsed the end of what turned out to be a long rectangular bar that ran down the center of the venue, which was also under some sort of roof but disconnected from the first roofline.

Under their feet, the decking turned into a finished cement floor ahead in the bar area and to outdoor green carpeting off to the left and right. Wear and tear on actual grass, Matthew figured, was the reason for this faux grass carpet that extended off in both directions, and squished and sloshed disconcertingly under his feet as he stepped to the left, out of the way of a small group of revelers who were on their way out. Groupings of low white Adirondack chairs were placed around umbrellas that were lit beneath, all along the streetside white board fence to the left. Matthew noticed that most of the noise and people seemed to be to the right of the entranceway and he shifted his attention in that direction.

If he were to try to describe Dock Side in a single word from what he was seeing so far, the word would be disjointed, he thought. He wasn't sure what he was expecting, but he was pretty sure this wasn't it.

"Where's the pizza place?" asked Danbury of Lanie.

"It's off to the right, down there," she said, pointing. "All of the food vendors are down that way. The biggest bar is straight ahead, with a couple of others off on the sides and seating all over."

As they walked past a couple of vendor trucks to reach the one in the far corner, the mingled smells of garlic and Italian spices told Matthew that they were in the right place and made him salivate, realizing that he was hungry. They had eaten dinner hours ago and he wasn't usually up and using energy this late at night. If he was hungry, he knew Danbury would be because the man could always eat more than Matthew, and that was saying a lot.

Danbury approached the vendor truck, flashed a badge, held up one of the laminated pictures, and a man from behind the counter inside stepped outside through the little door in the end to look at them. He was short and a bit stout, with dark hair and coloring. Matthew walked over to the group, which was now encircling the man, attempting to hear what was being said over the music that blared from somewhere and seemed to engulf them.

The man was shaking his head and gesturing, then nodding in agreement about something, so Matthew leaned in closer to try to understand what he was saying. The man said that he didn't remember the couple specifically, but that all pizzas the night before had been picked up. He couldn't guarantee that Ariel and Gavin had been the ones to pick up their pizza, but he said he didn't know who else would have.

Only after Danbury pressed him further to look up the order did the man oblige though somewhat grudgingly, Matthew thought, and slipped back into the vendor truck. Ignoring the hunger and fatigue that was starting to set in, Matthew turned to take in his surroundings more fully.

Running along the waterfront, the whole event center was long and not nearly as wide, an elongated rectangle that was over a block long, maybe two, he surmised. The main bar area was set in the center, as

Lanie had pointed out. It was also long and rectangular, with what looked like a finished cement floor and a high roof that looked like it belonged on a greenhouse.

A man and a woman were working opposite ends of the rectangular bar counter that surrounded them and another man was wiping down nearby high-top tables. There were patrons, sporadically, around the bar area and only three or four that he could see actually sitting at the bar. A couple with a baby stroller sat at a table between Matthew and the end of the bar, and they seemed to be arguing.

The pizza vendor reappeared from the food truck after a few minutes with a tablet. He explained that he was scrolling through the orders that came in online and by phone the night before. He located the one they were asking about.

"Here's one for Roberts," he said with a heavy accent that sounded to Matthew as if it had a Spanish origin, "They ordered two pizzas."

"Two?" asked Danbury holding up two fingers, "Dos?"

"Si, dos. If this is the right order, yes. One large pepperoni and mushroom, and one medium cheese. Monday nights, that's the special. Order a large and get a medium of equal or lesser value free," he added, sounding a bit like a commercial. "We try to keep the customers coming. During the week," he added.

"Yeah, that's theirs," confirmed Lanie. "Pepperoni and mushroom, that's Gavin's favorite pizza."

"And Ariel just likes pizza. She isn't picky," added Dr. Rob.

"Right," answered Lanie.

"But why two? Why the second one? Just because it was on special?" asked Danbury.

"I told them I wasn't hungry. Shawn did too, so it wasn't for either of us," said Lanie.

Danbury persisted, turning back to the vendor, "You're not sure if they picked it up, though? The two in this picture?"

The man just shrugged and said, "Earlier in the evenings, we have long lines. Every evening. Sometimes until midnight, we have lines. And even later on weekends. What can I say? They like our pizza."

"So I've gathered," said Danbury. "And they come a long way to get it." He thanked the man, handed him a card asking him to call if he saw them again or thought of anything else, and they all turned around as Danbury began to survey the surroundings as Matthew had.

"Let's go talk to the two at the bar," said Danbury.

"I think I'll talk to the guy cleaning the tables," said Matthew, as he pulled the pictures from the folder and walked over to greet a skinny guy wearing what was once a white apron that covered brown shorts and a beige t-shirt.

"Hi, we're looking for a missing young couple and I was hoping you could help me."

The guy straightened, wearily, from cleaning up beer spills on a high-top table and looked Matthew in the eye when he said, "I can try."

"We think these two were in here last night picking up a pizza between nine and nine-thirty or so. Did you see them?" He was immediately thankful to Leo for laminating the pictures as the guy took them both from Matthew without wiping off his beer-splattered hands first.

To his credit, the guy did study the pictures before handing them back and saying, "I might have. The redhead, I think I've seen her before. Maybe she just looks like somebody else, though," he added, picking up his towel and snapping it before going back to wiping off the table.

"Do you remember when you last saw her? This woman or the one who she might just look like?" persisted Matthew.

"Like a week ago, I think. Something like that," the guy answered over his shoulder, still wiping. "If it's her. I'm not sure it is. Pretty redhead, though. She was here a lot for a couple of months. I haven't seen her in a week or so, I think."

Matthew remembered the other two women who were missing before Ariel and wished he had pictures of them to show the guy. "If you see them come in or think of anything else, would you give me a call, please? I wrote my cell number on the back of my card there," he said, handing the guy one of his business cards.

The guy glanced down at it before shoving it in his back pocket and said, "Dr. Paine, huh? Good one!"

"Thanks," Matthew said over his shoulder as he went back to his group, now gathered at the bar.

He could hear the woman behind the bar responding to whatever Danbury had asked her as she studied the pictures of Ariel and Gavin. Matthew heard her say, "No, Courtney was here last night."

"What's her last name?" asked Danbury.

"DeBerry. Courtney DeBerry."

"Would she have been behind the bar all night?"

"Yeah, she'd have been working this end because Rod was here last night filling in. And he always works the other end if he's bartending."

"Rod?" asked Danbury, looking over his shoulder at the pizza vendor.

Matthew, too, had noted the proximity to the pizza vendor's truck, though there weren't many people at the high-top tables in between the two at this hour, he noticed.

"Rodney Rodríguez. He goes by Rod. For obvious reasons," she shrugged.

"But he's not here tending bar tonight?"

"Nope. He's the manager, so he's not usually behind the bar except to fill in for our breaks if we're busy. He had to fill in a full shift last night because we had another bartender out."

"The manager tends bar?"

"He used to be a bartender. He went back to school and got a business degree. Now he's the manager. He likes to remind us all of that regularly," she added, rolling her eyes with a pained expression.

"When will Courtney and Rod be back in?"

"Rod will be here by about ten in the morning, at least. Courtney is on a split shift tomorrow so she should be in around then too until one, when I get here. I've got the afternoon shift tomorrow and Courtney comes back about eight tomorrow night. Rod will probably be here the whole time, or at least in and out. He's here most of the time. You just missed him tonight. I think he left sometime after midnight."

"And you can't recall seeing either of these two before?" persisted Danbury, pointing to the pictures.

"Nope. I don't have a photographic memory, but they're not regulars anyway. Although…" she paused and leaned over to look back down at Ariel's picture on the bar. "She does look like someone who was here a lot. A regular. Haven't seen her for a while, though. A week or two, maybe. But it's not the same person. This one looks younger. Could be the younger sister, maybe."

"She doesn't have a sister," replied Dr. Rob. "She's my daughter, and she's an only child."

"Oh. I don't remember seeing the guy at all, though."

"Thanks, Ms. Delgado. We appreciate your help," said Danbury. "If you think of anything else, give me a call? Or text the cell number there. If you see them come back in, let me know?" he added, as he handed her a business card.

"Sure. I hope you find your daughter," she said to Dr. Rob, as she slipped the card into an apron pocket without examining it, and turned to check on the man sitting off to the right.

"We need to get some sleep. And come back in the morning," said Danbury. "Maybe by then there'll be some word from the Rydz driver. Maybe a new direction to look. But we'll need to split up. Cover the hospitals. There are several around. We need to take these pictures. Directly to the Emergency Departments. Find out who was working last night. Ask if they've seen either Ariel or Gavin."

The others just nodded consent as Danbury continued, "But first I want to finish a look around. There's a whole dock area over there. Where Ms. Delgado said patrons tie up. When they travel in by boat."

"Ariel told me about that," said Dr. Rob. "She joked that I should sail down and meet her here. She said that the night you all were here," he indicated Lanie as he spoke. "The night your group was down here, she said, there were so many boats along the waterfront that you couldn't see the river."

"That's true," said Lanie. "There were a lot of boats. A couple of really big ones. No sail boats that I saw though. I guess you'd call them yachts. Big power boats were taking up the whole waterfront so that, like you said, you couldn't see the river through them at all."

As they made their way around the bar to the waterfront, Matthew saw that there were a couple of large boats or yachts as Lanie had said, that were tied up farther down to the left. None were directly in front of Dock Side. The lights along the planked boardwalk that extended beyond the ends of Dock Side were glistening off of the bow of the first one, which otherwise looked dark. The second one had lights on and Matthew could see a blue flicker through the edge of the blinds that were drawn at the large windows. Someone must have a television on in there, he surmised, and he wondered where the power source was. He didn't see any hookups here so maybe they were operating off battery power, solar generated or something.

He made a mental note to ask about that, if Dock Side provided water and power for boats to tie up overnight or merely allowed the owners to come in for food and beverages. With a bar that stayed open all night, maybe the two things were synonymous, he thought, as they meandered down the boardwalk.

They walked the length of the boardwalk and back, but no one was out and about on the waterfront. Returning to Dock Side, the group was quiet as they circled the bar to the right, the opposite end from which they'd entered. They were about to exit when a chubby guy in white shorts and a sailor shirt came from somewhere off to the right. As he was about to rush by them, Danbury stopped him.

After flashing his badge, introducing himself, and explaining what he wanted, Danbury asked, "Do you work here?"

The guy said, "Hi, Detective. I'm JoJo. And yes, I'm on the wait staff here. I was just getting off for the night and going to collect my tips. Walk this way," he added, as he sashayed to the bar.

Matthew withheld the chuckle that was forming in his throat as he thought there was no way he could ever walk the way this guy was walking without throwing something seriously out of joint, or worse. He was working on rewriting the old Aerosmith song, *Walk This Way*, in his mind and realized that he was past punchy with the late hour. He kept the chuckle, the thought, and the revised song lyrics to himself as they followed JoJo back to the bar.

Angela Delgado, the bartender, had seen him coming and she met him at that end of the bar, leaned over, and handed the guy an envelope, "Here you go, JoJo."

"Thanks, Ang, you're an angel," he winked at her. Folding the envelope in half, he put it in the pocket of his shorts. Turning back to the group who had followed him over, he said with an appraising glance and smile, "Now, how can I help you, Detective?"

"Were you working last night?"

"I had an earlier shift last night so I was off long before now," JoJo answered, glancing at his watch. "But I did work last night, yes."

"Did you see either of these people?" Danbury asked, handing JoJo the photos.

"Oh, I did," said JoJo. "Last night, I'm pretty sure I saw this guy. He had on tight Polo shorts, converse sneakers, and a red Polo t-shirt."

Danbury looked at Lanie. She nodded and said, "Yeah, I couldn't remember what they were wearing when the police asked, but now that I hear you say that, I think that's right! His shirt was red, and he does wear a lot of Polo because I've heard Ariel tease him about it, about looking like a frat boy. He didn't pick any of it out. He said his mom bought it for him."

"Nice delts under that t-shirt," continued JoJo. "He was yummy. See that square jaw line? He's a looker."

Ignoring the last comment, Danbury perked up as he asked, "What about the girl? Did you see her with him?"

"Oh, I guess I did," said JoJo, waving his hand dismissively. "That's why I stopped looking after they came in. I mean, I guess that was her. I didn't get a good look. There was a little redhead with him, so it's probably her. She looped her arm through his and then he put his arm around her shoulders as they walked in. They were obviously together, so I went back to table eight to get their drink orders."

"What time was that?" asked Danbury.

"Hmm…" said JoJo, placing his hand under his chin, as if that would somehow help him to remember. "After nine, I think. Maybe nine-thirty? I had a group of divas at table eight and they came in around nine. They were doing shots and were on their third round by then. Girlfriends needed to slow down, I knew, or they wouldn't be walking out of here on those stiletto heels they were in. I was right, of course."

"Did you see them leave? This young couple?" Danbury asked, indicating the pictures.

"I don't think so. I got really busy and I don't remember seeing them after they first came in. They went down the other way, toward the food trucks. I was working tables at this end, so I don't remember seeing them after that."

"Had you ever seen them before? Either of them? Before last night?"

"Not that I recall," said JoJo. "At least not at any of my tables that I remember. And him," he pointed back at the picture of Gavin. "Him, I'd have recalled."

"Thanks so much for your help," said Dr. Rob, stepping forward and offering his hand. "The 'little redhead' there is my daughter and she's missing. They both are."

"Oh! I'm so sorry!" said JoJo, looking truly remorseful with this new information.

"Would you give me a call? Or a text. If you see either of them again. Or if you think of anything else that might help us to find them?" asked Danbury, handing over a card.

"I sure will," said JoJo, taking the card and slipping it into the same pocket as the tip envelope that he'd pocketed earlier. "And I'm sorry about your daughter," he added, quite genuinely, to Dr. Rob. "I hope you find her soon."

"Thanks. Me too," answered Dr. Rob as they watched JoJo sashay his way, though less enthusiastically, out of the front of the place.

"Now what?" asked Dr. Rob.

"Now we drop Lanie off. And then go check into our hotel," replied Danbury as he turned and went out of the front entrance.

*****

After dropping Lanie off at the ministry housing with more tears and hugs for Dr. Rob from her, Matthew and Danbury took both vehicles to the Holiday Inn Express north in Hialeah where Penn had gotten them a great deal with Danbury's badge. Parking, wi-fi, and breakfast were included. Matthew was thankful for the navigation on his phone because all of the streets around West 20th seemed to be similarly named by direction and number. Despite that confusing factor, it was an area he thought that he'd love to explore under normal circumstances.

They checked in, rode an elevator up to the fourth floor, and found their rooms. Matthew's room and Dr. Rob's rooms adjoined and had two queen beds each. Danbury's room was a king suite across the hall. Matthew had refrained from comment that Dr. Rob should have had the suite, since it was his credit card that was paying for it all, but he also realized that Dr. Rob could probably care less about it and he'd have given Danbury the moon to find his only child.

Matthew shook his head to clear the mean thoughts; he also knew that he was being petty because he was exhausted. Quickly plugging in his electronics, he managed a hasty shower to wash the plane and humidity off. Pulling out his laptop, he managed to get an internet connection through the hotel site long enough to upload the documents that he'd created to a new folder on his cloud account. He shared the folder with Danbury and Dr. Rob, inviting both of them to be editors.

Finally, he fell into bed and immediately into a deep sleep, though it wasn't dreamless so it wasn't entirely peaceful.

5 ~ GO AGAIN

Waking with a start to an annoying noise, Matthew had to orient himself and remember that he was in a suburb of Miami in a hotel room. Max was not curled around his head, and he was neither at his own condo outside of Peak nor at Cici's house in Quarry. It seemed like longer than the seconds it probably was, but he finally realized that the annoying noise was his phone. Not the alarm, but Facetime.

He rolled over to retrieve it from the nightstand and clicked to see Cici, brightly smiling at him from across an ocean. She'd been in London only a little over a month, but it felt like much longer.

"Good morning, Sleepyhead," she said. And then, leaning in, her smile faded as she asked, "Where are you? That's not my bedroom nor is it yours."

"I'm in a hotel. In a place called Hialeah. Outside of Miami. What time is it?"

"It's about a quarter after six, your time," she said.

"I'm surprised Danbury hasn't beaten my door down before now," he responded as he tried to push himself into an upright position.

"OK," said Cici and hesitated. "I guess I'm relieved that you're there with Danbury, and not shacked up with some woman," she said as she laughed and rolled her eyes. They both knew that wasn't Matthew's style at all. "But, what on earth are you doing in Miami?" she demanded.

"The short version? Dr. Rob's daughter was here for a summer service project and she's missing. We flew in last night. I think I hit the bed around two AM and I'm still not all here."

"So, Dr. Rob is with you too?"

"He is. Right next door in an adjoining room."

"Wow. I just talked to you yesterday morning. Things changed quickly for you over there."

"Yeah, you know how that goes. I guess I could have texted to tell you, but we flew down on the last flight out last night and it was already the middle of the night, your time." He wasn't sure why he felt like he owed her an explanation or anything else because they weren't officially together, but he felt a slight twinge of negligence on his part.

"So, what are you going to do? Are you there to try to find her?"

"Yeah, that's the plan. Though, Miami is a huge place and she was last seen in a busy downtown area last night. No, make that night-before-last," he amended. "What day is it anyway?"

"It's Wednesday, Matthew, hump day. But I'm on the other side of the pond so that does neither of us any good," she said with a twinkle in her eye and a pert smirk on her lips.

Matthew laughed, despite his exhaustion, and sat up on the edge of his bed. "It might take more than coffee and a shower to get me moving this morning," he said. "Too bad you're on the other side of that really big pond." He waggled his eyebrows at her and she laughed back at him.

"This does postpone your plans to fly over here, though, doesn't it?" she asked.

"It does," he answered and then she got very quiet. "Are you mad that I can't come to London now?" he asked.

"No. If you can help find Dr. Rob's daughter, of course I'm not mad. I'm just disappointed, that's all."

Cici was confusing these days, Matthew thought. They'd broken up over a year ago and only recently reconnected, and even then not purposefully. She seemed to be coming around to his way of thinking about the future. Sometimes it felt like they'd never been apart and they had the rest of their lives together. Maybe, he thought. Maybe they did, but right now, he knew he had more immediate problems to solve.

"I hope everything's OK over there?" he asked.

"Yeah, I miss you. But I'm fine. Let me know how it goes with finding Dr. Rob's daughter."

"I miss you too, Cees," he said, honestly, reverting to the name he'd always called her when they were dating. "I really do. And yes, I'll be in touch, just from Hialeah, Florida instead of Peak, North Carolina."

They both grew quiet for a moment before he continued, "I've got a busy day ahead of me though, so I guess I'd better go get that shower and get going on it."

"Yeah, I'll let you get back to saving the world. I'll just be here trying to get this client all set up to move operations to the US."

Matthew laughed at her. "I'm hardly saving the world, but honestly, I'll take saving just this one young woman. Dr. Rob is beside himself."

Cici pursed her lips and said, "I can't really imagine, and I'm pretty sure I don't want to. But go help him. He's a dear man."

"Yeah," Matthew chuckled, "He is. Have a good day, Cees, and I'll check in later."

"OK, stay safe down there. I love you and I don't want to lose you again," she added.

Matthew stuttered, "I love you too, Cees," in surprise, as they disconnected. Did she actually have him now? Did she think that she did? Yep, he thought to himself, definitely confusing.

*****

After showering and dressing in khaki shorts, a short-sleeved dry fit shirt, and leather deck shoes, Matthew meandered down to the lobby area in search of coffee with real cream and lots of sugar, and maybe even some breakfast. He found Danbury and Dr. Rob at a corner table, already deep in conversation. They hadn't discussed the time to reconvene this morning but the understanding was generally "early."

"Hey, Doc," said Danbury over his shoulder as Matthew approached. "We were just discussing the order of operations. For the morning at least. Thanks for creating the online documents. And sharing them. We can all update them throughout the day. Dr. Rob gave me Gayle Blevins' information. I added it. And added her as an editor. And I added a list of hospitals to check. Grab some breakfast and let's get on the road."

"We're going to pick up Lanie," added Dr. Rob, looking at Matthew. "We're heading downtown to canvass the hospitals in the area and then go to Dock Side at ten when Rod and Courtney DeBerry should both be there. Danbury has a call in to Sergeant Nelson and they're following up some potential leads on the other two missing women. Hopefully, he'll have heard something from the Rydz driver and that'll help. If so, that might change our plans but that's it as of now," he added as he ran his fingers down either side of the goatee that he had just started growing. The goatee was surrounded by a day's growth on the rest of his face this morning, so it was harder to tell that he was growing one.

Matthew hadn't taken the time to shave and he noticed, just before spotting the coffee urn and heading for it, that neither had Danbury. All of them were a bit scruffy. Matthew filled a thick paper travel cup with coffee, cream, and sugar and carefully snapped a lid on. Turning, he loaded a plate with biscuits and eggs from a buffet table along the wall and sat down, sipping his coffee. He said a quick prayer, both as a blessing for his food and for help in finding Ariel before it was too late. Danbury looked on impatiently and Dr. Rob stared at the table beneath him, apparently unseeing and lost in his own thoughts.

Loading the eggs into two biscuits and wrapping them in napkins to take them with him, Matthew stood up, tossed the paper plate in the nearby trash bin, and declared, "OK, let's go."

"Are you sure? You can eat your breakfast first," said Dr. Rob, hesitating and looking concerned.

"Nope. I can eat while we travel. We have lots to do, so let's hit the road. Hey, could you grab a couple of water bottles out of that cooler over there for the road?" he asked Dr. Rob. "We'll likely need those today and I'm out of hands." Dr. Rob nodded and headed for the cooler.

"Good idea," said Danbury, who had already risen and headed for the front door. He, too, paused to open the glass door on the refrigerated cooler in the lobby and pulled two water bottles. Matthew followed Danbury out and Dr. Rob trailed behind. Dr. Rob pulled up the address of the ministry, where they were to pick up Lanie. It was already in his phone from the night before. He half-heartedly offered to drive their rental car so that Matthew could eat. After a moment's discussion, Matthew climbed behind the wheel, munching on a biscuit and, downing the first one, and started the car.

They headed south on W 20th Street, which paralleled the Palmetto Express toll road. Lanie was waiting for them at the base of the steps dressed in running shorts, flip flops, and a tank top with her streaked blonde hair in a messy bun on top of her head. Matthew noted that her eyes were still puffy and she hadn't bothered with the makeup that had run down her cheeks the night before.

Lanie climbed in the back seat and offered to take over the navigation process so that Dr. Rob could help spot road signs and exit numbers, which they'd learned the evening before too quickly appeared without warning, so that Matthew could deal with the traffic. Driving in Miami during normal hours, they were soon to discover, was a bigger challenge than late the night before.

"Where to first?" asked Lanie.

They had a list of nearby hospitals that Danbury had added to the shared documents, Matthew explained. Lanie pulled up the first one.

"St. Gerard Hospital is north of their last known location, but the closest hospital," answered Dr. Rob. "Danbury put it first on our list, then the University hospital, which is just west of that. And then Grace, which is south of the river and Dock Side. They all have twenty-four-hour emergency rooms. That's where we start unless the Rydz driver tells the police differently."

"OK," said Lanie, after a moment's pause, "I've entered the address for St. Gerard's Emergency Entrance. After you pull out here onto East 17th Street, take a left onto East First Avenue. That'll take us south to either East Okeechobee that runs to the southeast or Hialeah Drive, due east. Let's take East Okeechobee. That looks like it's more direct. That's Highway 27. Then, we'll take Highway 112 across to I-95 and down. It's not the most direct route but, even with the heavy traffic on I-95, it looks like it's the fastest."

"OK, fastest is good," said Matthew, pulling out onto East

Seventeenth and following Lanie's directions south and east.

Finding the hospital was relatively easy but finding parking, once there, was a bit more challenging. After a couple of laps that felt like huge loops, they located free parking off of North West 16th Street and followed the signs to the Emergency Department entrance.

The hospital was busy. It took some convincing and displaying of professional credentials, such as they were, to get through the first layer at the reception desk and into the bays of the Emergency Department to talk to the personnel. A gregarious young summer volunteer finally ushered them back and found several of the staff who had been on duty there Monday night. None of them had seen Ariel or Gavin. After a string of head shakes from the staff, Matthew and Dr. Rob were ushered back out of the bays to the reception area.

On the way out, Matthew pulled the receptionist aside and asked discretely if she could contact the morgue to be certain that neither Ariel nor Gavin had been brought in without having been seen in the Emergency Department. After being assured by the Medical Examiner in the morgue that nobody even remotely resembling either of them had been brought in over the past two days, Matthew thanked the ME and the receptionist and joined Lanie and Dr. Rob outside.

"Well, one down," said Lanie, looking cheerful about it. "She's OK, Dr. Rob. I don't know how I know it, but I just think that we're not going to find her in an Emergency Room or," she hesitated. Then she choked out, "Or worse."

"I think so too but we need to be certain. What's next on the list?" asked Dr. Rob as they rounded the corner to the parking lot. "It was the university hospital, wasn't it?"

"Yep," said Lanie. "Wait. We don't even need the car. It's just right around the corner." She turned her phone around and back again as she was trying to get her bearings. "The address is 1400 NW 12th Avenue, so there are two Emergency Departments in this complex? That doesn't make any sense."

"It doesn't but let's check it out," agreed Matthew.

Having struck out, yet again, but happily so, they got back in the car to head south to Grace Hospital. Lanie navigated them through the traffic south and then back out onto I-95. A few turns later, and they were following the signs in front of and then around to the left of Grace Hospital. The Emergency Parking lot was along the waterfront and had a gated arm across it.

Stopping at the gate, Matthew started to tell someone on the other end of a square box, after pushing the button to talk, why they were there but the arm in front of them went up before he'd gotten much in the way of explanation out at all. He shrugged and pulled through into a small lot that was only about half full.

"Is that Biscayne Bay out there?" Dr. Rob asked, pointing at the water over the cement bulkhead on the other side of which they'd just pulled in. "The river where the event center is feeds in from that, right?"

"I think so," said Lanie, with a shrug, as she pulled up her phone to look. "It's not really well marked on here, but it has to be."

They parked and followed the walkway toward the loop in front of the Emergency Department entrance and, as they crossed the street they had just driven in on, Matthew's cell phone sounded. They all paused as he pulled it out of his pocket and said, "It's Danbury."

"Hey Doc," said Danbury. "We heard from the Rydz driver. He was supposed to meet them in front of Dock Side. He said he waited for a half hour. But they never showed. He gave up and left. Shortly after ten. Their last known location is still Dock Side," he added. "I'll head back that way. After one more stop in Brickell. Where are you now?"

"Lanie updated the online documents with who we talked to and what we learned so far, which is nothing really, except that they weren't in the ED and they aren't in morgues so far. We just got to Grace Hospital and we were about ready to go ask in their ED. We have one more hospital on the list, up in Miami Beach, which is farther away from Dock Side. But we can still check."

"Why don't you meet me at Dock Side. When you're done there," said Danbury. "It's on the way to Miami Beach anyway."

"OK, got it," said Matthew. "Any new information on the other two missing women?"

"A little. They're from Brickell. Both of them, originally. So far, there's no connection between them. One had just broken up with a boyfriend. She moved in with a friend in Wynwood. The other had just lost her job. Both had roommates. Neither of the roommates knows each other. Or the other of the missing women. We're on our way to talk to the boyfriend now. He's already given a statement earlier. But I want to hear it directly from him."

"Yeah, you usually look at boyfriends and husbands first, right?"

"Usually. But this is a little different. We have three missing. And no known connection."

"Unless the guy was getting rid of his ex and making it look serial. But that's a lot of trouble to go to just to get rid of an ex. There must be easier ways."

"I'll record the interview. In the shared documents. Then meet you at Dock Side."

"OK, we'll record whatever we learn here and see you there."

As he put his phone back in his pocket, the trio made their way into the Emergency Department and were hit with a blast of welcome cold dry air. It was already hot and humid, Matthew noted, and not yet ten in the morning in Miami. They explained what they wanted to the security guard on duty at the desk, but he seemed confused by their request. With a heavy Latino dialect of some unknown origin, he finally said, "Just a minute," and called someone on the phone to try to explain the request.

"Yes Ma'am," he said, "I'll do that."

As he put the phone down, he pushed something under the desk and they heard the double doors in front of them buzz and open.

"Go through there," said the security guard, pointing. "Dr. Mayer is the head of the ED. Go down this hallway and ask for her at the other end."

"Thanks," said both Matthew and Dr. Rob in unison and they started down the hallway.

6 ~ ONE STEP CLOSER, TWO STEPS BACK

Doorways led off to the left and right of the hallway as they walked along it but they kept going, as instructed, until the hallway opened out into a larger room that was partitioned with a desk in front of them. They approached the desk and asked for Dr. Mayer. The small dark-haired woman behind the desk motioned to someone behind her and a tall blonde woman with broad shoulders, probably in her mid-forties Matthew was guessing, stepped forward and introduced herself as Dr. Mayer.

Matthew and Dr. Rob introduced themselves and Lanie, and then explained why they were there.

"I was actually here Monday night into Tuesday morning," said Dr. Mayer. As surprise must have registered on their faces, she held up her hand and said, "I know, I know, and no, I don't normally work the overnight shift. I had three staff out, including my night supervisor, with some nasty stomach virus and I stayed over. I was here until about eight yesterday morning, so who is it that you're looking for?"

Dr. Rob pulled the laminated pictures from the folder and handed them over, "This is my daughter Ariel and her boyfriend Gavin," he said. "They've been missing since Monday night and we were wondering if you'd seen anyone who looks like either of them?"

Taking the pictures from Dr. Rob, Dr. Mayer ran her fingers through her short blonde hair in concentration. "It's hard to say," she said. "But we might have a guy who once looked like that. How tall is this guy?"

Dr. Rob looked at Lanie, who put her hand up in the air. "About here, I think?" she said.

"About five foot eleven?" Dr. Mayer squinted up her eyes at the measurement. "Maybe. I haven't seen a girl matching your daughter's description, but we did have a guy brought in shortly before dawn on Tuesday who could be this guy. He was pretty banged up, but that square jaw line is kind of distinctive."

"What happened to him? Do you know?"

"He wasn't conscious, so he was taken for an MRI and some scans. He had contusions on his face and head so skull damage and brain swelling were the concern. He was still breathing on his own and his heart rate was strong, so we ordered the tests. After that, I'm not sure. I don't think he had any identification on him, but let me check."

She picked up the phone, punched zero, and asked for the ICU. "Hi, this is Dr. Mayer in the ED. We had what I believe was a John Doe come in overnight Monday night. Do you have an unidentified male, or a young male, probably early twenties up there?"

"He's twenty," interjected Lanie.

"Yeah, he's twenty. Maybe five eleven?" After a pause, she said, "Yeah, that sounds like the same guy. Any identification on him?"

After another lengthier pause, she said, "Yeah, there are people here looking for a guy that might be him. OK to send them up?" And then, "Sure, I'll tell them."

As she put the phone down, she said, "Joan Haywood is going to meet you up in the ICU waiting room. She's a nurse on that floor and she can help you from here." She gave them instructions to reach the elevators, leading them through the Emergency Department and out the other side, and told them where to go when they reached the right floor.

Dr. Rob and Matthew both thanked the woman profusely and hurried toward the elevator.

"If it's really him, he can tell us where Ariel is!" said Lanie, hopefully, with a huge smile spreading across her face.

Matthew wasn't as hopeful, mainly because Ariel hadn't been brought in with Gavin and he reportedly wasn't in great shape when he was brought in. Glancing at Dr. Rob, Matthew saw that the man's face seemed to mirror his own thoughts. "Let's just see if it's him first," said Matthew as they stepped onto the elevator and punched the button.

As they stepped off the elevator, they were met in the vestibule by a pretty young nurse who looked not much older than Lanie. "Are you the group looking for the guy who came in Tuesday morning?" she asked.

"Yes," said Matthew, and introduced himself.

"I'm Dr. Richard Roberts," said Dr. Rob, stepping forward and extending a hand. "We're looking for my daughter and her boyfriend who disappeared Monday night. Your ED Director said that no young women matching my daughter's description came in, but a young man who was brought in might be the one we're looking for." As he spoke, he pulled out the pictures and handed them to her.

She scanned them and looked back up at Dr. Rob. "This could be the guy we have up here, but he had no identification on him, and he hasn't regained consciousness, so we've had no idea who he is."

"What can you tell us about his condition?" asked Dr. Rob. "I know HIIPA regulations prevent you from talking to just anyone, but if it's him, his mother will have just landed at MIA less than an hour ago. If we can identify him, we'll let her know."

"This way, Doctors," she said, as she led the way through double doors to the right and to a nurses' station just inside them. She rounded the corner behind the desk, stepped up to a computer screen, and started clicking keys.

"He has multiple facial contusions, so it'll be difficult to determine if it's him without something more to go on," she said. "He also has an epidural hematoma, fractures to the pterion region, so there's lots of swelling and he's been in a coma since he arrived Tuesday morning. We've been monitoring the swelling, ready to intercede if there's too much pressure."

"If it's not subdural, that's something," said Dr. Rob encouragingly as he turned to Matthew, who nodded in agreement. Lanie looked on in complete confusion.

"He's got a fracture here," said Matthew to Lanie, pointing to his temple, and there's internal bleeding and swelling of his brain, which they're watching closely because that can be dangerous if there's too much swelling. But it could be worse. If the swelling goes down, this is survivable."

"Oh," she said despondently, as she understood the seriousness of the injuries. "I was hoping to see him and talk to him and find out where Ariel is."

"Can we see him?" asked Matthew. "Maybe we can at least rule out this guy being Gavin."

"Or maybe Lanie can tell if it actually is Gavin," added Dr. Rob. "She's spent much more time with him recently at school and here than I ever have. Ariel has brought him home a couple of times and I took them to dinner a couple of times in Asheville. I've met him and his mom at the parent weekends each semester, but the last time I saw him was a couple of months ago. I know Ariel is over the moon for this guy, but I've really only been around him a handful of times."

"I'm not sure I can. I mean I'm not sure I can see him like that," said Lanie.

"It's OK, Lanie, you don't have to see him if you don't think that you can," said Dr. Rob. "I can at least go in first."

Lanie took a deep breath and said quietly, "No. I need to know if it's him, and I know that Ariel would want me to check. I need to know where Ariel is and if it's him, maybe that gets us closer."

"Do you know if he has any identifying marks?" asked Matthew, helpfully. "Tattoos or birthmarks? Anything? If he does, then maybe they can identify him or rule out that it's Gavin by those. Then maybe you don't have to see him at all."

"Not that I know of," said Lanie slowly. "He doesn't have any tats, I don't think. None that are visible anyway. And Ariel never mentioned him having any that aren't," she said and blushed profusely.

"This guy doesn't have any tattoos," confirmed Nurse Haywood as she clicked a few more keys. "At least none that were noted when he was triaged and then cleaned up and bandaged."

"OK," said Lanie, breathing deeply again, "I'm ready. Let's go see if it's Gavin."

She and Dr. Rob were led around the corner and down the hallway while Matthew pulled out his phone and called Danbury.

"I think we might have something," he said. "A guy was brought in to Grace Hospital in the middle of the night Monday night. He is pretty banged up but generally matches Gavin's description. He's suffered some head trauma so he's still unconscious. Dr. Rob and Lanie have just been escorted down to see if they can tell if it's him."

"OK," said Danbury. "Somebody will need to get his mom. If it is him. That's not something I'd want to tell her over the phone."

"Yeah, and we shouldn't have her driving in this crazy Miami traffic if her son is in the ICU," added Matthew.

"Agreed," said Danbury. "I can go get her. And bring her there."

"OK," said Matthew. "She's headed where when she lands? To the hotel?"

"Yeah, that's what Dr. Rob said this morning. I'll head that way. And pick her up. If they think it's him."

"OK, I'll let you know when they come back," said Matthew. "How'd the conversation go with the ex-boyfriend of the other missing woman?"

"He wasn't there. Hasn't been all week. Nobody seems to know where he is. He was questioned last week. By the Miami-Dade guys. But he didn't show up to work this week. He apparently lives alone. Nelson is running down his landlord now. But it doesn't sound promising."

"Wow, that makes him look guilty if he ran," said Matthew.

"Well, guilty of something. This is Miami, after all. Not Peak."

"Yeah, true. I'll let you know as soon as I know what Lanie and Dr. Rob think."

They disconnected and Matthew couldn't be still. He sat in one of the chairs just inside the waiting area, knee jumping and foot tapping. Then he got up and paced the small waiting alcove. He felt that he needed to be doing something productive so he sat back down and called Leo to check on Max. At least he was happy to get a good report on that front, he thought. Much to Matthew's surprise, Max had happily curled up around Leo's head in the middle of the night, and Leo was thrilled to finally have a pet to care for. Matthew shook his head in amusement as he ended the call and spied Dr. Rob and a tearful Lanie under his arm making their way back down the hallway toward him.

"It's him," Dr. Rob said as they approached. "We're all but positive. I need to call Gayle."

"Wait," said Matthew, holding up a cautionary hand. "Danbury said he'd go get her and tell her in person. Let me just call and tell him and then drop him a pin to get down here."

"OK, grand idea," conceded Dr. Rob. "Good plan."

Danbury picked up on the second ring and Matthew filled him in.

"I'll head back to Hialeah. And then bring her there," said Danbury. "Do you want to wait?"

Matthew quickly checked with the other two and said, "Yeah, we'll wait for you. I want to walk back down to the ED and see if anyone can tell us how he got here. The ED director said he was 'brought in' but I don't know how or by whom. I didn't think to ask because we didn't know it was him."

"OK, I'm on my way," said Danbury and disconnected.

Matthew dropped a pin with his location for Danbury to get to the hospital and turned to Dr. Rob. "I'm going back down to the ED to see if I can figure out how he got here and where he came from. Do you want to come down or wait here for his Mom?"

"I need some air," choked Lanie, tearfully. "I know it's hotter than Hades out there, but I really want to go out and sit on one of those benches we saw under the edge of the trees by the water."

"OK, I'll go with you," said Dr. Rob. "We'll go down with you," he added to Matthew as they all started toward the bank of elevators. "We can come back into the ED if it gets too hot out there," he added to Lanie. "We left water bottles in the car, but I'm sure they're warm by now," he grimaced.

"We're not getting any closer to finding Ariel, are we?" asked Lanie, disappointedly. "I was hoping we'd find Gavin in a room, propped up, watching television, and Ariel with him. But then, she'd have called or texted me, wouldn't she? She wouldn't have left me worrying about them if she could help it," she gulped air and Dr. Rob put an arm back around her shoulders reassuringly. The look on his face as he peered over her head at Matthew was anything but reassured.

They said nothing on the ride back down in the elevator. It was only as they approached the rear entrance of the ED and pushed the button to be admitted that they spoke again, asking for Dr. Mayer.

When the doors opened, Dr. Rob steered Lanie around the periphery of the room and back down the hallway leading out. Matthew approached the nurses' station where he was told that Dr. Mayer would be right with him.

She approached, looking at bit harried for an ED Director and apologized, telling him that they'd just had victims from a four-car-pile up brought in and they were still short-staffed.

"I'm sorry, I won't take up much time," he said. "We're pretty certain the young man brought in is the one we're looking for and I was just wondering how he got here." When she looked confused, Matthew clarified, "You said he was brought in, but by whom and how? How did he get brought in?"

"Oh, by ambulance. He was brought in on an ambulance."

"And he was alone. Just him, no other patients came with him?"

"Right, just him. He was alone in the ambulance and there were no others brought in with him."

"Not even to the morgue? Would someone who was DOA be transported through here? Or straight to the morgue?"

"I or one of the other physicians would have to call the time of death so, unless the person had been deceased for some time, even if they were dead on arrival, they'd still have come through here. Our Medical Examiner is a good friend of mine. We walk together in the afternoons, so I happen to know that there were only two elderly people in the morgue yesterday afternoon, both identified. They died here."

Matthew was certain that the relief must have been apparent on his face as he let out a breath that he didn't realize he'd been holding and

Dr. Mayer smiled at him. He summarized, "OK, the young man was transported in alone by ambulance. Do you know from where?"

"I don't," she said, shaking her head. "But the girlfriend of one of the paramedics works up on the main floor in patient billing. She can probably get you in touch with him and he can tell you where they picked up the patient."

Just then, the doors from the front hallway whooshed open and two sets of paramedics were rushing toward them rolling stretchers that were transporting incoming bloodied patients. Matthew suddenly remembered all the reasons why, after a rotation in an Emergency Department in his medical program, he'd opted against working in the ED. The stress level was unbelievable and the adrenaline levels of the medical staff who worked there had to be on overload most of the time.

Rushing toward the stretchers, Dr. Mayer called over her shoulder, "The paramedic's name is Pete. Don't know his last name, but his girlfriend's name is Elana Moreno." She'd reached the stretcher and started taking stock of the first patient, then the second. As the whole group with both stretchers was rushing back toward Matthew, she barked out questions and orders. Then, to Matthew, as she ran by, she said, "Come this way and you can take the back hallway out and an elevator up."

He had to jog to keep up, but when they reached the ED bays, she pointed off to the right as she and the stretchers were turning a corner to the left, and said, "That way. Go through those doors, and down the hall to Elevator B, then up a floor and follow the signs to patient accounting!"

"Thanks Dr. Mayer!" he said, but he wasn't sure she'd heard him at all as she was already around the corner and out of sight. Two other physicians in scrubs and lab coats rushed past Matthew to follow her as he headed to the back hallway and through the double doors to the right that she'd pointed to.

Finding Elevator B easily enough, Matthew pushed the button, eventually heard it clunk down to his floor, and watched as the doors slowly opened. Very slowly, he noted, in contrast to the frenzied rush he'd just left in the ED. He stepped inside and punched the button for the next floor up, hoping that he could gain some valuable information about where Gavin had come from before landing in a coma fighting for his life. He hoped fervently that information would help them find Ariel quickly, alive and well.

7 ~ GAINING TRACTION

As he exited the elevator, Matthew could see signs pointing in all directions. He found a kiosk with each floor labeled and located the area marked Patient Accounting. The hospital wasn't huge, but it appeared to Matthew to be a labyrinth of corridors and alcoves. He turned down a side hallway and continued along until he reached a sign over a doorway that identified the patient accounting area. Pushing through the double doors, he found an elderly woman with thick glasses seated behind a circular desk.

"May I help you, Sir?" she asked.

"Yes, I'm looking for Elana Moreno."

"She's around this corner to your right," answered the older woman. "But she's with a client right now. Do you have a billing issue? Can someone else help you?"

"No, I really need to speak with Ms. Moreno. OK if I just wait here until she's available?" he asked, motioning to a row of chairs across from the circular desk.

"Certainly, Sir."

As he took a seat, he realized that he hadn't asked if the woman would tell him when Elana Moreno was free or if he needed to check himself, but then she'd gotten on the phone so he'd missed his opportunity. She seemed to be doing more listening than talking and she was jotting something on a notepad as she said things like, "Ummm hmmm. OK, got it. Sure, I can check on that for you."

While she chatted away amicably with someone, a short stocky woman with thick dark hair that she kept pushing out of her eyes rounded the corner from the right and said, pleasantly, "Who's next?"

Matthew stood up, "I'm looking for Elana Moreno."

"You found her," she smiled up at him and extended a hand. "Come on back and I'll be happy to help you." He followed her back to a cubicle. She sat on one side of a desk that looked more like a counter and indicated the seat across from her for Matthew. "OK, what's your billing issue?" she asked, as she turned to a computer off to one side, ready to gather whatever information she'd need to properly bill him.

"I don't have a billing issue," he responded, as she raised her eyebrows in surprise. "Dr. Mayer sent me up to find you because she said your boyfriend, Pete, is the paramedic who brought in someone Monday night and I was hoping you could connect me to him."

She blushed. "Connect you to Pete?" she asked, and Matthew nodded.

"Pete is a friend of mine," she said slowly. "But I'm not comfortable giving out his information."

"Perfectly understandable," he answered, handing her his business card. "I'm Dr. Matthew Paine. I flew in last night from North Carolina because my colleague, Dr. Richard Roberts, has a daughter who came down here on a summer work trip and she's been missing since Monday night, along with her boyfriend. We're pretty sure we've found the boyfriend upstairs in the ICU, but he's badly injured and currently in a coma. My colleague's daughter is not here. I was hoping your, ah, Pete," he said, catching himself before saying "boyfriend" again, making her blush. "I was hoping Pete could tell me where the patient was picked up."

She hesitated, and he added, "You don't have to provide me with Pete's information, but could you contact him and provide him with mine? If he could just call or text and tell me the circumstances of that incoming patient, it could be vitally important in helping us locate the missing woman, preferably alive," he added for emphasis. "Her boyfriend up in the ICU isn't in great shape. He has severe head injuries and he came in as a John Doe. No identification. You can see why we need to determine his last whereabouts as quickly as possible."

"Yes, I see," she said, and quirked her mouth sideways. "I guess I could call him and give him this information and ask him to contact you."

"That would be great!" said Matthew. "I really appreciate your help. I jotted my cell number on the back of the card there. Or if Pete would be more comfortable talking to a police officer, we have a Homicide Detective who traveled down with us. I can give you his number if that would be better."

"No, no, yours is fine," she said. "There wasn't anyone else out there waiting so I'll call him really quickly for you." She reached into the bottom drawer of a metal file cabinet that was mounted beneath the desk, retrieved a big bulky purse, plopped it with a loud thud on top of the desk, and pulled a cell phone from it. After poking at it, she held it up to her ear and a moment later said, in a very professional tone, "Hi Pete. It's Elana. I need to talk to you about a patient issue. Would you please call me back ASAP? Thanks."

She put the purse away but left the phone out on the top of the counter. "I'll give him the message, Dr. Paine, and ask him to call you. I hope you find your friend's daughter."

"Thank you, Ms. Moreno," said Matthew, as he rose from his seat. "I really appreciate it. And I hope so too!"

He tuned and made his way back through the reception area and the elderly woman, who was off of the phone said, "Have a nice day!" He nodded, returned the sentiment, and stepped back out into the hallway wondering if he could get back through the ED and out to find Dr. Rob and Lanie or if he needed to take a different path entirely. He thought he could find them more easily if he went out of the front of the hospital and then off to the right and around to the parking lot than back through the maze of the hospital, so he headed in that direction.

He could smell coffee as he approached the main lobby and saw a small coffee shop to his left. Resisting the nearly irresistible temptation, he walked through the sunny vestibule at the main entrance that was fronted with a double story of glass windows, and out into the brightly lit June day. The sun was blinding and the humidity oppressive as he walked out, but he thought he preferred it to the twists and turns he'd made trying to find his way around inside.

As he rounded the corner and the Emergency Department canopy was to his right, he held his hand up over his eyes and squinted to try to see Lanie and Dr. Rob. He thought he could see them on an A-frame swing under the edge of the trees down by the bulkhead on the water. He headed that way, enjoying a slight tropical breeze that was blowing in off the water. That's what Miami heat was, he realized, it was stagnant. Just that little bit of a breeze from the water helped the heat index a lot.

The waves lapping against the bulkhead and the palm fronds whispering in the breeze were refreshing despite the humidity. As he was making his way over to the swing and enjoying the beauty of the day, his cell phone sounded from his pocket. Retrieving it, he answered, "Dr. Paine," and an uncertain male voice said, "Hi, it's Pete Eanes. Elana Moreno said you wanted to talk to me?"

"Hi Pete, thanks for calling me back. Yes, Dr. Mayer in the ED said that you transported a patient in late Monday night, or actually really early Tuesday morning. A young unidentified male who was unconscious with multiple contusions, particularly around his face and head."

"I did, yeah. We brought him in around five AM, I think. Somewhere around then. What else do you need to know?"

"Where you picked him up from and how you were called to the scene."

"We picked him up in an alleyway behind businesses on one of the roads off of Brickell Avenue. Southwest 9th, maybe? There are lots of restaurants around there and he was behind one of them by a big dumpster. I can check the log if you need to know exactly."

"Thanks, that would be helpful. Brickell Avenue? Isn't Brickell south of downtown Miami? Below where the Miami River comes in?"

"Yeah, it is. I'll check the log. Can I just text you the exact location?"

"Sure. And do you know who called you in? It wasn't likely to be him since he didn't have a phone on him and he wasn't conscious."

"I don't know. Dispatch can tell us. Do you need me to connect you to Dispatch?"

"I can get that information, I think, based on the location."

Pete gave him the precinct number and Matthew realized he had nowhere to write it down, but he could surely remember it long enough to give it to Danbury, who he planned to call next, and get it into their shared documents. The medical profession had well taught him how to document everything in detail, he thought, and that was coming in handy now.

"They can get me an address, too, so don't worry about that. But the guy in the alley, was he alone there when you picked him up?" asked Matthew. "We're looking for a young woman who was with him earlier in the evening. A petite redhead who's also missing. You didn't see her?"

"Nah, I didn't see a woman. There were a couple of concerned onlookers, but they weren't with him."

"Why do you say that?"

"They looked more like drifters. The guy we picked up was dressed in Ralph Lauren, not surfer rags like the guys watching from one end of the alley. He looked like he belonged there, in that trendy section in Brickell. They didn't. They were older, both male. I don't think they had moved him.

"Why do you say that?" asked Matthew.

"He had no wallet, ID, or phone, so there was no way to contact anyone for him, but if those guys had taken any of that, they'd have been long gone. So, they probably hadn't moved him. We were able to slide him on a board and get his neck in the collar to immobilize him in case he'd broken it. We weren't sure what we were dealing with so we were careful. As always. We did wonder where he came from and how he got in the alley. A bar fight gone south, maybe?

"Thanks, Pete. You've been very helpful. If I have any other questions, can I call or text you at this number?"

"Yeah, no problem."

"You have mine so if you think of anything else that could be helpful in finding the woman who was with him that evening, would you call or text?"

"Yeah, I can't think of anything else right now, but if I do, I will."

They said their goodbyes and ended the call just as Matthew walked up to the A-frame swing and Dr. Rob turned to him, "Anything? Any new information?"

"Yeah, we've got a general location," said Matthew. "I was just about to call Danbury. Just a sec, and I'll tell you both at once."

He called Danbury and knew that he was on speaker in the car as Danbury answered, sounding like he was in a hole or under the plentiful Miami water, "Hey Doc. I'm just getting into Hialeah. What's up?"

Matthew explained about the paramedic's information. Danbury said he'd pull over and quickly put the request in for the information from the dispatcher at the precinct Matthew provided to get a specific location and any information about who had called it in before he picked up Gavin's mom.

"A back alley," Danbury repeated. "Not likely a car accident, then. Unless it was a hit and run. And then he was dumped there."

"That part sounds plausible," said Matthew.

"Yeah, battered elsewhere, somehow. And dumped there. I'll bring the mom. Then we can go check out the location. Canvass the area. Maybe get some help from the Miami Dade guys. I'll let you know when we're close," Danbury added before abruptly disconnecting.

"They found Gavin in Brickell?" asked Dr. Rob. "Isn't that on the other side of the river from Dock Side where they were last seen?"

"It is," confirmed Matthew. "It's on this side of the river, just north of here, and Dock Side is on the other side. But we saw all of the bridges, so crossing it wouldn't be a big deal."

"And in a back alley?"

"That's what the paramedic said, yeah. Danbury's going to get an exact location and we'll go check it out after he gets Gavin's Mom here."

As they were conjecturing about how Gavin could have gotten into the alley and what had happened to him, Dr. Rob's cell phone sounded. "It's Gayle," he said as he pulled it from his pocket and answered it.

"Hey Gayle," he paused. "Yeah, we're here. We're pretty sure it's Gavin, but he had nothing on him, no phone, no ID, no wallet. He's in ICU in an induced coma now but he wasn't conscious when they brought him in, so we don't know yet what happened. He's in critical but stable condition."

He paused, listening, "That just means that they're monitoring him closely for brain swelling. I don't think they can accurately predict the prognosis yet, but I will say that it sounds like it could surely have been worse and that recovery is certainly possible from what we know so far."

After another few moments of hesitation, Dr. Rob added, "Sure, what's that?" And then he said, "Upper? We can check. OK, we'll see you in about a half hour. Yeah, got it, see you then."

As he disconnected, Dr. Rob stood up. "Danbury must be on his phone with Sergeant Nelson. Gayle said she overheard him mention something about checking dental records on someone and that made her think of one thing we can check to determine if this is Gavin. Gayle said he had braces as a young teen and they closed a gap between his top front teeth so he still has a dental appliance, a bar in place behind those top front teeth to keep them from shifting back."

"Do you want me to check, or do you want to?" asked Matthew.

Dr. Rob glanced back down at Lanie, "Are you too hot out here? Do you want to go back inside?"

"Yes, but No!" she said vehemently. "It is hot and sticky but I don't want to go back in there. I really don't."

"You could sit in the car with the air conditioner, if you'd like," Matthew said, handing Dr. Rob the keys. "I'll step back in and ask the security guard if he can call up and have them check. If this is Gavin, and we can track his movements backward, then maybe that gets us a step closer to finding Ariel too," he added, hopefully.

Matthew could feel the sweat dripping down the small of his back as he left the shade of the scrubby trees and walked back across the parking area, avoiding the asphalt and staying on the grassy edge as much as possible. He figured another thing they would need to do soon was find some water, chilled water. He was sure whatever was left in the car wasn't by now.

He approached the front desk of the ED and there was nobody behind it. He looked around but didn't see the security guard anywhere. This wasn't the time for the guy to be on break, he thought, a bit irritably and realized that the heat was getting to him.

"Excuse me?" he said to a woman over to the right who was working between two patients with a clipboard and asking them all of the usual intake questions. These patients clearly weren't critical and they were seated in large chairs with blood pressure cuffs and oxygen sensors hooked up.

"I'll be with you in a moment, Sir," she said. "Please have a seat in Chair 5," she added, motioning to the chair to her left.

"I'm not an incoming patient," he said. "Though I might be if I'm out in this heat too much longer," he added trying for some levity. When she didn't respond, he said, "I'm looking for the security guard who was here an hour or so ago. Is he still on duty? Or, how can I call up to the ICU unit?"

"Visitors go through the front entrance," she said, flatly, returning to her intake forms.

"Thanks so much for your help," responded Matthew, feeling as if the sarcasm was dripping from his tongue and through his teeth as he spoke, "I'll wait."

After what seemed like an eternity of pacing around the long narrow room, in which time he thought he might have indeed managed to get back around to the front entrance and up to the ICU unit to check for himself, the double doors whooshed opened and the security guard stepped through carrying a steaming cup of coffee. Matthew couldn't imagine drinking hot coffee much in Miami in the summer and he said so. The security guard, unbothered by the remark, simply said, "I'm from Costa Rica. We drink coffee all day, every day. Were you looking for me? How can I help you?"

Matthew explained the situation and the security guard said, "Just a minute and I'll see what I can do." He slowly and carefully set the coffee cup down on the desk beneath the top level of the counter and tapped some keys on the computer keyboard in front of him as he stared down with drooping hooded eyelids at the screen. Then he picked up a phone from the counter and lackadaisically poked a few more keys on there.

"Hello?" said the guy. "Yes, I'll hold." Meanwhile, Matthew could feel his impatience growing. His eyebrow shot up and he was fighting the urge to tap his foot in annoyance this time, not in concentration.

Finally, the guy said, "Hello? This is Tomás in Security in the Emergency Department. You have a John Doe up there that some people were just up to identify? Yes, yes, that's him. Can you check to see if there is a," he paused. "How you say," and he paused again.

"May I please speak with them?" asked Matthew, very formally, with his goal firmly in mind.

"Certainly, Sir," said the security guard, with apparent relief, as he handed the phone handset over the top of the counter to Matthew.

Identifying himself, Matthew made the request to check behind the patient's top front teeth and waited. He'd seen the configuration of the unit and knew that the nurse's station was in the center with the ICU units surrounding it, so the nurse he'd spoken with wouldn't have far to go. On the other hand, he'd also seen that most of the ICU beds were occupied up on that floor and he'd only seen two nurses.

Eventually, she returned to the phone, "Dr. Paine?"

"Yes, I'm here."

"The patient does have an appliance attached behind the top row of teeth."

"Thank you!" replied Matthew, gratefully. "His name is Gavin Blevins, he's twenty years old, and his mother Gayle has just flown in and she's on her way here now."

"Wonderful!" she said. "We've been worried about him up here, unknown, all alone. Tell her that she can park in the ED parking lot and come through that entrance if it's easier for her. We can tell her what we know of his condition when she gets up here."

"I'll do it. Thanks," he said, as he handed the phone back to Tomás. Maybe they were finally getting some much-needed traction on finding the two missing young people, he thought. One of them at least was most likely found. But what had happened to him and where was the other one? That was the question still turning through his brain as he walked back out to give Dr. Rob the update.

Lanie and Dr. Rob were no longer in the swing so Matthew crossed the parking lot to the Sonata. The tinted windows were up and he could barely see that they were inside with the air conditioning blasting. Just as he was about to join them, Danbury's rented SUV pulled up to the security arm. As the metal arm went up, Matthew raised an arm to flag Danbury down.

Danbury weaved his way over to Matthew in the small parking lot and pulled alongside as Matthew tapped on the window of the Sonata and pointed. Dr. Rob and Lanie slid out of the car while a woman who looked to be in her mid to late-forties climbed down from the big SUV and launched herself at Dr. Rob. There seemed to be a lot of that going around, thought Matthew. Under the circumstances, he could hardly blame them.

She held on for a moment longer than Matthew thought she should have. Stifling a sob, she pulled away and started firing questions. "Where is he? Can I see him? Where did they find him? In a brick alley?"

Momentarily stupefied, Matthew saw the dawn of understanding on Dr. Rob's face as he finally answered, "In an alley in Brickell. It's a suburb of Miami just north of here."

"Oh!" she said. "The big guy over there said something that I thought was 'brick alley' and then his phone rang and he's been on it ever since. He's not terribly communicative, is he?"

"Not so much," said Matthew stepping forward and introducing himself. "But he's a first-class detective so we cut him some slack," he added with a grin. "We confirmed that the young man up in the ICU has the dental appliance you told us about so you just need to give them a 100 percent on the identification."

"When can I see him?"

"Right now," said Dr. Rob. "I can take her up," he added to Matthew.

"Just introduce her to Tomás, the security guard, when you go in so that he'll know to let you through. If he questions it, tell him the ICU nurse said you could park down here and come through that way. She sounded like a force to be reckoned with, but I didn't catch her name."

Dr. Rob nodded and Matthew added, "I think Danbury and I are going to check out the alley. Why don't you hang on to the keys for the Sonata so that you can get back to the hotel when you want to? Or meet us later if need be."

Danbury was putting his phone back in his pocket as he stepped out of the SUV and approached the group, "It's too hot to stand out here," he said, giving voice to Matthew's thoughts. "We need to hit the road anyway. We have a location on the alley. No identity on the 9-1-1 caller. But we can listen to the recording."

"Lanie," Dr. Rob turned to the young woman, who had wrapped her arms around herself and was standing just back from the group. "What do you want to do? You can stay here with Gavin's mom and me, or you can ride with Danbury and Matthew to check out the alley. Wherever you're most comfortable."

When she hesitated, Matthew added, "We'll be happy to have you along, if you want. There's not going to be much to do around here." Unless Gavin wakes up, he thought, but he didn't say it out loud.

Dr. Rob had pulled the keys from the car and locked it and he was looking expectantly at Lanie, waiting for her to decide what to do.

"I guess I'll come with you, if that's OK," said Lanie cautiously to Matthew. "I really want to help find Ariel, if there's anything at all that I can do."

"We'll need your help anyway at Dock Side to talk to the Gen Zers," said Matthew, encouragingly. "We're Millennials, so they already think we're old and crazy."

Lanie half smiled at that and she hugged Dr. Rob and told him good-bye before following Matthew and Danbury back to the SUV and climbing in the back seat. As they watched Dr. Rob and Gayle Blevins make their way to the canopy over the ED entrance, Matthew turned to Danbury and said, "OK, what's the address and I'll navigate."

"Just a sec," said Danbury. "There's something else." He looked over his shoulder at Lanie and then said quietly, "They've found a body. But it isn't Ariel. They're all but certain," he added quickly.

Lanie choked on a sobbing breath, "What? Who is it then? Where?

When?”

“I didn’t want to say anything in front of you,” Danbury said to Lanie. “Or Dr. Rob,” he added. “Until we’re positive. The Miami-Dade guys are checking. They just got dental records. From the other two women. Both of them were missing before Ariel. They think it’s the first one. But they just got the dental records. To confirm it.”

“That’s awful!” sobbed Lanie. “Does that mean?” she choked and couldn’t finish the question she was trying to ask.

“It doesn’t mean anything yet,” reassured Matthew, wanting to console her but realizing that he didn’t know her well and he didn’t want anything to be misconstrued.

“Did Ariel cut her hair?” asked Danbury. “Since the pictures we have of her?”

“No,” said Lanie. “Everyone has always told her how beautiful her hair is. She’d never have cut it herself, unless ….” She couldn’t finish her sentence.

“The hair is shorter. On the woman they found,” said Danbury carefully. “And they think it’s dyed. Not naturally red. They think she has a more compact build. Stockier than Ariel.”

“Can’t they tell?” asked Lanie.

Danbury grunted, looking at Matthew for moral support before he answered, “It’s hard to know. They pulled her out of the water. We think she’d been in there a couple of days.”

“Oh!” said Lanie. “So she isn’t?” and stopped again, not knowing how to finish the sentence.

“It makes the identification much more difficult,” supplied Matthew. “But we have to assume it’s not Ariel and try to find her as quickly as possible.” And then to Danbury, he asked, “Are we still going to the alley? Or does this change that?”

“Nope,” said Danbury definitively. “It doesn’t change anything. We’re going to the alley. Then we need to go back to Dock Side. See what they can tell us. The folks who were working Monday night. We’re still looking for Ariel. And we’ll do our best to find her.”

“OK, good,” said Matthew. “Give me the address.”

Danbury read it off and Matthew punched it into the app on his phone.

"I've asked for video footage. Any cameras from that area," said Danbury. "The Miami-Dade guys are stretched thin. We might have to canvass for that ourselves."

"What do we know about the woman who was just found?" asked Matthew.

"Hey Lanie," said Danbury. "You want some ear buds? To listen to something on your phone? I picked them up at the airport. I have a brand-new set up here. They're corded. But they've never been used."

Lanie sighed deeply before she responded, "Yeah, I get it. You want to talk about things that you don't want me to hear. That's probably good, thanks."

Danbury reached down to a partitioned section of the console and handed back a packet with the earbuds, which Lanie gratefully took, opened, and proceeded to plug them in and then poke her phone. "I'll just be listening to my favorite music back here," she said. "Let me know if you need me for anything."

"Thanks, Lanie," said Matthew turning to Lanie and then back to Danbury as he saw her pop the ear buds in her ears, "OK, tell me what you don't want her to hear."

"The body that was found. It was washed ashore at Brickell Key Park. On the southern tip of an inverted triangular island. Brickell Key. Very upscale area. Just off the mouth of the Miami River. Offshore just north of here. There's a road over. Not far from where we're going now. Where Gavin was picked up. She wasn't in good shape. Initial estimate was two days. But fish had gotten to her. They won't know how long until the autopsy. And maybe not even then. Cause of death is also unknown. Nelson's team is handling that. Mostly. He is supposed to keep me in the loop. They're experts on the tides. Water temperatures. The weather patterns down here. We might need to make a trip over. But we'll see what they turn up first."

"Why now, if she's been missing for a couple of weeks?" asked Matthew. "Which woman do they think this is?"

"They think it's Dominique Rizzo. She was the first one reported missing. She's twenty-five and slightly shorter than Ariel. With a more compact build. She's a redhead, but dyed red. She's the one who just broke up with her boyfriend. They were living together in Brickell. Then she moved in with the friend in Wynwood. Then he moved out too. The Miami-Dade guys couldn't locate him, at first. But they found and questioned him. And now he's in the wind entirely."

"Wynwood? Where's that?"

"That's an up-and-coming area. Or so I'm told. It's north of Brickell. It's south of Little Haiti and a place called Model City. Some of the least safe areas around Miami. Location-wise, not great. But somebody is trying to make it trendy. Her new roommate was a friend she'd worked with. Several years back. But they hadn't seen much of each other. Not since Dominique moved in with the boyfriend. Not until Dominique moved in with her. And that's about all I know. I added information about her in our shared documents. But I left out details about the body. Those details are too grisly."

"Do you have access to the notes from the interview with the boyfriend? Maybe he's a nut job hung up on redheads."

"I have a transcript of it. I added it to our online documents. He didn't say much when questioned. He'd known Dominique for a couple of years. They'd dated on and off. Over two years or so. They'd moved in together nine months ago. Into one of those high-rise apartment buildings in Brickell. Neither could afford it alone, apparently. When they spilt, they both moved out. He said it was amicable. No hard feelings. At least not on his part. Dominique's new roommate says otherwise."

"Yeah? What did the new roommate say?"

"Maria is the roommate's name. That's also in our documents online."

"Wow, you've been busy this morning!" said Matthew.

"Not really," said Danbury, dismissively. "Mostly just copied and pasted. From files Nelson shared."

"What did Maria say that was different from the boyfriend's story?"

"That Dominique was heartbroken. I think that was the word she used. And that he was a skank. Again, her words."

"A skank? I haven't heard that one in a while. I might have to look that up."

"On the take. Selfish. In it for himself. Womanizer. Didn't care that he'd hurt Dominique. Multiple times. Maria did elaborate," he added with a smirk.

"Oh. Not a nice guy, huh?"

"Yeah, sounds like it. To read Maria's account, anyway."

"And you said earlier that there was no known connection to the second woman who's missing?"

"Both the boyfriend and Maria were asked about her. Katie Jones. The second woman reported missing. Both denied knowing her. Or ever having heard of her. Neither had heard Dominique mention her. And both were asked that question. Pointedly."

"What do we know about her? Katie?"

"That's in our shared documents too. Nelson's bio on her. With a picture. And a last address. But the short version? She's twenty-three, a petite redhead. But also dyed red. Bright red. She's a natural blonde from South Carolina. She's lived in Brickell. After college in Miami. She had just lost her job. Her roommate said she was depressed. Rent is high in Brickell. Katie didn't want to move. Especially not back home to South Carolina. She didn't have a serious boyfriend. But the roommate characterized her as a flirt. Particularly in bars. When the drinks were flowing freely from men."

"Bars. Interesting. When we go back to Dock Side, we could ask JoJo and Angela which of the two women they remember seeing. Maybe it's Katie if she was into the bar scene."

"It's likely Katie. If it's one of them. Katie is about the same build as Ariel. And her eyes are blue. Dominique was heavier. And her eyes are brown. Her face is also more rounded. Or it was. Before she was ceviche."

Matthew's head snapped around at that comment.

"Sorry, Doc. Occupational hazard. Distancing yourself from the personal element. Makes it easier to handle sometimes. If bodies are bodies. And not people."

"I guess I get that," said Matthew slowly. "The ED staff in hospitals does that sometimes too. I guess all first responders and emergency workers do it, dehumanizing victims as a coping mechanism so that they can deal with treating patients without their emotions getting in the way of analysis and correct action."

"Yup. Women turning up that way. It's tough to deal with. Even if you have a thousand times before. It doesn't get easier. My least favorite part of the job."

Matthew was quiet as he realized that Danbury was actually sharing his inner thoughts. Danbury, the Homicide Detective, who was normally exceptionally stoic, had a softer side. Well sort of, Matthew thought. Not that he wanted to get all sappy. Prying open the tightly shut lid on Danbury could be potentially dangerous. Did anyone really understand the man's thought process, he wondered? Did Penn? Did he have any family that he was close to who understood him?

Just then, Matthew heard the roar of a powerful engine coming up from behind them. He noticed two dots growing rapidly larger in his side view mirror. Turning, as they were stopping for one of the many lights that were prevalent in Miami, Matthew's jaw dropped and Danbury turned to see what he was looking at.

Up beside them pulled two cars, first a red Lamborghini Veneno followed closely by a dark silvery grey Pagani Huayra coupe with nearly neon blue trim. Matthew could initially only manage to point and say "Oh! Oh wow!"

Unashamedly, he put the window down and openly gawked. The guy in the Lamborghini waved up at him and, as the light turned green, both cars quickly became specs on the horizon of South Miami Avenue, then slid around a corner to the left onto an entrance ramp for Interstate 95, and completely out of sight.

Matthew was in awe of the sound the engines made as they roared away and he just continued to stare after them in silent appreciation for the sight he'd just witnessed, unbelieving that he'd actually just seen it. It was a sight, he thought, that he'd never seen before and one which he was not likely to ever see again.

Lanie pulled her earbuds out and asked, "What is it?"

"Just a motorhead," said Danbury. "Hey Doc, roll your tongue back up. Stop drooling on yourself," he added as he punched Matthew, good-naturedly, in the shoulder.

"A what?" asked Lanie.

"A car fanatic," said Danbury. "One who just saw two high end vehicles."

"Highest of the high end," said Matthew. "Millions of dollars' worth of cars just went by. They're both extremely rare. I've never seen either of them, except in car magazines. That Lamborghini was a Veneno."

"A what?" repeated Lanie.

"A Veneno is reportedly the fastest Lambo. It's a fiftieth anniversary Lamborghini that came out in 2013 and only a handful were made that year. It has a top speed of well over two hundred miles an hour and it can go from zero to sixty in just under three seconds. And the Pagani," added Matthew. "The top speed on that might be a little bit higher, the zero to sixty only slightly slower, and the doors are truly gull-wing. They open up and the car looks like a seagull when they're both up."

"Oh. Pretty wicked looking," said Lanie as if trying to sound appreciative but obviously unimpressed, and she put her earbuds back in.

Matthew sat lost in thought until the navigation system brought him back to the moment at hand, as the automated voice started providing instructions, and he helped to make the last two turns. Then they located a parking spot two blocks down from the alleyway they were going to examine and pulled in. They were parked along a busy downtown street that Matthew figured must parallel the waterfront on the other side. It looked safe enough during the daytime hours at least. He wondered if Lanie might rather stay in the car and listen to her music.

"Hey Lanie, do you want to sit this one out? Or do you want to come examine the location where Gavin was found? We don't know what we'll find down there. We can lock you in with the air on if you want to stay in the car."

"It might be just an alleyway," added Danbury. "But it might not," and he hesitated without saying that it could be a grisly bloody scene.

Lanie cringed visibly but said aloud, "I don't want to be left alone here."

Matthew assumed that the police hadn't gotten around to checking it out yet for myriad reasons. Because they had just learned of it themselves and the victim had, so far, survived. Because the Miami Dade Police had a decomposing body of their own to investigate. And mainly because Danbury had said that they were overwhelmed already. Dead bodies and probable murders usually trumped almost everything else on their agendas, he'd learned. Aloud, he asked Danbury, "The police haven't looked at this spot yet, have they?"

"Not yet. I told Sergeant Nelson about it. Right after you called. I told him we were going to check it out. He was fine with that. He knows we'll share what we find. If we find anything."

They all stepped out of the SUV and the doors slammed shut simultaneously. Matthew stole an appraising glance at Lanie. She did not look up for the adventure. He was suddenly wishing that she'd stayed behind with Dr. Rob at the hospital.

"Hey, Danbury," he said to the retreating back of the hulking man. "Didn't you say that we would need to canvass the area for video cameras?"

"Yeah, that would help. If we had footage to review. Any from this area. From, say ten Monday night to five Tuesday morning."

"Why don't you check the alley and Lanie and I will start asking around at the businesses that surround it, from all angles. Surely somebody recorded something that'll help, though if they hadn't had any reason to look, they might not know that they have it yet."

"Reason to look?" asked Lanie, hopefully.

"If they'd had a break-in or gotten called for a potential issue, they'd have looked at their video feed," explained Matthew. "But if the businesses were quiet overnight and everything looked normal in the morning, they wouldn't have had a reason to look and they might not have. It's so busy down here somebody had to have seen something. It's not like it's lonely and deserted in the middle of nowhere."

"Oh," she said. "That makes sense."

"Good idea," answered Danbury. "Divide and conquer."

"Exactly," said Matthew. "OK, let's go find this alleyway and then Lanie and I can start to check with the businesses all around it."

The long alleyway was bisected by three narrow streets crossing it. Even in the daylight hours, it looked dark and smelled dank. Several large trash dumpsters lined the walls along both sides. There were high rise apartments, hotels, and restaurants all around them. Occasionally, alleyways darted behind them to provide access for deliveries and trash removal, Matthew assumed. This must be one of many service entrances behind the big buildings.

"Huh," said Matthew. "Pete the paramedic said they found him beside a big dumpster. He didn't mention that there were so many of them. I'll send a picture and ask him which one." That held them up momentarily, but Matthew was happy to get a quick response from Pete.

"Looking from this end, Pete says Gavin was found on the other side of the fourth one down on the left, between the second and third ones from the other end. He'd have been at least partially obscured by the other dumpsters down this alleyway," Matthew observed. "It's a wonder anyone found him and called it in."

Lanie shivered at the thought. Matthew said, "OK, ready?" She nodded, and they parted company with Danbury to start canvassing the businesses on the streets around the alleyway. Matthew could feel the breeze from the ocean and smell the salty air blowing in between the buildings from the nearby coastline. He was also getting whiffs of food cooking on that breeze, the scent emanating from the restaurants around them. His stomach growled in response and he realized that breakfast had been a long time ago and it was indeed lunchtime.

"Tell you what, Lanie," he said, pointing across the street. "Let's go check out that brasserie across the street there first. If they have security cameras, maybe we can at least get an iced coffee and a croissant while we wait."

"OK, sure," she said slightly uncertainly. "Maybe I can eat something. I don't really eat much when I'm upset."

That fit exactly into Matthew's view of the world. He thought there were basically two sorts of people, those who ate voraciously when they were upset or worried, and those who lost all appetite. Lanie apparently was in that latter category. He had, over his few years practicing medicine, treated both.

They made their way across the busy street and Matthew looked up to see what he thought was a disguised small security camera above the door as they stepped into the softly lit and heavenly fragrant brasserie.

9 ~ UNSEEN

A camera was mounted over the awning above the door on the outside of the brasserie. It might have caught anything happening near the entrance to the alleyway across the street.

Matthew and Lanie went in and sat down. While they awaited both the arrival of the manager they'd asked to speak with and the iced coffee and savory crêpes they'd opted for, Matthew thought he'd use the opportunity to get to know Lanie and Ariel, by extension, through her.

"Dr. Rob said you and Ariel have been friends since early childhood," began Matthew, giving Lanie an opening to talk about her best friend.

"We have," said Lanie. "I barely remember a time when we weren't friends. We were in a playgroup together when we were little. About four, I think. Something like that. Dr. Rob and Ariel had just moved to Peak and my parents sort of befriended them."

"Ah, your parents have been friends a long time too then?"

"Well, sort of. My parents divorced when I was just starting middle school. That's a horrible time to turn a child's world up-side-down, by the way. My older sister rebelled and I just felt so lost. Our parents tried to share custody and both remain fully in our lives, but it doesn't really work that way. So that's when I started spending all the time I could at Ariel's. It's not that she had a whole family either. Her mom is kind of," she hesitated, looking for the right words. "Well, she's kind of flaky. She lives in Asheville now, which is a perfect place for her.

She fits in with all of those artsy people."

"Was she in Peak back then?" asked Matthew. "When you and Ariel were little?"

"No, I'm really not sure where she was, but I know Ariel didn't see much of her. Her grandmother, Dr. Rob's mom, really filled that mom role in Ariel's life. But her dad is so," again at a loss for words. "He fills the gaps, you know?" Matthew nodded, completely understanding what Ariel was saying. And if his memory served correctly, Matthew thought that Dr. Rob might have been doing a residency when Ariel was about that age, which would have made life incredibly difficult for the man.

"He's so solid and kind and genuine. He always puts Ariel first. Because I've always been part of the package, that includes me too. It was a nice change from the bickering my parents were doing back then. They tried to hide it from us. But it was so obvious that they didn't agree on much of anything. At times, they tried to outdo each other with gifts. At other times they were just checked out. Lost in their own world or pain or whatever and neither of them had any idea what my sister and I were really up to."

Her big brown eyes looked up at Matthew and watered as she added, "But Ariel and Dr. Rob have always been so close. I think she really tells him everything. And I think he listens and remembers it all. Now that she's in college, he gives more suggestions than directions. He's smart about that. Ariel is really headstrong and determined. If he tried too hard to control her, she'd balk. But she's a good person, so it's not like he's had to work too hard to keep her on track. She's really an amazing person. I've never known anyone else like her. And I don't want to lose her." Her voice cracked as she admitted, "I guess that sounds selfish." Lanie looked down at her hands where she'd twisted a napkin into oblivion.

"It doesn't sound selfish," said Matthew, trying to console her. "It sounds like a strong friendship."

"It is. She's the best. We've had little squabbles growing up but never anything serious."

"And you purposefully went off to college together?" he prompted.

"Yeah, we'd always dreamed of being roommates. I mean, for real, like in our own apartment. I was at her house so much back in middle school and high school that she called the second bed in her bedroom my bed. She'd say, 'I changed the sheets on my bed and Lanie's too,' or 'Just tuck Lanie's shoes under her bed so that you don't trip over them.'"

Lanie smiled through the tears, "They made sure I knew that I was always welcome there and treated me like part of their family. When we were looking at colleges, I think Ariel was worried about her mom. She decided that UNC-Asheville could give her the degree she needed and she could be near to keep an eye on her mom. We were both already looking at graduate school so where I got my undergraduate degree in psychology wasn't as important as where I'd go for graduate school. We applied and got in easily. We got the scholarships we wanted, and we decided that's where we were going. Together."

"And Gavin? Did he go from Peak to school with you in Asheville too?"

"No, Gavin's not from Peak. He's from somewhere up in the Appalachian Mountains, I think. He almost went to school up there, but he said he wanted a little more space. He and Ariel met right at the beginning of our freshman year at a rally. Gavin is more of an activist than Ariel. He's into Greenpeace and all of that, but he has some of the same ideas about helping people in poorer communities that Ariel does, so it was nearly love at first sight."

"What was he needing space from?" asked Matthew, now very curious and not entirely focused on his initial intent to learn more about Ariel, though learning more about Gavin, he realized, couldn't hurt either at this point.

"His Mom. He has an older sister who rebelled, growing up. Gavin and I have that in common. But his dad peaced out on them entirely. I don't think he even knows where his dad is. And his mom can be," she paused, searching for the right way to say something that probably wasn't positive.

"Oppressive? Controlling?" offered Matthew after a long pause.

"Needy," supplied Lanie at last. "Clingy. He said she called him all the time his freshman year, trying to get him to come home. She called late one night and said she heard a noise downstairs and thought someone was breaking into the house. I think that's when he lost patience with her and told her he was two hours away and by the time he got there she'd be dead, so she'd better call the police if she had an intruder."

Matthew found a bit of humor in that but stifled the urge to chuckle.

"And honestly," she leaned forward, conspiratorially, "I think she has a thing for Dr. Rob. She's probably ten years older than he is. He's so nice he won't tell her outright that it's not going to happen. Everybody but her can tell that it isn't! It embarrassed Gavin when they were up for parents' weekend this past semester. He started making a point of putting the three of us between them any time they were about to sit down somewhere."

"Huh," was all Matthew said to this as a tall slender woman who was tastefully dressed in a tailored taupe pant suit with a light cream blouse approached their table. Her hair was pulled back in a bun at the nape of her long neck and she extended a slender and perfectly manicured hand to Matthew.

"Bon jour. I understand that you wished to speak with me?" she said with what was either a genuine French dialect or, to Matthew's untrained ears at least, a great imitation of one. As he nodded, rising from his seat, she added, "I'm Lillian Toussaint, proprietor. How can I help you?"

Taking the proffered hand, he introduced himself, "Hi, Ms. Toussaint, I'm Matthew Paine and this is Lanie James. We're looking for information about a young man who was found, unconscious, in that alleyway across the street there." He pointed in the general direction from the front of the restaurant. "He was found very early, before dawn, Tuesday morning but he could have been there from any time after about ten Monday night. We're trying to determine how he got there and when. Did you see anything or anyone unusual during that time?"

She pursed her lips in thought and said, "I don't recall anything unusual. It was a quiet night Monday night. I don't remember anything out of the ordinary at all. We close at ten and we come in around five to reopen by six. I am afraid I am not much help during the hours you are asking about."

"Do you remember seeing this young man?" asked Matthew, as he reached across the table, picked up the folder, and pulled out Gavin's picture. "Or this young woman?" he added as he handed her Ariel's picture too.

"No, no, he is not familiar," she said as she flipped Gavin's picture behind Ariel's and studied hers more closely. "And she has a look that is familiar, but no, I do not believe that I have seen her either. I am sorry that I cannot be of more help to you."

Lanie had leaned forward, expectantly and she sank back into her chair as Lillian handed the pictures back.

"Maybe you still can," replied Matthew. "Do you have a security camera on the front of your building?"

"Yes, yes. Of course, the security camera. We can have a look, if you would like?" she asked, charmingly.

"Yes, please."

"It is a tiny space, my office. You will be more comfortable waiting here, no?" she said to Lanie, though it was obvious that it wasn't really a question.

"I'll be right back," said Matthew, to Lanie. "Don't drink my iced latte. Or, if you do, order me another one," he said with a wink.

"Sure, Dr. Paine, I'll save it for you," she said.

"Doctor?" said Lillian. "Of what sort?"

Thinking that he'd have to tell Lanie to just call him Matthew later, he explained to Lillian that he had studied osteopathic medicine and worked in a family practice in a little town outside of Raleigh, North Carlina.

"Ah, I see," she said as she unlocked a door along a hallway that led to the restrooms and, Matthew presumed, a back kitchen area. She motioned him into what was indeed a very small room. He caught a whiff of perfume in her wake, but he wasn't sure what it was. It was woody and earthy, but musky at the same time, and it had a definite appeal. He had seen larger closets, he thought, but he managed to slide to the front of a large heavily ornate wooden desk, which took up most of the room, and into a chair she'd motioned him to, with his long legs jammed into the back of the desk.

Lillian slid into a chair on the other side of the desk and pulled a keyboard over to her, clicking keys until she was apparently satisfied and then turned a monitor around so that they could both see it. "We'll start at ten," she said, "I will fast forward through. If you see something you would like to look at, I will back up for a better look."

The time between ten at night and about one in the morning was very busy with people coming and going on the sidewalks and streets. She stopped and backed up several times for Matthew to get closer looks at people passing but only two went down the alleyway and that was much later, about four-thirty in the morning. But those two were telling.

After backing up and forwarding several times, Matthew knew all there was to know about them from the video, though that didn't tell him what he wanted to know. What it did tell him was that they were likely the two guys that Pete, the paramedic, had seen watching from the end of the alleyway. It might also have told him who made the 9-1-1 call.

They looked to be revelers coming from one of the bars, as they meandered along the sidewalk and into the frame of the video, looking a bit unsteady on their feet. One of them looked less steady than the other as they turned and headed down the alleyway. Less than five minutes later, they had reemerged and were standing at the corner of the building, peering much more steadily, and even expectantly, back down the alleyway. The taller one, who seemed to be less inebriated, pointed and said something to the other. The second guy shrugged and leaned heavily against the building. Clearly, they were waiting for something or someone.

Then, at four forty-two, both men leaned closer into the opening of the alleyway ostensibly to get a better look, though the shorter of the two was still leaning heavily against the wall. Matthew leaned in too to get a better view of the monitor because he thought he could see a red flashing light reflecting up the alleyway. It was a long alley he'd seen spanning the back of three blocks, so he wasn't certain about that. The guys stood there for another twelve minutes before wandering down the sidewalk in the direction from which they were originally traveling and back out of the screen.

That was all Matthew was going to get from this angle, he realized, so he asked, "Have you ever seen these two guys before? Do they look familiar? I know it's a long distance and you can't see their faces."

"Not from this distance, no. I cannot tell if they are familiar. But their clothing does not look like that of one of our patrons. I have not seen anyone as shabbily dressed in here."

They did look a bit like vagabonds, Matthew conceded, but to Lillian, he said, "Can you capture just that section of the video?"

"Yes, yes. I can, of course."

"If I bring you a thumb drive, could you provide me with a copy? Or, if you'd rather, you can upload it to a site where we're storing information. I can give you access to it temporarily for the upload."

She readily agreed to capturing and uploading the video clip and gave him her contact information. He pulled out his phone and gave her momentary access to a folder he created on their shared site and sent her a link to it.

While she was working on the upload, Matthew texted Danbury and told him both where he was and what he'd learned about the two men in the alley. Then he handed Lillian his card with his cell phone number jotted on it. "If you think of anything else that might be helpful, or if you see anything unusual in the area, including the two guys in the video, would you contact me?"

"But, of course," she said with a smile that was disarming. "Perhaps you could join me this evening for dinner? Or perhaps for drinks? I would enjoy your company," she added alluringly as she stared into his eyes.

"I'm sure I would enjoy your company too," he conceded, somewhat to appease her and mostly, he realized, because it was true. "But I can't. We are working hard to find out what happened to the young man who was found in the alleyway and to find the young woman, Ariel Roberts, who was with him. She's still missing. But thank you for providing the video. It might help if we can find the two guys in it."

"Ah, that's a pity that you have no leisure time," she said pouting and stepping forward.

"I really don't," he agreed, as he stepped around her to prevent her from blocking him in her office. "This isn't a vacation trip and time is everything. It's critical that we find Ariel as quickly as possible."

After a few extricating exchanges back and forth with Lillian, he thanked her again for her help, rejoined Lanie, paid the bill, and took his food to go. He was eating his crêpe from the paper wrapping as they crossed the street to meet Danbury at the end of the alley.

Lanie said teasingly, "She likes you. She really likes you."

"She was very helpful, but I don't have time for any of that right now," he answered, matter-of-factly.

"Who likes you?" asked Danbury, looking longingly at Matthew's crêpe as he shoved the last bite in his mouth.

"Nobody," said Matthew, trying to chew and swallowing hard. He quietly told Danbury about the video he'd just watched and uploaded and about the two guys in the alley. "What did you find?" he asked.

"There's not much to see down here," Danbury said. "Looks like the action was at the other end. Or off of one of the narrow side streets. There are three of those. Eight entry points over the three blocks. Three entry points on each side. One at each end. Only one ruled out by your video. There aren't cameras on the cross streets. Not that I can see. So that leaves the other end. I don't think he was beaten here. There's no," he hesitated, looking at Lanie and then he tried again. "The area is clean. He can't have been brought in unseen. It's too busy in this area.

Taking a breath, Danbury considered for a moment and then added, "We need somebody to identify the two guys. The ones you saw in the videos. We need to do some more canvassing. But we also need to go back to Dock Side," he added, checking his watch.

"Yeah, to catch the other bartender before she leaves after the first half of her split shift. What was her name? Courtney, right? DeBerry?"

"I think that's right," said Danbury. "Impressive. Why don't you take Lanie and go back to Dock Side. I'll canvass this area more closely. You can come get me after. You know the drill. What to ask. How to read people. You do that well. I'll see if I can find more cameras. Or anyone who saw anything that night. He had to have been brought in. Unless he stumbled into the alley. And fell there. But that doesn't make any sense. Somebody had to have seen something."

"OK, I'll ask about camera footage from Dock Side too. JoJo saw them come in but nobody, so far, saw them leave. Somebody had to have, because, like you said, they can't have left unseen with that many people around that area either. Maybe the time they left will tell us something, or if they didn't leave alone. The Rydz driver was supposed to pick them up on the street in front of Dock Side, so maybe some of the people under the bridge saw them after they left."

"If they'll talk to you," said Lanie, finally speaking up again. "And if they're reliable. Many of them seemed to be kind of out of it. You could ask them if the sky was green and they'd tell you that it is if they thought you'd give them something for the information."

"Not surprising," answered Danbury. "That's a rough life. Let's do this," he added, as he handed the SUV keys to Matthew.

"OK, ready Lanie?"

"Sure, she said, sipping the last of her Frappuccino and looking around for a trash can to throw the cup away."

"I got it," said Danbury, indicating the rows of dumpsters down the alleyway as Matthew stuffed his wrapper into the empty cup and Danbury took it and walked away.

"He's kind of," started Lanie, after they'd walked up the sidewalk and they were climbing into the SUV. She hesitated, seeming unsure as to how to finish the sentence. "Abrupt," she finally said.

Matthew just grinned at her, amused that he was defending the guy for the second time today. "Yeah, he gets right to the point, but he's also one of the best detectives around, at least in the Triangle area of North Carolina." He left out the bit about Danbury being a Homicide Detective and he particularly hoped that those specific skills wouldn't be needed on this trip.

"Oh, and Lanie," he added, "Please just call me Matthew."

"OK, I'll try," said Lanie as she pulled up a navigation app on her phone to guide Matthew back across the bridge to the other side of the Miami River and then under the bridges and back to Dock Side. The area under the bridges was still cluttered with makeshift tents and there were some people milling about around them. Several were smoking something, passing it between them, something that Matthew doubted was medicinal marijuana.

Matthew parked in the lot they'd been in the night before and selected the information from the app for the SUV. An hour should be plenty of time to get in, ask questions, learn what they could, and get back, he thought as he selected that option. He felt an oddly hopeful surge of energy that he couldn't define as he and Lanie turned and walked down the sidewalk toward the river.

10 ~ OVERWATCH

As Matthew and Lanie turned left to walk down the street across from the waterfront toward Dock Side, Matthew thought that a distraction from worrying about Ariel might be a good thing for Lanie. "Are you interested in history?" he asked.

"I guess that depends on what kind."

"That sign up there," pointed Matthew, to the informational marker that he'd jogged over to take the picture of and then read the night before. "It explains the historical importance of the river for commerce and transportation. The bridges and ports along the riverfront were built by the railroad because the river brought supplies in and out, to and from the train. This river is fresh water, flowing from the everglades just west of here into Biscayne Bay and then out to the ocean beyond."

"That bridge over there that they're tearing down," he continued, pointing to the SW 1st Street Bridge. "It was built in 1929 as a double-leaf bascule bridge and they're reconstructing it."

"Huh," was all Lanie said. "What's a double-leaf bascule bridge?"

Matthew shrugged, thinking that he needed Dr. Rob for any discussions about waterway bridge operations, but he said, "I'm not completely sure except that I think both sides go up, vertically." He held his hands up to illustrate.

"Oh," said Lanie.

So much for the history lesson, he thought. He'd have to find other ways to distract her from worrying about Ariel. Her face clearly showed the strain and it was such a young face, he thought, to be so lined with worry.

They walked through the entrance to Dock Side and Matthew went straight through to the long bar area and turned right, remembering what Angela Delgado, the bartender from the night before, had said. Courtney DeBerry, the one he actually wanted to talk to, worked that end of it as well. It was the right end in more ways than just because it was literally the end closest to the food trucks, the location where Ariel and Gavin had been heading when they were last seen.

Approaching the end of the bar, Matthew noticed a cute blonde woman behind it who was creating what looked to be mimosas for the patrons at the far end. She had a bottle of Prosecco in one hand and was holding a champagne glass in the other while artfully pouring the champagne over juice that was already in the tall fluted glasses.

Motioning Lanie, who looked hesitant, to follow, Matthew sat down at the bar and waited. Normally, he'd have been waiting patiently, but his foot was bouncing on the rung of the bar stool and his leg was jumping as a result. He had tried to distract Lanie, but he realized that he needed the distraction as much as she did because he was also very worried about Dr. Rob's daughter.

He'd heard all of the statistics about missing persons and none of them were promising. The longer she was missing, the worse the odds would become for her safe return. He wondered if Gavin would regain consciousness anytime soon and be able to tell them anything further about what he had experienced, anything that would help lead them to Ariel.

Finally, the cute perky blond turned to him and asked, "What can I get you, Sir?"

"Do you have bottled water?" he asked, thinking that it would be good to actually purchase something from her if he wanted her help. His shirt was sticking to his back in the humidity, after just the short walk down the block, and a cold bottle of water for both of them would be a good idea, he reasoned.

"Perrier, Evian, or filtered?"

"Evian sounds good to me," he said and she nodded. "Lanie?"

"I'd just like some filtered water, please. Whatever you have."

"Coming right up," she said and took a few steps away to a row of undercounter coolers and pulled out the water bottles. "Here you go. Ice cold," she added as she handed them over.

"Thanks," Matthew said, as he slipped his debit card from his wallet and handed it to her. "I don't need a tab, but we might want one of each of these for the road."

"Sure thing," she said. "Do you want me to go ahead and run those too?"

Matthew nodded in response and asked, "Are you Courtney DeBerry?"

She froze in her tracks, looking back at him suspiciously, and asked a bit sharply, "Who told you that?"

"Angela Delgado, who was working last night. We're looking for a missing young woman and she said that you were working this end of the bar Monday night."

"Ohhhhh," said Courtney, coming back to the edge of the counter. "Sorry, I just get a lot of creeps in here, you know, working the bar and all."

"I'm sure," said Matthew, taking a swig of his water but thinking that her reaction was indeed a bit harsh and wondering if she'd had a bad experience with a stalker maybe.

"Angela texted me about that," said Courtney. "A young couple is missing, right?"

"Right," he said, deciding to skip the story of how one of them had been found. "I'm Matthew Paine and this is Lanie James. The missing young woman is her best friend," he added as he pulled the photographs from the folder he'd carried in and held them up for her. "JoJo said he saw this young couple come in Monday night somewhere around nine-thirty. They had ordered pizza, which was picked up from the pizza vendor down there," he thumbed over his shoulder to the far corner. "But nobody we've talked to so far saw them after that. Nobody saw them leave, so I was hoping maybe you had."

Courtney took the photos from him and examined them closely. "They do look familiar. But I can't place them. Maybe they were in here last Monday night," she finally said, slowly. "Maybe that is where I saw them. But I was on my evening break just before nine-thirty. So, I wasn't behind the bar."

"Who would have been covering this end of the bar for you?" asked Matthew.

"That would have been Rod on Monday. He fills in for our breaks usually, and sometimes he just gets stuck back here. He was working the other end of the bar Monday night, but things were slower so he filled in for me on this end too."

"We need to talk to him anyway. He's the manager, right?" asked Matthew.

"Yeah, he is. He's probably in the office over there," she said, pointing to her right. It was the only area of the outdoor event center that looked like an actual building, enclosed by wooden walls and a roof. Matthew had noticed it off to the left from the entrance the night before when he'd been evaluating the layout of the place.

"And are there cameras here?" asked Matthew.

"Oh yeah, there have to be. People pack into this place on the weekends like you wouldn't believe and the noise level is ridiculous. So, there are cameras everywhere," said Courtney as she pointed to one that was obscured in a corner beam overhead.

Matthew smiled, "Good," he said. "That's what I was hoping you would say. And the feeds are recorded?"

"They are," she said, as she started to gather some glasses around them and put them in the sink. "Rod can access the recordings from whatever time span you want from multiple angles."

"Perfect!" piped up Lanie.

"If you see the woman in the picture here or if you think of anything else that might be helpful, would you give me a call?" asked Matthew, handing over a card and pulling the laminated pictures off the bar and putting them back in the folder.

"Sure," she said, as she tucked his card into her pocket and then handed him his credit card and the receipt. "Just stop back by for your other water bottles on the way out. They'll be cold and waiting," she added with a smile as she saw the tip that he'd added for her.

Lanie followed Matthew back across the outdoor carpeting to an open entranceway between wooden walls that were above their heads. It was a foyer of sorts, an enclosed area off to the left side of the complex. Directly in front of them was the wooden building. There were bathrooms in the center, a door marked "Employees Only" to the left, and another marked "Management" on the right.

Matthew held up his fist to knock and then looked around. Seeing no one to ask, he followed through with the knock and was answered by a male voice in what sounded like a New Jersey dialect, saying, "Yeah? What d'ya want?"

"I'm looking for Rod. Um, Rodney Rodriguez," he clarified.

"You found him, but if you're sellin' anything, I ain't buyin' it, and same goes for donations," said the voice as the door swung open to reveal a man in his early forties and just a hint of cooler air from within the office. Rodney Rodriguez was an average height and looked like he might have once been athletic, but he now had a paunch forming in his mid-section. His dark hair was graying at the temples, and he sported a goatee that had gotten ahead of his hair in the greying process. Matthew looked down into the man's squinty dark eyes with prominent laugh lines at the corners. His ruddy complexion had obviously seen more than its share of the Miami sun.

"Hi, I'm Matthew Paine, and this is Lanie James," he said, offering his hand, which the man took as he looked up at Matthew suspiciously. "We're not selling anything or asking for donations, just a few minutes of your time. We're looking for a young couple that was in here around nine-thirty Monday night. Courtney DeBerry said she was on her break around that time and you were covering her end of the bar area."

"Yeah, I was," Rod responded and Matthew noted an odd quirk at the corner of his mouth as the man spoke.

"Do you remember seeing either of these?" Matthew asked, pulling the pictures from the folder and handing them over.

"C'mon in," the guy said, stepping inside. "And lemme look at 'em good." He flipped a switch to turn on an overhead light and flopped the pictures on a large metal desk. Circling it, he sat down and held each one up in turn. Matthew and Lanie stepped through, closing the door against the heat behind them. The office was only marginally cooler than the outdoor area under all of the fans, but anything was a relief in the heat and humidity that they weren't really used to.

"Yeah, I think I seen 'em," said Rod, after a moment. "Not at the bar. But I think I seen 'em come in. One of 'em was wearing red. I remember that."

Matthew nodded, encouragingly, because JoJo had also said that Gavin was wearing a red t-shirt and Lanie had confirmed it.

"It wasn't that busy Monday night," continued Rod. "And I was looking out the entrance wishing all this bridge construction wasn't scaring all my customers away when they walked in."

"Do remember seeing them leave?"

They guy tugged on the bottom of his goatee as he pondered the pictures. "I don't remember seeing 'em leave," he said. "But I wasn't staring out the front all night. I did have customers around that end of the bar to attend to. I just do that to fill in," he added. "I used to be a bartender here for some years. But then I went and got my business degree so I could manage it. I still fill in for breaks and if folks are out sick."

"You have lots of security cameras here, don't you?" Rodney nodded and Matthew asked, "Could we have a look at your recordings from those camera feeds from say nine-twenty until ten Monday night? Or, until we see them leave?" he amended, realizing that they had to have left, one way or another.

"Yeah, yeah, I can do that," he said, checking his watch. "We're not real busy right now. But it'll take me a minute or a few," he said, reaching over to retrieve a tablet that was on the corner of the desk. As he was looking up and around them, Matthew realized that there was a huge screen mounted on the wall behind where he and Lanie were standing that could be viewed from the desk where Rod was sitting.

They stepped to the side and watched the screen change from what looked to be a current feed of multiple camera angles to a login screen with a big logo that said OVERWATCH in large letters."

"Overwatch?" asked Matthew.

"Yeah, don't pick your nose or pull out a wedgie around here," said Rod, in a snuffling chuckle like he thought he'd made a funny joke. Maybe he had, thought Matthew, if he were back in middle school. He tried to look mildly amused and not as annoyed as he felt as Rod continued, "The cameras are always watching over the place. They record everything. The recordings are stored up in the cloud, so they go back a ways."

After Rod logged in, the screen displayed a list of folders and then files. He tugged on the bottom of his goatee with his left hand while he maneuvered on the tablet with this right. "Here we go. Monday evening. Nine-thirty, you said?"

"That's right," answered Matthew.

"I got all sorts of camera angles and we can view 'em one at a time or all in a bunch of boxes on the screen."

"Can you pull up the best view of the front entrance around nine-twenty? Then maybe we can follow them through from there?"

"Sure thing," he said as he did so. "Nine-twenty, here we go. I'll fast forward until we see 'em."

He sounded to Matthew like a mobster who needed a cigar hanging out of his mouth to complete the image. That image explained the odd quirk in the corner of the man's mouth. It was as if he were talking around a cigar that wasn't there. Matthew's mind started to write a goofy song about it, but he tried to clear the thought and focus on the screen, just as Lanie pointed and said, "There they are!"

Rod quickly froze the picture and backed it up so that they saw Ariel and Gavin just entering the doorway. She was looking up at him and laughing about something. Matthew noted that she had on the same sort of black running shorts with white trim that Lanie was wearing and what looked like a dark purple dry fit t-shirt. On her feet was a pair of running shoes, not flip-flops like Lanie wore. He'd add that to their online information files now that he had the visual, he thought.

They turned to the left on the screen, which would be to the right of the entrance, and walked out of the screen.

"Gimme a sec," said Rod as he tapped away on the tablet. "Here we go. This camera should pick 'em up next. I started it at nine-twenty-nine, just before they were out of the screen on that first camera."

Matthew caught himself leaning forward and purposefully leaned back so that Lanie could see and, as Rod had said, they walked into view. The angle on this camera was from above and they could see Ariel hook her arm in Gavin's. Gavin looked down at her and put his arm protectively around her shoulders, just as JoJo had said.

When they disappeared from that view, Rod pulled up another camera angle from a longer distance and Ariel and Gavin walked the length of the area and had almost reached the food truck, but it couldn't be seen from this camera angle, so Rod tapped on the tablet a few more times and then pulled up another camera angle.

"You really weren't kidding when you said the whole place was under camera surveillance, were you?" Matthew asked.

"I wasn't," said Rod. "In Miami, and with the bars, we see a little bit of everything. But we need to see it all. There's a sign at the front that tells ya that there's video cameras all over."

Matthew admitted to himself that he hadn't noticed the sign and wondered how many other people walked right by it without noticing. All the better, he thought, if people didn't realize they were being watched.

"Here's the next one," said Rod.

Ariel and Gavin were behind two other customers in line at the pizza food truck. Matthew watched until they'd claimed their pizzas, Gavin balancing a smaller box on top of a larger one, and turned back the way they'd come.

"Well, hell, if I'd known that, we coulda just fast forwarded the videos from the other cameras a little bit," said Rod, with a grimace. "But gimme just a minute."

He poked on the tablet a few more times and they watched as Ariel and Gavin walked back down the length of the venue along the front fenced-in wall. They had to lean in to look because the young couple was partially obscured by two guys walking parallel to them, but in front of the camera. When Rod pulled up the final view, they didn't see

Ariel and Gavin in the frame as they had expected.

"Can you back that up just a few frames?" asked Matthew.

"Yeah, sure," said Rod and did so.

"And play it slower?"

"Yep."

"There! Can you freeze it?"

Rod backed it up to where Matthew had pointed and froze the screen.

"There they are, but there are two guys walking out behind them. Right behind them."

Rod grunted and leaned over, "Yeah, that looks like Danny Boy there on the left. I dunno who that other guy is."

"Danny Boy?" asked Matthew.

"That's just what I call him. I think Courtney started callin' him that too 'cause he looks so Irish, but maybe it's because he drinks Irish Whiskey. I'm not sure, but he's a regular," answered Rod.

"OK, keep going until they're off the screen. Are there cameras outside?"

"You bet there are. All down the sidewalk."

As Rod started the video up again, they all watched the exit, but they couldn't see Gavin and Ariel at all with Danny Boy and the other guy, who was taller and broader with dark hair, behind them.

"OK, the outside camera?" prompted Matthew.

"Yup. Coming right up," said Rod, sounding like a bartender again. After a bit more poking on the tablet, he said, "Here you go."

The next camera angle was coming from above the entrance and caught the posterior view of exiting patrons. They saw Ariel and Gavin very briefly with the two men right behind them. Just as they were all about to exit from the camera range, they saw the guy Rod had identified as Danny Boy tap Ariel, who he was walking directly behind, on the shoulder. The next step took Ariel completely out of the frame and they were looking at Danny Boy's back.

The guy was motioning with his right arm at something beyond them, and he must have been talking to Ariel and Gavin. After a few more motions, they caught a glimpse of the side of Danny Boy's face as he turned to say something to his companion and then they were all off the screen.

"Where's the next camera?" asked Matthew, excitedly.

"That's it, if they crossed the street there like it looks like they were gonna do," said Rod. "Lemme see what I can do." He poked some more on the tablet and then they were looking along the outside sidewalk to the right, from an angle up above the fencing. People were still coming and going, but they saw neither Ariel and Gavin nor the two guys who had followed them out.

Rod backed up the camera feed to an earlier timestamp and looked again, but they still didn't see any of them, Ariel, Gavin, Danny Boy, or the bigger darker guy. Rod pulled up footage from the other direction along the outside sidewalk, but the result was the same, none of the four they'd been watching reappeared.

"Uh," grunted Rod. "I guess we don't overwatch everything, huh?"

"But it's a start," said Matthew, excitedly. "We know what time they left, we know the last person who talked to them after they left, and we know what they were wearing and what direction they went in."

"Yeah, they were walking toward the Bridge People if they kept going on the other side of the street the way they were veering off to the right there in the shot."

"The Bridge People?"

"Yeah, that's what people around here call them. The people who live under the bridges. It's like a whole community over there."

"OK," said Matthew, his brain on overload as he started processing all of the new information. Turning to Lanie, he said, "That's where Ariel and Gavin were going to meet their Rydz car, at the end of that street where it ends here at Dock Side, right? I saw that in the notes that Danbury added. But they're about twenty minutes early for that."

Then, as he was thinking through the next steps, he asked Rod, "Can you download clips of just those sections from your video in the cloud?"

"I could," said Rod. "But I've been pretty helpful so far. And I'm not sure if I'm violating anybody else's rights by giving you video of them coming and going."

"I'm not a lawyer," responded Matthew. "But I have a good friend who is. I think your sign out front covers you in that it notifies your patrons that they're under video surveillance. I can check that, if you need me to."

"Yeah, I'm gonna need you to do that before I hand over the video."

"OK. We also need to know about Danny Boy. And then go talk to the people living under the bridge, the Bridge People, as you call them. If I go take a picture of your sign about the video surveillance and send it to my friend, would you start pulling down the video clips that we just looked at? You only give them to me if my friend says the verbiage on your sign covers us."

"And how do I know that your 'friend' isn't just some quack that will tell me what you want me to hear?"

Having already anticipated that question, Matthew pulled up the information from Cici's legal practice in downtown Raleigh. There was a picture that accompanied biographical information for each of the lawyers in the firm, a long list of them, but he pulled Cici's entry up and showed it to Rod, "Here's the friend I'm going to contact. Do you want me to send you a link to this information so that you can call and confirm her identity?"

"Nah. Just because they say she's legit still don't mean that you're actually talking to her when you text. So that don't help any."

As he was saying this, Courtney DeBerry peeked around the corner of the office, "Hey, Rod, I'm leaving for the first part of my shift," she said. "I'm a little late getting out of here but I'll be back this evening."

"Hey, Courtney," said Matthew, before Rod could answer her. "Rod says you call one of your regular customers 'Danny Boy.' What can you tell me about him?

"Danny Boy?" she asked, suspiciously, checking her watch. "Why do you need to know about him?"

"He's in the video recording from the camera feeds here. On Monday night he walked out right behind Gavin and Ariel, the woman in the picture that we're trying to find. It looks like he was talking to them. He and another guy who was with him. He's the last person we can find to have seen them before they disappeared so I need to talk to him."

Then, choosing his words more carefully, as he saw Courtney's eyebrows shoot up, Matthew amended, "Maybe they told him where they were going or at least maybe he saw the direction they left in. It looks like they crossed the street and out of the range of the cameras from here. But I'm hoping that he can tell us where they went next at least."

"Oh, so you saw them on the video from the camera feeds?"

"We did. I was just asking Rod to provide the videos they appear in so that we have that to work from, but he seems to have an issue with the privacy of your patrons here."

"Isn't that what the sign out front is for?" asked Courtney.

"That's what I thought," said Matthew. "But I was going to check that with a friend of mine who's a lawyer."

At this, Courtney visibly cringed and then said, "We don't really need lawyers involved, do we, Rod?" And then she added sweetly, "Can't you just give him a copy of the video?"

Rod's mouth moved as if he were chewing on his imaginary cigar and talking around it, as he grumbled, "Yeah, I guess so."

"Thanks, Rod," said Matthew. "I really appreciate it."

"It'll take me a few minutes. What do you want me to do with it when I have those videos all together?"

"Put them in a folder. I can either go get you a thumb drive to load it onto," he said, making a mental note to pick up a few of those and have them on hand. "Or I can give you temporary access to an online site and have you upload them there."

"Yeah, that's a better idea," groused Rod around his imaginary cigar.

"While he's working on that," Matthew turned to Courtney. "Can I walk you out?"

"I don't need an escort, Mr. Paine," she said, curtly. "And I don't need to be protected."

"It's Doctor Paine," said Lanie, speaking up in his defense. "And he's a good guy, I promise you that. The best. He dropped everything and flew down here to help find my best friend Ariel. And he's not doing anything else but helping the police to look for her." Matthew noticed Courtney flinch at the mention of the police and wondered what she was hiding. In his newly acquired experience with crime investigation, he'd discovered that everyone was hiding something. If whatever she was hiding wasn't helpful to finding Ariel, he vowed to himself not to want to know what it was.

"Doctor Pain?" said Rod from behind the desk. "That's a good one!" he guffawed.

"Yeah, yeah, I know. Take your best shot if you want," said Matthew. "I'm sure I've heard them all before, but if you come up with some new material, I'd love to hear it." That had been his practiced response since childhood, long before becoming a physician, to anyone choosing to rib him about his last name.

Then, turning back to Courtney, he said, "Lanie can walk with us as your protection from being protected," and he followed Courtney DeBerry out of the office and toward the entrance.

Courtney might not want an escort, he thought, but he she couldn't stop him from walking with her. Normally, Matthew was very laid back and if he'd been interested in her romantically, he'd have taken no for an answer at the first hint of it. But this wasn't that. There was a young woman's life at stake and she was the daughter of a man he admired very much, a kind and caring man who was suffering immensely as he worried about his only child. So "no" wasn't an answer Matthew was prepared to accept just then.

Lanie followed as they headed for the big entrance. "Let's get something straight right now," said Matthew to the retreating Courtney's back. "I don't have any objective other than finding the missing young woman, Ariel Roberts. She's the only child of a dear friend, a kind and caring man who pours his all into treating children in our family practice in North Carolina."

She slowed slightly, as he added, "I don't care why you don't want to talk to the police or get a lawyer involved. I really don't." At this she stiffened but she stopped.

"I just need you to get me in touch with this 'Danny Boy' guy so that I can ask him if he knows where the young couple went when they left here Monday night," Matthew implored. "Any decent person would want to help us find her before it's too late," he added, figuring that his need to get Courtney to talk to him outweighed tiptoeing around Lanie's fragile feelings at that exact moment.

"You think I'm not a decent person?" she said, turning to face him, angrily. "Who are you to judge that? You don't even know me!"

Figuring that he'd struck a chord somehow with her but being less concerned about that than getting the information he wanted, he decided to pluck it harder. He charged on, "I didn't say that, but if you are, you'll help me. Tell me about this Danny Boy. What does he really look like, for example? I could only see his back and a quick glimpse of the side of his face in the video. Tell me where I can find him."

"I've got to go pick up my son," said Courtney. "And I'm late."

"What if your son disappeared?" asked Matthew, going for the jugular. "Wouldn't you want help finding him?"

Now furious, Courtney turned to face him, "You leave my son out of this! Daniel Rubio is in his early thirties, I'd guess. He's a medium height, maybe five-foot-eleven and a medium build. I'd guess maybe a hundred and eighty-five pounds or so. He has streaked blond hair, blue eyes, and a killer smile."

Matthew cringed visibly at her choice of words but he hoped it wasn't noticeable.

"He has a 1,000-WATT smile," she corrected, obviously having noticed Matthew's response to her words. "He showed up around here about three months ago and he's been a regular since then. I see him hanging out on a boat down that way a lot," she said, losing steam on her anger as she talked. "A big boat, a yacht, I guess you'd call it. He hit on me a little bit, like most of the creepy guys around here, you included," she flung at Matthew, who didn't bother to look offended or to contradict her because he wanted to keep her talking, angrily or not.

"Do you know who the guy was with him in the video? He was a bigger guy, taller and broader and his hair looked dark, but it's hard to know for sure from his back in the video."

"I don't. I usually see Danny Boy alone, unless he's wooed some doe-eyed girl or highly susceptible woman off to the boat and then she's usually drunk and swaying and he's usually all chivalrously holding her up, all the way back to the boat and then God knows what happens there. Danny Boy is very charming. I told him he could charm the skin off a snake, but I'm too worldly wise to fall for it and he said he isn't into blondes right now anyway," she turned to walk off.

"He said he isn't into blondes," repeated Matthew. "Is he into redheads?"

This stopped her in her tracks. She turned slowing back around in the entrance, her whole body tensed, and Matthew realized that she didn't have a poker face. She flushed and said, "Yeah, redheads. Why?"

"Because the young woman we're looking for is a redhead."

"But wasn't she here with her boyfriend? The guy in the picture?"

"She was, but Danny Boy approached her as she and her boyfriend were leaving. Do you have any idea why he'd do that if her boyfriend was obviously with her?"

"I don't! Why don't you ask him yourself?" she shot back.

"I'd love to if you can tell me where to find him. That's all I'm asking," pleaded Matthew.

Taking a deep breath, unclenching the fists she'd made, and relaxing her arms that were stuck stiffly straight down by her sides, she said, "He'll likely be in this evening. Around eight-thirty or nine, if I had to guess. I don't know who the guy was with him, but I think I've seen him here before too. Maybe Rod knows more about him. Can I go pick up my son now?" she asked, with some of the venom returning to her words as she stomped through the entranceway.

"Sure," said Matthew. "Just one more thing, though."

"What?!?!" she spun back around. "What else could you possibly want?"

"You do have my card. If you see either of them, would you call or text me? Please?" He realized that he wasn't above pleading with her, and then he added, "It's really important and you might be helping to save a young woman's life."

There it was. He'd thrown down the gauntlet, Lanie or no Lanie, and Courtney nodded her agreement. "I will," she said quietly. The reality of the situation as Matthew expressed it had taken the steam right out of her.

"Thank you," said Matthew to her back again as she rounded the corner at the sidewalk and disappeared beyond the fence and out of sight.

Matthew turned back to see Lanie staring at him with huge eyes. He hated that expression and he wished she could unhear what he'd just had to say to extract the promise from the angry bartender, but he put an arm around her shoulder and said, "We'll do whatever it takes to find her, Lanie. We will. Whatever it takes, including making people mad if they can help us."

Usually, Danbury had played the bad cop role to Matthew's "good cop," though Matthew had continually insisted that "notta cop" suited him far better, in the few instances that he'd helped to interrogate witnesses or suspects. And now Matthew could clearly understand why Danbury didn't relish the bad cop role either. It wasn't any fun, he found it entirely unsatisfying, and Matthew felt a bit empty and cold, even in the Miami heat, after having had to do it. He realized that Danbury might be right about his ability to read people. Usually, once he found those sore spots in people, he avoided them.

Lanie just nodded, her soulful brown eyes looking up at him pleadingly as he turned her around and they headed back to the office to get the video uploaded. She didn't know Matthew well enough, he realized, to know that he'd never have pressured someone and upset them as he just had Courtney without an extremely important reason, a life-or-death reason.

11 ~ GLITCHES

After getting the video footage uploaded securely to the shared files online and removing Rod's access, Matthew profusely thanked the guy. While he wasn't worried so much about Rod trusting him, he needed to come back that evening and he wanted to be welcomed. He was pretty sure that the guy had heard Courtney yelling at him and the last thing he needed was for the manager to ban him from the premises.

"Just one more question," said Matthew.

"Well, aren't you just full of 'em," responded Rod around the cigar that wasn't in his mouth.

"Do you recognize the guy who was with Danny Boy? Do you know who he is?"

"I've seen him here before. But I don't have a name, if that's what you're asking."

"Any chance he paid by credit card? Any way to track him that way?"

"Well, we'd have to know when he was using that credit card, wouldn't we? If I don't have a time, I can't check the system and I'm not going through any more video feeds. Not without a warrant."

"Thank you for your time and your help," said Matthew again, as he and Lanie stepped out of the office and closed the door behind them.

So far, he realized, they'd only confirmed everything that they thought they already knew about where Ariel and Gavin had been and when. Now knowing about Danny Boy presented other opportunities to get closer to their next destination. Matthew planned to pursue those as quickly as he could.

They picked up their water bottles to go and Matthew thought that no matter how mad he'd made Courtney, and he wasn't sure exactly why she was so angry with him to begin with she was as good as her word. She'd left instructions for each of them to be given a water bottle because they were prepaid.

Matthew had wanted to go talk to the Bridge People but he and Lanie were both sweaty and hot and they still had to go back and pick up Danbury. As they walked back to the car, Matthew asked, "Are you up to typing up what we just learned from the videos and from Courtney on your phone into our shared files? I can call Danbury and tell him we're on the way back and tell him about it, but we need to have it captured for later reference while it's all still fresh in our minds."

"Yeah, anything I can do to help find Ariel, you know I'll do it."

"OK, great," said Matthew. "And be sure to add a description of the clothing that Ariel was wearing. Did you notice what it was?"

"Oh yeah, shorts like the ones I have on, and her purple V-neck dry fit shirt with her black trainers." Matthew nodded his approval.

As they reached the big black SUV and climbed in, they left the doors open to let the heat out as Matthew cranked up the vehicle and then the air conditioning immediately afterward. Even in the shade of the overhead bridges, the black SUV had heated up to a temperature that Matthew didn't want to contemplate.

They closed the doors and Matthew used his phone to pull up the navigation app so that Lanie's phone was free for her to update the online files. Mostly remembering the path back, Matthew figured he could navigate without Lanie's help so that she could focus entirely on the updates. And then he called Danbury.

"Hey Doc," said Danbury, picking up Matthew's call on the second ring. "Any new information? Anything helpful?"

"Yeah, quite a lot," said Matthew and proceeded to tell him about his conversations with Rod and Courtney and about Danny Boy and the bigger guy with him being the last ones, so far, to have seen Ariel. "Lanie is putting all of that into our files now."

"They were headed under the bridges?" clarified Danbury.

"We think so. They were crossing the street out of range of the camera, so it's just a guess. That was the direction they were headed in across the street though. And it was where they were supposed to meet the Rydz too, so that makes sense. But they were early, so what doesn't make sense is why they never met the Rydz driver. He said he waited for them."

"Huh," was all that Danbury said.

"What about you? Learn anything new in the alley?"

"Yeah, a few things. And a few glitches. There were two other cameras. Down near the other end of the alley. Both were conveniently disabled. One had been completely busted up. The other was spray painted. Whoever did it knew what they were doing. And where the other cameras were. Because they weren't captured by either one. Prior to them going offline. The cameras were both working. Until they weren't."

"Ah, they suddenly stopped working?"

"Yeah, within about five minutes of each other. But here's the weird part. That was on Saturday. Gavin wasn't dumped there until Monday night. Or early Tuesday morning. So, it makes me wonder. What else was going on in that alley? Or how premeditated was dumping Gavin? It doesn't add up."

"Yeah, it really doesn't," agreed Matthew.

"And the trash was collected on Monday. So there isn't much in the dumpsters. But if there were any evidence, it'd still be there. I've been through them. I found nothing."

"You went dumpster diving?" asked Matthew, incredulously.

"Yeah, Doc. You do what you have to do."

"Oh, I do not want to ride back with the windows up in the car with you!" said Matthew, momentarily laughing at the thought of the huge detective, who usually looked like a misplaced mythical Viking, climbing around in dumpsters. He glanced at Lanie and suddenly returned to all business. "You found nothing at all that's helpful in the dumpsters?"

"Nothing."

"And no video feeds from the alley?"

"Not a one. The only one that I found is on an ATM. It's across the street. One of the little cross streets. Aimed diagonally at that other end of the alley. I've called Nelson to ask for that footage. Those are usually grainy at any distance. And not usually very helpful. If it picked up anything. Well, that's better than we have now. Even if it is grainy. And the alley. What I wasn't saying out loud before. When I said it was clean. I found no blood spatters. You said Gavin lost a lot?"

"Yeah, that's what the doctor said."

"I saw no signs of a fight. Or a struggle. And no signs of pools of blood. Or large blood spatters. And I looked up and down the alley. Not just where Pete said he was picked up. Gavin had to have been moved here. And beaten somewhere else. Maybe left here for dead."

"Maybe so," agreed Matthew solemnly, swallowing hard. As he caught Lanie looking at him in his peripheral vision, he abruptly changed the subject, "We'll be back there in eight minutes, according to my navigation," he added, holding the phone out from his ear to look. "Did you get lunch at least?"

"Not yet. And my stomach is complaining about that. Loudly. I can't go into the restaurants. Not like this."

"Those crêpes were really good. We can get you one of those if you want, but we'll have to send Lanie in if you want one. I had a bit of trouble extricating myself from the proprietor the last time."

"Oh?" said Danbury, but apparently decided not to enquire further. "Yeah, that sounds good. They'd be throwing me out. If I went in there like this," he joked.

After a moment, Danbury seriously asked, "Have you heard anything from Dr. Rob? Any update on Gavin?"

"I haven't, but I can call."

"Yeah, do. We need to get the cars swapped around. Leave the one that Gayle got. At the hospital with them. And pick up the one you were driving. Maybe go back to the hotel. Shower and regroup."

"Sounds like a plan," said Matthew. "I'll call him as soon as we're back. I've got turns coming up so I need to get back to my navigation. Meet you where I left you?"

"Yep," said Danbury, and he clicked off.

"Do you see any recent entries from Danbury in the files?" Matthew asked Lanie. "I forgot to ask if he'd updated them."

"Yeah, but it's terse. It says cameras were disabled on Saturday, dumpsters were emptied on Monday morning but contain nothing useful now, the alley is clean, and Nelson is checking an ATM camera for him."

"That's pretty much what he just told me. OK, good, those are current. At some point, we'll need to sift back through all of the information in there."

"For what?" asked Lanie, pensively.

"To look for connections or anomalies in the information we've collected so far. Sometimes, answers or at least the right questions are right in front of your nose and you miss them."

"You do detective work regularly?" queried Lanie, surprised.

Matthew chuckled. "Medical diagnosis is sometimes very much like detective work. The difference is that once the detective builds the case and the suspects are apprehended, he gets to hand it all off to a DA and hope that he's built a solid case to get a conviction. Doctors, on the other hand, have to work the treatment plans they create for patients, and then re-evaluate and tweak them if the first plan doesn't work." He paused before adding, "But to answer your question, I am a medical consultant with the Raleigh Police Department and I've worked with Danbury on two previous investigations."

"Really?" asked Lanie. "So you do have experience."

"I do and recently," he added. "I thought I'd have a bit of a lull this summer, but then Ariel disappeared. Obviously, this isn't one of Danbury's cases because he's from North Carolina, but he agreed to come down and help Dr. Rob find Ariel."

"Everybody loves Dr. Rob," said Lanie.

"Everybody does," agreed Matthew. "He's a great guy."

"Some people maybe a little too much," added Lanie, as they were pulling in to park along the curb a bit closer to the end of the alleyway than they'd been previously. "Like Gavin's mom," she added.

Matthew grinned and said, "Yeah, I can see that. But I'm guessing she's going to be too worried about her son to be too interested in hitting on Dr. Rob right now."

"You'd think so, wouldn't you?" asked Lanie. "From what I've seen she might use it as an excuse."

"Oh," said Matthew, and then, "Hey Lanie, if I give you some cash or my credit card, would you be willing to go get Danbury a couple of those savory crêpes?"

"A couple? Those things are huge."

"You obviously haven't seen Danbury eat. The guy eats anything, so just pick something you think looks good. And he says he's really hungry. Oh, and a couple of bottles of water, too, one for each of us," he said, holding up his empty one as she nodded her agreement. He pulled out his wallet and peeled off three twenties and handed them to her as she slid off the seat, slamming the door shut behind her.

Matthew watched her cross the street and enter the brasserie, where he figured she was safe, before sliding out into the oppressive heat and humidity himself. He kept watch, over his shoulder, of the entrance to the brasserie while walking to the end of the alleyway in search of Danbury.

Danbury appeared, walking slowly in the heat, and looking more drained than Matthew remembered having seen him.

"Hey man, have you had any water?"

"Nah, not since earlier today."

"Come get in the car. Lanie's bringing food and water bottles. I'll text her to bring an extra one for you. I'm betting that you're dehydrated."

"Yeah, probably so. Afghanistan is a tolerable dry heat. At least compared to Miami," he joked.

Matthew knew that Danbury had been a Marine or, as Danbury had told him, "Once a Marine, always a Marine." And Matthew knew that he'd been in the middle east, evidently in some sort of clandestine operation that he could only partially talk about. He figured the guy could usually take care of himself but in his medical mind, Matthew was seeing signs of dehydration and he wanted to rectify that quickly.

Matthew started up the SUV and cranked the air up full blast, aiming all of the front vents at the driver's seat. Then he slid out, abdicating the driver's seat to Danbury, who he knew had a control issue when it came to driving. "I'll go get the water bottles now," he said. "Be right back," and he could see the heat like a dark mirage rising in waves from the asphalt pavement as he crossed the street.

As he stepped into the brasserie, the cool of the place was a welcome relief. He motioned for Lanie and asked if she could get four water bottles immediately. He waited a moment and then she brought them to him at the door. He thanked her and reluctantly stepped back out, feeling like he'd walked into a wall of the oppressive Miami humidity.

He climbed in the passenger seat, still watching the exit of the brasserie, and handed Danbury a water bottle. Matthew watched in amazement as Danbury uncapped it and downed it in what looked to Matthew like two swallows.

"What?" asked Danbury, seeing Matthew's face.

"Nothing, man. You needed that."

"Yeah, I guess I did. Do you have another one?"

Matthew handed him a second bottle, which Danbury uncapped and sipped more slowly.

"I'll check in with Dr. Rob while we wait for your lunch," said Matthew. "Are we going there next to get the other car and then drop the one Gayle Blevins got later?"

"That's the plan. As long as they agree to it."

"OK, I'll ask," said Matthew as he poked at his phone and waited.

"Hey, Dr. Rob," he said.

"Matthew! Have you had any luck with finding their trail from Monday night?"

"A little. I can tell you about it when we get there, if you want. We're headed your way if we can pick up the Sonata. Danbury needs to go back to the hotel to shower. I have a couple more stops to make. Then I'll go back to the hotel too. We can get refreshed, regroup, and then bring Gayle's car back there when we head back out for the evening."

"Yeah, good plan. I can't do anything else here so I'll come with you and help with the car shuttle."

"How is he?"

"No change since this morning. Gayle has been in and out several times and she sits with him as much as the staff will allow. I haven't been back in and I really want to come help in the search for Ariel. I feel utterly useless just sitting here. Hey Matthew, here comes the doctor out to give us an update. I'll see you in a few minutes. Text when you're here and I'll come down and meet you in that same parking lot."

"OK, get the keys to Gayle's rental car from her and tell her we're going to swap them out."

"Will do. Bye Matthew."

Matthew was about to answer, but realized that Dr. Rob was already gone. Lanie was coming out of the brasserie carrying a bag and three more water bottles. She was struggling with them, so Matthew jumped out, quickly crossed the street, and took two of the water bottles from her.

"I thought maybe we could each use another for the road," said Lanie. "I hope you don't mind because you don't have much change."

"No problem, that was a good call," he told her as they climbed back into the big SUV and she handed Danbury his crêpes from the backseat.

"It was cool to watch them make these," she said. "I just kept thinking that I wanted to share that with Ariel, but," and she choked, unable to complete her thought aloud.

"We'll find her," said Danbury, swallowing the half of crêpe that he had just bitten off at once. "We'll keep working until we do."

Lanie watched transfixed as Danbury downed the second half of that crêpe and started on the next one. "Wow," she said, looking at Matthew. "You weren't kidding."

"About?" said Danbury between the next three bites that finished off the second crêpe.

"Dr. Paine, I mean, Matthew," she corrected herself. "Matthew said that you could put away some food. Those crêpes were huge!"

"Eat when you can. Sleep when you can," said Danbury.

"Because you don't know when you'll get a chance to do either again," finished Matthew for him.

"OK," said Lanie, as she settled back into her seat and buckled up. "I'll keep that in mind. Where to now?"

Matthew explained the plan to her and pulled up the navigation app on his phone while Danbury pulled away from the curb.

*****

When they arrived in the parking lot at the hospital, they looked at each other, all equally loathe to get out of the air-conditioned vehicle. Though Danbury's dumpster aroma that permeated the interior wasn't exactly a pleasant one, it was preferable to the scorching temperatures on the outside.

"Dr. Rob said he'd meet us down here. I just texted to tell him that we're here. I'll take the Sonata back with us and meet you at the hotel, but I have two more stops to make first. There's one last hospital with an Emergency Department near downtown Miami that we haven't checked yet. It's over on the beach. And then the one in Hialeah. I know we don't think they came back that way, but I want to be certain. Lanie? You riding with Danbury or with me?"

"With you!" she answered a little too enthusiastically. "No offense," she said to the big detective. "But you kind of stink."

The laughter that erupted was a welcome relief to the tension they'd been feeling all day. Even Lanie laughed with them and then Matthew teased, "Yeah, I was trying not to mention it, Lanie, but now that you do, he is pretty ripe, isn't he?"

"Hey, I took one for the team," said Danbury, in mock injury.

"Oh yeah, and we appreciate that," said Matthew. "And now if you can take one shower for the team, that'd be so much better."

They'd made Lanie laugh and Matthew smiled over at Danbury appreciatively. He had taken several for the team already, Matthew thought, and who knew what they had yet ahead.

12 ~ Prognoses

Dr. Rob approached the SUV and climbed in beside Lanie momentarily so that they could all talk together.

"What's the update on Gavin's prognosis?" asked Matthew.

"They're still monitoring the swelling but there's a lot of internal bleeding around his brain due to the TBI. His GCS is an estimated seven, and they're contemplating either an Epidural Hematoma Aspiration or potentially even a craniotomy if the pressure gets any worse."

"In English, please?" pleaded Lanie.

Dr. Rob had probably purposefully provided information over Lanie's head, thought Matthew, and perhaps it was because Dr. Rob wasn't up for the explanation to the woman who he considered as his other daughter.

Matthew summarized for her, "TBI just means traumatic brain injury. Because he has a serious head injury. They're still monitoring him closely and just discussing possible procedures, one of which is more complicated and invasive than the other, if he should need it. His Glasgow Coma Score, or GCS, is in the good range for him coming out of the coma. It just means that he's somewhat responsive instead of totally unresponsive."

"Thank you" mouthed Dr. Rob, without saying it aloud, as he sank back into the seat, clearly exhausted.

"Oh," said Lanie, seeming to ponder that information.

"Don't get too comfortable, unless you want to ride back in the stinky car," said Matthew to Dr. Rob, trying again to lighten the mood. "Danbury went dumpster diving for evidence, so you can come back in the Sonata with Lanie and me if you want. But I do have a couple more stops to make, so I'm not going straight back to the hotel yet."

"I'm fine right here," said Dr. Rob, the tension and exhaustion showing in both his face and his demeanor. "As long as Danbury doesn't mind chauffeuring, I don't have to move at all."

"No problem," said Danbury, smirking at Matthew, as he and Lanie climbed out.

Lanie must have seen Dr. Rob's exhaustion too, as she reached in and patted his hand, "We'll find her," she said. "Danbury and, uh, Matthew have both promised that we won't stop looking until we do."

Dr. Rob clasped her hand and held on for a moment, smiling reassuringly at her. "Thank you, Lanie," he said and then settled back into the seat as he let go of her hand and she leaned out and closed the door. Matthew thought he'd aged years in just days as Dr. Rob looked strained, which was not a description normally applied to him or his boyish grin.

Matthew assumed that Dr. Rob wanted the unabridged prognosis on their progress so far, which was as much why he wanted to remain in the car with Danbury, away from Lanie, as anything else. As he and Lanie opened the doors of the little Sonata, they couldn't begin to get in.

"Well, I guess it's heat over stink," said Lanie as she fanned the heat waves coming out of the car and stepped back to escape them.

"Yeah, I'll get some air going," Matthew said, climbing in and starting the car. "But you can wait there a minute if you want." After a minute or so, Lanie reluctantly climbed in but then turned the vent full in her face, which was already pink from the heat that was radiating up from the asphalt parking lot. The forecast for the high of the day was only ninety-one, thought Matthew, but it felt like 120 degrees in the shade to him. The inside of the car had probably been well above that, he surmised, before they'd opened it up.

They discussed their destinations and Lanie was pulling the address for the hospital over on the beach from their online notes and putting it into the navigational app on her phone as they followed Danbury out from around the hospital and turned right onto the main road. Matthew didn't expect to find Ariel at the hospitals but he knew that they had to rule it out definitively before meeting the others back at the hotel.

The car was quiet on the drive, except for the occasional voice from the navigation app telling them when to turn, as both were lost in their own thoughts. Mount Hermon Medical Center was located in Miami Beach proper, and the traffic seemed to be getting worse as the afternoon shadows grew longer. That stood to reason, Matthew thought, and marveled at the fact that it could still be Wednesday. It felt more like a week, and not merely a day, since he'd gotten involved and flown into Miami on a moment's notice.

They had been traveling north but then headed east to cross Biscayne Bay on 195 to get over to the beach. As they should have expected, traffic was backed up on the bridge and nothing was moving particularly.

"Lanie, if you want, you can pull up your play list and we'll listen to your music."

"Really?" she asked.

"Sure. It's plugged in anyway, so why not?"

She brightened a bit at this possibility and said, "I have multiple play lists, but there's one that's more relaxing. It'll be good for being stuck in heavy traffic."

"OK, whatever you want to play," he answered.

After a few extra pokes at her phone, Lanie had the car filled with music and Matthew silently wondered if this was her relaxing music, what her energizing music would sound like. After listening through a few songs, he decided that it was eclectic. He'd have to give her that much. And he liked that. His taste in music was varied, though his favorites were old rock and some of the heavier metal rock.

Matthew particularly liked jazz for relaxation, which is what he was hoping for but hadn't heard yet in her collection of what she considered to be relaxing music. He listened to classical, pop, and sometimes even blue grass. His tastes were diametrically opposed to Danbury's and they'd had a few tense moments over the music selections when they'd traveled together previously. Danbury preferred the old mournful country that Matthew despised and Danbury detested Matthew's older and harder rock equally as much. They could agree on newer country and pop, which is where they landed most of the time.

Lanie, Matthew soon realized, had some crooners, a bit of hip hop, a couple of pop songs, and some retro dubstep in what she considered to be her easy listening collection. He was smiling to himself at what he considered a ridiculous label for the playlist just as the traffic ahead opened up and they navigated off to the left to get to the hospital. As always in and around Miami, parking was at a premium and he had to download yet another app to pay for it.

They made their way around the hospital to the Emergency Department entrance, explained why they were there, and went through the scrutiny of Security there before finally being taken down a hallway that opened out into the triage rooms for the ED. Matthew knew, from personal experience during one of his clinical rotations in medical school, that the ED would get busier in a few hours as people got crazier at the end of the work day. But he was thankful that there were three staff members behind a semi-circular nurses' station and they were happy to talk to him.

After reviewing the picture, the nurses all said they hadn't seen Ariel. Two of them had been on the night shift Monday night and the other on Tuesday night. While Matthew and Lanie discussed what was next on their agenda, one particularly helpful older nurse whose name tag said Judy Crew, helpfully called the morgue for them, just to be certain. Matthew noticed that she had a huge overbite in her otherwise prevalent and sparkling smile.

"How tall is the young woman? And what's her approximate weight?" asked Nurse Crew, as she put one hand over the receiver.

"About five-foot-four and maybe 100 pounds or so, right Lanie?"

Lanie nodded apprehensively and the nurse relayed the information over the phone.

"Nope. Nobody down there even close to her description," she confirmed. "So that's good news. Did I overhear you saying that you were going to Hialeah next?" she asked, helpfully.

"We are," answered Matthew. "To Hialeah Medical Center."

"We have an Emergency Center with specialty care there too. I can make a quick call, if you'd like, and save you a trip."

"To the one on East Twenty-Fifth Street?" asked Matthew.

"No, that's Hialeah Medical Center. This is on West Twentieth Avenue, up north of there."

"Oh. I didn't have that one on our list. That would be great," he answered. "Thank you. I really appreciate your help."

They waited while she placed the call, asked for a specific person in the Emergency Department, picked up the picture, and gave an incredibly accurate description of Ariel, just from the photo and the height and weight that Matthew had provided.

"Sure, I'll hold while you check," said Crew. Then, back to Matthew and Lanie she added, "Nobody who was on shift Monday night or last night saw anyone matching the description of your young lady come in, but they're checking the morgue to be certain. Their incoming patients have been mostly Hispanic over the past couple of days. They've seen a couple in the right age group, but with dark hair, eyes, and skin. None of them sound at all like the young woman you're looking for."

Nurse Crew pulled the phone back under her chin as she thanked the person she was speaking to and put the phone down.

"Nope. Nobody there who comes close to the description of your friend," she said, happily. "I guess that's good news for you."

Matthew and Lanie both thanked her and Matthew handed her a business card with his cell number jotted on it, "Would you give me a call or text if anyone matching that description should come in?"

"Oh, you're a doctor? Certainly, Dr. Paine," she answered. "If I can help in any way at all, just call the ED and ask for me. I'm here until eleven tonight and then back again on Thursday night this week."

Matthew wished that everyone in Miami was as helpful as Nurse Crew. Had they been, they could probably have made a lot more progress on the investigation in half the time. Lanie was subdued as they made their way back out to the car and cranked up the air conditioning again. Matthew was amazed at how quickly it had heated back up in the late afternoon sun.

"OK, next stop, Hialeah Medical Center and then back to meet up with everyone else," said Matthew as Lanie pulled up the online documents from which she copied the address and pasted it into the navigation app on her phone. The automated voice on the app droned over the speaker system until Matthew suggested that Lanie pull up her happy play list. "You have one of those, right? The stuff you listen to that just makes you happy?"

"Sort of," said Lanie, poking at her phone until the car was filled with hip hop and pop music, none of which Matthew recognized. It seemed to improve Lanie's mood and that was his primary objective. While he drove he had time to ponder what they'd learned so far and the myriad questions they still had to answer. It seemed to him that every time they got one question answered, it just led to more questions.

If Ariel and Gavin were headed under the bridge when they left Dock Side, why were they headed there? And did they make it that far? If they did, why didn't they meet up with their Rydz driver just twenty minutes later? How did Gavin end up in the alley with surveillance cameras that had been disabled more than two days before, and why leave him there? What had happened to Ariel while he was being beaten and dumped in an alley?

So many questions, thought Matthew, with so few answers. He glanced over at Lanie, who was sunk down with her arms wrapped around her knees, which were pulled up to her chest. She looked much younger than her 19 or 20 years. Matthew wasn't sure how old Lanie was exactly. He hadn't asked, but he knew that Ariel was 19 and Gavin 20. At that moment, Lanie looked much younger than either.

After what seemed like an eternity in slow moving traffic, they finally heard the navigation app voice announce that they'd arrived at their destination. "Well, if 'drove right by' means we've arrived, then I guess she's right," said Matthew, taking his next left to circle back as he realized that he'd just passed the entrance to the hospital.

He was truly amazed to find a free parking spot without having to download an app or pay to park. They made their way in through the Emergency Department entrance and repeated the process of explaining why they were there, though the security scrutiny seemed to be less intense at this hospital. Led pretty quickly through a set of double swinging doors, they squinted in the brightly lit hallways that seemed to form a giant square around a central desk, where they were taken, introduced, and then abandoned by the security guard.

"How can I help you?" asked a tall solid-looking nurse behind the desk.

Lanie pulled out the picture of Ariel, handing it to the nurse, as Matthew introduced them and explained that they were looking for the young woman pictured there who had been missing since Monday night.

"I just came on shift and I wasn't here this week until this afternoon. I normally work three twelve hour shifts on the weekends," said the nurse whose name tag said Gina Dias. "But I'm filling in tonight. Let me see who might have been here since Monday night," she said, taking the photograph and showing it to the collection of people behind the counter. Some were at computers, pecking away, others were just passing by, one had just pushed a stretcher into an alcove and left it, and another seemed to be restocking a case.

Though Matthew and Lanie couldn't hear what they were saying, each person Nurse Dias presented with the picture studied it and shook their heads. When Dias returned with the news that nobody had seen a young woman come through who matched that description, Matthew asked the question he'd dreaded having to ask at each hospital, and Dias helpfully called the morgue to be sure Ariel hadn't somehow bypassed the Emergency Department and been taken straight there.

When she turned and reported that Ariel was not down there, Matthew let out a breath he didn't realize that he'd been holding and thanked Nurse Dias for her help. Handing her his card, he asked her to contact him if anyone matching that description came in.

As they left the hospital, Matthew realized that he was hungry. He was beyond tired from the long day, lack of a full night's sleep the night before, and driving in all of the heavy traffic with the crazy drivers in Miami. They had certainly lived up to their reputation for cutting you off without warning and crossing multiple lanes of traffic.

Matthew hoped a quick shower and some dinner would revive him because he knew they still had lots of work to do and they were racing against an unseen clock to find Ariel. The prognosis for her survival, the longer it took to find her, became more dismal.

13 ~ RECOUP AND REGROUP

"Do you want to come back to the hotel with us or do you want to go back to where you're staying for a while?" Matthew asked Lanie when they'd gotten back to the car and cranked up the air conditioning again. "We won't be there long, I don't think. Danbury will have showered and changed and he might not even still be there. I'll check, but we do need time to regroup and discuss our next steps. I want a quick shower, and we need to grab something to eat. I know I need to be back at Dock Side this evening and I still want to go talk to the Bridge People, which we didn't have time to do earlier."

"I'll go where you guys go," said Lanie in a resigned voice. "I wouldn't change clothes or anything if I went back to Conexiones Saludables anyway. Believe it or not, I think I'm getting used to the heat and humidity down here."

"OK," said Matthew, as he gave her the address of the hotel for her nav app and then called Danbury.

"Hey Doc, where are you?"

"We're back in Hialeah. Ariel has not been seen at Mount Hermon Medical Center over on the beach or either of the hospitals here in Hialeah. I left contact information with all of them, just in case she comes in. We're coming back to the hotel if you're still there."

"Yeah, in the lobby," said Danbury. "We're reviewing the video feed. The one from the ATM. With Sergeant Nelson. And he's looking at the videos we collected. There is something going on in that alley. He doesn't think it relates to Gavin. Or Ariel. I'm not convinced of that. Dr. Rob has been on the phone with Gayle. He's agreed to pack some clothes for her, reluctantly. He wanted the hotel staff to do that. But she wasn't having it. Then he'll take her car to her. As soon as the hotel manager lets us in her room."

"Good. I want a shower and something to eat. Then I was thinking I'd go back down to Dock Side and try to talk to this Danny Boy guy. I want to find out what he said to Ariel and if he knows where they went after they left or had anything to do with their disappearance. Courtney DeBerry called him Daniel Rubio somewhere in her ranting. Maybe you can run background on him."

"Already on it. I saw that in our files. Where you'd added it. Nelson's team is working on that. He requested background on Rubio. If that's really the guy's name. We'll see what his team digs up."

"And I want to go talk to the Bridge People," said Matthew.

"The Bridge People?" asked Danbury.

"That's what people at Dock Side call the community of people who live under the bridge," explained Matthew. "Anyway, I want to see if any of them can tell us if they saw Ariel and Gavin Monday night, if they made it that far."

"Yeah, that's my plan too. What's Lanie going to do? Is she with us? Or Dr. Rob? Or back to where she's staying?"

"She says she's with us," he answered, looking over at Lanie, who nodded her agreement.

"And I want another look at that alley," said Danbury.

"Tonight?" asked Matthew.

"Yeah, there's something weird about it. And it feels like I should know what it is. But I can't place it. It's like it's right there. But I can't get my mind around it."

"I understand that completely," said Matthew. "OK, we're close. I'll see you in about five minutes," said Matthew and disconnected the call.

"Sounds like you already regrouped," said Lanie with the first half smile that Matthew had seen from her in several hours.

"I guess we did. But I still want a quick shower and something to eat. Aren't you hungry?"

"Yeah, but for the first time, like ever, I don't want pizza."

Matthew chuckled at her attempt at humor and agreed with her.

*****

After the requisite shower, they opted to get Cuban sub sandwiches from a local place that Nelson recommended. They were as good as he'd promised and between that, the shower, and a quick change of clothes, Matthew was feeling refreshed. On Danbury's insistence, he had loaded the magazines and popped one into each handgun. He couldn't use an ankle holster to conceal the 1911 wearing shorts, but he holstered the Glock at his waist in the lobby as they were on the way out. Lanie watched this process with apparent trepidation but said nothing.

The group had split back into thirds. Dr. Rob took the car that Gayle Blevins had rented, along with a bag of the things she'd asked him to bring her, back south to Grace Hospital. He said he'd at least check in with the medical ICU staff before joining the others anywhere else.

Lanie and Matthew took the little Sonata back to the parking lot under the bridges near Dock Side while Danbury took the SUV, now dubbed by Lanie as "the stinky car," to Dock Side to begin the evening. Then, he said he planned to go back to the alley south of the river to do a little surveillance on his own.

Having the parking process down by now, Matthew added the Sonata to his PayByPark account and set both it and the SUV for an hour, which he hoped would be sufficient. He knew that he could always update it remotely if Danny Boy didn't show up on his usual schedule or if they needed time to talk with the Bridge People after they found Danny.

As they approached the event center, it was lighting up the evening sky as it had the night before. Danbury peeled off to the left, working his way through the crowd, and Matthew and Lanie headed to the right end of the bar to see if Courtney DeBerry had seen Danny Boy yet.

When they approached, Matthew was dreading the encounter but the bartender surprised him entirely.

"I was hoping I'd see you this evening," she yelled over the din as he and Lanie found spots on the only two stools left at the bar.

"Oh?" was all that Matthew could manage to splutter in his surprise.

"Yeah, I owe you an apology. I was really rude this afternoon."

"Oh, OK," he yelled back, and laughed. "I was going to apologize to you, too. I don't normally ever give anybody such a hard time. It's just that time is critical right now in finding Ariel."

"I understand. I was just late getting my son from the babysitter. Usually, my mom or my sister has him, but they were both tied up and I had to get a sitter. She was sending me threatening texts about charging me double and never sitting again if I didn't come pick up my son. I was a little stressed with the delay."

Matthew was thinking that the woman was a Jekyll and Hyde type, charming and friendly behind the bar but a barracuda when she was out from behind it. What he yelled back, sympathetically, was, "You're a single parent? That must be rough. I hope you didn't have to leave him with the sitter again tonight."

"Nope. My mom has him tonight. I'm picking him up in the morning. Now, what can I get you before I get back to these two guys down here waving their mugs around impatiently," she tilted her head in their direction without pointing at them directly. Matthew noticed that she had never looked at them directly or made any sort of eye contact. She must be well practiced at seeing the whole end of the bar in her peripheral vision, which might come in handy tonight, he hoped.

"You want anything, Lanie?" he asked.

"Can I have a Coke?"

"One Coke and a seltzer for me, in a bottle, please," said Matthew. Before she could disappear, he added, "And let me know as soon as you see Danny Boy."

"Sure thing," she smiled at them. "Coming up."

Matthew saw Danbury making his way through the crowd, coming their way. He stopped by long enough to verify that Courtney would tell them when Danny Boy showed up and to say that he was going to go sit at the other end of the bar so that they could cover most of the venue that way. Matthew agreed and Courtney slid the drinks in front of them before disappearing again.

When she got a momentary break in customers, she sidled back down their way and said, "No Danny sightings yet, but he'll likely be here. He's here most every night, at least for a little while."

"Thanks. Hey, remember you were telling us that you were away from the bar Monday night around nine-thirty on your break?"

"Yeah, I usually take my break about then, why?"

"Do you remember if Danny was at the bar when you left or, more importantly, after you returned?"

She flipped a towel between her hands as she pondered that. "I did see him that night, but he was at one of the high-top tables with a couple of other guys, not at the bar that night. And I know I saw him before I went on break, but I don't remember seeing him afterward. You saw him in the video leaving, though, right?"

"Right. I was just wondering if he came back."

"Oh. Not that I remember. I had taken some leftover hor d'oeuvres that had been out too long to some of the Bridge People about that time. They weren't bad, just not fresh," she added, apologetically.

"The 'Bridge People'," muttered Matthew and was surprised that Courtney had heard him over the din when she answered him.

"It's what everyone around here calls the people who live under the bridge," she said.

"Yeah, I've heard that."

Lanie, Matthew observed in his peripheral vision, had leaned forward expectantly and she said, "Some of the other people here the last time we were here called them that, but it was mostly in a condescending way. It made Ariel mad."

"Yeah, I know," said Courtney. "It used to affect me the same way. Most of us around here are just a paycheck away from being under the bridge ourselves, so there's no room for judgment as far as I'm concerned."

"Great way to look at it," said Matthew, sipping his seltzer but noting that Lanie was still leaning forward in her seat, looking tense.

"Now I just take food out to them whenever we have some that's not good enough to serve paying customers but isn't bad enough to throw out," continued Courtney. "With all the food vendors here, we don't have a real kitchen, but we have a variety of hor d'oeuvres brought in to the bar several times a night," she motioned to a row of warming ovens with glass fronts sitting along the top of the counters in the center of the bar behind her.

"When each new batch comes in, we're supposed to throw out the rest of the last one, if there's anything left. But I take my breaks after restocking and take the food that's still good out to the Bridge People. The last batch for the night usually comes in shortly after nine on most week nights, so I was probably out delivering the leftovers about nine-thirty or so."

Suddenly, Lanie jumped up so fast that Matthew had to catch the stool to keep it from knocking into the people stacked up behind her as she shouted triumphantly, "Anna!"

As Courtney and Matthew both looked in surprise at her sudden outburst, she explained, "I know why Ariel wanted pizza from here! I know why she got two! She was taking one of the pizzas out to Anna!"

"Who's," Mathew began to ask as Courtney was in the process of explaining.

"The girl under the bridge. She's about fifteen, I think. She lives in one of those pods under the bridge," Courtney supplied.

"Exactly!" said Lanie. "I don't know why I hadn't put that together before, but that's why Ariel was here. Matthew, we need to go find Anna!" she shouted passionately over the din of music and revelers.

"OK," said Matthew, as he pulled his wallet out, handed Courtney a twenty-dollar bill and said, "See that guy down at the other end of the bar? The tall blonde guy in the white t-shirt?"

"You mean the cop?" asked Courtney.

"How'd you…" began Matthew.

She waved him off and said, "I can spot them a mile away. Ex-military, too, I'd bet."

Matthew's amazement must have shown clearly on his face he realized, when she laughed and said, "I've been bartending a long time. Didn't have you pegged for a doctor."

Regaining his composure, Matthew said, "His name is Danbury. Could you tell him if Danny Boy shows up? We need to go find a girl under the bridge. Lanie, do you know what she looks like?"

"Yeah, I met her at the same time Ariel did that first night we were down here. Ariel could talk to her. My Spanish isn't nearly as good as hers but I'm learning."

"OK, then let's go," said Matthew to Lanie as he picked up his bottled water. Then, back to Courtney he said, "Keep the change."

Making his way with Lanie in tow through the crowd and down to the other end of the bar, Matthew leaned in to tell Danbury where they were going, that Courtney would get word to him if Danny Boy came in, and to tell him that she'd immediately made him as a cop.

"Huh, OK," was all that Danbury said in response.

"I'll call if we need you under the bridge."

"OK," Danbury said again. "I'll sit tight. Until you get back. Or for another hour or so anyway."

Lanie led Matthew through the groups of people and out the entrance before she turned and said, "I can't believe I didn't think of this before!"

"You thought of it now, Lanie, so let's just go find this girl. Hablo Español?" he asked as he came up alongside her on the sidewalk across the street and was stretching his long legs to keep up with her much shorter ones that were moving fast.

She laughed at him, which was a nice sound to his ears, "You mean ¿Hablas Español? Si, hablo un poco. Solo un poco," she added, putting up her thumb and forefinger closely together to emphasize the point. "But several of the people there spoke Spanglish the other night, so I'll do my best."

"At least we can stop yelling at each other to be heard now," he said, as they rushed around the corner of the street that ended at the waterfront just down from Dock Side.

"Yeah, my throat hurts from yelling back there," agreed Lanie.

One of the party busses that Lanie had mentioned earlier was parked at the curb and there were groups of people who looked like they were waiting to board it all along the sidewalk. Just as they were passing the revelers, music cranked up on the party bus and Matthew muttered, "And then again, maybe not."

Beyond them, there were other revelers who didn't appear to be part of the party bus crowds. They were dancing in the street behind the bus and one guy was attempting to sing along but failing miserably, in Matthew's opinion.

As they approached the first guy, Lanie looked at him closely and then moved on. Matthew too noticed the vacant look in his eyes and the poor guy was all but drooling on himself as he attempted to dance to the music. The next guy, the one who was attempting to sing, looked more promising. Though the tune was anything but on key, he seemed to know the words.

Trying to stay in front of the gyrating guy long enough to speak to him, Lanie said, "Hola, my nombre es Lanie."

"Don't be spewin' all that, Missy. This here's America," he answered in English.

Lanie looked over her shoulder at Matthew triumphantly. Back to the dancing man, she asked, "Is Anna around tonight?"

"Who wants to know?" he asked back, as Lanie was dodging the spit that flew liberally as he spoke. Matthew wasn't sure if his presence would help or hurt but he stepped up behind Lanie and, somewhat reluctantly, stuck his hand out, "Hi, I'm Matthew Paine." As the man ignored the hand, Matthew withdrew it and continued, "This is Lanie James. We're looking for a young woman who was bringing pizza down here to Anna Monday night. Have you seen her?" he held up the picture.

The man glanced at it and said something indistinguishable before turning and spinning until Matthew thought he'd fall over. When the spinning stopped and the man looked like he'd regained most of his balance, Lanie tried again, "Is Anna around tonight? Have you seen her?"

"Maybe so," said the man. "I ain't her keeper." He reached up to put one grimy arm around Matthew's shoulders and said, "But you and me, we're brothers. Brothers," he added, with emphasis as he reached over and relieved Matthew of the bottle of water, uncapped it, and chugged what was left of it before handing the bottle back. Then, jumping back like Matthew had slapped him, he screwed up his face and scowled, "What the hell kinda drink was that?"

"Seltzer water," said Matthew, relieved that the guy had let go of him that easily. "Have you seen Anna tonight?"

"Don't know," he said, flipping the bottle cap back before he started howling to the music again, dancing and gyrating away toward the bus.

Giving up on getting any help from him, they moved farther along the sidewalk. Heading toward what had looked from a car driving by like a tent city, Matthew now realized that it was clumps of configurations, juxtaposed cardboard, boards, tarps, sheets, and who knew what else. It looked like a huge but badly planned out city composed of patchwork quilts.

As they approached, a couple of women who looked to have had hard lives so their ages were impossible for Matthew to discern, glanced at them warily and then ducked down and disappeared into the depths of the mound that they probably called home. Two men were sitting under the bridge passing something between them that they were smoking as they contemplated the meaning of life.

"Nah, man, I don't need nothin' else. I ain't payin' no taxes. I'm all set. Set for life," Matthew overheard one say to the other as he and Lanie approached. Thankful to find English speakers, for whatever good it would do them, he introduced himself and Lanie again.

"We're looking for Anna. Have you seen her this evening?" he asked.

"Whatcha lookin' for Anna for?" said the other disheveled guy who didn't look at all like he had everything he needed for life.

"We're looking for a young woman who's missing. We think she brought a pizza down here to Anna Monday night and we need to know if Anna saw her."

"Yeah, I think she's around somewhere. Probably in there with her brother," he said, pointing to the other end of the large mound that had an opening which looked like a tent, two blankets hanging side by side and forming an overlapping slit in the center.

"Thanks, Man," said Matthew, mimicking their vernacular, though not intentionally. He had turned so quickly away that he missed seeing the guy's hand out, looking for payment for that small bit of information.

As he and Lanie made their way to what appeared to be an opening in the end of the mound, they looked at each other, unsure how to proceed. What exactly was proper protocol under these circumstances, wondered Matthew. There was nothing to knock on. If he called out, would he spook whoever was within? He looked at Lanie and said, "Maybe you can call out to her?"

"Anna?" said Lanie. The tent quivered, as if an occupant within had moved.

"Anna, are you here?" asked Lanie, and then quickly tried to correct herself. "Anna, estas aqui? Mi nombre es Lanie."

After waiting a few moments with no reply and no further movement from within the tent, Lanie tried again. When they still got no response, she asked Matthew, "Now what do we do?"

"Maybe we should have brought them a pizza," he said.

He had just gotten the words out when a dark head poked out and around the corner of the tent and repeated, "Pizza?"

14 ~ BUILDING BRIDGES UNDER BRIDGES

Matthew and Lanie both turned back to the tent, nodding. "Si, pizza," responded Lanie quickly, before the dark head could dart back into the tent. Slowly, the young face of a girl appeared around the edge of the tent as she looked up at Lanie and then looked around, presumably for the pizza, Matthew thought. When she saw him, she withdrew fearfully, so he stepped back and gave Lanie some room to work on drawing the girl back out.

In a safer environment, like at home in Peak, he'd just go get a pizza but he was not about to leave Lanie here alone. After a few minutes of stilted exchanges between Lanie and Anna, Matthew reached over and touched Lanie's arm, "What kind of pizza? I'll text Danbury and get him to order one. We can bring it out to her with some drinks, Coke or whatever she wants, if she'll tell us if she saw Ariel."

After a few more exchanges, Lanie stepped back and reached for the folder with the pictures that Matthew was holding and pulled the pictures out to show the girl. Matthew overheard Lanie ask Anna something and then Anna responded with, "Si," and then an inexplicable string of Spanish as the girl pointed and gestured. When she was finished, Lanie turned to Matthew, looking confused as Anna repeated, "Pizza?"

Lanie turned back, trying again, and probably asking Anna to slow down, Matthew assumed, though he couldn't hear, from behind her, what she said. If she was speaking Spanish, he figured he wouldn't have understood much of it anyway, even if he could have heard her.

He'd taken French in high school and college and he realized now that he should have worked on his Spanish. He would have, he thought, if he'd had a little more notice that he'd be jumping a plane and heading to Miami where that language was known to be prevalent.

While Matthew waited, he could see that Anna was earnestly trying to communicate. Both she and Lanie were gesturing quite a bit and he hoped some understanding was happening on both sides. At one point, Anna turned and pointed into the tent, gesturing while she spoke. Lanie pointed at Matthew, and said something back, excitedly, but Anna shook her head and responded vehemently. He couldn't understand the words, but he got the meaning. Whatever it was that they were talking about, Anna did not want him involved in it.

Finally, he stepped forward just a bit, trying to give Anna the look he gave the small children who he was treating at his office, and then asked, "Lanie, what did she tell you about Ariel?"

"Anna was some help there. Ariel was here Monday night. She brought pizza and asked if Anna needed anything else. Anna asked for shoes for both her and her brother, and Ariel said she'd bring her some. But then she hasn't come back."

"Did she see which way they went?" asked Matthew hopefully.

"They went back toward Dock Side, and she thought they were getting on the party bus. I know they wouldn't have done that, so that's as far as I can get with where they went," she said, miserably. "It doesn't help much, but at least we know that they made it this far."

"That's good work, Lanie. What kind of pizza does she want?"

"We need enough for her and her brother both. He's in the tent. And he's injured. But she completely refused to take him to a doctor or a hospital and she doesn't want you to look at him either. I told her you were a doctor, but she still said no. I think she thinks we'll take him away from her or something. Oh, and I'm not sure what kind of pizza, so just a medium cheese, I guess. And a couple of Sprites, maybe?"

"OK, I'm going to text Danbury and ask him to bring a pizza and a couple of soft drinks out. We can circle back on Danny Boy if he isn't there yet. Can you keep working on getting her to let me see her brother? Do you know what's wrong with him?"

"Not really, no. I'll try to ask," she said, turning back to Anna, who had fully emerged from the tent at some point during the conversation. She was a wisp of a girl, who looked to be maybe eleven or twelve years old, and nothing like the fifteen-year-olds that Matthew had treated back home in Peak. If Courtney had been right about her age, thought Matthew. Anna was in dirty shorts and a t-shirt with flip flops so sparse that her feet might as well have been bare. Her face was clean and her long dark hair was tied back in a strip of cloth.

While Lanie was trying to talk to Anna, Matthew pulled his phone out and sent the pizza and drink order to Danbury.

"No Danny Boy yet. I'll order. And bring out. Unless he shows. Stay tuned," was the text that Matthew got back. Thinking that Danbury texted just like he talked, Matthew responded with a thumbs up on the text. Then he turned back to Lanie, who seemed to be having some success with Anna, as the words were more and the gesturing less.

Finally, Lanie must have convinced the girl that Matthew could help because Anna got bold, stepped forward, and said, pointing first in the tent and then at Matthew, "Brother. Broke foot. Man fix?"

"Si," said Matthew. Then, to Lanie, he confirmed, "Her brother is in the tent?"

"Yes."

"Will he come out? Or do they want me to…" he didn't finish his sentence because Anna had turned and poked her head back into the tent opening and said something in Spanish, which caused a second dark head to slowly poke out of the makeshift tent. As the boy looked up, Matthew could see that her brother was younger and smaller than Anna. "Pedro," said Anna, pointing at the boy, by way of introduction.

"Mi nombre es," he said, repeating what he'd heard Lanie say earlier as he glanced at her for confirmation. She nodded before he continued. "Matthew. Mi nombre es Matthew."

He wished, once again, that Dr. Rob was here dealing with the two children. Dr. Rob had a way with their youngest patients that Matthew had always admired. He could calm a screaming child in record time and he would manage to break the language barrier, thought Matthew, in ways that he himself felt inadequate to manage.

"Did you tell them that we have pizza on the way?" he asked Lanie.

"I did. Anna said she's hungry and so is Pedro. I think she said they hadn't eaten today."

"Where are their parents?"

"Anna wouldn't tell me. I'm not sure that she even knows. That's probably why she completely refused the hospital visit too."

"There'd be a lot of questions about their parents, their address and all of that. Without the answers, Child Services would get called in. I'm not sure that would be a bad thing, except that they might get separated, which is probably what she fears. Let's see what we can do to help."

As Matthew began to kneel on the sidewalk to lessen the gap between his huge six-foot three-inch frame and that of his tiny patient. He beckoned the little boy forward, as Anna said something and darted past Pedro into their dwelling. She reappeared with pieces of cardboard and said, "asiento."

Pausing, Matthew looked at Lanie who provided, "Seat. She's trying to give you a seat off of the pavement."

"Gracias," said Matthew to Anna, taking the proffered pieces of cardboard and placing one under his knees and another for Pedro across from him. As Pedro stepped from the tent, he too was in shorts and a dirty t-shirt. He had no shoes on, and Matthew could see a rag wrapped and tied around the end of his left foot that was dirty and saturated in what looked like dried blood.

"Lanie, can you ask when and how the injury happened?"

"I can try," said Lanie, turning back to Anna.

After a few false starts, some vigorous head shaking on Anna's part, and finally "Si, Si!" after Lanie said something that must have been right, Lanie turned back to Matthew.

"It happened last night," she said. "That was the easy part to understand. The harder part was that he stepped on a broken glass bottle on the sidewalk and sliced the bottom of his foot open. If Ariel had managed to get shoes for them and get back here," she stopped before completing the thought.

"Can you get him to sit down here and prop it up so that I can see it? I'll need the light from your phone aimed in this direction to get a good look."

"Sure, I'll try."

After a bit of conversation back and forth, Anna turned to Pedro and motioned, saying something to him in Spanish. The boy promptly plopped down on the piece of cardboard on the sidewalk, leaned back on his hands, and propped his left foot up on his right knee in front of Matthew.

Lanie held her phone up with the light she'd turned on, and aimed it at Pedro's foot as Matthew carefully untied and unwound the layered wrappings. Wishing for gloves at that point, Matthew was afraid to leave and come back because he didn't want to spook them and send them into hiding. He had none of the supplies he normally carried in his cars with him at home in Peak down here in Miami anyway.

Lanie looked away as Matthew revealed the wound, a gash across the bottom of the boy's foot that wasn't very wide but it was, as he could see as he probed, deep.

"This really needs stitches," announced Matthew. "If the cut was last night, we need to get this stitched up as quickly as possible. I think his tendon is OK, but it looks like he's nicked an artery. That needs to be stitched up so that it doesn't continue to bleed. Then it all needs to get closed up cleanly so that it doesn't become infected."

"They're not going to go to the hospital," said Lanie. "Anna was pretty clear about that earlier. But I'll try to explain and ask."

"Yeah, that's the best I can do here. I don't have any of the supplies that I carry with me in my cars at home. I didn't fly down with any of that," he said, mildly chagrinned.

As Lanie explained to Anna what needed to happen, Matthew watched as Anna vehemently shook her head. Knowing that the refusal translation was coming next, Matthew contemplated his options. Leaving this child in his current condition wasn't one of them, so before Lanie had even turned back to him, Matthew was on the phone with Dr. Rob.

Skipping the small talk, Matthew provided the update on Ariel's whereabouts Wednesday night and Lanie's sudden epiphany as to why Ariel was all the way down here from Hialeah. He did enquire about Gavin, but as soon as he heard that there was no change in his condition, he ploughed ahead with what he needed to know, "Dr. Rob, how comfortable are you driving in Miami night traffic alone? And how well can you sweet talk the nursing staff around there?"

Dr. Rob hesitated at the odd question, and then answered, "I'm fine in the traffic. I've driven in it before. But why would I need to sweet talk nurses?"

Matthew quickly explained his dilemma and his plan, to which Dr. Rob readily agreed, just as Matthew knew he would when there was an injured child involved.

"I'll drop you a pin now to our location. You'll have to go around the corner from here to park and then walk back around. Unless," he said, looking over his shoulder. "There are party buses here that take nightly tours of this area. One had just pulled up when we walked down here. If there's one of those there, maybe you can pull in behind it without attracting too much attention. Honestly, I think you'd have to do something drastic down here to get a ticket. I've watched the idiocy of drivers right in front of police cars today and been amazed that nothing happened. I guess the police have more pressing things to deal with."

"Like finding missing women, I hope. And for that, right now, I'm thankful," said Dr. Rob. Then he added, "OK, I'll explain the situation to Gayle and get her to call if she needs anything. She's already found the coffee shop and the cafeteria and she's planning to spend the night here anyway. I brought her everything she would need for a couple of days, so I'll be there as soon as I can."

"Thanks, Dr. Rob," said Matthew, and they said their good-byes and Matthew clicked to disconnect the call.

Turning to Lanie to explain his plan, Matthew then asked Lanie to explain it to Anna, who initially looked concerned at the news. But Lanie kept talking and finally the girl nodded in uncertain agreement, saying something quietly in Spanish.

"What did you just tell her?" asked Matthew, who had caught a few words here and there, but nowhere near enough of them to understand the exchange.

"First, just that you want to help Pedro here. She wasn't agreeing to that. But then I thought to tell her that the father of the woman who brought her pizza Monday night was on his way and he's also a doctor. That seemed to do the trick."

"Dr. Rob," muttered Matthew. "He isn't even here yet and kids are responding."

"What?" asked Lanie as Matthew realized that he was tired and he hadn't meant to say that out loud.

"Dr. Rob just has a way with children in the office that I've always admired and sometimes envied," confessed Matthew. "He can calm them down and console them, somehow. But he isn't even here yet and his coming is what put Anna at ease."

"Oh," chuckled Lanie. "I'd love to try to make you feel better and tell you that I don't know what you mean. But I totally know what you mean. Ariel is an only child, but Dr. Rob is one of those few people who should have had at least two or three more."

"Yeah, I can see that," answered Matthew, thinking that was very insightful on Lanie's part and sincerely hoping that Ariel was still an only child out there somewhere and that they'd find her soon, somehow.

Pedro started squirming a bit and Matthew asked Lanie, "Can you tell him that he could lie back if they have a blanket, but that he needs to keep that foot propped up? The less swelling we have when Dr. Rob gets here, the better. I'll text Danbury to bring us some ice and a plastic bag if he can get one."

"OK, sure. I'll tell them."

As Lanie turned to explain this to the young brother and sister, Matthew texted his request to Danbury, who quickly texted back, *"On my way now. I'll ask."*

After a few more minutes, Danbury arrived with an extra-large pizza, five drinks, a paper bag containing paper plates and napkins, and a plastic zip-closure bag full of ice. Matthew walked down to meet him as Danbury juggled it all to hand off drinks and the ice bag.

"Here's the ice. Courtesy of your bartender friend. She sent some wipes too," which he retrieved from the pocket of his shorts, handing the little plastic package over. "I guess for hand washing. She had them in a huge purse. Locked in a cabinet. Behind the bar," Danbury shrugged, seeming to be confused by this.

"She has a son," explained Matthew. "These are probably baby wipes, but I'll take them. Why the huge pizza? They just needed a medium."

"Well," said Danbury, "I figured we could have a piece. They can share an extra-large. It smelled really good."

Amused, Matthew just chuckled because of course that's what Danbury was thinking, the man who could always eat. Matthew saw the fear register on Anna's face at the approach of the hulking Danbury, and then Lanie leaned over and said something to her that seemed to calm her fears. That something, Matthew realized, contained the word pizza. He knew how to communicate that much with them, at least, and gain some trust and cooperation. He'd remember that for future reference if he needed to talk to them again. Speak softly and carry a big pizza.

After they had all gotten seated in a semi-circle on pieces of cardboard on the sidewalk beside the tent, Matthew handed out a wipe to each of them and then divvied out the plates and napkins. Everyone was happily munching on a slice of pizza, as Matthew filled Danbury in on what Anna had told them about seeing Ariel and Gavin and thinking that they got on the party bus; and that Lanie knew that wasn't the case.

As Matthew pondered what he'd just reported, he asked, "Why do you think Anna thought they were getting on the party bus? Did they just disappear into a crowd that was standing there?"

"Good question," said Danbury, who had realized that Lanie was the only one there who could somewhat effectively communicate with them. "Can you ask Anna?" he asked Lanie.

"Sure," she said, wiping her mouth off with a napkin. She turned to Anna and Matthew understood a few words of the question, but none of the response. Lanie's reaction to it, however, was telling. After a few more exchanges, Lanie turned back excitedly to report what she'd learned.

"Anna says she thought they got on the party bus because two men approached them. She thought they were selling tickets to ride the bus, and then they disappeared together down the sidewalk into the crowd outside the bus. But the description she just gave me sounds like the two guys who followed Ariel and Gavin out of Dock Side!"

"I've got to get back there!" said Danbury, jumping up and shoving the last tidbit of his pizza crust into his mouth. "Let me know when Dr. Rob gets here. Specifically, when you're done. Then you can watch the bar. If Danny Boy hasn't shown yet. So that I can get to that alley."

"OK, will do."

*****

The pizza was finished and Pedro was looking sleepy as Matthew jumped up suddenly. He'd finally seen Dr. Rob arrive and he walked quickly down the sidewalk to meet him, taking one of the proffered bags of supplies.

"Sorry that took so long," Dr. Rob said. "First, I had to convince Gayle that I'd be back to check on her later and that I'd bring the car back anytime she wanted it. Then I had to convince the nursing staff to let me talk to the head of nursing to get approval to remove supplies. That nearly took an act of Congress."

"I'm sure," said Matthew. "And I don't blame them. We'd respond exactly the same way if strangers showed up in our offices claiming to be physicians and asked us for supplies. Thank you for doing that." He quickly filled Dr. Rob in on what Anna was able to tell them and that Danbury was working on locating the two men. He added, as they approached Anna and Lanie, "Pedro is right over here."

Matthew noticed that the first thing Dr. Rob did was to kneel in front of the boy, getting down on his eye level, and introduced himself in Spanish. Matthew knelt beside him and with some help from Lanie they explained what they needed to do. The boy looked up fearfully but, sitting on a piece of cardboard, Anna slid in under him to put his head in her lap. She stroked his hair and crooned something to him in Spanish, nodding to the two men to begin work.

As Matthew opened the bags that Dr. Rob had brought, he was

amazed, "You thought of everything, didn't you?"

"Except for the sterile environment," he said, looking around. "And some strong lighting, I did the best I could. And you can really thank the staff at Grace Hospital. After I explained the situation, and the Head of Nursing gave her consent, supplies started appearing from all directions."

"Let's hope it's good enough," said Matthew, wiping a bead of sweat from his brow with the back of his hand. He'd noticed that Miami weather didn't vary as much by night and day as the weather back in Peak did. It was still hot as the evening was turning to night. The variability, as far as he could tell, went from hot at night to scorching during the daytime hours and then back again without any relief in between.

Pulling on some gloves, after washing his hands as best he could with sanitizer and wipes, Matthew removed two syringes from one of the bags. Both of them were labeled, so he selected the one he wanted first. One was a numbing compound for the foot and the other was an antibiotic, both dosed for a boy Pedro's size, he knew. He asked Lanie, who was holding an LED flashlight that Dr. Rob had procured from somewhere, to translate as he explained what he was doing. He gave the first shot on the foot to numb the area as Anna crooned to Pedro and a single tear slipped down his right check. After a moment, Dr. Rob began the work of cleaning and prepping around the injury.

Moving up the boy's body, Matthew asked Lanie to explain as he cleaned off a spot and gave Pedro the second shot, the antibiotic that he hoped would be enough to prevent the initial phase of infection. Pedro also needed real shoes, he thought, just as Anna had asked of Ariel initially.

Pedro had whimpered at first, with any pressure on his foot near the puncture. When that ceased, Pedro's anxiety eased, and they were able to prod the foot without Pedro's objection, Dr. Rob and Matthew went to work. After cleaning and then rinsing the gash with saline and suturing the nicked artery, they sewed the gash neatly closed.

Dr. Rob gently wrapped and bandaged the foot and, turning to Lanie said, "Thank you, Lanie, for the lighting. You're a trooper."

Matthew noticed that Lanie had been looking away through most of it, and only glancing back occasionally to be sure that the light was in the right location. He saw that the young woman glowed at Dr. Rob's praise, though she said nothing.

"OK, can you explain to Anna that she'll need to change this dressing daily? Just the wrapping. Ask her if she saw what I did when I put it on there. I'll leave some betadine to bathe it with and all the wraps she'll need for the next two weeks."

He waited while Lanie spoke, first haltingly, and then picking up the items and pointing as she explained his instructions to Anna.

"Equally importantly," added Dr. Rob, "is this boot." He pulled a sock and a child's Velcroed boot from one of the last bags, placing it on Pedro's foot as he showed Anna how to position it. "Tell Anna that he needs to wear this constantly unless she's changing the bandage or he's got it propped up with ice on it. He needs to elevate the foot tonight and as much as he can for the next few days. If they have access to ice, applying that will keep the swelling down."

As Lanie tried to convey this information to Anna, Matthew said, "I know Courtney, the bartender down at Dock Side, brings food to them from the leftover bar appetizers. Maybe she can slip some ice out to them, as she comes and goes to work too. I can ask."

Picking up the trash from their makeshift operating area and then pulling off his gloves, stuffing it all in one of the bags, Matthew said, "Thanks for gathering all of the supplies and coming down here on such short notice. As usual, your presence calmed the children."

"I'm happy to have had the opportunity to help. This would make Ariel so happy," said Dr. Rob, tearing up. "This is exactly what she came down here this summer to do, to build bridges and understanding about available healthcare and why it's so important. Working to eliminate food and healthcare deserts and helping the underserved population to find both is what she most wants to do."

"It would make her happy. It's what she's all about. We'll tell her about it when we find her," Lanie added, with passion.

Smiling at them both, Matthew said, "I need to go relieve Danbury. Do you want to come sit with me at the bar when you're done? We're still looking for Danny Boy to make an appearance tonight, unless he already has," he said, pulling out his phone but seeing no new messages from Danbury.

Dr. Rob glanced at Lanie as he said, "We can come for a few minutes at least. We all need to wash our hands really well, even with the gloves."

Matthew agreed, adding, "Good plan. Then we can figure out who's going where from there."

He understood what Anna was saying as she was thanking them profusely, "¡Gracias, muchas gracias!"

"De nada," replied Dr. Rob as he still knelt on the sidewalk and asked Lanie to explain the dosing on the dropper of the liquid Children's Tylenol and an antibiotic that he was leaving with them. He instructed Lanie to ask Anna if she had any questions before they left for the night. He looked over his shoulder at Matthew and said, "You know we've got to figure out how to get these stitches out if they won't go to a hospital and we're gone in two weeks."

"I have an idea about that," said Matthew, thinking about the nurse, Judy Crew, who had been so helpful to them at Mount Hermon Medical Center. Maybe he could set up a proxy. And a woman would be far less threatening, though she'd need to bring a burly escort with her to come down here, he thought.

"I do too," Lanie piped up. "Unless you have something specific that you need for me to do tomorrow, or if you find Ariel tonight, I think I want to spend the day back at Conexiones Saludables tomorrow. I think I can get Marianna, our director, to gather supplies for Anna and Pedro, including shoes. She already goes to Little Havana, so this should be a breeze."

"Great idea, Lanie," said Dr. Rob. "She might be able to arrange for the stitches to come out too."

Lanie smiled, again glowing under Dr. Rob's praise.

"I'm going down to relieve Danbury at the bar," said Matthew as he turned to head back down the sidewalk toward the brightly lit event center.

"We'll be along in a minute," said Dr. Rob, as he reached behind Pedro's ear and made a quarter appear. Then, to Lanie, he said, "Tell him that he was very brave."

As Matthew wandered back down the sidewalk, passing the other pods and their residents, he heard a delighted Anna chime in, "¡Yo también!" which he thought was her asking to be next for the quarter trick.

As he walked along, Matthew was whistling the tune that was running through his head. He was wishing that he had change in his pocket to jingle. If he had, he'd have left some extra quarters for Dr. Rob to pull from behind the children's ears. He hadn't used cash much since he'd been down here, he thought. Well, none that he'd gotten any significant change from anyway, he amended, as he wondered both how much longer they'd be here and what the eventual outcome of their search for Ariel would be. He stopped whistling long enough to offer a silent prayer that they'd find Dr. Rob's daughter unharmed, both physically and emotionally.

As he returned to Dock Side, Matthew noticed anew how well lit the place was. How could anyone just disappear from here, unnoticed, he wondered. It was lit like daytime all night and there wasn't anywhere to hide around the periphery that wasn't well lit. There were no shadows to lurk in, at least in the area surrounding the event center. So how, he wondered, could not one but two young adults disappear. One of them not to be seen again at all for days, while the other was in the hospital as yet unable to tell them what had happened.

He desperately wanted to know the answer to that question, he realized. Even if Dr. Rob's daughter weren't involved, he knew he'd want to know the answer. But he wanted answers all the more because Dr. Rob's daughter was involved and he desperately wanted to find her alive and well, he thought as he entered Dock Side and headed for the restroom to wash up.

15 ~ IN PLAIN SIGHT

After locating the restroom and washing his hands and arms up to his elbows thoroughly with soap and hot water, Matthew found Danbury back where he'd been before, sitting at the opposite end of the bar from where Courtney was working. That was probably a good idea, he thought. She had figured out that he was a cop pretty quickly. Matthew worked his way through the thick crowd toward Danbury.

"Got him all fixed up?" yelled Danbury above the noise of the crowd and music as Matthew slid in to stand beside him. There was no stool available.

"Yeah, Dr. Rob and Lanie are finishing up with them now and they'll be back in a few minutes," yelled Matthew back.

"Good," yelled Danbury. "You got this then?"

"Yeah, I think I'll go find one of those high-top tables on Courtney's end so that she can let me know when Rubio, AKA Danny Boy, gets here. I need to thank her anyway for sending out the ice and the wipes and ask if she'll deliver more ice at intervals to them over the next couple of days. I can tell her what to look for and to let us know if his foot gets infected. I assume she speaks Spanish so she can ask, but I don't know that. I'll also update the timeline in our online files with the newest information about the last sighting of Ariel and Gavin."

"Good plan."

"I'm going to put us all in a group chat and share my location with the group so that we can stay in touch since we're splitting up so much. If you need anything when you get to the alley, just text the group."

"OK. I'll share my location too."

"Oh," said Matthew, as Danbury tossed cash on the bar and rose to leave. "Can you share Sergeant Nelson's contact information with us? I didn't get that last night."

"Yeah, sure. You should have it."

"Thanks, I'll let you know if Rubio shows up. I can talk to him and see what he knows about their whereabouts. If he's innocent, he'll tell me. I think I won't mention that we know he was with them last on the way back from the Bridge People."

"Good plan. Don't spook him. We don't want him in the wind. And call or text me. If you need my help. Or Sergeant Nelson's. Here," Danbury added, as he shared Nelson's contact information.

"Got it," said Matthew, pulling his phone from his pocket and clicking to add the contact. "Are you coming back here?"

"Not planning on it. Shouldn't he be here by now? Didn't your bartender friend say he usually is? That he makes an appearance before now?" asked Danbury.

"Yeah. I guess I'll hang out another couple of hours," Matthew said, checking his watch. "And then call it a night if he doesn't show by eleven or so."

"OK, see you in a couple," said Danbury as he turned and made his way back through the heavy crowd.

It wasn't a weekend, thought Matthew, and this place was crowded enough on weeknights. He'd hate to see what it was like on a Friday or Saturday night. He realized that he had no desire to know. This crowd was making him wish for his quiet life in Peak. He hadn't enjoyed a bar scene or nightlife like this in a long time, he thought as he made his way to the other end of the bar. Probably ever, he amended his own thoughts. And the humidity. And the fact that the heat was still at least eighty degrees and probably a lot more didn't help matters in the crush of the crowd.

Muttering "Pardon me," as he made his way through to the bar at the other end. He doubted that anyone could hear his southern politeness. He finally got within earshot of Courtney DeBerry.

"Hey, thanks for the ice and the wipes," he yelled across the bar, pulling the rest of the package of wipes from his pocket and handing them to her. "That helped a lot. Could you maybe take ice out to them when you come and go? Any time you get the chance?" As she nodded, he continued, "That kid sliced his foot open pretty good and they were terrified of going to a hospital and vehemently refused. Do you know where their parents are? Anna wouldn't tell Lanie."

She shook her head, "No, they wouldn't tell me either."

"Thanks," he said, "If they don't take good care of that foot, it can still get infected. If I tell you what to look for, could you keep an eye on him?"

Courtney rolled her eyes at him and yelled back, "Sure thing, Dr. Paine, anything else I can do for you?"

Though he caught the full brunt of the sarcasm, he responded, "Maybe a cold bottle of water? And let me know if you see Danny Boy? I'm going to try to grab the next high-top table that vacates over this way," he yelled, thumbing over his shoulder.

"Yeah, I can't really get away from the bar, but I can text you if I see him."

"Great! Still have my card?"

"It's back here somewhere, but I already put you in my contact list," she answered over the din.

"Thanks!" he yelled, surprised at this admission. "I can text you what to look for with Pedro's foot."

"You got it," she answered, handing over a water bottle and thanking him for the ten-dollar-bill he'd slipped her, telling her that he didn't need change. Then she quickly turned away to refill the beer glass of a patron who was waving the empty one wildly in the air and looking more and more annoyed with her.

Matthew forced his way back through the crowd that was about six or seven people deep around the bar and noticed that the patrons were all more than a little inebriated and nobody cared that he wasn't offering the southern mannered pleasantries as he did so. Miami, he thought, the land of constant contradictions. Here at Dock Side people were inebriated and celebrating while just down the street people were living in makeshift tent pods under bridges and struggling for survival.

Some of Miami, he'd heard, was divided by location. There were places just west of I-95 where there was abject poverty, cross I-95 to the east between that and Highway 1, and living conditions got a bit better and safer. Then cross Highway 1, closer to the water and it's a land of overabundance with Ferraris and Lamborghinis on every other corner. Or so he'd been told, though some of that he'd seen with his own eyes.

Spotting a high-top table at which a man and woman seemed to be settling up their bill and putting cash in a plastic folder, Matthew headed that way. As soon as they vacated the table, he sat his water bottle down in front of one of the seats and tipped two more chairs against the table to keep them from getting pulled away by other patrons. This table was a bit farther away than he preferred and was closer to the river, though he could see only snatches of it through the rows of boats tied along the boardwalk there. Courtney had said that she'd text him if Rubio showed, so he'd have to take her at her word, he thought.

As he settled in at the table, he pulled his phone out and created the group chat, naming it *A Recovery Team*. He wanted a name that wouldn't be discouraging but be obvious at the same time. Pinning it to the top of his list of chat contacts, he shared his location with it. Then, he pulled up the PayByPark app and added time for the car he'd driven, the Sonata. Next, he went to the shared documents and started typing in, albeit slowly on the tiny phone keyboard, the new information that they'd learned this evening.

After a few moments, he saw the notification that Danbury had also shared his location and Matthew clicked the *Find All* app and selected *People*. Danbury had made good progress in what must not be terribly insane traffic on a Wednesday night in Miami. He was across the river and nearly at the opening of the alley. Danbury was probably sitting at one of the myriad stoplights, Matthew noted, as Dr. Rob and Lanie appeared in the crowd around the bar. He stood and lifted his hand to signal them over.

As Matthew motioned to the two chairs he'd leaned against the table, they pulled one out on either side of him and sat. Lanie looked disoriented and Dr. Rob just looked sad. Matthew wished he could fix that for the man, but he leaned over and yelled, "I created a group chat with all of us in it and shared my location. I'll send a group text so you can see it."

After Mathew had done so, Dr. Rob pulled his phone from his pocket and said, "Got it. Good idea. I'll share my location too." Quietly, Lanie followed suit.

"You know," yelled Dr. Rob. "As I look around this place, I can't help but think that it's so public, so well lit. How could Ariel and Gavin just disappear from here in plain sight?"

"I've thought the same thing," yelled Matthew back, laying his cell phone, face up, on the table so that he could see any incoming text from Courtney. "Maybe they left here. If they hadn't missed their Rydz, I'd say that was the obvious answer. But why wouldn't they have taken the ride out that they'd already scheduled and might have already paid for?"

"That is the question," yelled Dr. Rob. "It'd be grand if we could come up with the answer!"

As Dr. Rob inevitably turned to stare out at the boats, because his passion and favorite pastime was sailing, a thought came to Matthew. "Wait a minute!" Matthew yelled. "I'm pretty sure that Courtney said this 'Danny Boy' guy took young women out to a boat in the evenings! I wonder if that's how he got them out of here? By boat, not by the street. That waterway, in either direction, isn't as well-lit as the street and sidewalks around the event center. It doesn't go very far inland, though, or at least the sign I read said it's not a very long river. Only five and a half miles before it finds its source in the Everglades."

"I thought of that," yelled Dr. Rob back. "But Ariel has never been as enamored of boats or sailing as I am. In fact, I think she mostly tolerated it, just to humor and spend time with me on the weekends. She wouldn't be excited about going to see some guy's boat. And she was with Gavin. She'd want to get right back to the ministry, I'm thinking."

"You're right!" piped up Lanie. "She would want to get back and she wouldn't willingly follow some guy out to a boat."

Just then, Matthew's phone lit up and he held it up to read the text message from Courtney. He'd put it on vibrate because he figured he couldn't hear it above the racket in this place anyway, so he slipped it into his pocket and stood. "He's here!" he yelled to Dr. Rob and Lanie. "I'm going to make my way over to the bar. I'll be back after I talk to him."

Nodding his thanks to Courtney as he went by, he spotted the guy in the lime green collared shirt that she'd indicated was about half way down the bar on the street side. The guy's streaked, dirty blonde hair and bright blue eyes were obvious just as Courtney had described, even from a distance. Matthew knew from her earlier description that Danny Boy was in his early thirties, medium height around five eleven, medium build, around 185 pounds, and had a 1,000-WATT smile.

Matthew steeled himself, yet again, to defy his normally calm and laid-back demeanor for a confrontation that he'd never, under normal circumstances, want to have. He told himself that it was for Ariel and Dr. Rob and he determined that he was going to do it anyway, as much as he really didn't want to. As he approached, he saw that Danny Boy had turned his infamous smile, charmingly, on a young woman who Matthew noticed was smiling coquettishly up at him.

"Hey, Danny Boy! How's it going?" Matthew yelled, jovially, as he approached and tried to look just slightly drunk as he said it to push his way through the remaining layer of the crowd around the long bar.

Danny turned from the woman and the 1,000-WATT smile morphed quickly into an arrogant sneer as he looked at Matthew and said, "Do I know you?"

"Not yet," replied Matthew honestly.

"Then bugger off, Mate," yelled the guy, turning back to the young woman.

That was interesting, Matthew thought, because nobody so far had mentioned that the guy had a British dialect. Or was it Australian? It was so noisy that Matthew wasn't sure. It could even be South African for all he was able to hear of it.

Pushing his way through two more people to stand beside the young woman, purposefully towering over and crowding Danny Boy,

Matthew looked down at him, "I'm afraid I can't do that, Mate," he added for emphasis. "I need to talk to you."

"About what?" the guy asked, clearly agitated.

"About a friend of mine who was here on Monday night. You stopped her on the way out, she and her boyfriend."

"I talk to lots of people here, so what?" asked the guy.

"I need to know what you talked to her about and where she went after you parted company," he said, tactfully but trying to maintain his tough guy act. "Do you remember talking to a young couple?" he asked. "She's a petite redhead and he's best recognized by his square jawline, apparently," offered Matthew helpfully. He didn't show the pictures from the folder under his arm because he didn't want to spook the guy, at least not just yet.

"I talk to lots of people, like I told you. I probably just offered them a tour of the bay," said Rubio, noncommittally. "I do boat tours of Biscayne Bay. And how would I know where she went next? If they said no, they'd have gone on their way and I mine. Now best be on yours, Mate."

"You mean yacht tours, right Babes?" asked the pretty blonde woman, who was obviously inebriated and slurring her words badly, as she clung to his arm on the other side of Matthew. "I want a full tour of that, too," she pouted. "Right now. I want to see the yacht too."

"Excuse us, Mate," said Daniel Rubio, with a smirk and a nod as if Matthew should fully well know and appreciate why he needed to leave them alone just now.

Matthew thought he'd be better off following them at a discrete distance than continuing to hem the guy in with more questions, so he just nodded, trying to look like he understood completely, and stepped back to let them pass.

Being six-foot-three had its advantages because he was able to see over a good bit of the crowd and follow in their wake. He was half wishing that he had Danbury's extra inch or two, as he momentarily lost sight of them. But then he was happy that he didn't when he saw Rubio just ahead looking back over his shoulder. Matthew was able to quickly step behind another tall guy in the crowd and he didn't think

Rubio had spotted him following them.

They continued on to the waterfront. Once they'd hit the boardwalk alongside the river, he could see that the young woman was leaning heavily on Rubio and he was half dragging her along toward a big boat that was tied down near the end of the boardwalk to the left. Maybe she wasn't really in her right mind, Matthew thought. Maybe she'd had some coercion to want to go with Rubio. Maybe he'd slipped her a roofie or something. That could explain a lot, thought Matthew, as his phone vibrated in his pocket.

Standing just beyond the pool of light cast by the last street light in the shadows of some heavy brush along the end of the boardwalk, Matthew was watching to see which boat they'd boarded. He waited until they were aboard and had gone below deck before he pulled his phone out, with his hand cupped around it to block out as much of the light from it as possible. There was an urgent message from Dr. Rob to come toward the bridge that was under construction down along the other end of the boardwalk.

Matthew wasn't that far away from their location, now that he was clear of most of the crowd out here on the boardwalk. He decided to pursue Danny Boy and the woman first and then circle back to Dr. Rob and Lanie. Staying in the shadows, Matthew made his way down to the boat they'd boarded first. He could see lights on within but the occupants weren't up on the deck, so he slipped around behind the massive boat and got pictures of the stern. Then he slipped back through the shadows out along the riverfront in front of Dock Side and down to the other end of the boardwalk where Dr. Rob and Lanie were waiting for him.

As he approached them, Matthew could see that Lanie was obviously shaken. Rob pointed into the shadows of the construction site of the old SW 1st Street Bridge and said, "We heard screams, coming from down there."

"Screams?" asked Matthew, realizing that he was pulling his gun from the holster, handing Dr. Rob the folder with the pictures in it, and was ready to run that way as he asked the question. When had he become the guy who ran toward screams with a gun, he wondered. Just as that thought flitted through his mind and he'd turned and started walking that way to investigate, a woman came running headlong at him, as fast as she could on wobbly legs, and nearly ran into Matthew. As he caught her, he could see that her face was as white as the sheets on some of the sailboats he'd seen down here, and she couldn't seem to catch her breath. When she finally did, she pointed back under the bridge and said, "Body! There's a body down there!"

"A body?" asked Matthew. "Whose? Where?"

"Down there in a hole on the other side of the old bridge. I don't know whose, but there's a body!"

Matthew's gaze followed the direction in which she was pointing, beyond the area that was fenced and corded off with the construction effort and he asked, "How'd you get in there?"

"Around the fence," she answered, nearly collapsing against him. "You hang onto the end. Then you step around it and swing out over the water to the other side."

"Did you see anyone else down there?" he asked.

"No. But I heard people. They were going the other way." She gasped for breath as she added, "Two guys, one with a deep voice."

"Were you the one who screamed?" asked Matthew and she nodded. "Where were the guys you heard talking when you screamed?" he asked, pulling her over to a bench along the waterfront and sitting her down there.

"They were gone. At least, I guess they were. I heard their voices a while before I saw… it," she stammered. "The body."

"You went down there alone?" Again, she nodded. "Can you tell me where you saw it?"

"On the other side of the old bridge," she answered. "There are holes, some of them pretty deep. They run along beside the old bridge from the water out to the street. It wasn't the one right next to the water," she was sobbing now. "But maybe four or five back from it."

"Dr. Rob, what did you do with that LED flashlight?"

From the one remaining bag that Dr. Rob carried with a few items in it, he pulled the flashlight, which he handed over to Matthew. "I told them I'd bring this and the suture kit back tomorrow," he said.

"Can you get her some water?" he asked Lanie, who nodded as Matthew handed her a ten-dollar bill. "I'm going to go check it out."

Neither Lanie nor Dr. Rob looked excited at this prospect, though neither did either of them object as Matthew headed off in the direction of the end of the fence and grabbed hold. Suspending himself over the river, he pulled himself back around the other side of the little section of fence and onto the ledge at the top of the bulkhead there.

He decided that the moonlight would be good enough until he reached the set of holes. He didn't want to risk being spotted by the LED flashlight if anyone else were still around. The scream would have alerted them if they were. If the nearly hysterical woman could see down the hole to see a body by moonlight and Miami light pollution, then so could he.

Finding the row of holes as she'd said, he began examining them. The first three from the river back toward the road were empty. But he could see something in the bottom of the fourth hole and it did look like a body under a blanket or some sort of covering. Matthew paused and looked around to see if there was anyone watching him, but he knew that with all of the construction equipment and piles of debris, he couldn't know for certain one way or the other. He decided to risk it and turned on the flashlight, shining it down the hole.

What he saw in the bottom of the hole made his blood run cold.

16 ~ MANTRA

Matthew couldn't climb down into the deep cylindrical hole to examine the body, but from under one end of what looked like a dirty tan tarp he could see feet. They were bare and clearly belonged to a woman, small in size. The toenails of one foot that was upturned just slightly were painted a vibrant pink. Protruding from under the other end of the tarp was bright red hair. It looked dirty and matted but it was definitely bright red.

Knowing that Ariel's hair was a deeper more natural coppery auburn color and wasn't that bright stop sign color of red, Matthew breathed slightly more easily. He turned off the flashlight and looked around him once again. A weak light was being cast by a streetlight nearly a football field away down along the street, but the circle of its glow beneath didn't reach anywhere near where he was standing. Otherwise, all was dark and he saw nothing moving so he turned on the flashlight, clamping the end of it between his teeth, pulled out his phone, pulled up his camera, and snapped a couple of pictures with one hand, all while still clutching his Glock firmly in the other.

Turning, he put his phone back in his pocket. His nerves were on edge and he thought he heard snaps and cracks behind him. Looking all around, his head swiveling first in one direction and then the other in broad sweeps, he went back the way he'd come. Holstering his gun, he slipped the flashlight into his pocket and quickly and nimbly swung around the end of the fencing. As he approached Dr. Rob, he could see that the man was watching him in horror, so he shook his head decisively to let him know that the body was not Ariel's.

"There is a body in the hole," said Matthew. "But it is NOT Ariel."

"Are you certain?" asked Dr. Rob, dropping to the bench in relief.

"I am," said Matthew as he pulled his phone out and texted Danbury, sending the picture too. He'd already learned not to call if Danbury was off on surveillance. A ringing phone could give away a position and turn the stalker into the stalked. Danbury would have silenced it, he thought, but it might still vibrate noiselessly in his pocket.

They waited ten long agonizing minutes, while Matthew paced. Eyebrow raised in concentration and deep in thought, he paced back and forth in front of Lanie, Dr. Rob, and the woman whose name he hadn't even asked. All seated in a row on the bench. He was holding his phone waiting for a response and then remembered that he could check Danbury's location. He pulled up the app, but Danbury's location wasn't registering and the app said that he couldn't be located. Matthew wasn't concerned, figuring that Danbury had probably done the sane thing and turned off his phone if he was doing surveillance.

Matthew decided that time was of the essence, so he chose the next best option and called Sergeant Nelson, thankful that he'd gotten his contact information from Danbury earlier. There were two numbers for Sergeant Nelson on the contact information that Danbury had shared and, when Matthew got a voicemail message on the cell number, he called the precinct number and asked for Nelson. The very helpful young male voice on the phone said that Sergeant Nelson was out and asked if he could take a message.

"The message is that we just found a dead body," said Matthew, providing his name and the exact location. "I have the woman here who found the body. She said that she heard men's voices leaving the construction site shortly before finding the body in the hole but she said she didn't see anyone. She just heard them."

Turning away to pace a little farther, he added, "I'm here working with Detective Danbury trying to locate Ariel Roberts, the third redhead to be reported as missing from this area. Can you please tell Sergeant Nelson that I think maybe the body is that of Katie Jones, the second redhead who was reported as missing? Her hair is dyed bright red, so I don't think it's Ariel Roberts, who we're searching for. I can only see her feet and the bright red hair sticking out because she's under a tarp about five feet down in a cylindrical hole."

As he paced back to the bench, Matthew could see that Dr. Rob had given up any semblance of control and his face was in his hands and his elbows on his knees. Lanie had one arm around him and she too looked stricken. "Yes, I'll hold," he said to the dispatcher he'd been connected to.

A few moments later, Matthew heard a gruff voice answer, "Sergeant Nelson. What is this about a body of another redhead?"

Turning away from the bench, Matthew filled him in. Nelson promised that he was on his way. Matthew continued to pace, running his splayed fingers through his short, wavy brown hair, frustrated that there was no comfort to offer any of the occupants of the bench and annoyed with himself that he didn't know how to try. The woman who had found the body identified herself as Rebecca Aimes when the dispatcher asked for the identity of the person who'd made the discovery. Now she seemed to be in shock. She stared straight ahead, unblinking, at nothing.

After what seemed like an eternity, Matthew heard police sirens in the distance and he pushed his way through the crowd out to the front of Dock Side, flagging down the police cruisers. There were three of them, two clearly marked, and a third unmarked. Parking them at the curb in the no parking zone, Sergeant Nelson got out of the unmarked car and came over to Matthew. "Show me," he said simply.

Matthew led him back to the bench and introduced him to Rebecca Aimes. She was responsive enough to answer Nelson's questions and she continued to give her statement to a uniformed police officer as Matthew led Nelson and two other officers back around the fence, swinging carefully out over the water and onto the ledge on the other side of the fence. "I'm sure there's an easier way to do this," he said. "And you heard Ms. Aimes say that the voices she heard left in the other direction, but this is how she said she got over here."

He took them to the hole, shining the flashlight down it.

"How did you get involved with this?" Nelson asked Matthew, who had visibly cringed at the body in the hole.

"Tonight? My colleague Dr. Richard Roberts from our medical

practice back home and Lanie James, his daughter's best friend, were out here by the water. They heard Rebecca Aimes scream."

"Why were you down here tonight?"

"We were here to find and talk to Danny Boy. Daniel Rubio, the guy that Danbury asked you to check out. He's apparently a regular here and he was seen approaching and talking to Ariel and Gavin twice on Monday night. He's the last person we can find to have seen them, but he's not admitting to it."

"Where is he now?"

"Last big boat on the other end of the boardwalk. At least, that's where he went with his conquest for the night. She didn't look like much of a conquest. She was pretty out of it. He was all but carrying her down the boardwalk. Here," added Matthew, pulling out his phone and showing Nelson the pictures of the stern of the Yacht with the name, '*Playbuoy*' from Miami, FL clearly displayed on it.

"It's not wrong," he added.

"Can you send me that?" asked Nelson.

"Sure," said Matthew and proceeded to do so.

"OK, we'll take over from here," said Nelson. "You can take your friends back to your hotel now, if you'd like. They look tired and so do you."

"Mostly just really worried, I think," replied Matthew. "If this is Katie Jones and they're showing up dead in the order that they disappeared…" He left the rest of the sentence hanging because he had no desire to complete it. "I need to go find Danbury. He went back to that alley where Gavin Blevins was found."

"He did? When?"

"Over an hour ago now," said Matthew, checking his watch. "Nearly two hours ago. Something about it was bothering him and he wanted another look."

"Huh," was all that Nelson said, as he turned his attention back to the hole, as if dismissing Matthew by default or forgetting that he was still standing there.

Taking that as his cue to leave the police work to the qualified,

Matthew turned to leave and he overheard one of the other officers mutter, "Are these holes for footings for the new bridge? What, is this? Like a bad old mobster movie where they were going to pour cement in over her?"

As Matthew went back the way he had come, swinging himself around the end of the fence, he saw the officer who had been talking to Rebecca Aimes now talking to a man in a white lab coat, motioning to him and a second man with him to go around the other way. Apparently, thought Matthew, the forensics team was quick to respond around here if the police were already on the scene.

Telling Dr. Rob and Lanie that they were free to go, he also admitted that he was going to look for Danbury. It wasn't like the guy to be silent this long, particularly given that Matthew had texted telling him about the body that they thought to be the next redhead victim. Dr. Rob insisted on going with him, and Matthew eventually acquiesced. Lanie just nodded, though she looked less than thrilled with a trip back down to the alley.

Stopping back by the bar, Matthew told Courtney what to look for on Pedro's foot and asked her to notify him if she saw any of the symptoms that he described to her. Then he texted her that same list of descriptions, just to be certain she had it.

"Nobody mentioned to me that Danny Boy had a dialect, British or Australian, or whatever it is," Matthew yelled across the bar to her.

At that, Courtney laughed and yelled back, "Danny Boy can turn on whatever dialect he thinks will lure in the lady he's got his eye on. That's how he got his nickname. The night that Rod and I gave him the name, it was an Irish accent he was going for. That and the blond hair and blue eyes earned him the nickname and, as far as Rod was concerned, that was that. It stuck."

"Oh! Thanks again for all of your help! Hey, could we get four more water bottles to go, please?" he asked, handing over his debit card this time.

"Sure thing. Be right back."

After he'd signed the receipt and left a healthy tip for the young bartender, the single parent who had been helpful, he picked up the water bottles and met Dr. Rob and Lanie on the sidewalk in front of the entrance where they were waiting for him. He handed each of them a water bottle and Lanie said softly that she wanted to ride back to the alley with Dr. Rob. Not surprising, thought Matthew. That gave him some time to get lost in his own thoughts as he drove out from under the bridges, through the late-night traffic, and over the bridge heading for the alleyway.

His mind returned to the two artificial redheads who had been reported missing before Ariel. They allegedly, both had been found dead in the same order as they'd been reported missing. His mind wandered and he realized that it had landed on Cici, his ex-girlfriend and the other half of his very complicated relationship. She was a strawberry blonde and her hair shown coppery in the right lighting too. He shivered, thinking about the woman in the hole, who looked to be small framed like Cici, but maybe not as extraordinarily so. Cici, though her feisty personality made her seem like a huge presence and she was a force to be reckoned with in the courtroom, stood only five-feet tall in her bare feet.

He shook the thoughts of her from his mind, or at least he tried to, as he arrived. He parked along the curb down near the brasserie again. Dr. Rob, who hadn't explored the area earlier that day, pulled in directly behind him. Matthew knew that the brasserie would already be closed, though he wasn't sure why it closed so early because restaurants all around the area were still open. Maybe it was a French thing, he thought.

Though the business was dark and empty for the night on the inside, parking in front of it was directly beneath a bright street light. There were also little lights on posts along the sidewalk. As they climbed out of the cars, Matthew was pretty sure he saw the SUV that Danbury had been driving down the street on the other side of the entrance to the alleyway.

Pointing out the big black SUV, Matthew led the way as they headed toward it. Just as they reached it, they heard loud noises, which Matthew took to be three shots in rapid succession, ringing loudly through the thick, mostly stagnant, night air. It sounded like it had come from the alleyway and all three of them jumped and ducked behind the big SUV. Matthew peeked above the back windows quickly and then made his way to the front and peered in. Danbury wasn't in the vehicle, nor did any of his personal items appear to be there.

"There's no sign of him here," said Matthew quietly to the other two. As he started, still ducking beneath the windows, back down to the other end of the SUV toward the alleyway, they heard a grunt before at least two vehicle doors slammed and an engine revved, tires peeling out in the other direction from the alley.

Not again, thought Matthew as he pulled his gun from the holster and peered around the back of the SUV. It wasn't close enough to the opening of the alley to afford him a view down it, so he motioned for Dr. Rob and Lanie to stay put as he slipped across the sidewalk and along the side of the stucco building, the front of which would be on the next perpendicular street. Peering quickly down the alleyway, he couldn't see much because it wasn't well lit, but what he did see made him cringe. Part way down, he saw what looked like a pair of large feet sticking out from behind one of the many dumpsters, but on the right this time.

Slipping back to Dr. Rob and Lanie, he told them in couched terms what he feared he'd find down the alley. Because Danbury was missing, he knew that he had to go look. He told them to stay put but Dr. Rob insisted on coming with him.

"Lanie, let's get you safely locked back in the car first," said Matthew, and Dr. Rob nodded his agreement.

Matthew could see Lanie's fear and the internal struggle. On the one hand, he was sure she didn't want to be left alone, even in a locked car under a bright street light. But on the other, she'd already expressed her revulsion to what she'd previously dubbed as the creepy alley, even without tentatively finding another corpse and potentially that of someone she had actually met.

Gulping hard, Lanie nodded her agreement and the three of them crossed the street to get her as far away from the alley as possible, up the sidewalk on the other side of the street where they'd parked perpendicular to the alleyway. As they were locking Lanie in the car that Gayle Blevins had rented, Matthew shared Sergeant Nelson's contact information with the group.

"We'll likely have to use this anyway if I find what I think I will in this alley, but if you hear any more shots, if anything else happens, or if we don't check back in about five minutes, call it," Matthew admonished Lanie. "Don't hesitate, just call it, OK?"

Lanie, who hadn't spoken aloud since they'd arrived, just nodded and closed and locked the door. Matthew and Dr. Rob crossed the street to access the shadows from the end of the building on the other side and headed back to the alleyway.

"Dr. Rob, I'm pretty sure I saw feet sticking out from behind one of the dumpsters on the right, about the third one down the alley. They look to be large feet. I just don't want them to be," he choked on the end of the sentence. "Danbury would never have let anyone get the drop on him. He's too good at what he does, he just wouldn't have," finished Matthew, resolutely trying to convince himself along with Dr. Rob.

As they rounded the corner into the alleyway, Matthew led the way, with his Glock at the ready. As they reached the third dumpster down on the right, Matthew could indeed see large feet sticking out at an odd angle from behind it. Slowly, he crept up while keeping his head on a swivel to watch his surroundings constantly. As he peered around the dumpster, he could see the body of a large man with dark hair.

Breathing out a huge sigh of relief, he turned to Dr. Rob who was on the other side of the dumpster still, and whispered, "It isn't Danbury. But it is a body. We have to check," he added as he and Dr. Rob slipped along beside the large man with their backs to the wall and Matthew's Glock pointed outward.

Matthew held the gun steady and kept watch while Dr. Rob knelt and felt for a pulse, first on the wrist and then the neck. He looked up, shaking his head, and stood up beside Matthew. "After I saw the hole in his forehead, I wasn't expecting to find a pulse," said Dr. Rob.

"I'm sure it's grisly," said Matthew glancing quickly down at the prone figure in the dimly lit alleyway, "but can you get a picture of his face?"

Dr. Rob pulled out his phone and took several pictures, with the necessary flash lighting up their corner down beside the dumpster, while Matthew stood watch with the Glock still poised in front of them.

"Thanks. Let's go back to Lanie and call Nelson," said Matthew, his head still on a swivel as they made their way back down the alley and out onto the street.

"Maybe we should tell Lanie to just take that car and go back for the night. It's late, she's exhausted and we could be here for a while," said Dr. Rob, practically.

"If you're sure you don't want to go with her?" asked Matthew.

"Yes, but no," said Dr. Rob. "I dragged you into all of this mess down here so I'm not leaving you here to deal with it. Especially without Danbury."

"I came down here willingly," said Matthew. "But if Lanie is comfortable driving that little Accent back alone, I would be happy for the company. She's right, that is a creepy alley."

Lanie had been watching their approach and she opened the door as they walked up. "Well?" she urged.

Matthew decided to let Dr. Rob handle explaining things to Lanie while he called Sergeant Nelson.

"We don't have an ID on the vic yet, but we have her out of the hole and the forensic team is working on it," said Nelson when he answered, as if in reply to the question he assumed Matthew was calling to enquire about but hadn't given him the chance to ask.

As Matthew explained about the alley, the abandoned SUV, the shots they'd heard and the vehicle driving away, Sergeant Nelson asked all of the usual questions.

"No, we didn't see the shooter or the vehicle that he or she left in," answered Matthew. "But I wasn't finished yet. There's a body in the alley, but it's not Danbury. It's a big guy with dark hair. Probably the victim of the gun shots we heard, given that one shot was placed cleanly just above and between his eyes, probably at close range. But we didn't stick around to examine him more thoroughly. We just checked for a pulse, found none, and then called you. Otherwise, we didn't disturb the scene at all."

After a momentary pause, Nelson asked, incredulous, "How is it that you are always the first person on the scene for these bodies that keep turning up?"

"Actually, I was the second one on the scene for that last one that you're still working on and I wasn't there at all when you found the first redhead," Matthew reminded the somewhat miffed police officer. "And I was looking for Detective Warren Danbury, who we still haven't located, when I found this one."

After a long sigh, Nelson said, "OK, I'll bring part of the forensic team and be right there. We just got the portable lights in to see this area, but I'll order more to be sent there. Stay put. We'll want to talk to you when we get there."

"I've told you what I know, but OK, we'll wait for you to get here. I wasn't going anywhere anyway. I still want to find Danbury tonight."

Nelson clicked off without further comment and Matthew turned to see Lanie hugging Dr. Rob tightly and they were both in tears. He wasn't sure what had transpired except that, with all of the bodies and missing people surrounding Ariel's disappearance, finding her alive and well or at all was looking less and less hopeful.

"Yes, I promise to text as soon as I'm there," Matthew heard Lanie say as he approached and the two pulled apart.

Thinking two things at once, Matthew grimaced. He knew that he should still be hopeful but as he felt his own hope waning, he felt the sudden strong urge to check in with his mother. He wasn't at all a mama's boy and he knew that Jackie Paine worried about him a lot, which is why he was surprised that he'd suddenly want to talk to her in the midst of this mess. But he knew that she prayed at least as much as she worried, likely more, and maybe that's exactly what he needed right now to reignite his waning hope.

After seeing Lanie off, he and Dr. Rob climbed in the Sonata and locked the doors to wait. "I heard Lanie agree to text as soon as she's there. We need to create a new group. One without Danbury in it for now. In case he's followed somebody somewhere, we don't want his phone giving him away if we're texting back and forth. And if he hasn't disappeared on his own," Matthew added and then hesitated. "We don't want anyone else seeing our texts, where we are, or what we're working on or learning."

"Good plan," said Dr. Rob. "I'll add you and Lanie into a group and text her to use that one."

"Thanks. Hey, mind if I make a quick call?" he asked Dr. Rob. "I know it's late and this might sound a little weird but I really want to talk to my mom and ask her to get her Bible study group to pray for Ariel. I don't understand exactly how this works, but she calls them her prayer warriors and apparently this group of women will pray for each other's families and friends diligently without having to have ever met them."

"Sure, Matthew. That'd be grand. I'll take all of the help that we can get to find my daughter!" he said, and choked a bit on the end of that sentence.

"Oh, and would you add those pictures of the deceased in the alley to our shared files? Figuring out who he is might help us figure out where Danbury is. Maybe. Though Danbury didn't shoot him."

"How do you know that?"

"That shot wasn't in self-defense. It was at close range. The shooter got too close for that to have been self-defense."

"Oh. That makes sense. I'll start updating the files with what we know now," answered Dr. Rob.

"Thanks. If Nelson's guys get here before I'm off the phone, would you just take them down or point to where the body is? Nelson said he'd have more questions for us, but this is more important right now."

"Yeah, I can do that."

Matthew poked a few buttons on his phone and when he heard his mom's voice, alarmed, on the other end, his first words to her were, "I'm fine, Mom. I'm sorry it's so late, but can I talk to you for just a minute?"

He could hear the relief sweep her voice as she said quietly, "Sure, son, hang on."

He could hear the shuffle of slippers and robe and whatever else as he waited. After a few minutes, she said, "OK, I needed to slip out of bed and downstairs so I wouldn't wake your dad. I'm in the sun room now so we can talk. Thank you that those were the first words you uttered to me, but something must be wrong or you wouldn't be calling after midnight."

"I'm not even sure where to begin," but he tried, telling her the story of catching the quick flight into the Miami International Airport through the tracking of Ariel, finding Gavin but unconscious, and the two other redheads, both reporting missing before Ariel, and both having been found dead.

"Oh, son!" she exclaimed and he knew she'd just hit her knees as his story unfolded. His guess was that she'd remain there long after he'd gotten off the call with her and then she'd text or email her Bible study group and they'd all do likewise as soon as they saw the prayer request.

"Where are you now?" she asked. "Are you safe?"

"Yes, I'm safe. Danbury is also missing and Dr. Rob and I came down to the alley that Danbury came back to check looking for him. We can't locate him, but the SUV he rented is here and," he hesitated, "and someone else has been killed in the alley. It's not Danbury. We're in the car waiting for the police to get here."

"Oh Matthew!" she said.

"I know, Mom. I'm really sorry to wake you up and lay all of this on you so late at night. I should have thought to ask you to get your Bible study group praying for Ariel long before now."

"Yes, you should have," she agreed. "But I can get the request out quickly. A few of our group might still see it tonight. Some of the early birds will see it by sun up. And they will all start praying as soon as they do. They'll be asking for updates, so text or call me when you find her, OK?"

Matthew agreed.

"Or if there's anything specific you need us to pray about as you learn more. It sounds like you need hope right now, you need sleep, and you really need to find Ariel quickly."

"Exactly. I knew you'd know what to pray for."

"It's my honor. And Matthew," she started.

"Yes, Mom, I'll be careful and be as safe as I can," he answered, knowing exactly what she was going to say.

"I was going to say that, yes," she said. "But I was also going to tell you that I'm proud of you for caring for other people, helping where you can. And, most importantly, I love you, son."

"I love you too, Mom. And thank you."

"Of course. Good night, Matthew."

"Good night, Mom."

Dr. Rob turned and looked at him. "I need to call and update my mom too. She pretty much raised Ariel when she was little and I know Mom's worried too. She was ready to get on the next flight down here, but I told her to wait. There's nothing she can do down here. I wish she'd get together with your mom and this group of hers. She needs the support right now."

"That's a great idea. I'm sure my mom would be happy to support her through this. We can connect them in the morning, if you want."

"Parenting isn't for wimps," said Dr. Rob. "I've always known that, but the things that moms have to endure, and they never stop worrying."

"No, I guess they never do," agreed Matthew. "Mine doesn't, but she prays at least as much as she worries, probably more. As much as I hated dragging her out of bed after midnight, I just felt my hope waning and I knew I needed to get that back."

"And did you?"

"It's coming back," he said, looking over at Dr. Rob and smiling a tired smile. "We'll find your daughter. We'll keep looking until we do." It had become their mantra, Matthew realized as he said it. Having repeated that mantra several times, he was entirely unsure, following the day's events, exactly what keeping it would entail.

*****

After being questioned relentlessly by one of Nelson's uniformed officers, Matthew and Dr. Rob were finally told that they were free to go but not to leave the area in case there were more questions. Matthew had assured the officer that they had no intention of leaving until both Danbury and Ariel were found. The officer then assured Matthew that they were actively looking for Danbury and the two women whose bodies had been recovered moved finding Ariel higher up on their priority list as well.

Matthew had refrained from rolling his eyes at that last statement because of course he thought that finding Ariel should have been a top priority to begin with. He also realized that he was exhausted and he didn't want to say anything caustic, so he and Dr. Rob left the scene to the police and drove back to the hotel. They agreed to meet in the breakfast nook in the morning to regroup and both hoped to get a decent night's sleep as they went to their adjoining rooms.

Checking his email and text messages and seeing nothing at all from Danbury, Matthew texted him one last time. Then he locked the Glock in the room safe, washed up for the night, and collapsed into bed. Sleep was instantaneous but restless. In his dreams, he saw a nondescript shadowy presence that was chasing him down a dark never-ending alley which he couldn't see the end of. He was running from something in the dreams, one dream after another, but he could never see what or who it was that he was running from.

Matthew awoke and rolled over to check his watch on the nightstand. It was four AM, the sun wasn't up yet, and he was in a cold sweat, feeling exhausted. His muscles were tensed and sore all over, and he was not at all rested. He crawled out of bed, turned down the thermostat and heard the rumble of the condenser crank up a notch on the air unit, though he'd had the recirculate fan on all night to combat the stagnant air of Miami.

Wandering into the bathroom, he splashed warm water on his face and wiped around his neck with a warm wet washcloth. Hoping that would do the trick, he got back in bed and fell into a sleep of oblivion for a few more hours.

17 ~ Down One, Stalled Out

Wondering what the annoying noise was that was invading his peace, Matthew realized it was his alarm that he'd set for seven-thirty. He was meeting Dr. Rob in the lobby at eight. He felt heavy and tired as he dragged himself out of the bed and into the shower.

Opting for a pair of khaki shorts and the hiking shoes he'd worn down on the plane instead of the flat leather boat shoes he'd had on the day before, he added another dry fit shirt to his ensemble, ran his fingers through his hair, and considered himself mostly ready to meet the world for the day. He figured he'd come back up to brush his teeth and retrieve his Glock from the safe after a breakfast he was planning to actually sit down and eat this morning, so he wandered downstairs.

As he expected, Dr. Rob was already down there, though Matthew checked his watch and noted that he was actually three minutes ahead of schedule himself. Even from a distance, Dr. Rob looked weary, haggard, and not at all well rested. Working his way through the breakfast buffet, Matthew selected eggs, turkey bacon, and two biscuits to put together himself as well as the requisite coffee with heaps of sugar and cream.

As he sat down with Dr. Rob, Matthew greeted him and then said a silent blessing over his breakfast as well as their day. They needed to find Ariel quickly, he knew, and now Danbury too. Ariel had been missing for at least three days, depending on how you calculated it, since it was Thursday and the last sighting of her was Monday night. It felt like much longer, he thought, as he dug into the biscuits he'd assembled. It felt like weeks not days.

"This feels weird without Danbury," admitted Matthew. "But we need to come up with our plan for the day, at least start out with one, though we know it could change depending on what we learn as we go."

"I was thinking that too. I don't really know what to do next, so I was hoping you had some ideas."

"Yeah, I want to call Nelson and see if he was able to talk to Danny Boy and if he'll share the identities of the young woman and the big dark guy that we found last night. I'm sure he would have with Danbury but we're not cops of any description so, even with our vested interest in finding Ariel and Danbury, we might have to figure some of this out on our own. And he likely won't want us probing around without Danbury so I need to tread carefully there."

"That makes sense."

"Then, I want to go back down to Dock Side and see if Courtney, Rod, Angela Delgado, JoJo, or whoever is working, can ID this guy from the pictures you took last night. If Nelson provides us with a name, so much the better. But even if he doesn't, I'm betting they know who this guy is, or at least they've seen him before. I have a theory about him, but I need to verify it before I mention it to Sergeant Nelson. Lanie said she was staying put at Conexiones Saludables for the day, right?" asked Matthew, trying to pronounce the name of the ministry but realizing that he'd probably butchered it badly.

"Yeah, she is. And I think that's best. All of the bodies and missing people were really getting to her last night. I was worried about her driving back by herself but more worried about her staying. A day, at least, to focus on the children that she works with will be better for her, I think. And I know she wants to try to get some ongoing help worked out for Anna and Pedro."

"Yeah, I'd like to check in on them today too. What about Gayle? Does she need anything today?"

"I don't think so, but I can check with her before we leave. I want to check on Gavin anyway."

"We can go get her car from Lanie or get another key to Danbury's SUV from the rental agency if we need it, though I didn't want to move it, just in case he came back for it today. And Nelson put a police placard in the window so it wouldn't get towed."

"Yeah, I saw them break into it and do that last night. Or, I guess it was this morning. That was thoughtful of them."

"Well, I'm sure they wanted a look inside to be sure that there wasn't anything there, no sign of a struggle or…anything. But you're right. At least we don't have to worry about that. OK, so I'm going up to brush my teeth and get my Glock. I'll call Nelson and see if he'll talk to us if you can check in with Gayle."

Dr. Rob just nodded as Matthew added, "Meet you back in fifteen?"

"OK," agreed Dr. Rob as they both stood and dumped their plastic plates and cutlery into the trash. Matthew refilled his coffee before heading back upstairs. He'd finished most of it on the way and was just opening his door when his phone went off. It was Cici FaceTiming him.

"Good morning, is it safe yet? I didn't wake you this late, did I? I mean, I know you're not exactly on vacation down there."

"Good afternoon, Cici. Yeah, it's safe. We just had breakfast, Dr. Rob and I, and I was coming up to brush my teeth and check in with Sergeant Nelson. He's the local Miami-Dade police officer we've been working with down here, the guy heading up the investigations."

"Investigations? Plural, as in more than one?" asked Cici, who Matthew knew missed nothing. "Why isn't your buddy Danbury working with him?"

Matthew quickly gave her the update on the other two women, missing before Ariel and both turning up dead. At least, he explained, he was pretty sure that was both of them, unless there was another young woman missing who he didn't know about. He also shared that Danbury had suddenly disappeared the night before.

He could hear the genuine concern and fear in her voice and see it all over her face as she said, "Matthew, please, please be extra careful. I mean, I know you're normally cautious by nature but you don't know what you've stumbled into down there. If Danbury is missing then," and she didn't finish her thought, at least not aloud.

"I know. If somebody can take him down or out, then I'm no match for them. I know, Cici, believe me, I know. But I can't just go home and leave Dr. Rob by himself or Danbury who knows where." He could hear the desperation in his own voice so he was sure it was also in his face and that she hadn't missed it.

"I understand that, it's just that," she started to explain but she actually choked up before she could finish. "Matthew, I miss you. I love you. I've been thinking a lot about you, about us. I know I won't be back home for a while, but when I am, I really want there to be an us again."

Smiling despite the seriousness of the rest of the circumstances, Matthew answered honestly, "Cees, you know that I love you. I've never stopped loving you. Breaking things off with you was the hardest thing I'd ever had to do. I want there to be an us again too, but only if we can get on the same page about our life plans because I don't think I can go through breaking up with you again."

"I feel exactly that same way," she said, and they got quiet as they just looked longingly at each other.

"I guess I need to let you get back to your search. Just please promise me that you'll be more careful than you've ever been. And I understand what I'm asking of you," she teased him. "You've always been Mr. Safe. It's one of the things that I love about you. But please be Mr. Extra Safe," she pleaded, quickly returning to seriousness.

"I promise. And I'll check in with you later and let you know how things are going. It's taking time to learn things. I didn't think this would be instant and I knew that the outcome might not be a good one when we came down here. But I'm not ready to give up yet on any of it."

They said their good-byes and Matthew called Nelson to see if there was any update on Danbury or Ariel. Hesitant at first and particularly cagey when Matthew asked about the body that he and Dr. Rob had found in the alley, Nelson did finally share that he had no update at all on Danbury. The man had disappeared without a trace. In some ways this was good, thought Matthew. Nelson said that there was no blood found in the alleyway, except for that of the victim, the guy they'd found that Nelson wouldn't talk about. Nelson either didn't know the identity or he wouldn't share it, because Matthew could sense him shutting down when asked about it.

"Were you able to talk to Danny Boy? I mean, Daniel Rubio."

"He was already gone," said Nelson. "By the time we got down there, the boat was gone."

"He might have gotten spooked by all of the police presence. What about the woman in the hole beside the bridge?" asked Matthew, changing the subject.

After a few moments of hesitation, Nelson finally spluttered, "You were right. It's Katie Jones. But don't share that with anybody. We have only found one of her parents to notify. The story that a young woman was found dead is out and all over the news this morning, but her identity isn't yet. Why did you think it was Katie?"

"Three things. The description of the dyed bright red hair and the description of her being petite."

"But you couldn't see anything but hair and her feet under the tarp and you said that you didn't climb down there and disturb anything, right?"

"Exactly. Her hair was red and her feet were tiny. And unfortunately, it fit the pattern. What's worrying me is that the killer didn't leave the amount of time between capture of those first two women and the time of their deaths consistent. Unless you have times of death that say otherwise, he killed them both quickly, days apart and not a week apart like they were reported as missing. And both pretty quickly after Ariel was reported missing."

"That's only two things. What was the third?"

"The pattern itself. The pattern of missing redheads," answered Matthew, meaningfully.

"What's your point?"

"We all need to redouble our efforts to find Ariel. She might have only a day or two left, if she isn't," he left the thought hanging because he couldn't finish that sentence. They all seemed to be doing a lot of that on this trip, he thought. He swallowed hard before continuing, "We have to find her and without Danbury, our efforts are hindered. He has the expertise that we need to find Ariel. And we can't even find him. I mean, I need his expertise to find HIM!"

"I understand that frustration. I lose lots of valuable officers to the private sector all the time."

"The private sector?" asked Matthew, taking a breath and trying to calm down.

"Oh yeah, look around you. All of these multi-million and billion-dollar properties down here need security. The people who own them, who fly in and out from all over, they hire security guards and body guards too. It's a huge business down here and it pays a lot better than the police force. And there's nothing I can do about that."

"Ah," said Matthew. "I get that. On a smaller scale, this is a huge setback for our little team of searchers. Being down the most important team member hinders our efforts at moving forward with finding Ariel, never mind finding Danbury himself."

"Are you saying that you think somebody removed him to keep you from finding Ariel? That's a stretch."

"No, I'm not saying that at all," replied Matthew, wondering how Nelson had made that huge leap of logic that he hadn't intended. "It might not even be related. From all we've seen going on down in that alley, it might just have been wrong place, wrong time for Danbury. But it surprises me that anybody could have gotten to him."

"Yeah, I agree, if somebody got the drop on him. That wouldn't be easy to do, would it?"

"From what I've seen of the guy, I wouldn't think so, no."

"I will tell you this much," said Nelson, conspiratorially. "The bullets that killed the guy in the alley didn't come from Danbury's weapons. At least not those he has registered in North Carolina. Does he have any that are not registered? Do you know?"

Realizing that Nelson had just verified his assertion that the guy in the alley had indeed been shot there, Matthew answered, "I have no idea. Danbury has always carried a service weapon back home, but he would have brought his own down here, right?"

"If he's a by-the-book kind of guy, yeah, he'd have left the issued one at home. Unless he carries a personal weapon on the job."

"He is by-the-book, which is why my best guess is that he's carrying his own weapon and it's registered. Whether it's what he carries on the job or not, I don't know. I didn't know you could carry your own personal weapon on the job."

"In most places you can. If you do, you have to register it with your department and then it becomes subject to a monthly formal inspection."

"He asked me about my weapons and told me to bring them both. I never thought to ask about his," answered Matthew, a bit sheepishly, realizing again how much he didn't know about Danbury. "He was a Marine, and he always likes to be in control, so it wouldn't surprise me if he used his own weapon that he could choose and completely control on the job."

"Good. I didn't think he'd have unregistered weapons, but I appreciate you verifying it. The bullets don't match anything that would have come from the weapons registered to him in North Carolina. We checked, just to be sure."

Matthew was certain that there was still something that Nelson wasn't telling him, but the fact that Danbury wasn't suspected of any foul play was a good thing. There were probably a lot of things that Nelson wasn't telling him, he thought, which he might have shared with Danbury, had he been here.

"One last question," said Matthew. "Were you ever able to dig up any information on Daniel Rubio, the guy who was the last person we know of to see Ariel Wednesday night? Danbury said your team was working on it."

"Oh yeah. We're looking for him. His real name is Daniel O'Rourke and he jumped bail in Nebraska four months ago. That big boat you saw him on the other night does not belong to him, but both he and it have disappeared."

"Huh. I can see him disappearing easily enough," said Matthew. "But I'd think a yacht would be a lot harder to hide."

"Down here," replied Nelson. "You'd be surprised. There are canals wide and deep enough for it and more docks on restaurants, houses, and apartment buildings, not to mention boat yards and marinas with storage and dry docks than you can shake a stick at."

As he was promising to stay in touch and keep Nelson updated if they learned anything helpful, Matthew's phone was ringing again. He'd managed to unlock the safe in his room and pull out and holster his Glock with one hand while talking to Nelson, but he thought he'd never get back downstairs to Dr. Rob at this rate. But then he noticed that the incoming call was from his father. Chagrined, he was pretty sure that he was in for a reprimand about calling and waking his mother after midnight the night before and probably keeping her up all night.

Slipping into the bathroom to attempt putting toothpaste on his toothbrush with one hand while holding the phone with the other, he was pleasantly surprised to hear his father sounding concerned, asking how he was doing and offering support.

"Your mom told me about Dr. Rob's daughter missing down there. Is there anything you need, son? Anything we can help you with from here?"

"Thanks, Dad. Actually, there is one thing. Dr. Rob's mom is up there in Raleigh somewhere, probably worried sick. She helped raise Ariel from infancy, I think because Ariel's mom skipped out on them. Dr. Rob is concerned that his mom might not have a good support system in place. It would be great if I could connect her to you and mom and you guys could check on her."

"Sure, Matthew. Can you text or email us her contact information?"

"Yeah, I'll get it from Dr. Rob and send it to both of you. I'm meeting him back downstairs in a few minutes to head back out and continue looking for Ariel, and now Danbury. Both seem to be dead ends right now," he cringed at his choice of words. "I'm not really sure what more we can do but we have to try. Ariel might well be running out of time."

"OK, I'll watch for that contact information and we'll get in touch with his mom."

"Thanks," said Matthew. And then he added, before they could disconnect, "I love you, Dad."

Sounding surprised, Joc Paine responded not particularly quickly but resolutely, "I love you too, Matthew. And I'm proud of you."

Surprised by the entire conversation, Matthew realized that he told his mother that he loved her pretty regularly and far more easily, but he was less effusive with his verbal admissions of love in his father's direction. He wasn't sure exactly why, but now that he realized it, he figured it would give him something to ponder when his mind wasn't quite so full of more time-sensitive issues.

Finally heading back downstairs, Matthew pondered his conversation with Sergeant Nelson. He knew there were a couple of things about the conversation that he'd found unsettling or at the very least incomplete. Who was the guy in the alley? The dark-haired big guy had been, as Matthew had assumed, shot in the alley. What wasn't Nelson telling him about that and why was he withholding that information?

When he'd asked Nelson about the guy's identity, Nelson had stopped answering entirely and Matthew had to tread carefully to get him to open up again. Annoyed that Nelson was at least partially stonewalling him, he wondered if the anonymous man could have been the one with Danny Boy the night that Ariel was last seen with the two men. And if Danny Boy AKA Daniel Rubio AKA Daniel O'Rourke didn't own the big yacht that he was taking the young women aboard, then who did? And what was Danny Boy doing with it?

Maybe Dr. Rob could help him find an answer to that last question from the pictures he'd taken of the stern of *Playbuoy*. He didn't know how boats were registered and if that process was anything like how cars were registered, but he knew Dr. Rob would know, at least how that worked in North Carolina.

"Sorry, Dr. Rob," Matthew said as he entered the lobby and saw him waiting. Dr. Rob rarely looked impatient about much of anything but this morning was an exception to that. "I got on the phone with Nelson and then my dad called. Speaking of which, if you can text me your mom's contact information, my dad said he and my mom would be happy to connect with her and check on her for you."

"That's grand!" said Dr. Rob. "I'll do that," he added as he pulled his phone from the golf shorts he was wearing and poked at it until Matthew heard a ding on his own phone.

They each pulled a water bottle from the glass refrigerated case in the lobby before heading out the front doors. They'd learned to drink water as much as they could whenever they could find it in Miami. Matthew quickly forwarded the contact for Dr. Rob's mom to his own parents with a heartfelt note of thanks to them for checking on her.

"Where to first?" asked Dr. Rob, obviously depending on Matthew's previous experience working with Danbury to guide their next steps for the day.

"Let's go get Gayle's car from Lanie while we're close by here. We can drop it back here, but that gets it back in our hands if we need it later today. We can compare notes on Gayle and Gavin and what little Nelson shared on the way."

"OK. I'll text Lanie and tell her that we're coming to get the car. I checked in with Gayle. She doesn't need anything today from here and she said she doesn't need the car right now. She's excited that Gavin is starting to show some increased signs of responsiveness so that's great news. I'm still hoping he can tell us what happened to him, where he was at the time, and how he and Ariel got separated."

"That would be ideal," said Matthew.

"It might lead us straight to her," said Dr. Rob hopefully.

Matthew thought that nothing so far had been that easy so he didn't hold out much hope. But he didn't admit that to Dr. Rob as they pulled out of the hotel parking lot and headed out into another scorching June day in Miami.

Matthew had a heavy feeling about going back to the event center. It was the locale closest to where Ariel had last been seen and there had been clues about her whereabouts that had come directly from people there. Admittedly, it was the place that he thought they should go. He just didn't want to be back there.

18 ~ UNHAPPY RETURNS

Matthew shared the information that he'd learned from Nelson and the things he still wanted very badly to know with Dr. Rob as they made their way back to Dock Side. Dr. Rob added the sparse new information to their shared files.

"One thing that stands out is that boat," said Matthew. "I saw Danny Boy blatantly take a woman out to it and he wasn't trying to hide the fact. Nelson said the boat wasn't his but both he and the boat have disappeared. Is there any way to find out who does own it? If Nelson knows, he isn't sharing that information with me."

"Hmm…" said Dr. Rob. "There's no DMV listing for boats that we can get access to. I'm pretty sure that boats in Florida are registered through the FLHSMV."

"The what?"

"I think it's Florida Highway Safety and Motor Vehicles. It's like the DMV department back in North Carolina. You register your boat the same way you'd register your car."

"With so much water down here, I guess that makes sense. But you said we can't check that, right?"

"Not that I know of, though the state information would list the owner. There's the Coast Guard site. I can do a PSIX vessel search on it by the boat name. Let's see if they have a listing for *Playbuoy*. They should, but it might not provide much information."

After poking a few buttons, Dr. Rob reported, "I see a vessel with that name and I do see the HIN number and primary vessel number.

It's a Coast Guard number, so it doesn't show it being registered in Florida necessarily. It's still in active status, but this report doesn't show anything about ownership or current location."

"You lost me. HIN and vessel number? Coast Guard number?"

"HIN is the Hull Identification Number. The HIN was put on by the manufacturer and it can positively identify a boat. Like if there's a dispute about who a particular boat belongs to, you can check the HIN for a positive identification of the boat. It's like the VIN on all of those expensive sports cars I hear that you've been drooling over down here"

Matthew just grinned. "And the primary vessel number?"

"That number can either be a state-issued number that shows the state it's registered in by the first prefix letters in the string or it can be a Coast Guard documentation number, which is the official number. If it's the USCG official number, as in this case, then the first two prefix letters are CG. The official number stays with the boat for the lifetime of the boat and that identification number has to be prominently and permanently displayed on the boat. Another thing to check might be if they have AIS on the boat. It's required on commercial boats and highly recommended on recreational boats."

"AIS?"

"Automatic identification system. It's a device boats use to send a signal to allow other boats in the area to see them. It also includes boat size, direction, and speed. I expect that a yacht has an AIS transponder that is registered with the Coast Guard too. I'm pulling up the website for the marina where my boat is, just inland of the Pamlico Sound. It has a link to AIS information so it'll show all of the boats that have AIS in that area. I should also be able to move down and check this area too from it," said Dr. Rob as he was poking his phone.

"How does that help us?"

"It might give us the current location, though AIS itself is about collision avoidance. You can see all the boats around you, how fast they're going and their direction. The system will warn you of collisions. It's especially handy if you're out on the ocean at night or in a storm when visibility is limited. But it should also show us the location and destination of a particular vessel if you know the name."

"Name, yes, location apparently not," said Matthew.

"Wow!" said Dr. Rob. "There are a LOT of boats down here and a lot of big ones too! Some of these big ones are probably cruise ships coming and going from the Caribbean and the Gulf of Mexico and likely some cargo ships. I'll show you when we stop, but there are an unbelievable number of boats down here! You can tell a lot from this website. For example, I just clicked on one and the website tells me that it's a cargo container ship en route to Freeport, Bahamas. I can see its speed, that its draught is 13.3 meters, and its past track."

"OK," said Matthew, taking it all in. "So how does that help us?"

"Well," said Dr. Rob. "You can also search for boats, so I just put in *Playbuoy* and I see two of them. I'm checking the details now."

After a moment he said flatly, "Oh."

"What's wrong?"

"One is in Ontario Canada and the other is up on Lake Michigan. Both are pleasure craft, smaller vessels on lakes."

"What does that mean for locating the one down here?"

Dr. Rob took a deep breath and sighed. "AIS can be turned off from the boat, if say you didn't want people knowing the location of your favorite fishing hole. Or if you were trying to do something sneaky."

"Oh, so it doesn't help us."

"It doesn't right now. But I can keep checking to see if it shows up."

As they pulled into the parking lot under the bridges that were around the corner from Dock Side and parked again, Matthew's heavy feeling returned, the dread of the crowds and noise and confusion. It had dissipated during the drive as he was learning all about how boats are registered and potentially located from Dr. Rob. Taking a deep breath, Matthew entered the parking space on the app online on his phone to pay for parking before they stepped out into the oppressive Miami heat. It wasn't as bad under the bridges as it would be out in the sun, he thought, and it was a sunny day so far.

The two men were quiet as they rounded the corner and passed the north side of the bridge where they could still see a corded-off area, in which the police had been working late into the night before. There was a bored-looking sentry officer still on guard. He'd managed to pull his car over the curb and alongside the row of holes to keep the curious away from the area. They must not have everything they needed from the area, thought Matthew, and if construction was scheduled for the day, it had been halted.

As they entered the now too familiar event center, the first person they saw was JoJo scurrying by with two stacks of glasses. Matthew turned to follow him toward the bar as he slipped through the raised bar opening, placing the glasses on the counter that ran down the center of the long bar which surrounded it, and turning to drop the bar top closed behind him. As he did, Matthew stepped up and greeted him.

"Hey JoJo, I'm Matthew Paine. I talked to you late Tuesday night."

JoJo nodded and said, "Hi again. Of course, I remember you."

"This is Dr. Rob, my colleague and, more importantly, the father of the missing young woman that we're searching for."

"Oh my!" said JoJo. "You haven't found her yet?"

"No, but we could really use your help, JoJo, if you're up for looking at a less than optimal picture of a guy. To see if you recognize him."

"Less than optimal?" repeated JoJo.

"Well, the guy's kind of dead," answered Matthew, looking at Dr. Rob, who had pulled his phone out to pull up the picture.

"Oh!" said JoJo. "Oh, no!"

"I'm not saying it's pleasant, but if you know who this guy is, it might help us find a couple of missing people," added Matthew, thinking that he would go farther in that.

"Well, when you put it like that," said JoJo. "It's just a picture, right?"

"Right, a pretty close-up picture of his face," answered Matthew.

Taking a deep breath, and seeming to steel himself for the task, JoJo said, "OK, OK, I'm ready. I can do this,"

Dr. Rob held his phone up and JoJo quickly glanced down, eyes bugging out as he saw the picture of the guy with the hole in his forehead. He looked away as if he might be sick.

"Yeah, I've seen that guy," he finally said. "Big guy like that is hard to miss. And he had a voice to match. Really deep voice and pretty gruff."

At this, Matthew leaned forward, "When was the last time you saw him here?"

"Um, it would have been Sunday," he said decisively.

"This past Sunday? How do you know?"

"Unlike lots of other places around, we don't have happy hour, per se. Instead, we have daily specials on drinks. Sundays are three-dollar tall beers and I was serving lots of those when I saw him."

"What else can you tell us? Was he alone? How long was he here? What was he doing? Anything at all that you can think of," said Matthew. "Even the smallest detail might turn out to be helpful," he added as he noticed that Dr. Rob had his phone out and was typing away in their shared files during this exchange.

"He wasn't alone. There was another guy with him, one who's here a lot, a guy they call Danny Boy. And I've seen the big guy in here a few times before. With another guy, not Danny Boy. This guy was older, mid-fifties, maybe. Distinguished looking, with a pocket square in his jacket pocket. Who even wears a jacket down here anyway?" asked JoJo.

"OK, let's start with this past Sunday," said Matthew. "Were you his server?"

"Not exactly. They got drinks from Courtney at the bar, then sat at one of the high-top tables over there," JoJo pointed to the waterfront on the left in the general direction of the path that Matthew had followed Danny Boy along the night before to get to *Playbuoy*. But that might be too much of a conclusion to draw at this point, thought Matthew, trying to keep to the facts and learn as much as he could from JoJo.

"OK, they got drinks and went to the table. Any idea what time that was?"

"Pretty early," said JoJo. "I was only here until six on Sunday so maybe about four-thirty or five? Something like that."

"And then what?"

"I checked on them a couple of times to see if they wanted anything else. Danny Boy was just about to answer the first time I asked, when the big guy cut him off and said something like, 'We're good for now.' They looked like they were having a serious conversation, so I just went to the next table to check on table sixteen."

"Did you happen to overhear any of their conversation? Anything at all?"

JoJo stopped to consider this. "I got the impression that they were arguing about something but that the big guy was clearly in charge. I think I heard him say something about screw ups. No more screw ups or something like that. Oh, and that he'd better get it right this time! I remember the big guy telling Danny Boy that just as I was walking up to check on them. He was handing back Danny Boy's phone, I think, as he said it."

"That's very helpful, JoJo, anything else?" asked Matthew, impressed with the guy's recall if he really was right about all of this. There was a sure-fire way to find out with the security cameras all over the place. They had a date and a time, so getting a better look at the guy should be easy enough.

"Not that I can think of."

"Were they still here when you left at six?"

JoJo stopped to ponder that. "No, they couldn't have been," he said. "Because I brought the tall beer special to three women at that table just before I left. So, they were gone by six."

"Did you see where they went?"

"I didn't," answered JoJo. "I really hadn't thought about them being gone until you asked me just now. But I do pay attention to people because they move around a lot while they're here, so I have to keep track of them to get the drink orders right."

Pondering this information, Matthew asked, "Did you see them come in?"

JoJo thought about that a few moments and then said, "I'm not sure. They were coming from the waterfront, when they went to the bar, but I don't know where they were before that."

"I think I do," said Matthew, but he didn't elaborate. "Thanks, JoJo. You're right, you do pay attention to people. What can you tell me about the older gentleman that you saw with the big guy earlier?"

"I've seen him in here a couple of times too. He looks very uptight and self-important," said JoJo. "But then that last description covers half of certain sections of Miami," he added with a wink.

"I'm assuming that you never heard names for him or the big guy?"

"Not that I can recall," said JoJo. "But if I did, I wasn't paying attention to their names. I operate by descriptions, like big guy, dark hair, deep voice, drinking vodka on the rocks. Or blonde guy, white smile, drinking Irish whiskeys like water."

"You said Courtney was here Sunday night?" asked Matthew, looking around.

"Yeah, I think she and Matt were working either end of the bar on Sunday evening. But neither of them is here now," he added, answering the next part of the question that Matthew hadn't yet asked.

Matthew had noticed Angela Delgado at the other end of the bar pouring mimosas, but this end seemed to be unattended at the moment. It was Thursday morning after all, he reasoned, so maybe most people didn't start drinking for the day until later. Maybe. But this was Miami and he'd already learned in the short time that he was here that any assumptions he had in Peak or Raleigh didn't necessarily apply here at all.

"How long are you around today?" asked Matthew, thinking that he wanted to go ask Rod for more video feeds but he wanted to be sure that he could ask JoJo anything else that came to mind.

"We're here today until seven," he said, including Angela in the sweep of his hand. "And then a bigger team comes in for the night."

"Is Rod in the office, do you know?"

"Yeah, I think so."

"Thanks, JoJo. You've been a huge help."

"You're welcome. Always happy to help," he said before returning to his stacks of glasses behind the bar.

"Let's go talk to Rod and see if he can pull video from Sunday afternoon," said Matthew.

"OK, that sounds reasonable," answered Dr. Rob as he followed Matthew off to the left, across the faux grass carpeting and into the covered foyer that housed the doors to the restrooms, office, and whatever limited kitchen area there was.

Knocking on the office door, they heard a gruff, "Just a minute," from within.

After Rod had obviously taken his own sweet time about getting to the door, he opened it, but stood in the doorway, blocking entry and attempting to block the view into the office beyond him.

"Hi Rod, Matthew Paine," he said, reaching for his hand to shake, politely.

Hesitating, Rod took his hand and shook firmly but briefly.

"And this is Dr. Rob, my colleague from North Carolina and the father of the young woman we're looking for," he added, meaningfully.

"Oh," said Rod as this last bit of information seemed to take out of him some of the angry steam that he seemed to have been building up. "What can I do for you?" he finally asked, as if he were duty-bound to ask but not really volunteering to be helpful.

"We're looking for another patron, a sporadic patron I think. He's been seen here a couple of times according to your staff. We'd like a quick look at your video feeds."

"Well, that's pretty wide open. I don't have all day to look at those," he said. "I have a business to run, here."

"We have a date, time, and specific location," answered Matthew a bit triumphantly, having anticipated this objection and enjoying the moment of being able to completely diffuse it.

"Oh," said Rod, still looking put out at the intrusion. And Matthew immediately understood why as he added, "Fine, come on in."

A brunette woman, skinny, but voluptuous in all the right places, probably in her mid-forties, Matthew thought, was sitting in a chair behind Rod and just putting on stiletto heels. She stood as they entered and said, "I'll catch up with you later, Rod."

"Fine," said Rod, shooting Matthew and Dr. Rob a look of obvious annoyance.

Giving Dr. Rob a knowing look at what they had just interrupted, Matthew turned to Rod and said, "This past Sunday afternoon, starting about four-thirty, the high-top tables near the waterfront to the left of the bar. Can you show us the video surveillance?"

"Yeah, yeah, yeah," said Rod around the imaginary cigar in the corner of his mouth as he slipped behind his desk and pulled over the tablet, poking away at it as if he were taking his frustration out that way.

"OK, Sunday, four-thirty, river view," he said as he looked up at the screen and first Matthew and then Dr. Rob turned to look at it too. They hadn't bothered to have a seat and Rod hadn't offered them one anyway, so they were standing on either side of the big screen on the wall, which Matthew realized was a much better vantage point anyway.

"There they are," said Matthew, indicating the two men walking from the bar to sit at the table. They were facing the river front so the camera caught the side of their faces.

"Yeah, that's Danny Boy and some other guy. Now what?" asked Rod.

"Two things," said Matthew. "I want to see where they came from, where they went when they left, and a better angle of that big guy's face that we can freeze and get a good look at."

"That's three," said Rod irritably. "Why do you need to see his face?"

"He did ask," Matthew said, turning to Dr. Rob. "I guess he does deserve to know."

Dr. Rob nodded and pulled his phone from his pocket, queueing up the picture of the face of the dead guy from the alley.

"We need to know if it's this guy," answered Matthew as Dr. Rob held up the phone for Rod to see.

"Good God! Is he…" he started and then stopped up short.

"Shot in the head? Dead?" Matthew supplied. "Very much so."

After a moment to recover from the shock that Matthew had intended to give him, the guy crossed himself. Catholic, Matthew thought, though he wouldn't have guessed that.

"It," Rod said and then started again. "That looks like him. The guy I've seen here. He is a big guy. Huge. He hangs off of the bar stools and the chairs at the high-top tables. But I don't think it's fat. He looks like a former linebacker. Hell, he could be for all I know."

"Do you know who he is?"

"By name, no. I've just seen him a couple of times. Guy like that, he stands out in a crowd, you know?"

"I'm sure. OK, so can we get a better shot of his face and track him forward and backward?"

"Yeah, lemme see what I can do," said Rod, much more helpful now that the shock of looking into the face of a dead man had worn off.

After a few back and forth starts and stops and switching cameras several times, they were able to see that Danny Boy and the big guy had come from the direction that *Playbuoy* had been tied the night before when Matthew had followed Danny Boy that way. They had departed the same way initially, though they then parted company and the big guy had turned at the waterfront and headed back through the event center to the front entrance.

It was at one of these cameras as he was leaving that he looked up just briefly and gave them a perfect shot of his face. Without having to be asked, Rod froze the image and enlarged it. All three men just stared at the screen. Were he a gambler, Matthew thought, he'd put a lot of money on facial recognition software matching the two faces. It was their guy.

"I guess you want me to upload all of this to some link you give me again?" asked Rod around the imaginary cigar that seemed to be more prevalent when he was agitated.

"Please," said Dr. Rob politely. "We'd really appreciate it."

Before anyone could say anything else, Matthew had his phone out, creating a new folder, and giving Rod access to it as he'd done before. "OK, all set. You should see an invitation with a link."

"OK, I'm capturing them. Give me just a couple of minutes."

"Thanks, Rod. We'll go get water bottles to go from your bar and be right back," said Matthew.

Matthew's mind had been racing trying to assimilate all of the new information. As they walked out, he said as much to Dr. Rob, "I needed a minute to just think and connect the dots."

Turning to Matthew, Dr. Rob asked, "I have a few ideas too but what are you thinking?"

"I'm thinking that this guy is Danny Boy's boss in whatever business they're operating, and I doubt that it's chartered tours of Biscayne Bay. And the deep voice that JoJo said this guy has, I mean had," he corrected himself. "Could it be the same deep voice that Rebecca Aimes heard leaving the construction site on the other side of the bridge?"

"Good point. I was already thinking about the relationship between the two and what JoJo said about the big guy telling Danny Boy that there could be no more screw ups."

"Exactly. That sounds menacing to me. What would Danny Boy have screwed up? Danny Boy wasn't involved in her murder or dumping her body. At least he wasn't directly involved in dumping her body because I had just seen him board the yacht. If this big guy was involved in dumping Katie Jones' body in the hole by the bridge, then that adds lots of possibilities," concluded Matthew.

"Yes, it does. Starting with if he killed her."

"And if he did, why? And if he did, was he involved in abducting her? From what I saw of Danny Boy last night, it'd be much more likely that he was the abductor," postulated Matthew.

"I know we're getting ahead of ourselves here because we have no evidence directly tying this big guy into any of it yet," added Matthew as he considered the scenario. "Except that he was shot in the alley where Gavin was found and where Danbury was headed when last heard from. But for the sake of argument, let's continue down this line of logic and speculation."

"OK," said Dr. Rob. "So where does that take us?"

"If the big guy was Danny Boy's boss in an abduction operation and he has been taking women, then there is a pattern. I'm sure there are more women missing in Miami right now for various reasons than we can shake a stick at, as Nelson said about hiding a yacht down here. But the three we know about, we can tentatively connect two of them to Danny Boy and this big guy, whoever he turns out to be. And they have at least one thing in common."

"The red hair," said Dr. Rob.

"Exactly. Courtney told me earlier that Danny Boy said he wasn't into blondes just then, or that he had a thing for redheads just then, or something like that. Then three of them in as many weeks were reported missing. Two of them have been here. Well, we know that Ariel was last seen near here."

Matthew paused before adding, "And it's logical to conclude that whoever the bartender, Angela Delgado, and the busboy said the picture of Ariel looked like was either Katie or Dominique, the other two missing before Ariel. From the pictures and the descriptions, we were betting on Katie earlier. Her roommate had said she was a flirt when it came to getting free drinks from men in bars. She could easily have been slipped something in one of those drinks if she encountered the wrong guy."

"True, but Ariel doesn't drink. She's not old enough and she's seen what it's done to other people in her life so she's just not interested in any of that," said Dr. Rob.

"Maybe another method was used on her to get her away from here then."

"Maybe," said Dr. Rob. "But doctoring a drink wouldn't have worked on her. That much I know for certain."

"We need to check the pictures of Katie and Dominique with Angela and the busboy while we're here. We do have pictures of them in the files on Katie and Dominique that Danbury got from Nelson and uploaded before he disappeared."

They had started walking toward the bar and Matthew was pulling up the files of the other two women to access their pictures when he suddenly stopped in his tracks. "Younger, prettier, the only true redhead, she didn't drink, and she wasn't in distress," he said aloud.

"What's that?" asked Dr. Rob.

"The screw ups. Danny Boy's screw ups. If we follow that line of logic and what the three women have in common, those are the outliers. Ariel was younger and prettier than the other two and the only true redhead. And," he added, gaining steam on his theory, "she was the only one not in distress of any sort."

"Distress?" asked Dr. Rob.

"Dominique had just broken up with her live-in boyfriend and had to move out of Brickell. Katie had just lost her job and was afraid she'd have to move home to South Carolina and out of Brickell. Ariel was just here for the summer, she was with Gavin, and she wasn't in any sort of distress. But she was younger, prettier, and a true redhead. And, according to JoJo, it would have been just the night before when Danny Boy had been admonished by the big dark guy not to make any more screw ups. So what if they snatched Ariel, despite not being in distress, but because of those other characteristics that the other two didn't share?"

"Huh," said Dr. Rob. "That's a grand theory. And that line of logic makes complete sense."

"To extend that logic and to give us more hope of finding Ariel, what if the first two weren't what they were looking for, whoever that ambiguous 'they' might be, but Ariel is?"

"By that, you mean that they aren't likely to kill Ariel too."

"Exactly my point. But it's all conjecture based on circumstantial evidence. Now if we just had real evidence to prove any of it. But let's start by showing these pictures to Angela Delgado to see if she's seen either of the other two here. And JoJo. If he's seen them, he will certainly remember them. As he said, he does apparently have an eye for people. And an amazing memory for their descriptions. Danbury would call him an excellent witness."

19 ~ BLINDING DARKNESS

As they made their way back to the bar, Matthew held his hand along the right side of his face, shielding his eyes against the morning glare and wishing that he hadn't left his sunglasses in the rental car. He realized, with the sun coming in at that angle from the east, they might not do him much good. They approached the bar and waited patiently for Angela to finish refilling drinks and both men looked surprised when they heard a huge belch from the other end of the bar. Angela turned, seeing their expressions, and looked amused.

"If only that were the worst of it," she said quietly as she draped a towel over the end of the bar in front of them before asking, "What can I get for you?"

"Yeah, I bet you've seen it all," said Matthew, with a smirk at her comment. "Two bottles of water and a quick look at a couple of pictures, if you don't mind?"

"Sure," she said, reaching under the bar and handing up two water bottles. "You were in here showing me pictures the other night," she said. "There are more?"

"Just two more," said Matthew, and then glanced at Dr. Rob. "Or maybe three, if you're up for it."

Before Matthew could reach for his wallet, Dr. Rob had pulled a twenty-dollar bill out of his and tossed it on the counter. "Keep the change," he said.

"Thanks," said Angela, "Now what did you want me to look at?"

Matthew assumed that was exactly the reaction that Dr. Rob was hoping for in tipping almost as much as the cost of the water bottles. He had his phone at the ready and he pulled up the pictures that Danbury had copied in from the police files of Dominique and Katie. "Have you seen either of these women?" he asked, beginning with the picture of Dominique and then scrolling to Katie. When she didn't answer immediately, he handed her the phone so that she could scroll between them and zoom in to get a better look.

"I'm pretty sure I've seen this first one in here," she said. "But it's been a couple of weeks ago. She came in a couple of weekends in a row and she was pretty wasted the last time I saw her here."

"Do you know when that was?" he asked.

Angela screwed up her face in concentration. "I'm not sure," she finally said. "But it's been at least two weeks and probably more like three. And this one," she added, scrolling to Katie's picture and rolling her eyes. "This one was here a lot up until maybe a week or so ago. I don't remember exactly when I last saw her, but she was a regular here for a month or more. I think her name is Cassey or Cathy, something like that."

"Katie?" asked Matthew.

"Yeah, I think that's right!"

"Were they alone? Can you remember if anyone was with them, either sporadically or consistently?"

"The first one there," Angela began.

"Dominique," Matthew supplied.

"Dominque, OK," said Angela. "She was in with another woman several times. They seemed to be together, anyway. I mean, not together, together, but friends. Like they'd come clubbing together."

"But no men with them?"

"Nobody consistently with either of them that I can remember, though in this crowd I'm sure they were hit on more than once. But the other one," she added. "Katie. She was surrounded by men constantly and she seemed to be enjoying the attention. She left here pretty bombed more than one night in a row. I don't know how they do that, drink themselves into oblivion and then come back the next night and do it all again."

"Did she leave alone?"

"That I can't say. She did have another woman with her a couple of times, the same other woman, I mean. I think she might have been the DD until she got tired of it and I hope Katie got a ride after that because she wasn't ever in any shape to drive by the time she left."

"Katie wasn't ever the designated driver?" asked Matthew, just to be sure he'd appropriately pegged her as a binge drinker before her untimely death.

"God, I hope not!"

"This last one, if you're up for it, is less pleasant," said Matthew. "We already know that he was here, but what we don't know is who he is. You did well with Katie's name. Do you think, if you've served him before, you'd know a guy's name?"

"Maybe," she said. "If he was memorable in some way and if he told me his name. Like I said, Katie was a constant regular for a month or so. Her name, I'd heard. What's unpleasant about this picture?"

"It's a little grisly," said Dr. Rob. "The guy in the picture is dead."

"You mean he's dead IN the picture?" Angela asked, horrified.

"Yeah, that's what we mean," said Matthew. "You don't have to look at it if you're not up for it. We can describe him to you, if you'd rather do it that way. He would have stood out in a crowd for several reasons."

"OK, let's do that," said Angela, the look of horror fading from her face.

"He's a big guy. Tall, probably a couple of inches taller than I am," said Matthew. "And he's much wider. Not fat, I don't think, just broad. He has dark hair and a really deep voice."

"That sounds familiar," said Angela. "I think he's the guy that JoJo calls 'the hulk' because he looks like he's just about bursting out of his clothes all the time. But I don't know his real name. I've seen him here a couple of times with Danny Boy. He's the only man I've ever seen Danny Boy with, ever, come to think of it."

"Yeah, that's the guy," said Matthew. "If we had a time range of when he'd ordered drinks, would you be able to search for a credit or debit card if he used one."

"If he ever bought the drinks, sure. But I don't remember that he ever did. Danny Boy bought drinks for both of them, and he has a running tab that I think he settles up with cash every other day or so."

"Running, huh? I hope he's already settled up his most recent one." Before she could ask what he meant by that, Matthew said, "Have you seen him today? Danny Boy?"

"Nope. I haven't."

"Thanks for your help, Angela. We really appreciate it." Then, turning to Dr. Rob, he said, "Let's go see if Rod has that video and picture uploaded. That should help."

"Aren't you going to ask JoJo about the guy's name?"

"Yeah, I guess we could before we leave, but he said that he's not good with names, just descriptions, so that's a long shot. But you're right. It's worth the ask."

"Why don't I go ask JoJo while you check the upload process with Rod?"

"OK, good plan. I'll be sure to remove his access as soon as I know it's all there. I didn't give him access to the whole site anyway, just the one folder I created for the upload."

*****

After obviously annoying Rod again, Matthew checked the videos and the face capture, thanked the guy, removed his access to the site and, just as he was turning to go find Dr. Rob, realized he had at least one more question for the guy. Or, as it had gone so far, the answer to one usually led to multitudes more.

"Hey Rod, one more question. Do you have power and water hook ups out here for the boats that tie up along the river front? I didn't see any, but I'm not sure what I'm looking for."

"Nah, the boats are usually day or evening trips and they're on their own for any of that."

"It looks like some spend the night here."

"Most have water tanks on board, sewage tanks too. And most of them also have huge batteries with solar power, so they can come and go and stay as long as they like. As long as they don't cause any problems, they can tie up for the night. Some of them would cause a lot worse problems trying to get out of here after drinking for hours, so everybody wins if they just stay."

"They don't have to register with you to tie up here?"

"Nah, as long as there's room on the riverfront, they just grab a couple of cleats out there by the boardwalk and come on ashore."

"What about *Playbuoy*, the boat that Danny Boy was on? Was he always coming and going from the boat? The same one?"

"I've seen that guy come and go from all directions and I didn't follow him out to see which boat he got on, but yeah, I have seen him aboard that one, *Playbuoy*."

"You don't have showers or anything here either, do you?"

"Nope. Not running a hotel, just an event center with bars and food and music."

"Do you know how long *Playbuoy* was tied here at a time?"

"I'm tellin' you, I don't keep tabs on the guy," said Rod, with growing annoyance as Matthew's one more question had turned into a barrage of them.

"Thanks for your help. The police might have more questions for you later, but I guess that's it for me for now."

"The police? They're not so good for business. The other night when they were here, we half emptied out right after they got here," he said around his imaginary cigar. "What else do you want to know?"

"Nothing right now," answered Matthew, realizing that he'd just been handed Rod's weak spot for getting information. "But I appreciate your help."

"Sure thing, no problem," answered Rod, conciliatorily.

As he wandered back out into the heat to find Dr. Rob, Matthew shaded his eyes against the sun and wondered at what point he should contact Sergeant Nelson and tell him about what they'd learned. He definitely had a few questions for Dr. Rob first, though, about boating and how to find what you'd need to perhaps live on one in this area, or at least tie one up in a permanent location if you had other living quarters nearby. It wasn't here at Dock Side. Of that he was now certain.

Spotting Dr. Rob talking to a busboy at the other end of the bar, Matthew sidled on over that way and listened in on the end of the conversation, which seemed to be somewhat fruitful. He heard Dr. Rob asking what it was that Sebastian said that upset Danny Boy, so this sounded like definite progress.

"Something like, 'no more screw ups, Rubio! Get it right this time or there won't be a next time!'"

"And then Danny Boy called the other guy Sebastian?"

"Yeah, he said something like, 'I got it, Sebastian, I got it. I'm working on it. Just give me another week.'"

"And then what?" asked Dr. Rob.

"I didn't hear what the big guy said back because they were already out onto the boardwalk by then, but Danny Boy didn't look happy about whatever it was."

"Thanks, Obadiah, that's helpful," said Dr. Rob. "If you think of anything else, would you give me a call or a text?" he asked, handing over a card. "My cell number is on the back there."

"Oh, you're a doctor from North Carolina? I've always wanted to go there. I hear Myrtle Beach is a great place in the summer."

"Thanks so much for talking to me, Obadiah, I really do appreciate it."

"Sure. I hope you find your daughter."

"Thank you, me too."

Matthew noted that Dr. Rob had refrained from pointing out that Myrtle Beach is in South Carolina, not North Carolina, and didn't react at all in the process. As soon as they'd walked clear of the busboy, whose name was apparently Obadiah, Matthew complimented him on that.

"Sounds like you got some new information. Good job on not even cracking a smile when the guy was talking about wanting to come to

Myrtle Beach in North Carolina. That was impressive."

"I learned how to do that long ago," said Dr. Rob. "I had a young patient, a little girl who was about four or five when I was just starting out. She said something like, 'when I was little,' and I laughed. The little girl looked genuinely wounded so I learned, then and there, never to laugh when someone is being earnest in what they're saying, no matter how ridiculous it might sound."

"Ah, the wise words of Dr. Rob," Matthew said. "Let's go order a pizza and then walk down to the boardwalk. I want to hear what you just learned and I want to see if there's anybody around down there. Nelson said that Danny Boy and *Playbuoy* are gone, but maybe somebody else tied up down there knows where they went. Rod says there are no hookups for water or sewer, no power. So, I'd assume that anybody tying up down here would do so only temporarily."

"Likely so. You could stay for a little while, but it's not sustainable for long without a water source and electric hookup."

"You'd either need an apartment or hotel locally, and a place to tie up and then a means to get to that location, or a marina or some place to get those resources, then?"

"Yeah, one or the other."

"I wonder which Danny Boy was using. *Playbuoy* is huge. Wouldn't that limit the places it could go?"

"Somewhat. I'd assume, for example, that it wasn't going up river, but out into the bay or along the coastline somewhere. There are deep water boat slips along the shore of the bay. But the ones that I know of are some that Ariel told me about when she was trying to lure me down here with my boat this summer."

"Hmm…" pondered Matthew. As he placed the pizza order, he was thinking that he'd love to go somewhere to get out of the heat and study a map. He'd downed the last of his water bottle and tossed it into a nearby recycling bin. Maybe the map that Dr. Rob was looking at earlier which showed all of the boats would show where a few of them were in more isolated areas. Though he wasn't sure what he'd be looking for, he hoped that Dr. Rob would know.

"Tell me what Obadiah had to say. That sounded promising."

"Just that he was pretty sure he'd heard Danny Boy call the big guy 'Sebastian' as they were leaving the table headed for the boardwalk. Obadiah walked up behind them to clean the table and flip it for the next patrons and he overheard a little of the conversation. I guess you heard the rest. It was mostly what we'd already heard about Danny Boy screwing up something, though Obadiah added that Sebastian said that Danny had one last chance to get it right before he lost any more chances."

"And this was the night before Ariel was here? The same night that JoJo overheard part of that conversation?"

"It was. Sunday evening."

Matthew stopped in his tracks on the way out to the boardwalk and started talking fast. "We need to sit down and update our timeline. That could be the reason for the break in the pattern. If Danny Boy had snatched two redheads who were in distress, but who weren't true redheads and the big guy, Sebastian, had given him an ultimatum, then maybe he got desperate and snatched Ariel, who wasn't in distress. But he didn't have time to exploit the distress anyway. He had to act quickly. He'd have had to take Gavin out somehow to take Ariel from him, and he dumped him in the alley."

"But how could he have gotten them both at once?" asked Dr. Rob.

"You're right. He couldn't have. He had to have had help," said Matthew.

"OK, that makes sense."

"So, let's play that out. Two guys approached Gavin and Ariel for the second time as they were leaving Anna and the Bridge People. We know that. Anna didn't see where they went, but if there were two guys, then snatching both Ariel and Gavin and then dumping Gavin would have been more possible. They couldn't have gotten them back through here to the boat. There were too many people and Ariel and Gavin would have objected."

"If they were conscious, they would have. And if they weren't, they couldn't have been moved through this crowd without the whole thing being seen and people questioning it," added Dr. Rob to Matthew's theoretical scenario.

As they walked onto the boardwalk and headed to the left, Matthew saw a yacht that he was pretty sure was tied up the first night he'd wandered down this way. It was the one that had been dark inside, just in front of the yacht that he was now pretty sure had been *Playbuoy*, where he'd seen the blue light inside, and before that vessel had any significance to him.

He explained this to Dr. Rob, who immediately threw a hand up in greeting to the guy who was working on a piece of equipment that was unrecognizable to Matthew up on the deck. The guy waved back and greeted them and, after initial introductions, Dr. Rob and the guy started talking boating. In his usual humble manner, Dr. Rob explained that he'd just gotten a larger sailboat back in North Carolina the year before, but it was nowhere near the size of the yacht that this guy was standing on.

The guy, whose name was Nick something that Matthew didn't catch, invited them up on deck. Nodding to Matthew, Dr. Rob climbed aboard and Matthew followed. Nick and Dr. Rob talked boats, navigation systems, favorite ports, trips they'd taken, and charting while Matthew stood patiently listening and wondering what Dr. Rob was up to. He knew that Ariel was his primary concern, so Matthew wasn't sure why the sudden detour into boating small talk, until it suddenly became crystal clear.

"We walked out here looking for a yacht I really wanted to see, *Playbuoy*. I've heard a lot about it," said Dr. Rob honestly after the initial chatter, which Matthew now assumed was to build nautical credibility. "It's similar in size to this one, isn't it?"

"Probably slightly larger," said Nick, grudgingly. "It's here a lot. I'm in and out of here a good bit too, entertaining both clients and some of my top sales team members."

"Have you seen it recently?"

"I think it was here night before last. The guy who sails it is a piece of work."

"Oh?" was all that Dr. Rob said to encourage him.

"From what I've heard, he's not the owner, though who in their right mind would trust that guy with it, I can't imagine. He thinks he's

God's gift to the female gender."

"Ah, a lady's man," said Dr. Rob. "The boat is appropriately named then."

"Yeah, but like I said, I don't think it's his."

"What makes you say that?" asked Matthew.

"Just snatches of conversation I overheard the other night."

Matthew knew that he needed to tread carefully, so he said noncommittally to Dr. Rob, "To charter it, I guess that's not who you'd need to talk to."

"What did you overhear?" asked Matthew of Nick. "Anything that might help us find the boat or the real owner?"

"Not much," said Nick. "Just some big guy reading the guy who's always on it the riot act about not screwing up anything else or he'd lose the privilege of the boat."

"Like a parent?" asked Dr. Rob.

"No, more like an employer, but that guy wasn't the boat owner either."

"What makes you say that?" asked Matthew and then clarified, "We'd really like to find the owner."

"No knowledge of the boat for starters. The 'front' of the boat is the bow and anybody who sails one would call it that. 'Port' is left, and anyone who owns or sails one would call it that."

"I see," said Dr. Rob. "Definitely not the owner. Do they charter it much? Do you know?"

"Not that I've heard about, but I haven't been paying attention since *BizNick* here keeps me plenty busy."

"Huh," said Dr. Rob, "Any idea where it's docked when it's not here?"

"I'm pretty sure I've seen it over at Atlantic Miami Marina. But I don't think it was even transiently docked in one of the slips there. I think it was just taking on supplies and using the pump-out service."

"That's too bad," offered Matthew to Dr. Rob. "I know you really wanted to see it."

"Yeah, I did. I'm not down here for very long and I'm running out of time to find it."

"I might be able to help you," said Nick after a moment's hesitation. "I don't think that guy who has it out here is always at the helm, at least not for longer voyages. I think they hire a captain that I've used too when I want a relaxing cruise. I can give you his contact information, if you want to check with him."

"That'd be grand!" said Dr. Rob enthusiastically.

The guy disappeared below and after a few minutes, returned with a card and handed it to Dr. Rob. "Here you go. He's one of the best, even for longer trips down to the Islands. I'd highly recommend him. And he might know where *Playbuoy* is docked."

"Thanks, Nick, I really appreciate that." Said Dr. Rob, pulling a card from his wallet and handing it over. "If you see it, would you let me know? Text, call, whatever."

"Oh, you're a doctor up there in North Carolina. How do you like it up there?"

"It's a place I love calling home," said Dr. Rob. "In Peak we're just a couple of hours from the coast, closer to some of the inland waterways and a few hours in the other direction to the mountains. Something for everyone."

"Nice. I should plan a trip up one of these days. I'm from Georgia, but I haven't traveled north much, at least not by water."

"If you do, give me a call. I can give you a rundown on the best spots to dock and places you should see. Our intercoastal waterway is grand and the outer banks are beautiful."

"I'll do that," said Nick, and with that, they shook hands and Dr. Rob and Matthew disembarked.

"That must have been exhausting," said Matthew, noticing the haggard look that Dr. Rob emanated as they headed back across the boardwalk. "That light-hearted trivial conversation with Nick back there."

"You have no idea. But boaters are talkers when it comes to talking boating. They'll help each other out. As soon as it was clear that he wasn't fond of Danny Boy, I figured that he'd tell me whatever he knew about the whereabouts of *Playbuoy*. I just wish he knew more."

As they made their way back toward the front and angled left to pick up the pizza, they passed the bar and Matthew stopped long enough to purchase four water bottles and ask for a cup of ice from Angela. Their conversation stopped as they got the pizza, napkins, and paper plates.

"I wish we knew more too," Matthew picked up the thread of conversation as they headed toward the portico over the entrance. "It seems like there are tiny points of light that we catch a glimpse of every now and again, revelations of some sort. But we're otherwise wandering around in the dark and I hate that."

Just as he said it, they'd stepped out from under the shade of the event center into the full brunt of the sun that was rising toward mid-day.

"Ugh," answered Dr. Rob. "That's the most blinding darkness I've ever seen. After checking on the children, calling this captain and maybe going by the Miami Atlantic Marina, what's next today?"

"Calling Nelson with the information about the association of our dead guy, presumably Sebastian, and Danny Boy, who's currently not around. I wonder if Danny Boy knows that Sebastian is dead? Maybe that's why he's in the wind."

"You sound like Danbury," said Dr. Rob.

"And then there's finding Danbury!" said Matthew. "That alley is another place we should probably be watching, but I'm agreeing with Lanie now. It's creepy."

"Do you think that Ariel and Danbury both being missing is related? I mean, Gavin was found in that alley where Sebastian was found, if that really is his name. Then Danbury was headed there before he disappeared. That alley ties them together, at least marginally."

"I don't know what to think, but it does all seem intertwined. And you're right that this darkness is blinding," answered Matthew as they crossed the street to go check on Anna and Pedro. On the way down the sidewalk, Matthew called Sergeant Nelson, leaving an urgent message to call back when the guy didn't pick up.

They passed myriad Bridge People, mostly adults of a variety of ethnic backgrounds, and approached the pod tent that Anna and Pedro apparently called home.

"Now what?" asked Dr. Rob as they stopped in front of the tent pod and confronted the issue that Matthew and Lanie had the night before.

"Just watch," said Matthew quietly. Then, more loudly, he said, "Hola Anna, Hola Pedro," and they saw the tent pod wiggle slightly with motion from within. Then, Matthew said enthusiastically, "Pizza!"

The response was immediate as both children appeared from within the tent and their eyes lit up when they saw that Matthew indeed held a pizza in his hands and he was holding it out to them. He handed it to them along with the water bottles, plates and napkins. After Anna brought out the requisite squares of cardboard for their "asiento," the children plopped down and dug in.

Dr. Rob checked the bandage and they said their good-byes amidst profuse thanks in Spanish.

"I think we really need to find some place to sit down, enter the information we learned this morning, including the contact information for that captain, call him to see what he can offer, and regroup. Maybe we can search maps online and find places near Dock Side where *Playbuoy* might be more permanently located if the captain doesn't know."

"That sounds like a good plan. Any thoughts on where?"

"I do have one," answered Matthew as they turned the corner heading back to the rental car in the parking lot under the bridges.

20 ~ SAFETY BRIDGES

Matthew was heading for one place that was familiar and where they'd be warmly welcomed but out of the Miami heat, the brasserie just across the street and up half of a block from the entrance to the alleyway. As he drove under the crossing bridges by the pods of the Bridge People, his cell phone sounded and he flipped it up to look.

"Sergeant Nelson," Matthew said aloud.

"I can get it on speaker and hold it up," offered Dr. Rob.

"Yeah, thanks, I didn't bring a dash clip for my phone," said Matthew as Dr. Rob poked to connect the call and put it on speaker.

"Hi, Sergeant Nelson. We've just left Dock Side and I'm driving. You're on speaker phone but Dr. Rob is the only other person in the car."

After that very brief greeting, Matthew dived right in, telling Nelson what they'd learned at Dock Side about the connection between Danny Boy and the large man they thought to be the dead guy from the alley. Matthew momentarily omitted the conversation about the last chance and the previous screw ups that was overheard by the staff and a fellow boater, except to tell Nelson that Danny Boy was overheard calling the big guy Sebastian. Matthew explained that they had a grainy picture of the guy's face as well as videos of the guy with Danny Boy Sunday evening.

"Huh," said Nelson, and then got quiet. Matthew waited him out and finally Nelson said, "Can I get a copy of your picture of this guy's face? Facial recognition can confirm if it's the same guy we found when we ran his prints.”

“Sure, I can send that as soon as we stop, if you’ll tell me if it’s the same guy.”

“Uh, yeah, I guess I can do that. It’ll save us the time of having to go behind you and collect that evidence ourselves,” said Nelson grudgingly.

“What can you tell us about his identity? Or whatever else you know about him?”

Again, Nelson hesitated, “He’s been arrested previously for trafficking but nothing has ever stuck. Looks like he’s got some powerful friends who’ve provided legal support and gotten him released on some technicality or other.”

“Had,” said Matthew pointedly. “He had some powerful friends. Maybe now he’s crossed one of them, which is why he was shot and left in the alley. Or maybe he outlived his usefulness in some way, or made too many demands, and they put an end to him. Do you have a line on Danny Boy or *Playbuoy*?”

Nelson didn’t immediately answer and when he did it was with a question, “How much do you know about him? O’Rourke?”

“Danny Boy? Not much. I met him once briefly. The staff at Dock Side characterize him as a charming womanizer. You said he went by O’Rourke in another state and was running from some charge or another and that *Playbuoy* didn’t belong to him.”

“Yeah, Nebraska.”

“He had a thing for redheads there for a while, which fits with the disappearance of all three women, two of whom have since been found murdered. And he was seen in the company of the other guy who just turned up dead, I’m pretty sure, so I’d say he should be a person of interest at the very least.”

As they headed south over the Brickell Avenue Bridge, Matthew glanced in the rearview mirror and suddenly exclaimed, “What the?”

Before he could finish his expression of surprise, a large black SUV that he had spotted racing up behind them, weaving in and out of the Thursday afternoon traffic, ploughed into the back of the little Sonata, sending it joltingly forward.

Matthew braked in time to miss hitting the car in front of them but the drawbridge was slippery so it must have been by mere millimeters, he realized, as he straightened up and tried to stay in his center lane. He processed that information quickly as he became hyper aware of everything around him, the location of all of the cars on the bridge, the distance to the low metal barricade beside the far-right lane that he'd swerved slightly into, particularly the pedestrians on the walkway beyond the barricade along the edge of the bridge, and the bridge rail on the other side of them.

"Hang, on, Dr. Rob!" Matthew yelled as he braced for another slam from behind, this one aimed at the rear driver's side bumper and designed, Matthew thought quickly as he held onto the steering wheel literally for dear life, to send them careening over the side of the bridge. That he'd managed to drop his speed after the initial contact and that his front tires had just grabbed cement on the other side of the metal grating in the center of the bridge probably helped with the impact of the second hit, he thought, as everything seemed to turn to slow motion around him.

The car, though sliding sideways, remained on the bridge and Matthew hung on, steering into the turn and trying not to spin out of control. Cars scattered in all directions around them on the bridge but somehow he managed to collide with none of them. Two others collided into each other as they made a space for the Sonata, now headed in the other direction back into the traffic head-on over the center of the bridge.

Managing to pull the Sonata through the forced turn and then more slowly the rest of the way around in front of the cars that had all stopped, Matthew steered to the edge of the bridge and down the far-right lane. He limped the car down the side and off the bridge before pulling over onto a slim shoulder of the road against a curb in front of a white building that shone blindingly in the sunlight.

What Matthew hadn't seen behind him was the driver of a Porsche Cayenne backing off the gas and swerving to stop completely when he saw the little Sonata spin, turning back toward him, head on. An Alfa Romeo came alongside the Porsche from behind, having missed the purposeful ramming, and wandered haplessly into the fray.

Turning to Dr. Rob as the Sonata wobbled to a stop along the curb,

Matthew asked, "Are you OK?"

Dr. Rob just nodded, his face ashen and his eyes huge. Matthew assumed that his face looked similarly distraught.

"Did you see where they went?" Matthew asked as he pulled his Glock from his holster, ready to defend himself if the black SUV was still around and coming back to finish them off, unbelievably in broad daylight.

"They were weaving on through the traffic and they kept going," said Dr. Rob.

"Oh," said Matthew, looking around before he holstered his Glock. "Where'd the phone go?" he asked, realizing that Dr. Rob wasn't still holding it.

"I'm not sure, but I've got mine in my pocket," said Dr. Rob reaching a shaking hand into his pocket to retrieve it.

"Good. Can you call Nelson back?"

"Yeah, I saved his contact information from the group chat," said Dr. Rob, poking his phone and then holding it out so that Matthew could hear it as it went straight to voicemail.

Just then, they could hear Matthew's phone sounding from somewhere in the back seat. Unbuckling himself and turning around, Matthew managed to fish it out of the floorboard behind him. "Nelson," he said, poking to answer it.

"What the hell just happened?!" they heard Nelson's voice demand.

"Somebody just tried to run us off the bridge," said Matthew. "We spun around and managed to get turned back around and down the bridge on the south side where we were heading, but I don't think the car is drivable for far. And there was a second collision on the bridge when two cars that were behind us tried to avoid hitting us head on as we spun around. It's a miracle that's all that happened."

"OK, we're on the way. Do you need a bus?"

"A bus?" asked Matthew knowing that this sounded familiar but unable, at that moment, to place the terminology.

"An ambulance. Are you injured? Anybody in the other cars injured?"

Matthew turned around in the seat to look behind him, "I see three people standing outside of the two cars that collided and I think we're OK. Dr. Rob?"

"I haven't really taken stock," Dr. Rob confessed as he stretched arms and legs and twisted his torso and turning his head from side to side. "I'm going to be plenty sore where that seatbelt bit into me, but I'm really glad I had it on. We need to go check on the people on the bridge," he said, opening the car door as the medical training and practice from a couple of decades kicked in and was overriding any personal aches and pains.

"Me too," Matthew agreed, as he'd done the same stretches and twists when retrieving his phone. "But I don't think I have any serious injuries."

"Did you see what hit you?" asked Nelson. "Did you get a license plate or a good look at the driver? Anything that would help us find them?"

"They went through the traffic down the bridge heading south," answered Matthew. "It was a big black SUV, a GMC, with some sort of bar on the front. Like a cattle bar if we were out west somewhere. That was the only distinctive thing about it that I noticed."

"Heavily tinted windows," added Dr. Rob.

"That's common here," responded Sergeant Nelson. "What else? Did you get a look at the driver at all?"

"There were two people in the front seat, and my impression of them was the Blues Brothers."

"Huh?"

"You know, that really old movie from the nineteen eighties, I think. John Belushi and Dan Aykroyd."

"OK," said Nelson slowly.

"They were both male, one lower in the seat with a more rounded face than the taller one who was driving, but both wore sunglasses and hats. Dark hair, I'm pretty sure, but it happened so fast, I'm not positive. I didn't see a front license plate. I didn't see the back of it at all as it went by because I was a little busy trying to straighten out and not spin off the bridge," he said, his adrenaline turning to anger. He looked over at Dr. Rob, who shook his head and shrugged, indicating that he hadn't seen anything else that was helpful either.

"OK, sit tight, we'll be right there," said Nelson.

"Hey Sergeant Nelson, one more thing I hadn't told you yet," said Matthew, deciding to give him all of the details from the morning while he had the chance. "Multiple people at Dock Side heard the big guy, Sebastian or whatever his name turns out to be, telling Danny Boy, I mean O'Rourke, that he'd screwed up again and that there would be no more screw ups or he wouldn't get another chance."

"Huh," said Nelson. "Who told you that?"

Matthew told him about JoJo, the busboy, and the guy named Nick on the other yacht that was tied up there a lot of the time that *Playbuoy* had been.

"We'll check it out. I'm on the way and we're sending an ambulance," he said, and Matthew could already hear distant sirens approaching as he and Dr. Rob climbed gingerly out of the car and walked a bit shakily up the bridge to check on the occupants of the other two cars.

A guy who was pacing, angrily beside what had been a nice blue Alfa Romeo Stelvio Quadrifoglio turned when he saw them coming. Matthew thought he could almost see steam coming out of the guy's ears as he stormed toward them. "Was that you going the wrong way on the bridge?" he yelled at them.

"Only after a hit and run," said Matthew, holding out his hands, innocently, to ward the guy off. "After we were hit twice by a big black GMC SUV and spun around at the top of the bridge that they had just tried to run us off."

"Oh," said the guy, losing steam. "I saw that SUV weaving through traffic coming up the bridge. He nearly took my front end with him."

"Did you get a look at it?" asked Matthew. "Like at the license plate number or the driver or anything?"

The guy shook his head and gestured dismissively. "It's Miami," he said, as if that explained everything about the plethora of crazy drivers and the completely inconsiderate and often dangerous things that they did.

"Are you injured?" asked Matthew, realizing that adrenaline can mask injuries sometimes. "The police and an ambulance are on the way."

"I don't think so, just my car," said the guy as Matthew saw the vein in his forehead pop out at the reply.

"Was anyone else injured?" asked Dr. Rob, slipping past Matthew where he'd stopped when the guy confronted him.

"I don't know. I was the only one in my car, which is now probably totaled," said the guy through clenched teeth. "And the two people in the car that hit me when you came through the wrong way are out of their car up there," he added.

Dr. Rob went up the edge of the bridge to check on them and Matthew saw, beyond the Alfa Romeo, a grey Porsche Cayenne beside which two other people were standing. Traffic was probably already backed up as far down the street as you could see, he thought, because the two cars, splayed at odd angles, were blocking all but a partial section of one lane of the three lanes across the bridge in this southern direction. Pedestrian foot traffic had also slowed, as onlookers gawked at the cars.

A police car had made its way up the north bound lanes and arrived on the other side of US 1. Two officers had climbed out and they were headed his way, Matthew observed. A fire truck was making its way up the shoulder of the road, lights flashing and a horn blaring. Matthew could hear more sirens from what he thought was the other side of the bridge.

As the police officers approached, Matthew walked over to meet them, introduced himself, and told them he'd just gotten off the phone with Sergeant Nelson. He told them what had happened on the bridge and they reiterated Nelson's instructions to stay put while they talked to the people involved in the other accident on the bridge. Running his splayed fingers through his hair with one eyebrow raised, Matthew looked at the Sonata and wondered where the officers thought he'd go and how he'd get there. On foot maybe? He was trying not to show his obvious annoyance with this whole process. It wasn't their fault, and he'd far rather they be looking for the vehicle that caused this whole mess than dealing with the mess at the moment.

He knew they'd have to call the rental agency next and he wasn't looking forward to that conversation any more than the prolonged one that he knew he'd have to have with the police. Thinking back to their late-night arrival, he was happy to recall that Dr. Rob had agreed to the full insurance on the cars. That would come in handy right about now, he thought.

Two EMTs or paramedics arrived on foot at the top of the bridge from the other side. They had parked the fire truck in the inner lane on the bridge amidst the traffic still flowing, though now less freely, over the bridge on the north-bound side. The occupants of the fire truck were quickly added to the fray as Matthew was sure they were evaluating the four other victims of the hit and run, the three people from the two cars and now including Dr. Rob, for potential injuries. Foot tapping at least as much in concentration and thought about what to do next as impatience and annoyance as he considered all of this, Matthew finally turned and wandered up onto the bridge to go through the rest of the process alongside everyone else.

Shortly after a barrage of initial questions, Nelson showed up on the scene and the questions started all over again.

*****

Several hours later, after many questions were repeatedly asked and answered including some discussion of charges against Matthew which were discussed and dismissed, and he and Dr. Rob were tired, hungry, sweaty, and exhausted. The rental company delivered a replacement car, a silver Toyota Corolla this time, and the Sonata was being towed away. The other two cars on the bridge had already been removed and traffic was flowing more freely.

"At least nobody should know we're in this car and be trying to run us off the road," said Matthew, adjusting the mirrors and his seat, after they climbed into the Toyota.

"I heard you and Nelson talking about how they knew who we were and where we were before. The conjecture on that is that they followed us from Dock Side?"

"Yup. But neither Nelson nor anyone else seems to have any plausible theories about why. Or who they were for that matter. Clearly it wasn't an accident. The SUV was seen by the other two drivers weaving in and out of traffic until the driver reached us. And the driver of the Porsche saw him ram us both times, so he'd stopped when the Alfa Romeo came up beside him. I missed all of what happened behind us after the second impact," concluded Matthew.

"How is any of this related to trying to find my daughter?" Dr. Rob demanded in obvious frustration.

"If I knew that, we might have a better shot at finding her faster," commiserated Matthew. "And without Danbury, it's harder for sure. But we'll find them both," he asserted. "We will."

"Where were we going anyway? You never did say."

For some reason, probably due to the stress of the past few hours, this question struck Matthew as entirely funny and he started laughing and, after a few attempts at an apology, couldn't seem to stop. After a moment, Dr. Rob joined in and both men felt better after the laughter. Spending a few minutes getting acclimated to the new car, they were happy to have the air conditioning, which worked exceptionally well, blasting at full power.

As he pulled away from the curb, Matthew answered, "I was heading over to the little brasserie where Lanie and I ate the first day we were down here. I thought we could scan some maps on our phones and maybe create a list of places to search for *Playbuoy*. I do wonder if that wouldn't be easier by boat? I'm sure there are multiple businesses down here that provide water tours of the area, and it'd be easier to see places a boat might hide from another boat. Did you get a good look at it?"

"At *Playbuoy*?"

"Yeah."

"No, I really didn't."

Matthew grimaced, "You're the one who needed to see it. You could identify it long before I could if you had. To me it's just a huge boat."

"What about that marina where Nick mentioned seeing *Playbuoy* taking on supplies and using the pumping service? Miami Atlantic Marina. We could ask there and maybe somebody does water tours out of that area."

"Good idea. Could you look that up while I park?" The brasserie was just a few blocks from the bridge they'd nearly been run off of and Matthew was relieved to see it. Somehow, it looked friendly and inviting in a place that was otherwise feeling hostile to him now.

"Sure."

As Matthew parallel parked at the curb, Dr. Rob said, "OK, I found it. It says it's located adjacent to Government Cut. It doesn't mention tours specifically but brags of great fishing, sailing, and cruising with no fixed bridges and plenty of deep water. The sailing I knew about. It's where Ariel wanted me to sail down to this summer while she was here. She'd researched it and sent me information about it earlier. I didn't pay too much attention but just told her that we were busier than usual and I didn't think I could get away this summer," he choked on the last of that statement.

"I wish I'd looked more closely," Dr. Rob added after a moment. "Anyway, apparently you can also stay there on the waterfront, presumably without staying on the boat at a slip."

"I hate that it took her disappearance to get you down here too, Dr. Rob, but you can tell her that when we find her." Matthew asserted. Then, pensively, he added, "Government Cut. Where is that? Can you see it on a map?"

"Yeah, it's slightly north of us now. It cuts between Fisher Island to the south and the southern tip of Miami Beach to the north. The marina is just around the tip of Miami Beach on the western side of the island where it's more protected from storms. To get there by land we have to go back across that bridge that we just came over," Dr. Rob said with a grimace, "and then up and over to Miami Beach on the A1A."

They were quiet as they got out of the car and Matthew glanced down the block to see Danbury's rented SUV still parked at the curb on the other side of the street across from the alley. He'd gotten the second key from the rental agency when they picked up the wrecked Sonata and dropped off the Toyota Corolla without too many uncomfortable questions about why an extra set was needed. Matthew had considered moving the SUV. There was still hope, he thought, that Danbury would return himself to reclaim it and need it to be where he left it.

As they walked into the brasserie, the smells immediately made Matthew's stomach rumble. He was hungry, thirsty, and in serious need of refreshment, he realized, as they found a table in the back corner and plopped down into their seats.

A young woman that Matthew hadn't seen on his previous visit came to take their order and the first thing they both wanted was plenty of water with plenty of ice. After that, the savory crêpes were calling Matthew's name, he decided, and opted for the seafood one again. When near the ocean, fresh seafood was the obvious choice, he'd always asserted.

Dr. Rob opted for the chicken cordon bleu crêpe and they both made trips to the men's room while they awaited the arrival of their late lunch and before they began their planning.

"OK," said Matthew, "Let's check out that boating map you had up earlier."

"The AIS map?"

"Yeah, have you checked it to see if *Playbuoy* showed up anywhere?"

"Not since the bridge incident," Dr. Rob admitted. "I checked it several times this morning prior to that."

"Maybe we can start there," said Matthew. "If we could find it that way, it'd be great. But maybe we can at least figure out where to look if it's still not online with that AIS system."

"Based on where the other boats are located?" asked Dr. Rob, pulling up the AIS tracking on his phone and poking his phone to zoom in near their area. "I see lots of large ships in Biscayne Bay and a few upriver, but *Playbuoy* isn't showing up in the search."

"Yeah, I was thinking we'd look for less populated places where maybe a bigger boat or two are located. I don't know. You're better at all of this than I am. Where should we be looking?"

"Let's go upriver first, just to see if we can rule it out. Here's one that's twenty-one meters a little farther up the river from Dock Side. I don't think we can rule the upriver route out entirely."

"That's about sixty-nine feet?" asked Matthew, doing some quick math in his head.

"Yeah, almost. Here's another one farther inland. But no, it's a ferry, so it'll have a shallow draft. I do see some tugs and cargo ships up the Miami Canal that's inland from the river and goes up north of the MIA airport. The canal must be pretty deep, though it doesn't look very wide through there. I see one that's sixteen meters off on the Tamiami Canal that's south of the airport. How long would you say *Playbuoy* is?"

"I thought it was about the size of the one we were talking to Nick on today but he said it was bigger. How big do you think that one was?"

"*BizNick*? Yeah, I'd say that one is about that same size, a seventy-foot Princess."

"Huh. Then *Playbuoy* is longer than seventy feet."

"Apparently. Nick didn't say by how much but that helps some. I see some much bigger ones, like sixty-one meters or about two hundred feet," he added to spare Matthew the calculations. "If I look back downriver into Biscayne Bay, I see some that size tied up at the outer dock of the Miami Atlantic Marina. And lots of them around twenty-one meters or seventy feet all along the inner slips and a couple of thirty-five meters. But that's like a hundred and fifteen feet, a lot bigger than *BizNick*."

"To get out to the Miami Atlantic Marina from Dock Side, you'd have to get under multiple bridges, including the one we just about went off of, US 1," Matthew added. "I wonder how that works. Is there a schedule that they open on? Or do they open when a boat large enough to need them to open arrives?"

"There must be a schedule, but let's see if we can figure that out," said Dr. Rob, just as their belated lunch arrived and all conversation ceased, except for a quick blessing that Matthew offered over their food and their efforts to find Ariel.

Matthew thought he was picking up Danbury's habits as he ordered a second crêpe, this one filled with Nutella like he'd had in France several years before. While they were waiting for the dessert crêpe to arrive, Dr. Rob was poking around on his phone. Matthew offered to split the crêpe with Dr. Rob, but the elder doctor just looked at him incredulously when the second large crêpe appeared at the table.

"I found the schedule for the bridges opening," said Dr. Rob. "The Brickell Avenue Bridge, the one that we just about got knocked off of, has a twenty-four-foot clearance without opening. The timetable I just found says that none of the bridges open during three time slots each day. In military time, it's 0735 to 0900, 1205 to 1300, and 1635 to 1800. That's basically the morning and afternoon drive times and lunch. Otherwise, the Brickell Avenue Bridge will open only on the half hour and the hour Monday to Friday. We're assuming that was Monday night if Danny Boy took Ariel out by boat."

"Would the bridge need to open for *Playbuoy*?"

"Great question. The yacht specs don't usually list the bridge clearance, just the length, the beam or width across, and the draft. But if you think about it, a three-story building could be thirty-three feet in height. It could be close."

As the waitress reappeared with their check, Matthew asked her to add two water bottles to go to the order and he handed her his credit card. Dr. Rob reached for his, but Matthew held his hand out, "You've picked up almost every expense for this trip so far. I think I can get a lunch and water bottles at least."

"Thanks, Matthew," agreed Dr. Rob graciously. "I appreciate your coming down here at all."

The slender lithe waitress returned quickly with their water bottles and the bill, which Matthew signed and slipped his credit card back into his wallet.

"OK, back to the bridge opening. At night the bridge could open every half hour anyway, so it's still very possible that the boat went out Monday night, either out to the bay or inland up the river, and came back before we arrived and I saw it. We know it's been out to the marina in the bay before, at least according to Nick. Let's go ask around there and see if anyone who might have serviced it earlier has seen it lately. Maybe they even saw something or someone helpful," Matthew added more hopefully than he felt.

21 ~ AQUATIC HAYSTACKS

Both men cringed as Matthew drove back over the Brickell Avenue Bridge and Matthew looked all around as he made the hard right turn following the road as it became Biscayne Boulevard Way. Traffic came to a complete stop and they eased through one stoplight after another as the road made another hard turn to the left between tall buildings and then the landscape opened up on the right to reveal a park along the waterfront.

As they approached the Bayside Marketplace entrance in their slow crawl through the area, Matthew pointed quickly to the top of a huge yacht that was visible momentarily through the trees, "How big do you think that one is?"

"Probably a good hundred-and fifty-footer," replied Dr. Rob, turning to look before the buildings of the marketplace obscured the view.

"Bigger boats can get into this area too. I'm starting to realize that Nelson was right about the number of places to tie a huge yacht down here. That's just one more, like the needle meets the proverbial haystack."

"That should be the turn off to Port Miami there to the right," pointed Dr. Rob, "but we want to turn right at the next big intersection and get onto MacArthur Causeway and then over onto the island. We'll pass the Coast Guard Station on the right just before we get onto the island and it's directly across from the Miami Atlantic Marina. Doing anything too illegal over there would take some nerve."

"Isn't one of Al Capone's mansions on one of those islands to the left over there?" Matthew asked after they'd made the turn onto the causeway and were crossing over to the island. "Speaking of illegal."

Matthew followed Dr. Rob's instructions as he navigated them onto the island and then off to the right. Though he was expecting to see a grand entrance into the Miami Atlantic Marina, there seemed to be multiple drives leading into what looked more like an area than a central location. Turning into one of them before they left the area, Matthew parked and added the information for the Toyota to pay for parking.

Slipping out of the car into partial glaring afternoon sunlight and partial shade from the surrounding buildings, Matthew snapped a picture of the license plate to complete the parking payment transaction. Stretching as they walked toward the waterfront on the bay side of the island, they looked around and Matthew was incredulous that the parking area wasn't heavily populated. He was wondering how that could be in any place at Miami Beach as they wandered out onto the boardwalk.

The piers were lettered and one of the directional signs listed a dockmaster at Pier E, so they followed the boardwalk in that direction. As they walked along, rows of long piers ran out perpendicular to the boardwalk and there were more massive boats tied along them than Matthew could begin to count, as he shaded his eyes from the sun glinting off the water and momentarily tried before giving up entirely.

"Lots of needles in this huge aquatic haystack," he muttered as they walked briskly down the boardwalk, despite the heat and despite the fact that the other people around them were meandering down the boardwalk at a much more leisurely pace. Some were eating ice cream, couples were holding hands, and none of them seemed to notice the two men looking around to get their bearings.

"Now what?" asked Matthew as they reached a walk-through covered gateway that was labeled Pier E. There was nobody in sight who looked like they were watching over it at all.

"Let's just walk up and see if anybody shows up," said Dr. Rob. "Aside from this being Miami, boaters will work at their own pace, generally anyway.

"I bet if I do something totally forbidden somebody will show up," said Matthew with a devilish glint in his eye, "but then they might not want to answer our questions cooperatively."

With an eyebrow raised and foot tapping in both deep thought and general impatience, Matthew looked around pointedly for someone who might be in charge of the piers, the promised dockmaster. After more than ten minutes, when he was ready to give up and start canvassing the restaurants and shops along the boardwalk, an older man whose name tag read simply, Jim, meandered over to see what they needed.

Biting back all of the snide comments that came to mind about why the guy wasn't at his promised post and was in no hurry to get to it after seeing them appear there, Matthew politely stepped back and allowed Dr. Rob to start the questioning process. Dr. Rob, Matthew reasoned, understood this world and he knew what to ask about slip rental and services for transient yachts.

Once again, after shooting the sparse Miami breeze with the guy about boating in general, and the Miami Atlantic Marina specifically, Dr. Rob broached the subject of *Playbuoy*.

"There's a boat down here that I particularly wanted to see before I return to the North Carolina coast," he began. "It's probably considered a mid-sized yacht by the standards of the boats I see here. I can't tell you much about it except the name is *Playbuoy* and it's over seventy-feet long. Have you seen it?"

"Yeah," said Jim, scratching his chin in thought. "There's a Hargrave 101 that we've serviced a couple of times with that name I'm pretty sure. It's only done a transient overnight once or twice and I haven't seen it tie up here in a couple of weeks. The one I'm thinking about," he added and hesitated momentarily, "I think it's out of Miami and I think the name is *Playbuoy*. It's thirty meters or so, about a hundred feet."

"Is there any way to check? I'd love to talk to the owner."

"Why? Is it for sale?"

"It just might be," said Matthew, taking up the conversation. "I hear that the current captain isn't all that reliable and the owner might consider selling it."

"Oh that guy? If it's the one I'm thinking about, unreliable is a good description. It looks all clean and shiny, but it needs some basic maintenance, which I recommended, but he wasn't having none of it. Let me see what I can find," he said, turning to a computer screen behind him in the little booth that Matthew hadn't noticed being there.

"Yeah, it was in about three weeks ago, took on supplies and water, added two new batteries, filled up on fuel, and got a pump out service. But the engines needed to be checked. They're diesel and one of them sounded off to me. And I do have an ear for it. Not something you want to neglect for long. Too many hours on them before maintenance and all of that."

"Any idea where it had been or where it was headed? Anything that might help us locate it now?" asked Matthew.

"The guy wasn't real chatty," complained Jim. "He wanted to get the supplies, get the pump out, and be on his way. He didn't tie up for long. He headed back out but that don't mean much," he added.

"Back out? Into the bay?"

"Yeah, out into Biscayne Bay."

"And from there he could go almost anywhere, right?" asked Matthew.

"Yeah, the bay is pretty big. There are canals inland and the river. You could go to the keys from here, over to Bimini for a day trip, or even over to Freeport if you're feeling adventurous. Just go out and to the south here, then out to sea."

"Can you leave the bay up to the north?"

"You can but you wouldn't want to risk it."

"No?" asked Dr. Rob.

"No, Haulover Inlet is up there and it comes by its name honestly. Some days are calmer up there, but the ones that aren't, those aren't worth the risk."

"Oh!" said Dr. Rob. "Why is it so rough?"

"There's a strong tide up there going out through that narrow channel with strong winds from onshore. That and shoaling makes for a rough ride. Smaller vessels shouldn't attempt it and it can be rough even on these bigger ones. But you could travel around up north on the rivers if you wanted to."

"I see. Mind if we look around a little?"

"I guess that'd be OK," said Jim. "If you're in the market for a boat, there are three or four nice ones tied up down Piers A and B. One of 'em is almost as big as the Hargrave 101 you're looking for. There are signs on the docks and on the bows of all of 'em with contact information."

"Thanks, Jim," said Dr. Rob, shaking his hand. "I appreciate your help. Hey, if you happen to see *Playbuoy*, would you give me a call? Or a text is fine too. My cell number is on the back there," he added, handing the guy a card he'd pulled from his wallet.

"No problem. You have a nice day now. And if you do buy one down here, we are a full-service marina, so there's no need to take it any place else. We can do repairs, deliver supplies, dry dock, whatever you need."

"Thanks, I'll remember that," said Dr. Rob as he and Matthew turned and went back down the boardwalk in the direction they'd come from.

"I don't see any need to check anything else out here," Dr. Rob was saying, as Matthew was thinking again that making small talk must be exhausting given the current circumstances. They veered toward the parking area where they'd left the Toyota. It was in a wide area between two buildings that were blocking most of the afternoon sun and it was unbelievably sparsely populated for a summer afternoon in Miami Beach.

As they approached the car, a big black SUV, one that Matthew recognized on sight, spun into the parking lot. It made an abrupt arc until the passenger side was closest to Dr. Rob and Matthew. A gun barrel protruded from the window and shots rang out through the heavy afternoon Miami air.

Hearing the whizzing of bullets that rained overhead, the thwack of them hitting the brick wall above and behind them, and the chink and pinging of the bullets connecting with the metal on the rear of the car, Matthew pulled a stunned Dr. Rob down between the front of the Toyota and the wall of the building it was nosed up to.

Finally, they heard the screech of tires as the SUV spun out of the parking lot and back down the street to the left in the direction it had come from.

"Are you OK?" asked Matthew, as he stood up and tried to see the license plate on the retreating vehicle. Of course, it had been obscured, he realized. It was blacked out with some sort of cover, as best he could tell before it disappeared as quickly as it had appeared. Dr. Rob rose beside him and brushed himself off, speechless.

"I, I think so," he finally stammered as Matthew looked him over. "Thank you. I think you just saved my life," he said slowly.

"I doubt it. I think if they'd meant to kill us, we'd be dead," answered Matthew.

"What was that then?" asked Dr. Rob, who seemed to be still in shock.

"I think that was a scare tactic, but I'm not exactly sure what it's supposed to be scaring us off of. If it's finding Ariel, they can forget it!" he said, feeling anger surpassing the initial shock.

Just then, a guy got out of a parked car a few spots away. Because it was parked on the other side of one that was empty and, like most of them in Miami, had heavily tinted windows, Matthew hadn't noticed that there was anyone else around except a few gawkers on the boardwalk. Hopefully, he thought, some of them were calling 9-1-1 as the guy from the car came jogging across asking, "Are you OK?"

Something in the back of Matthew's mind gave him an added jolt, but it didn't immediately register. With the shock of just having been shot at adding to the accumulation of all of the other things he'd been worrying about since he arrived in Miami, his brain was slow to process the reason for its own objection to the approach of this guy.

As the guy sidled up alongside Dr. Rob, appearing to onlookers to be concerned about the two men, he reached one hand under the windbreaker jacket that Matthew now realized he should not be wearing on a sunny day in Miami in June, which was akin to an

August day in North Carolina. He flashed a gun and then put it in Dr. Rob's back from under the jacket, telling Matthew, "Don't even think about drawing that gun you've got holstered under your shirt there or I'll shoot him."

The other reason that the back of Matthew's brain had registered an objection suddenly came to the forefront of his mind. This guy was Daniel O'Rourke, AKA Daniel Rubio, AKA Danny Boy in the flesh. The hunted had become the hunter and Matthew could feel himself growing angrier about this.

O'Rourke put the arm that wasn't attached to the hand holding the gun affably over Dr. Rob's shoulder and said, "Come with me." Then, over his shoulder to Matthew, he added, "Back off and stop asking questions about disappearances if you ever want to see any of your friends again."

Moving Dr. Rob smoothly away, he added, "And do not try to follow or this guy will look like Swiss cheese." Gone was the British, Australian, or whatever dialect the guy had been going for the first time Matthew had met him. It was replaced by a midwestern one, influenced by too many mobster movies. Al Capone's nearby house notwithstanding, Matthew thought the guy might be serious and he wasn't planning to take any chances on being wrong that the influence was purely gangster movies. He realized that he still didn't know what the guy was wanted for in Nebraska.

Stepping back in front of the Toyota where they'd ducked when the shooters drove by, Matthew understood what was happening as the guy ushered Dr. Rob back to the car he'd just gotten out of. Shoving him in, the guy slid in beside him, forcing Dr. Rob over the console and into the passenger side of the car. The gun was likely still trained on him, Matthew thought, though hidden now by the closed car door. The shooting had been a diversion, one designed to get them off guard and separated. And it had worked all too well. Dr. Rob had been snatched right under Matthew's nose and he was powerless to do anything about it.

Matthew stood, hands up, meaning to portray two different things to two separate audiences. To Daniel O'Rourke, he wanted to look completely compliant in not reaching for his gun and not aiming to follow. To the onlookers from the boardwalk, he meant to imply that he wasn't standing still there with his companion leaving the scene of his own volition and he posed no threat to them. He hoped that someone from the boardwalk was getting the license plate that he couldn't see as the nondescript silver sedan whipped around the other way and back out of the parking lot, following in the path of the big black SUV.

As he dropped his hands and his mind raced with the next course of action, Matthew caught the strong scent of gasoline and looked down around the car to see it pooling rapidly under the rental Toyota. Surely car explosions were mostly in the movies, but at the very least, the shooter had rendered the car undriveable. Turning from the fumes and taking a deep breath to steady his nerves, Matthew pulled his cell phone from his pocket and called the only person he knew of in Miami who could help in any way at all now, Sergeant Nelson.

As he walked back to the boardwalk to see if anyone got license plate information, Matthew was surprised to hear a voice on his phone. He realized that he had not gone straight to Nelson's voice mail this time.

"Sergeant Nelson," he said. "I need to report a shooting and an abduction."

"Lemme guess," said Nelson tersely. "You're at the Miami Atlantic Marina. I've just gotten a report of shots fired."

"I am," said Matthew, not sure if he was feeling that he'd been chastised like an errant child by the police sergeant, but knowing full well that he was angry regardless. Through clenched teeth, he added, "And I have now been shot at, the replacement rental car is damaged and undriveable, and Dr. Rob was just hauled off in a second car at gunpoint by Daniel O'Rourke."

"Daniel O'Rourke?" exclaimed Nelson as this revelation clearly got his attention. "I was sending a unit, but I'll be right there. Sit tight."

As the phone line went dead, Matthew realized that Sergeant Nelson had omitted a few important questions, starting with if anyone had been injured, and he was thoroughly tired of being told to "sit tight" or to "stay put" by the guy. He wanted, no, he needed answers. And he needed them now.

As he approached the little clusters of onlookers on the boardwalk, their reactions were mixed. Some looked on with concern and others backed away in fear. Matthew singled out one particularly able looking large guy and asked, "Did you see that?"

The guy nodded and Matthew continued, "What did you see?"

"A big black SUV pull in, shoot at you and the other guy with you, and then another guy in a little silver sedan whisked away the other guy. Was he injured? Is he headed to the hospital?"

"No. Did you get a license plate?"

"There wasn't one on the SUV."

"The car then. Did you see the license plate on the silver car?"

"No. But that guy over there was filming after the SUV left, so maybe he got it," he answered, pointing to the next clustered group on the boardwalk. As Matthew approached that group, he heard distant sirens and he knew he didn't have long before the police arrived and took over. From that point, they might or might not tell him anything that they learned, though he was betting more heavily on the might not alternative at this point.

"Hey, did you just record what was happening over there after the drive-by shooting?" he asked the guy who'd been indicated and was still holding a cell phone aloft.

"Yeah," said the short dark guy, who was probably in his forties and had a paunch in his mid-section that suggested a lack of activity in his life. He pushed up a pair of thick glasses as he stepped back, as if unsure how to handle Matthew's enquiry.

"Did you get the license plate on that little car in your video?" asked Matthew.

"Yeah, but I didn't get a good shot of either of the guys."

"That's OK, I know who they are. Would you mind sharing that video with me? The police are on the way and they'll want to see it too. But I'd really appreciate it if you'd share it with me now. Please?" added Matthew, holding out his phone imploringly as the guy pulled back reluctantly.

"I, I guess," answered the guy.

"Great," said Matthew as he held up his business card that he'd pulled from his wallet to add credibility to his request and handed it over. "My cell number is on the back there."

"You're a doctor from North Carolina?" asked the guy, incredulously.

"I am."

"Well, OK. I'll send it."

"Thank you. I would explain what just happened but I think the police will want to hear your version of the story untainted by that. And Sergeant Nelson would likely be very annoyed with me if I explained it to you anyway. I'll let him filter what he wants to tell you," said Matthew as he heard the ding on his phone and knew that he had the video in his possession.

"Thanks again," he said as he turned to face the police cars, two of them this time, both marked and neither of them Sergeant Nelson's unmarked car just yet. Three officers approached and the fourth one veered off to closely inspect the Toyota Corolla, where the gas leak gave away the location of the shooting without needing to ask that question.

As Matthew stepped forward and introduced himself, he thought he recognized one of the officers from earlier. Danbury had said the police force in Miami was stretched thin. Matthew figured it must still be an imposing size to cover an area the size of the sprawling metropolis.

"Ah, yeah," said one of the officers. "The doctor from North Carolina who came looking for one of the missing women."

"Yes," agreed Matthew. "And I haven't found her yet and now the two people I came down here with are both also missing!"

*****

After Matthew had answered the same questions repeatedly, first for the uniformed police officers and then for Sergeant Nelson, he called the rental car agency and reported the damaged car. After a row with the manager about going through two cars in one day, a discussion which Matthew was not in the mood to have, they offered him another rental car.

Declining delivery of another one, Matthew told them where to retrieve the Toyota. He gave them Nelson's contact information in case they needed permission to move it and told them where to find the key above the sun visor. From the Toyota, he retrieved his phone cord, sunglasses case, the folder with the pictures of Ariel and Gavin that had become a fixture with him, and the keys to the car that Gayle Blevins had rented. He was happy to see that Dr. Rob had left those behind. Opting for a Rydz, he figured he needed to get back down toward Brickell where Danbury's rented SUV was still parked and retrieve it. Afterward there was a long list of things to do next.

He needed to check on Lanie and Gayle and he really wanted to contact Leo back home to check on his cat Max, but he didn't want to have to explain to Penn that Danbury was missing. That was just one more conversation that he didn't want to have. He needed to get the car that Gayle had rented back to her somehow, he thought. He dreaded having to tell either her or Lanie that Dr. Rob was now also missing and that he'd been ushered away right under Matthew's nose. That thought still made his blood pressure rise in fury, an uncommon occurrence for Matthew, who was normally even tempered, laid back, reliably calm, and emotionally solid.

Given all that he'd been through recently, he realized that he'd probably been angry more in those last three months than in the past three years combined. He needed a break from all of the drama, he thought, and it couldn't come soon enough. His peaceful life back in his condo, the repairs on which should be finished any day now, his cat Max, and his collection of instruments, some of which would need to be replaced now, were all sounding like paradise to him in the midst of hot and tropical Miami. But he couldn't go back home alone, not without Ariel, not without Dr. Rob or Danbury, and he had no intention of doing so, at least not yet. He hoped not ever.

Waving an arm at the Rydz car, Matthew identified it from the description and the license plate on the app and, with everything else that had just happened, checked it all twice to be certain before he climbed in. He confirmed the address of the brasserie for the driver but he couldn't fully relax yet, knowing that he had a lot still to do. He began by calling Gayle.

It was a jubilant Gayle Blevins who answered the call and said that

Gavin had regained consciousness and was able to talk to her a little bit.

"That's excellent, Gayle! I'm on my way down now. We can figure out how to get your car back to you too, if you want to get back to the hotel or anything."

"I'm going to get one closer to here because they're telling me that Gavin still has a long road of recovery ahead and I want to be close by until they release him for travel home. But I would appreciate getting the car back. I could really use that now. I'd love a shower and a real bed for a night now that he's recovering."

"OK, I'm on my way and I can take you to get it or ask Lanie to help deliver it to you if you want."

"What about Richard? Can he help you get it to me?"

It took Matthew a moment to realize that she was referring to Dr. Rob. Matthew had heard Ariel call him Dad but everyone else, including their senior partner Steven Garner, called him Dr. Rob. Matthew wasn't sure how he'd acquired the nickname, but it had stuck solidly. Richard Roberts was pretty much exclusively called "Dr. Rob" by everyone. Everyone but Gayle Blevins apparently.

"Ah, he's not available at the moment. I was just checking in on you and Gavin," Matthew stammered, trying not to upset the woman any more than she already had been by the horrific experience with her son. "I'll head down there and we'll talk when I get there. Why don't I bring the car now?"

"That would be lovely," she said. "If I call the hotel and check out by phone, will you bring the rest of my things from the hotel room?"

"Sure. Just tell them to let me into the room or have them pack them up for you and leave them at the front desk for me."

"I'd rather you pick them up yourself if you don't mind. There shouldn't be much, if anything, unpacked anyway. Richard brought me some of it earlier. There's just my suitcase and another bag, probably still both on the bed unless he moved them. That's it. I hadn't unpacked anything before finding out that you'd found Gavin."

"OK, I'll get those and be there as soon as I can," he said and quickly got off the phone with her before she could inquire further about Dr. Rob.

Looking around, he realized that they were on the bridge back over to the mainland and there was plenty of time to reroute his destination. He leaned forward and asked the driver if they could change course and head west to Hialeah instead of south to Grace Hospital. After a bit of stammering and some argument about how things are done, the driver finally acquiesced, though he was still muttering under his breath in Spanish. Matthew gave him the address of the hotel.

Sinking back into the seat, Matthew felt exhaustion wash over him and he allowed himself a few moments to close his eyes and try to relax. Try as he might, he couldn't clear from his mind the image of Dr. Rob being ushered away at gun point. Maybe Gavin could tell him something that would help him find them all. He certainly hoped so.

22 ~ ALONE IN MIAMI

Arriving at the hotel, Matthew thanked the Rydz driver and checked first with the front desk. One of the managers escorted him up to Gayle Blevins' room and watched as he picked up the suitcase and the smaller bag from the bed, glancing around to be certain that really was all she'd left behind. Satisfied, he thanked the manager and went to his own room long enough to shower quickly, change out of the sweaty clothes he'd had on all day, and brush his teeth. He glanced through the steam on the mirror at the stubble that had started to take over his face and knew he had more important things to worry about than that.

On his way out, he dropped off one of the plastic laundry bags that were always in hotel rooms but which he'd never actually used before, containing what looked like a week's worth of dirty clothes. He realized the bag contained clothes from only a few days but he wasn't sure how that was possible. It felt more like weeks than mere days. With the heat and humidity in Miami, he thought he could change clothes every hour on the hour and still feel sticky and sweaty.

Instead of making progress on finding Ariel, he felt like he was being sucked backwards into some unseen muck and mire, like sinking into quick sand, which was poorly named anyway because descent into it was anything but quick. It was slow and painful or so he'd heard. As he descended in the elevator, he was contemplating how it was possible to have lost two more people in as many days since he'd arrived.

He walked out to the parking lot and put Gayle's bags in the trunk of the Huldai Accent. Cranking up first the little Hyundai and then the air-conditioning on full blast, he pulled up the location for Grace Hospital on his cell phone and plugged it into the charging port in the car. He was missing the navigators who had helped him to keep his eyes on the road amidst the crazy drivers and roads turning off suddenly at odd angles. He was thankful to have been to the hospital before so that the route was a somewhat familiar one.

Thankful that the trip down to the hospital was uneventful, though he checked mirrors constantly and wondered how he'd know if he was being followed, he parked in the Emergency Department parking lot as he had before. When he arrived upstairs, having been cleared through the Emergency Department entrance as he'd been told that he could do, he finally found Gayle Blevins crossing the hall from the ICU to the waiting room.

"There you are!" she said as she rushed over and hugged him. "I'm so glad to see you. The staff here has been great, but I've felt like an island with no familiar faces from home."

The woman was apparently a hugger, he thought, as he refrained from pointing out that he was hardly a familiar face because she'd never met him before coming to Miami. Instead he said, "I left your bags from the hotel in the trunk of the car and the car is in the Emergency Department parking lot where we were before. Here's the key," he said, handing it over. "How's Gavin doing? What are the doctors saying?"

"He's conscious, though really tired, so he's still sleeping a lot. It doesn't take much at all to wear him completely out," she answered.

"That's normal. His body has been through a huge trauma and it's trying to heal itself. It'll take time for him to build stamina again, to do even small tasks without tiring easily."

She just shook her head and laughed at him, "You sound like Richard," she said. "Always the doctor."

Matthew wasn't sure whether that was a compliment or just a statement of fact, so he said, "I guess it is an occupational hazard. Gayle, can we talk a minute?" Leading her the rest of the way into the waiting room and over into a corner, he sat down.

"What's going on?" she asked warily.

"Have you asked Gavin about what happened to him Monday night?"

"I haven't. He keeps asking for Ariel and I haven't known what to tell him," she answered, obviously distraught. "The staff here says we need to keep him calm and, like you just said, give him time to heal."

"Gayle," began Matthew, "I don't know how to tell you this, but we might not have time. I need to talk to him and get him to tell me anything he can remember of Monday night."

"N n no," she stammered. "We can't upset him like that."

"I haven't told the police that he's awake," said Matthew. "And I won't, for now. But I need to know what he can remember. Anything and everything that he remembers. It literally could be life or death for Ariel, for Danbury, and for Dr. Rob."

"Richard? What are you talking about? Where is he?"

"I wish I knew," confessed Matthew, "but that's part of why I need to know what Gavin can remember from Monday night." Haltingly, he told her how Dr. Rob had also been abducted right under his nose without him being able to stop the guy or even slow him down.

"Oh, my God!" exclaimed Gayle Blevins.

"Exactly," said Matthew. "That's why we need to know whatever Gavin can tell us and I think it'll be easier for him to tell you, with me there, than the police. Don't you?"

"Absolutely. What do we tell him about any of this? About Ariel and now Richard?"

"That's a good question. We need to have a strategy about that, a script of sorts, and then stick to it," answered Matthew. "Consistency in whatever we decide to tell him is key, but I'm counting on you to know how much he can take versus how much not knowing is already upsetting him. We haven't found Ariel," he hesitated, "but as far as we know, she hasn't been killed," he amended. "See, that's exactly what I mean by having a plan. How much information do we share with him and how do we state it to cause him the least amount of angst?"

"I see your point. OK, let's just tell him that Ariel is not here right now and we're not sure when she'll be back. That's the truth, or at least a form of it. If he presses to know if she's OK, then what?"

"As far as we know, she's physically just fine," said Matthew.

"I hope and pray that she is!" said Gayle Blevins. "I know my son and as far as he's concerned, the sun rises and sets in that girl. He loves her like he's never loved much of anyone else in his young life. He's had crushes on girls and dated in high school, sure, but this is different."

"Yeah, I know Dr. Rob said they were inseparable, and Lanie said they hit it off from the first time they met. We do need to be careful with how we phrase things. Let's work that out and then go talk to him. I'm not family, but I am a doctor so hopefully that won't be a problem here."

Gayle Blevins took in a deep breath and said, "OK, as soon as he wakes back up, we'll go in. Let's figure out what we're going to tell him."

*****

"Gavin?" said Gayle, as she stepped into his room that was growing dim in the gathering shadows of the early evening. "Are you awake?"

"Hey Mom," he said, opening the one eye that wasn't still swollen closed. "Yeah. I guess I'm in and out a lot, huh?"

"It's OK, sweetheart. That's what you're supposed to do now. Sleep when you feel like sleeping. Richard's associate Dr. Paine is here to talk to you."

"Dr. Paine? Really? That's really his name?" he asked, amused.

"Matthew Paine," he said, stepping into the room and slipping over beside the bed.

"Sorry," said Gavin, apologetically. "I didn't realize she meant that you were here here, like right now."

"It's OK," said Matthew grinning down at Gavin. "Give it your best shot. I think I've heard them all before but if you come up with some new material while you're recuperating, I'd love to hear it."

"Nah, with a last name like Blevins, I can't say too much," said Gavin.

"I don't want to stay too long and tire you out," said Matthew, deciding to get to the point. "But I need to talk to you about Monday night."

Matthew could see the panic rising in Gavin's face at the mere mention.

"It's OK, sweetheart," said Gayle, as she flitted to the other side of the bed and reached out for Gavin's arm that was not attached to myriad lines and monitors. Stroking his arm with her fingernails as she had told Matthew that she'd done when he was a boy to comfort him, she added, "Just relax and try to remember."

"You got a Rydz down to Dock Side and picked up two pizzas, right?"

Gavin nodded through tears that were starting to gather in his eyes.

"And you took one to Anna, the little girl under the bridge, right?"

Again Gavin nodded.

"And then you were supposed to get the Rydz back to Hialeah with the large pizza, right?"

Gavin choked when he answered, "Yeah, we were going to heat it up and share it with Shawn and Lanie."

"You were walking back toward Dock Side from under the bridge to catch your Rydz car and then what happened?"

Gavin's body shook and Gayle looked up helplessly at Matthew as she continued stroking Gavin's arm.

"She's dead, isn't she? I couldn't stop them. They killed her, didn't they?"

"As far as we know, Ariel is alive and physically just fine," said Matthew, providing the response that he and Gayle had rehearsed. "But she's missing and we need to find her. Which is why we need you to tell us anything and everything you can remember. When you were walking back to Dock Side, what happened? You didn't get back there, did you?"

"No," Gavin shook his head miserably. "Two guys had stopped us on the way out to offer us a free tour of Biscayne Bay to see houses of the rich and famous. Some mess about being the thousandth customer at the pizza truck this month."

"And how did you respond?"

"I didn't have to at first. Ariel thanked him politely but told him that we were down here to work and we didn't have time to go goofing off on a boating tour of Biscayne Bay. Houses of the rich and famous wouldn't have interested her at all anyway."

"And then what?"

"He was pretty persistent, so I took her by the arm and just said, 'Thanks, but no thanks,'" and we kept going to deliver the pizza to Anna. We talked to her for a few minutes and she asked Ariel to bring her some things. Ariel said she would and we were talking about either borrowing the Ministerios de Conexiones Saludables van or getting another Rydz Tuesday afternoon after we'd finished working for the day to get the things Anna needed and then get back down there with them."

"OK and then what?"

"It was really noisy out there because the party tour bus was parked there by the sidewalk. It's open on the top and music was blasting from it, so, I didn't hear them coming up behind us."

"Who?"

"The two guys who'd offered us a free ride on the boat on the bay."

"Then what happened?"

"One of them, the shorter blonde one, he got right up next to Ariel and stuck a gun in her side and put his arm around her shoulder. He told her to just keep walking or he'd shoot her. I didn't think he would right out there with all of those people but they were all pretty wasted, it was really noisy, and it was already dark except for the lights from Dock Side ahead of us. I kept walking with her. I was hoping to be able to get her away from them."

"What did they look like? One was shorter and blonde, you say?"

"Yeah, but not that short. He's probably about my height. And the other was huge and dark, dark hair, dark eyes, dark skin."

"Is this the guy?" asked Matthew, being careful to pull up the grainy picture of the guy from the Dock Side video on his phone and not the one from the alley.

"Yeah, that's the big guy. He didn't say much, he just shoved me and grunted. I guess I was shocked and I dropped the pizza. I think I saw some of the Bridge People who were dancing in the street pick it up behind us and tear into it. But I'm not sure about that. You know how it's all so slow and crystal clear, but fuzzy all at the same time?"

"Yeah, I do know," said Matthew, thinking back to nearly getting run off the bridge and Dr. Rob's abduction at gunpoint. "It's like it all slows down into slow motion and it's clear and then afterward it's like it's hazy and it happened so fast you're not sure what just happened."

"Yeah, just like that," said Gavin.

"OK, what happened after that?" persisted Matthew.

"That's where it all gets fuzzy," said Gavin.

"It's OK," said Matthew, noticing from the monitor that Gavin's heart rate was up and wanting neither to stress him unnecessarily nor to have the staff come running in and shoo them out. "Just tell us what you can remember, whatever you can think of. Any little detail might be important. Take a breath. Take your time."

"It's OK, sweetheart," said Gayle, stroking his arm with her fingertips and repeating Matthew's instructions. "Just take your time. Breathe."

"There was a truck parked on the curb on the other side of the street from the party tour bus," continued Gavin after a deep breath. "These guys steered Ariel toward it and then onto the sidewalk on the other side of it from the party bus people, between it and a brick building. I remember reaching for Ariel and then the big guy punched me in the face. Then there was this pain in my head. I tried to reach for her but things were all muddled in my mind and then everything went black. I woke up here today. And I don't remember anything else. Nothing in between. I don't know how I got here, or what happened to Ariel," he started sobbing. "I couldn't stop them. I couldn't help her. I should have been able to help her. I should have stopped them!"

"It's OK, Gavin. They caught you completely by surprise. None of us would have been able to stop them," said Gayle, stroking his arm.

"She's right," said Matthew, who knew all too well. And then he repeated, as they'd rehearsed, "None of us would have been able to stop them."

"The best we can do now is to find her," said Gayle.

"Can you remember what the truck looked like?" asked Matthew. "How big? What color? Did you see a license plate? Any markings on it?"

Gavin gulped air and Matthew hated upsetting him this way. He shared in his agony in that moment at not being able to stop Dr. Rob's abduction or to find Ariel or Danbury. Gayle had perched on the bed beside Gavin and Matthew dropped into the chair beside him where Gayle had earlier been keeping her vigil willing him to wake up. The guy probably wished he hadn't awakened, thought Matthew, with what they were having to put him through now. Matthew had dropped his head and was running splayed fingers through his hair when he heard Gavin continue quietly.

"It was white, silvery white," Gavin finally whispered. "It was boxy. Like with a cab up front that wasn't attached, but not like an eighteen-wheeler or anything. Not nearly that big. Front axles on the cab and another under the boxy truck part. I remember seeing those as I was falling, the axels. And the smell. There was a nasty smell, I think as they opened the back of the truck. But I'm not sure. I don't know what it was, but that's the last thing I remember. The very last thing was that smell."

"OK, so the truck was some sort of service vehicle? Or smaller transport truck?" asked Matthew, trying to narrow down the description.

"Yeah, I guess. I think there was some kind of logo on the side of it but the light from Dock Side was hitting it at an angle when we walked up. I didn't get a really good look at it. It had a red circle with something blue at the bottom and then something brown inside of it. I don't know what it was. I don't know if it had letters on it. I don't know if they took Ariel in it or if it was just there. I don't know. I just don't know," Gavin said desolately.

"You're doing well, Gavin," encouraged Matthew. "Think about what else was around you. Were there any other people on the sidewalk? Any other cars around? Was there a driver in the truck?"

"I couldn't see if there was anyone in the truck cab," said Gavin. "There was a car a little way in front of the truck, parked at the curb too. I guess it wasn't a car. It was bigger. Like a big SUV."

"That's good, Gavin, what did it look like?"

"It was big and dark, dark blue or maybe black, I think."

"A black SUV in front of the boxy truck. OK, did you see any other people at all?"

"People," he hesitated. "No, but there were feet."

"Feet?"

"In front of the boxy truck. I saw them when I was falling but I don't remember landing. Either somebody caught me or I blacked out before I hit the sidewalk. I remember falling, the awful smell, the axles on the truck, and the feet in front of it. That's it. That's all that I can remember, even the hazy parts. I mean, all of that was hazy."

"How many feet? How big? Anything you can tell me about them at all?"

Gavin closed his eyes momentarily, Matthew hoped in concentration and the monitor beside him bore out that supposition as his heart rate was still elevated but not alarmingly so. Matthew continued to watch it closely.

"Two sets of feet. Dark shoes, dark pants, men's feet. They were aimed toward the truck," answered Gavin, triumphantly opening his eyes. "I didn't know that I knew that, if that makes sense."

"It does," said Matthew. "You were traumatized and injured so I understand why it's all hazy. But you've done well. Anything else? Can you remember anything else?"

"Somebody yelled," he said. "But that might have been me. I'm not sure."

"That's great. You've done really well," Matthew repeated. "I'll keep the police away as long as I can but the hospital staff might have already notified them that you're awake. They might have been required to. I'll ask them not to if they haven't yet."

"You rest now, Gavin," said Gayle as Matthew was getting to his feet.

Looking down at Gayle, he added, "I'm going to go talk to the staff and then I need to go get Danbury's SUV. If Gavin thinks of anything else, anything, whether it seems important or not, please text or call me?"

"I will," she said, with tears in her eyes. "I promise that I will. I'll be right back, Son," she said to Gavin and slipped out into the hallway behind Matthew.

"Just find them. Please find them," she begged.

Matthew tried to dismiss the hopeless feeling that was starting to overwhelm him as he said quietly, "I'm not a detective, not even close. But I'll do my best to help the police to find them."

Matthew went over to the nurses' station to request that the police not be contacted and the nurse on duty replied indignantly, "I have no intention of it! It was all I could do not to run you out of here just now. Didn't you see his heart rate shoot up?"

Raising an eyebrow at her talking to him, a doctor, that way, he admired her care for her patient and simply said, "I did and I watched it closely as it came back down from that point on. I wouldn't have upset him if it weren't absolutely necessary to try to find his missing girlfriend and two other people who have also disappeared down here while we were looking for her. I appreciate the care you're giving him. Keep up the good work," he added as she seemed to deflate when he didn't reprimand her and instead walked away toward the elevator, pulling up the Rydz app on his phone.

He stepped outside to wait for the Rydz car, out of the growing chaos in the Emergency Department, and wandered toward the bulkhead along the waterfront. The hospital was situated on the southern portion of Biscayne Bay overlooking Key Biscayne. The sun was sinking and the reflected glow in the clouds that he was watching through the palm trees indicated a beautiful sunset on the way.

Matthew had been alone many times in his life and he was usually very happy and content in his own quiet company. He'd felt lonelier in crowds of strangers, but in this moment he realized that he couldn't recall a time when he'd felt quite so alone before.

It wasn't that he was incapable of continuing to search for his friends alone, he knew, but mostly that he understood what doing it now without any of the others meant. Without the resources or the information that Danbury provided and without the nautical knowledge and the knowledge of Ariel, which Dr. Rob provided, it just became exponentially more difficult.

The tropical ocean breeze and the water lapping against the bulkhead should have been consoling, he thought. In this moment, it wasn't at all. He didn't seem to be able to move forward with finding Ariel, Danbury, or Dr. Rob, but neither could he go home without them. He shivered in the Miami heat.

23 ~ Bat Signal

Matthew arrived back at the rented SUV after the sun had mostly sunk beyond the horizon, which he couldn't actually see through the buildings anyway. He agreed with Lanie that the alley just behind it gave him the creeps. A warm glow still lit the approaching night sky as he unlocked the SUV and started to climb in.

He wasn't sure what it was, but something stopped him in his tracks and beckoned him into the alleyway. If he were in a horror movie right now, Matthew thought, everyone in the cinema would be yelling, "Don't go down there!" And yet, like in every scary movie he'd ever seen, he ignored that, relocked the SUV, and walked slowly down into the alley, looking all around him as he went.

He stopped beside the spot where he'd found the body of the big guy, Sebastian, if that name was to be trusted. The guy who'd likely beat up Gavin and helped Daniel abduct Ariel. Gavin had been found, on the opposite side of the alleyway, just a bit farther down, presumably left for dead. Was this also where Danbury had been when he'd disappeared?

Considering the information that he hadn't yet pursued, Matthew wasn't sure if any of it would lead him anywhere worthwhile. There was the white-haired, uptight, self-important man who had been seen with Daniel O'Rourke. Could he be the sea captain? If not, then there was also the sea captain who might know where *Playbuoy,* and therefore Daniel O'Rourke, were. But did Matthew really want to find Danny Boy now? Would finding O'Rourke help him to find Dr. Rob? Maybe, he thought, but he was on his own to find the captain now too.

Pondering what Gavin had shared, Matthew wondered who the two sets of feet belonged to. The ones Gavin described in front of the boxy truck where he and Ariel had been led. If he were forced to bet, his money would be on the guys who in his mind had become the Blues Brothers, the guys driving the big black SUV with the bar on the front of it that had tried to run him off the road and then shot at him. And what about the foul smell that Gavin mentioned? He hadn't shared what it smelled like and Matthew was annoyed with himself for not asking Gavin when he had the chance.

Mostly in that moment, he felt a bit hopeless knowing that he was alone now. That feeling welled up within him as he stopped, looked up to the sky that was quickly darkening, and said aloud, "God, I could use some divine intervention right about now."

His phone dinged from his pocket just after he'd spoken. He pulled it out, not expecting much in the way of help, but he saw that he'd just gotten a text from Justin McMillian, his life-long best friend since early childhood.

Nobody from their friend group back home in North Carolina really knew what Justin did exactly, though they all assumed it was with one of the alphabet soup agencies of the US government. Neither did any of them know why he disappeared for weeks or months at a time, and they'd all given up asking. He wouldn't tell them anyway.

The only one of their group of friends who had seen him in action a few months before, Matthew had relied on Justin's expertise in rescuing Cici from captors. Justin had taught Matthew a few useful tricks in the process. But that was as it should be, thought Matthew, because he and Justin had always been the closest of the group of friends, living parallel lives even when they'd been periodically out of touch for a few months here and there growing up. Matthew and Justin had grown up together in Raleigh from age three and stayed in touch even after Justin's mom had moved him to the other side of town.

Opening the text from Justin, Matthew was stunned to read, *"Turn around, walk back up the alley, turn left."*

The next thing that Matthew saw was the happiest sight he'd seen in at least two days. Justin McMillian was waiting for him on the sidewalk to the left of the alleyway. Justin's dirty-blonde hair had darkened over the years from the tow-head blonde of their childhood, but his boyish grin had never changed, thought Matthew, though admittedly he saw less of it these days.

The relief that flooded through Matthew at seeing Justin went well beyond seeing his best friend appear suddenly, unbidden, in an odd place over seven hundred miles from home. Justin had always had a sense of adventure growing up, but in a soft-spoken and geeky way like Matthew. And Matthew knew that he'd been in some sort of military special forces. Who he worked for now was anybody's guess but if there was anyone Matthew would most want to have help him find his missing friends, it would most definitely be Justin.

"Justin! How did you find me? Why are you here?" asked Matthew, closing the distance between them quickly and giving Justin a big brotherly bear hug. Justin stood about an inch shy of Matthew's six-foot three-inch frame and was equally muscular, though Justin's were the longer leaner sort that were built more for endurance than bulk.

As they patted each other roughly on the back, Justin asked with a boyish grin, "Didn't you put up the bat signal?" Then, turning quickly serious, he added, "Follow me."

He crossed the street briskly and Matthew followed as they headed for the brasserie. "I didn't but I'm glad you're here."

"Let's go where we can talk," said Justin over his shoulder. He walked into the brasserie, nodded briefly and said, "Thank you," to Lillian Toussaint, who nodded back. Matthew saw her smile fleetingly at him as they walked past her and a busboy, whose nametag Matthew saw said Nathan. Both seemed unsurprised by the intrusion. Matthew followed Justin down the long back hallway behind the seating area of the brasserie and past the marked restrooms and the tiny office that Matthew had been in earlier with Toussaint.

The hallway jacked to the right and ended in front of them. To the left was a huge metal door, corporate looking and not at all like the rustic wooden doors and hallway they'd just passed through. Justin slid aside a panel in the metal door casing, punched in a key code, and opened the door motioning Matthew through. Closing it softly but firmly behind them, Justin stepped back into the lead and Matthew followed him down a long brightly lit cinderblock hallway that was painted a glossy off white with shiny concrete flooring beneath their feet. They passed corporate-looking metal doors set in metal frames on both sides of the hallway, each with keypads or badge readers of varying sorts. Matthew followed as they exited through an outside door at the end of the hallway.

As they stepped outside, the heat and humidity hit them again like a punch to the gut, though there was a slight evening ocean breeze blowing in off the water. Matthew could see that they were in a parking area that was bordered by tall buildings on three sides, including the one they'd just come out of, and a bulkhead that was being slapped by water from the bay in front of them. The water was sparkling with reflected lights from street lamps along what appeared to be a boardwalk and the sky was reflecting the last glints of sunset that was coming from the west behind them. Matthew could smell the ocean brine on a momentary breeze. It was a nice change from the stagnant air of most of Miami.

There were multiple industrial-looking vans and trucks parked sporadically around the parking lot. As Justin motioned him over to a white unmarked utility van, a panel in the side instantly opened for them. They climbed into the back of a large panel van and Matthew could see a counter-like surface around the periphery with computer screens all around above the counters. Some were displaying grids of what looked like feeds from cameras in multiple locations and others had files and some had lines of what looked like computer code running across them at a speed impossible to read.

A scruffy-looking guy was already in the van seated at a keyboard on the wrap-around counter so it was overly crowded in Matthew's opinion, as he and Justin climbed aboard. Justin seemed not to notice.

"Now?" asked Matthew, and Justin nodded. "We've got a mess down here and I don't know what to do next. We came down late Tuesday night because Dr. Rob's daughter Ariel is missing. Two other women who generally match Ariel's description were reported missing before Ariel, and they have both been found murdered. Last night we found a man's body in the alley that I just came out of. And now Danbury and Dr. Rob are both missing. I know who snatched Dr. Rob because it happened right under my nose at gunpoint and I couldn't do anything about it. The local Miami Dade police are on it, but they haven't been very successful so far."

"Tip of the iceberg," said Justin. "It's a lot more complicated than that. I can enlighten you on some of it but not all. Your missing people stumbled into a much bigger international operation. That's why I'm here. You've had help all around you, you just didn't know it," he added. As he spoke the guy at the counter, a lanky wiry man with longish hair and a scraggly beard, turned from the computer screens and stood up behind Justin. Matthew thought the guy looked familiar but he couldn't place him. He was wearing an FBI jacket, which seemed incongruent with the rest of his appearance, thought Matthew.

"It wasn't because he didn't want to tell you," said the man. "He had to await proper clearance to read you in."

The guy didn't sound like he looked either, assessed Matthew.

"This is Jett Johnson," said Justin, as Matthew shook his hand. "Obviously FBI. He was down here under cover but his cover was blown and his contact is in the wind. I think you've already seen him in a video from the brasserie over there."

"One of the two men in the alley Wednesday night, the night Gavin was found!" said Matthew, drawing the obvious conclusion and putting the pieces together. "You found Gavin and called 9-1-1?"

"I did. And then I waited to be sure an ambulance took him away from here. I saw the feet sticking out from behind the dumpster and went to check his pulse. My companion that night was my contact, but I figured he was too strung out on the drugs he deals to object to me being the Good Samaritan. I think now that I was wrong about that. Your friend had a pulse so I called it in and waited, just to be sure he made it safely out."

"He did get out OK and he's finally out of a coma. He'll have a long road to recovery but thanks to you it sounds like he will recover. I just came from the hospital," said Matthew and then asked, "You didn't see how he got there? Or if anyone else was with him?"

"Just what I've told you," he said and then looked askance at Justin, who nodded.

"We've had surveillance on this alleyway from one of the brick buildings down near the other end because there have been paneled vans in and out in the middle of the night, pickups and deliveries that we're interested in. One of the camera systems that went down Saturday night was ours and it was disabled from the inside, not like the ones that were busted and spraypainted down on the street," Johnson said. "You can draw the obvious conclusion. Our operation has been compromised."

"A third camera system?" asked Matthew.

"Right. Not one of the two visible ones," answered Johnson. "Our cameras were disguised in the brickwork on the third floor of the warehouse in back of the restaurant where we'd been running surveillance. Its software was disabled and we're still not sure if it was a hacker from without or a mole from within. Too many people knew about the operation. It started with a vice team from the Miami police working a local drug problem. But then they discovered that it was much bigger and the DEA and FBI were brought in. We had to move the operation and cull down the number of people who knew about it. Most of them think we just folded up and left."

"Ah," said Matthew. "Why is everybody so interested in this one alley?"

"We've had it under surveillance for several months now. Some goods have been exchanged between panel vans and trucks down there late at night."

"Goods? Like drugs? Or weapons?"

"Like that," said Johnson elusively. "And then it developed an international interest. That's when Justin showed up a couple of weeks ago and we've been working jointly since then."

"You obviously know lots of things that I don't need to know. All I care about knowing is how to find the three people who are now missing, the last one taken right in front of me this afternoon in exactly the same way that I've now learned the first one was taken, at gun point. Except that it was in full daylight this time and they didn't beat me up and dump me in an alley for dead. They just got us off guard by shooting at us first."

"Ariel Roberts was taken at gun point?" asked Justin, seemingly surprised that he didn't know this.

"She was. Like I said, Gavin just came out of a coma and he was able to tell me the last that he remembered from Monday night."

"She was officially reported as MIA Tuesday night, but had actually been missing since Monday night," summarized Johnson.

"Right, since a couple of hours before you found Gavin in the alley. The abductors were two guys who have been loosely identified by compiled information from Gavin, Anna, a girl that Ariel had been talking to under the bridge just before she was taken, and security footage from Dock Side. I think they are Daniel O'Rourke, who goes by Daniel Rubio or Danny Boy locally, and the big guy who was murdered in the alley, Sebastian. If that really is his name."

Matthew took a breath and then continued, "The two guys had already approached Gavin and Ariel as they were coming out of Dock Side with the pizzas. The guys offered them a free boat tour on Biscayne Bay to see the houses of the rich and famous, which Ariel and then Gavin declined. Gavin and Ariel walked up the sidewalk and took one of the pizzas to Anna under the bridge. They were on their way back down the sidewalk to catch a Rydz car back to Hialeah. There was one of the open-air party buses that does tours around that area parked along the sidewalk there and it was noisy."

"Gavin said that O'Rourke walked up beside Ariel, pulled a gun on her, put his arm around her shoulder, and told her to come with him. Just like I watched O'Rourke do to her father this afternoon. Gavin went along to try to help her, but as soon as they got behind a boxy delivery truck parked across the street, Sebastian punched him in the face and then somebody cold cocked him from behind, likely with the butt of a gun, by the looks of his injuries."

"There were just the two guys?" asked Johnson.

"That's all Anna saw and all that Gavin saw at first. He didn't see other people, but he said he saw feet approaching in front of the boxy truck after he'd been hit. From the direction of a black SUV that was parked in front of the truck. There are lots of those around, I'm sure, but one of those tried to run me off the Brickell Street bridge earlier today and it was from the same one that the shots were fired at us a couple of hours later."

"What about the truck that they walked behind? Did Gavin see anything that could identify it?"

"Sort of," said Matthew. "He said it was a boxy truck with a detached cab, small with only two axels. It was silvery white he said, and the side had some sort of logo, a red circle with a blue line under it and something brown in the center of it. It might have had lettering but he wasn't sure."

He saw Justin and Jett Johnson exchange a glance and then Johnson leaned over the keyboard, clicking to pull up an image on one of the big screens. It was poorly lit but the image looked like Gavin had described.

"That's what he described," said Matthew.

"That's what we've been seeing in the alley," said Johnson. "The brown blob in the center of the circle is a loaf of bread."

"It's a small fleet of delivery trucks from a defunct bakery business," added Justin. "There were five or six of them. The trail on what happened to them after an auction of assets when the company went out of business is completely cold."

"It provides perfect cover for illegal activities," added Johnson. "Nobody thinks twice about seeing a bakery delivery truck parked or backed up somewhere. It's almost invisible."

"The guy in the alley who you called Sebastian. You heard the gunshots when he was killed, didn't you?" Justin asked Matthew.

"We did. Dr. Rob and I found him and checked for a pulse but there was none. We didn't expect to find one after Dr. Rob saw that there was a bullet hole in his forehead," admitted Matthew. "It was dark so we didn't see the rest of the gore at the scene thankfully. We took pictures of his face to try to identify him and then left."

"He was triple tapped. Likely a professional hit," Justin spoke up.

"That makes sense," said Matthew. "We heard what I thought were three rapid shots. You didn't have the alley under surveillance at that point?"

"We were in the process of putting cameras on the edges of the rooftops to get eyes back on the alley when that went down," said Johnson. "We have witnesses after the fact but no camera coverage of the actual event."

"You had people on the rooftops when we went down there to check on the guy?"

"We did," said Johnson. "The guys on the roof saw you and your colleague check the guy, get the pictures, and get out."

"Wow," said Matthew, which was all he could think to say. "Did they see who shot the guy?"

"Vaguely," said Justin. "As you saw it was dark down there. They observed three shadowy figures enter the alley from the narrow cross road at the other end from here. Johnson's team went back to working on the cameras on the roof of this closest building on the left. They were under orders to get up there, get the cameras operational, and get out. So, they weren't watching the guys on the ground until they heard the shots. Then they slid back to the edge of the rooftop and looked down in time to see two of the guys running from the alleyway at that far crossroad where they'd entered. Then they saw you enter from the other end and they thought you might be professional, the way you were covering your approach and checking on the guy."

"Professional?" echoed Matthew.

"A cop. Or a private detective or something."

"Did you laugh at them?" asked Matthew in complete amazement.

"No. And I didn't correct them either," said Justin. "I just vouched for you so that they didn't track you down and interrogate you."

"I had a little bit of training from an expert a few months back," smiled Matthew, indicating Justin. "But that's as close to 'professional' in that line of work as I'll ever be. And thanks for sparing me the interrogation. I guess I could still be locked up some place answering questions if you hadn't."

"Likely," said Johnson, matter-of-factly. "Is there anything else you can tell us about your involvement down here? Anything else we might not know yet?"

Matthew gave them a summary of everything he knew so far. He shared the online documents they'd been updating until earlier that day with Justin, who shared them with Johnson, who pulled them up on the bigger screens in the van. After they finished poring through them, Justin said, "I can answer a few of the questions you've asked there."

"We've been watching *Playbuoy*, too, but only from this end when it's left the river and headed out into the bay. We hadn't followed it upriver to know where it went, so that's helpful information."

"It isn't docked there," pointed out Matthew. "Like we said in the documents, it's just been tied up there frequently. There aren't any services like water or power or anything there."

"Yeah, it gets those amenities just south of here," said Justin. "Just south of Vista Point, which is just south of where we are now. There's a condominium building owned by the same shell corporation, Royce Consolidated, that owns this yacht you've been watching. Ownership of the corporation is yet to be determined because it's tied up in multiple layers of shell corporations and subsidiaries. But if you follow *Playbuoy* and pay attention to who lives in the penthouse of the condominium unit, you can get a pretty good idea. There again, real names are obscured several layers deep."

"So, whoever owns *Playbuoy* and the condominium building is really good at covering their tracks," summarized Matthew.

"They are, but we have some hackers working with us who are some of the best," said Johnson. "And they're working on peeling away the layers of that onion right now. The biggest help they've given us so far is to tie Royce Consolidated to two other shell corporations that are registered in Bimini and one of the other Out Islands of the Bahamas. One of those corporations ships in and out of Freeport to some scarier places on this planet. That's where Justin comes in."

"Out Islands?" asked Matthew.

"Think of them like our Outer Banks at home in North Carolina," said Justin. "They're just a string of islands, about a hundred miles long, that are, except for Bimini, east of Grand Bahama. They mostly run south east of the Bahamas and south east of Nassau."

"Here," said, Johnson, clicking a few more keys and bringing up a map. "Maybe this will help."

"Ah," said Matthew. "OK, so there's Bimini just offshore from here, to the south west of Grand Bahama. How long does it take to get there by boat?"

"It depends on the boat," said Johnson with a grin. "It's only about fifty-five miles off the Miami shore. You can get all the way up to Freeport in a little over two hours with the right boat."

"And the other Out Island?"

"It's not a named island, as far as we can tell. It's privately owned by one of the shell companies associated with Royce Consolidated. It's just off the coast of Grand Bahama," said Johnson.

"It's on this west side closest to us, like Bimini," clarified Justin. "About twenty miles south and slightly west of Grand Bahama. There are deep-water ports in little towns all along the coastline of Grand Bahama on this southwestern side of the island. Johnson's hackers uncovered records of a water craft belonging to a subsidiary of Royce Consolidated, the subsidiary that owns the unnamed island, coming and going from the Lucayan port on this side of Grand Bahama and also a port on the east side."

"It's not *Playbuoy*," added Johnson, seeing Matthew's inquisitive look. "It's a commercial craft of some sort. Registered in the Bahamas, but it's been here in Miami several times over the past couple of months and from here to a shipping company on the eastern side of Grand Bahama Island, Freeport Shipping and Trading Company. They're a shipping agency that provides services not just for shipping, but for storage, both dry dock and container. Our hackers have gone through multiple layers of shell corporations from Royce Consolidated and found a connection there too. There are brokerage and port agency services between Royce and Freeport Shipping and Trading. It's very convoluted, but if you look at the shipping and trading company's web site, they are all about servicing the customer. Anything related to shipping that their customers need, they'll provide. From crews to maintaining and storing the vessels and any cargo involved, they do it all. It's pretty clear that they ask no questions about any of it."

"OK," said Matthew, feeling slightly like his tired brain might explode at any moment with this plethora of seemingly unrelated information. "But what does all of this have to do with the missing people I'm looking for?"

"Everything," said Johnson. "From the bread trucks to the owner of *Playbuoy* and the condominium to the owners of the island and the corporate registration on Bimini."

Suddenly, it all clicked like a bright light bulb being switched on in Matthew's mind.

24 ~ REVELATIONS AND RESOLUTIONS

"What you're saying is that they're shipping illegal goods," said Matthew to Johnson. "Like the weapons and drugs that I mentioned earlier which you didn't exactly confirm, but neither did you deny. And they're handing off in this alley, taking them to the dock at the condominium and either out to Bimini or the other island between it and Grand Bahama. Then they go to Freeport Shipping and Trading or maybe they go straight there from the Miami shore and then out to the scary places around the world that you mentioned."

"The alley is just one point of hand off. And there's just one team working that chain. There are lots of teams working lots of other chains, but yes, that's what we're saying," confirmed Justin. "There's a whole chain involved in the hand off so that the guys who provide the goods have no idea where they go after they hand them off to the next people, the next link in the chain. And then the next hand off happens and the next. There's no linkage between them if one or two people in the chain are caught and definitely no way to track them to the top of the chain. Each link knows only of the link before and the link after and as little as possible about either of those."

"And this ties into the missing people the same way?" asked Matthew.

"We believe that it does," confirmed Johnson. "Snatching and trafficking goods of the human sort out of the US isn't at all easy and it's not normally even possible. But this gets them around the entry and exit points that are tightly controlled with national security."

"There's a whole process involved in trafficking people. Women in particular can be ordered on the dark web. They are snatched, drugged, housed in various places around the world, then cleaned up and videotaped so that the buyers can see them.”

“Ordered?”

“Yes, unfortunately,” said Justin. “In this case some sicko likely wanted a young petite redhead.”

“And the first two who were snatched weren’t real redheads so they were killed.”

“That’s what we’re thinking. Because they couldn’t be returned to their lives without creating a major incident. Not in this country. The police would be called in and the media would have a field day trying to find the abductors. The only other option if they’re not wanted by whoever placed the order, and not otherwise transported out would be to kill them,” said Justin with a grimace. “And something in their chain has been disrupted, which is why we think they killed these two women. Somebody at the bottom of the chain had them, without being able to hand them off, and they didn’t know what else to do with them.”

“Aside from all of the other disgusting aspects, that’s ridiculously complicated for just one woman,” observed Matthew.

“These people have deep pockets,” said Justin. “You have no idea how much money they offer for the right woman and redheads are rarest. Asian women and those of other dark-haired ancestry are much more commonplace on the human trafficking black market. Snatching girls in some other countries is commonplace and families will even resort to selling their daughters if they’re financially poor and see no other way to survive.”

“Younger women and girls are told all sorts of things about where they’re going and how their dreams will all come true to garner their cooperation,” added Johnson. “In many cases they’re drugged and they don’t know where they are or how they got there when they’re cleaned up to be sold.”

“Women can be ordered like you’d order a pair of jeans online,” said Justin in disgust. “By size, height and weight, hair color, eye color, all of that.”

Matthew had a fleeting thought of his little niece back in North Carolina and pushed the thought quickly aside before he became too angry to concentrate. The thought just served to strengthen his resolve to understand this horrific process and find Ariel. "But these women had to be held here somewhere before transport," he said, with one eyebrow raised and his foot tapping in concentration.

"Why do you say that?" asked Johnson, leaning forward in his seat.

"Because the two women who were reported missing before Ariel both turned up dead here. In Miami," said Matthew. "They weren't transported off-shore. If they had been, why bring them back to Miami to kill them or to have them be found here?"

Justin and Johnson exchanged another glance and Justin said, "I told you we'd have to explain more than just the basic operational process to Matthew. He'll fill in any blanks that we don't."

Johnson just shrugged, "Your call," he said and turned back to the monitors.

"You're right," said Justin to Matthew. "We have reason to believe that people have been trafficked in and out of the high-rise condominium that's owned by the subsidiary of Royce Consolidated. We think it's a holding area before shipping them out. And it's not about volume at this level. It's about specifics, finding exactly what the buyer wants. We're not talking about lots of women coming and going from there. Just a select few."

"Ah," said Matthew. "Could Ariel still be there? And how do Danbury and Dr. Rob fit into that pattern? Any idea where either of them is?"

"Maybe. They probably don't. And not yet," said Justin, responding in the order that Matthew had asked the questions. "We're not sure if Ariel has been moved. We're working on that."

"But you think that they have her or at least have had her, there?"

"We do. There seems to be some disruption in their process flow, like Justin mentioned, and we're not sure why. That's all just from some chatter we've picked up in the past two days," added Johnson, chiming back in. "Warren Danbury, we believe, left with one of the trucks of his own volition."

"You mean he purposefully disappeared?" asked Matthew, gawking at the guy.

"He was last seen climbing aboard one of the shipping containers in the alley. Late last night. When was the last time you heard from him?" asked Justin.

"I hadn't heard from him for several hours last night," said Matthew. "But I hadn't tried to contact him either until nearly midnight, I think. That was after seeing O'Rourke board *Playbuoy* with the blonde woman and calling Nelson then dealing with the police after the body of who we now know to be Katie Jones was found in the hole under the bridge. I just assumed that if Danbury was doing some sort of surveillance that his phone would be silenced or turned off completely, so I wasn't too worried until we got to the alley, found his truck, and then the guy that was shot down there."

"Up until last night, goods had been moved between trucks that were backed in opposite sides of the alley from the little side streets coming in from the north and going out to the south. But last night, nothing was moved between trucks. Instead the drivers changed. A container truck was pulled into one of the side streets and across the alley from the north and just left there shortly before midnight," said Johnson.

"We don't know where the original driver went, but about fifteen minutes later two guys backed one of the bread trucks down the narrow access street on the north side of the alley, got out, crossed the alley, and then climbed into the waiting container truck. They drove it out to the south, like the other transactions. Twenty minutes later, we could see just the front of what looked like a black SUV in the alley behind the bread truck. There were three guys who then headed this way into the alley. You know the rest," said Justin.

"Danbury left the alley IN the container truck?" asked Matthew incredulously.

"We think he broke into it and got in it, and nobody saw him get back out," confirmed Johnson. "But remember, we didn't have the cameras back up and running. This information came from a lookout on the rooftop who was waiting for the cameras and the installation team to arrive."

"He got in between the time it was dropped off and fifteen minutes later when it left?" asked Matthew.

"Right," said Johnson. "He had time to get back out if he'd wanted to. It took him more time to break in and close the doors securely behind him than it would have taken him to get back out of it."

"Huh," said Matthew. "OK, so let's assume that Danbury is still in control of his fate, just given that information. What about Dr. Rob?"

"That one is a complete mystery so far," said Justin. "We have no theory as to why he'd be taken."

Matthew ran his fingers through his hair, eyebrow raised and foot tapping as he thought through that statement. "OK, so let's get back to Ariel. You think she was transported from the bread truck to the alley maybe? Or some other way?"

"We'd have seen a swap like that in the alley. And it would be harder to do anything unseen," said Justin. "We think the bread truck took her straight to the condominium."

"And then up to the penthouse without being seen?" asked Matthew skeptically. "And potentially back down and out again? How is that possible?"

"There's enough big money in Miami to make almost anything possible," answered Johnson. "People brought in and out by helicopter, boats, cars. You just wouldn't believe."

"I've seen a few of those cars," said Matthew, "including a Pagani and a rare Lamborghini. Aston Martins and Ferraris are plentiful and it seems that Mercedes, BMWs and Porsches are pretty common place down here."

"Matthew is a motor head," explained Justin to Jett Johnson.

"We've got pictures of one that maybe you can identify," said Johnson, excitedly returning to the keyboard and tapping to pull up a collection of photos of a sleek black sports car from various angles, except directly from the back where a license plate should be displayed.

"It's been modified," said Matthew, leaning in for a better look. "But I think that's a Koenigsegg One, that's right up there in price with the Lamborghini Veneno and the Pagani Huayra that I saw the other day. It's over a million easily, maybe two. Why? What does this have to do with anything?"

"It's been seen coming and going from the private area of the parking garage beneath the condominium," said Justin. "We just got these pictures earlier today and there was a big debate over what that was. But it might be important because of the other question you just asked, how anyone could be brought in and out of the condominium complex undetected. There's a private parking area beneath the bottom floor of the building with a private elevator that goes straight to the penthouse."

"Ah," said Matthew. "So, the owner of the car is likely the owner of the condo and the yacht?"

"Very probable," said Johnson, who had been furiously tapping at a keyboard. He then turned and added, "I just sent our team that information to run down. If they can figure out what it is and if it's as rare as you say, then maybe that's another angle to come at and try to figure out who really owns the condominium building and the yacht too."

"I did have one more lead to follow up on about the yacht that you'll see in the notes there. Dr. Rob added the information shortly before he was abducted so it's near the end," added Matthew.

"About the captain who might have been hired for *Playbuoy* and was seen at Dock Side in the company of the big guy who was killed in the alley?" asked Johnson. "I already sent the name off to our team and they sent back a picture that matches the description of the older gentleman who you said the waiter JoJo saw at Dock Side. The one your documents said that JoJo described to you as being self-important and dressed in a blazer in Miami."

"Yeah, that one," said Matthew, incredulously.

"He's a reputable sea captain from what they could determine," said Johnson. "He's retired from the cruise industry and he picks up odd jobs, but he's selective, so only on yachts that he really likes. One of our guys is off to go talk to him now."

"Wow," said Matthew, impressed. "It makes a huge difference in making progress on an investigation when you have teams of people to work on it."

"Hey, don't sell yourself short," said Justin. "You and your friends learned a lot in just a few days and then probably got too close to the truth for somebody's comfort."

"So, what's next?" asked Matthew. "How do we find Ariel?"

"We've got teams currently watching the little unnamed island, Bimini, Lucaya, and Freeport. The Freeport Shipping and Trading Company has been under close surveillance since early this morning," said Justin. "I'll be notified if our teams find anything in any of those locations. We'll take an extraction team over immediately by chopper if they find Ariel or any other evidence of human trafficking. Otherwise, I'm going over myself by boat at first light in the morning."

"Anything I can do to help?" asked Matthew, which drew a warning glance at Justin from Jett Johnson.

A loud pinging noise turned Johnson back to the monitors before Justin could answer. "What is it?" Justin asked instead.

"An alert. The DEA is just reporting counterfeit pills circulating in this area that contain at least two milligrams of fentanyl. That's considered a lethal dose. Most of the wealthier drug users have naloxone on hand. More commonly known by the original pharmaceutical name, Narcan. You can buy it from the pharmacy without a specific prescription here in Florida. Wealthier users probably also have fentanyl test strips to test the drugs before using them. All users and their friends and family should have both on hand. Mount Hermon Medical Center and Saint Gerard Hospital have been flooded with overdose patients in the past couple of hours."

"OK," said Matthew slowly, "Why is that relevant to our situation?"

"Because the remaining pills that the victims had on them are marked exactly like some that we've seen exchanged in the alley," said Johnson. "Not in the vans lately but handed off person to person a week or so ago."

"They have clear and unique markings on purple and orange striped capsules," added Justin. "Very difficult to miss if you've seen them. And very unusual that dealers would put that much fentanyl in a pill that they're selling. They're not usually trying to kill their best customers."

"Yeah, that's what I was thinking," said Johnson. "I wonder what our friends at the DEA will make of that?"

As they were pondering that thought, Justin's phone dinged and he poked it, read a message, and said, "It's go time at zero four hundred."

"Where?" asked Johnson.

"Freeport," said Justin.

"Assist?" asked Johnson.

"Alpha team."

"No locals?"

"No intel on them. Small unit anyway."

"They cover all of the Bahamas?"

"Yeah, Bimini included."

"By air?"

"No, under cover op."

"By water at zero four hundred?"

"Yeah, don't want to spook them."

"Not yet, huh."

"Right, that's the plan," said Justin. "It's more recon. Nothing concrete yet."

Matthew just stood there, looking from one to the other of them, like he was watching a fast-paced game of ping-pong and trying to understand the exchange that he'd just clearly heard but hadn't quite as clearly understood.

Turning to Matthew to explain, Justin said, "We have a team going over to Freeport to check out the Freeport Shipping and Trading Company more closely in the morning. They're leaving by boat at four AM. It's an undercover operation so we're going in as prospective clients."

"You're going?" asked Matthew.

"Yeah, I'll be up and out early."

"And you?" he asked Jett Johnson.

"FBI," said the guy, as if that explained everything. Matthew looked confused so he then added, "The Bahamas isn't far from US soil, but that's another country. I handle domestic, not international."

"Oh," said Matthew.

"I'll be mainly in the background on this one," said Justin, apologetically to Johnson who looked enviously at him, as if he got to have all of the fun. "Mostly observing and reporting back. Unless they need my expertise. I'll be wired with all sorts of electronics in case they do."

"Your expertise?" asked Matthew.

Laughing, Johnson replied, "This guy can hack his way into or out of anything. I'm just glad he's on our side! You didn't know that? How do you think he knew exactly where you were, where you'd been, and with whom?" To Justin, he asked, "Haven't you ever told him what you do?"

Justin just shrugged. "I try to keep all of that separate from my personal life so that I don't drag my friends and family into anything. This guy, though," he added, indicating Matthew. "This guy seems to drag himself into things regularly these days."

As Matthew started to object, Justin said, "Last month it was, what, money laundering and another trafficking ring that you stumbled onto? And now this?"

Incredulous again as to how Justin knew about all of that, Matthew realized that he had been so relieved to see Justin that he hadn't thought beyond that to wonder how the guy knew where he was when. He looked at his life-long best friend with different eyes, as if seeing him for the first time through an entirely different lens. Matthew wondered what else he didn't know about him.

25 ~ DARKEST HOURS

Justin had invited Matthew to stay with him in a nearby hotel but Matthew protested that he didn't have a change of clean clothes. He had changed mid-day, but he still felt the effects of the Miami humidity. As they discussed logistics and how Matthew could help, his stomach growled loudly.

"You haven't eaten," said Justin, more as if stating an obvious fact than asking a question. "You've always been bad about getting so involved in what you're doing that you forget to eat."

"Guilty. But I did have a late lunch," said Matthew, raising an eyebrow because Justin had an unbelievable memory and knew him better than nearly anyone else, with the possible exception of Cici and his parents, so it was pointless to argue with the guy.

"Want another savory crêpe?" asked Justin. "I know where we can get one."

"Don't they close at ten?"

"Yeah, but it's not quite ten yet and we can get special favors anyway."

"Apparently," said Matthew. Then he added jovially, "I'm not sure I want the details on that."

"We need more water bottles out here anyway," said Johnson, nudging a cooler that Matthew hadn't noticed under the counter with his foot. "But I'm on it. What kind of crêpe would you like?" he asked Matthew.

"Ah, the chicken cordon bleu that Dr. Rob had this afternoon looked good."

Johnson turned back around, poked some buttons on his phone, and ordered three crêpes and a half dozen water bottles.

"Didn't you just eat?" Justin asked Johnson.

"Yeah, but you never know when you're going to get to eat again," said Johnson and repeated his version of Danbury's mantra to eat when you can and sleep when you can because you don't know when you're going to get the opportunity to do either again.

"OK, seriously," said Justin to Matthew. "Why don't you hang down here for the night? It's a lot closer to the action than your hotel up in Hialeah. We can get you some spidey man pjs from one of the little shops down here if that's the issue," he joked like they had when they were boys. After a bit more good-natured ribbing, Matthew gave in and agreed without bothering to wonder how Justin knew that he had been staying in Hialeah. Maybe it was in the online documents that he'd shared but he didn't think so.

"My needs are pretty simple," said Matthew. "A clean pair of boxer briefs, maybe a t-shirt, toothbrush and toothpaste, and I'm good to go. I can wash this dry fit shirt out in the sink and it'll be dry by morning."

"Yeah, you don't seem to need a razor these days," Justin ribbed Matthew, indicating his scruffy face.

Reaching up and rubbing the thick growth of stubble on the side of his face, Matthew just shrugged. "No time lately."

"We're staying just down the boardwalk here," said Justin. "There's a little boutique on the first floor of the building that has lots of t-shirts on display and they have beach clothing in the window so they probably have what you need. The hotel has the signs up about providing any incidentals that you forgot so that should take care of the toothpaste and toothbrush. I've got two queen beds in my room so you can bunk with me. It'll be like old times, minus the bunk beds we had when we were kids."

Then changing the subject entirely, Matthew said, "I would like to find a pharmacy to pick up a few supplies."

"What? Is all of this giving you a headache?" Justin asked, in rare form this evening, Matthew thought.

"No, I just usually have a first aid kit, kind of like an old-fashioned doctor's bag in my cars at home. I didn't travel with it and I've already needed it, so I want to pick up a few things to have on hand."

"Oh yeah, the kid with the busted food under the bridge," said Justin. Before Matthew could begin to formulate the question about how he knew that, Justin had moved on. "Sure, no problem. There's one of those big chain pharmacies across the street on the next corner down, inland from the hotel. If they don't' have it all, we can find another one."

"By the sounds of things with those fentanyl-pills on the incoming ED patients, we should probably stock up on naloxone too. I question its effectiveness against the hyped-up version of the synthetic opioid that you were describing, but it's better than nothing."

"OK, make a list and I can help," said Johnson.

That took Matthew by surprise and, as he turned to Johnson, his face must have shown it.

"What? I can be helpful," Johnson said. When both Justin and Matthew just stared at him, he added, "I have a nephew who ODed on an opioid at a frat party his freshman year in college a couple of years back. He'd be dead right now, but for a girl who had naloxone in her bag and she wasn't too high to think to use it. It's what I thought had happened to your friend down the alley until I saw that he'd been beaten. It's why I waited after I called 9-1-1. I had to know that he was being taken care of."

"Ah," said Matthew, awkwardly. And then sincerely, he added, "Thanks. You probably saved his life."

The ping of an alarm sounded and Johnson spun back around to the monitors, "It's just Nathan," he said, clicking more keys to open the back panel of the van.

Over Johnson's shoulder, Matthew could see a monitor with a view of the parking lot around them and the guy he'd assumed to be the busboy in the restaurant was approaching with two bags. Nathan appeared in the doorway and handed the bags into the van to Matthew and Justin.

"Wow, that was fast," said Matthew.

"Just add it to the tab?" asked Nathan.

"Yeah, thanks, Nathan," said Justin as the panel on the van was closing again.

The group got quiet momentarily as the crêpes disappeared. "OK, all set?" Justin asked Matthew.

"Yeah, I guess so. Do we need to move Danbury's rental SUV?"

"Let's leave it, just in case," said Justin. "It's within walking distance if we need to get it later. And I see your sergeant buddy marked it with a Miami-Dade police placard so it's safe enough where it is."

*****

Matthew had gathered the supplies he needed with Jett Johnson's help when the pharmacy across the street didn't have exactly everything. He opened the packaging and arranged the supplies in a faux-leather backpack that he'd bought in the gift shop as neatly as possible for quick and easy retrieval. He'd managed to find six doses of naloxone, four nasal injection and two vials with syringes to be manually injected intramuscularly or subcutaneously. Knowing about the recent opioid problems and that sometimes it takes more than one dose, he wished he'd found more.

In the gift shop he'd also found chargers for his phone and watch and a pair of red silk boxers, which was all they'd had in his size but about which Justin had teased him mercilessly. A tie-dyed "I heart Miami" t-shirt, his only choice in an XXL which was the only size long enough for him, completed his purchases from the gift shop.

Having showered, packed the medical bag, washed his dry fit shirt out in the sink and hung it on the back of a chair at a desk in the hotel room, he and Justin were talking logistics about the next day. Justin kept stopping just short of including Matthew in the plans for the next day until after Matthew heard a loud ding on the computer that Justin had his nose in sporadically since they'd gotten back to the room.

"Finally!" said Justin, triumphantly. "I've just gotten clearance to have you come with us tomorrow, if you're willing," he added. "It took nearly an act of Congress, but my superiors have agreed that having a physician along in the background with me could be beneficial if we find anyone there who's there against their will and needs medical attention. If we meet with any opposition, the alpha special forces team will be both manning the yacht and on another vessel nearby."

Not having to consider this for very long, Matthew simply asked, "Where else would I be and what else would I be doing? I just need to make a quick call and send a couple of texts. Tell me what I can and can't tell them."

"Bare facts," said Justin, and provided a quick list of things that Matthew could disclose.

After calling Lanie to update her on as much of the situation as he could tell her, reassuring her not to worry, he sent a text to his parents. He provided them with a quick update and asked them to give his little niece Angelina, who had claimed him as her person almost from birth, a hug from him.

Next he texted Cici and told her that he'd be out of cell range for the FaceTime chat that they had most mornings and that he'd let her know when he was back in range.

"There. That should do it for updating concerned parties," he announced as he turned his attention back to Justin and they planned how the morning would play out. They'd bought protein bars from the pharmacy and there would be water bottles aboard the boat they were taking over, but it otherwise wouldn't be stocked with food Justin told him. That would be breakfast at least. The boat they'd travel over on would be a huge yacht, purportedly being brought into Freeport to find out about shipping and storage services as well as overwintering there. Justin and Matthew would both be posing as crew members aboard the ship, Justin as a navigational expert.

The situation would have been amusing to Matthew, had it not been so dire because he had yet to take Dr. Rob up on his offer of a weekend aboard his sailboat and Matthew's knowledge of boats was seriously lacking. Sure, he knew the port from starboard and bow from stern, but that was about the extent of his knowledge, he thought.

"Is it red right returning?" he asked Justin. "And returning from what? Sea? Across a lake? I'm not sure I'm fit to be a deck hand or anything else aboard a fancy yacht but I'll do my best to look the part and have my medical bag below just in case it's needed."

"That's all you have to do," said Justin. "I'll be at the ship's controls but with a few additions to the standard navigational equipment up on the bridge. We'll have a variety of equipment on board from diving gear to night goggles to heat sensors and a lot in between."

Having completed their inventory of gear assessment and tactical planning, Matthew was restless with nervous energy and he'd stepped out onto the balcony to appreciate the ocean breeze and the view of the bay from the twenty-seventh floor. The night was dark. If there was a moon up there, he couldn't find it. The stars were also obscured but he wasn't sure if it was due to cloud cover or the abundant light pollution from Miami. Maybe it was some of both, he decided as he spotted what he thought was a lone star in the night sky.

Without Justin, Matthew realized that he'd have had very little hope of finding Ariel or Dr. Rob or even Danbury. Until Justin had found him, he'd had no idea how truly hopeless that venture was. The night still seemed dark, but he held a glimmer of hope now that it was merely the darkness before the dawn and that the new day would shed new light on finding his friends.

26 ~ BREAK OF DAWN

After a restless night of tossing and turning with his adrenaline pumping too much to sleep, Matthew got up at three AM and he and Justin took turns showering. He pulled his dry fit shirt, which had lived up to its name, from the back of the chair and put his clothes from the day before over the silk boxers that Justin was still ribbing him about. He brushed his teeth and ran his fingers through his short, thick, wavy brown hair and considered himself ready for the day, whatever that might hold.

Matthew strapped his holster under his shirt and slung his new medical bag over his shoulders. Justin picked up his backpack that contained his computer, their protein bars. Matthew was not going to ask what else. Soundlessly, the two men left the hotel room just after three-thirty, made their way down the hall, down the elevator, and out the door onto the boardwalk at the water's edge. Following Justin along the boardwalk, which was lit at intervals by faux gas lights on low posts, they came to a set of docks. They were long docks, Matthew soon realized, as he and Justin turned out onto the middle one and walked to the end.

There was a massive yacht tied there and under the weak dock lighting, Matthew had noticed a lift on one side of the stern that contained what appeared to be a cigar power speedboat and lifts with at least two jet skis on the other. He wondered how many feet in length the yacht was and had a sadness in the pit of his stomach thinking that Dr. Rob would know and would be excited about exploring and learning more about the vessel.

Without ceremony they climbed aboard and opened darkly tinted sliding glass doors, stepping through into a salon with plush leather seating all around. There was a long table at one end and Matthew could see a wet bar on the other side of it. Doors led out of the room on either end, but he wasn't sure where they went because they were all closed.

"I need to get up to the bridge and set up some equipment," said Justin. "Why don't you come up with me and I'll introduce you to whoever is already here. They should all be. We were to be the last to board."

"Sure," said Matthew, following along behind as Justin opened a sliding door beside the wet bar and stepped through. They climbed up, turned on a platform, climbed again, and landed on a larger platform. Turning, Matthew saw what looked like a very sophisticated cockpit to his untrained eye. There were gadgets, instruments, and monitor displays across a huge dash panel that was wrapped in surround windows. It was still dark out and there wasn't anything to see yet through the windows.

Two men seated in front of the controls turned around and Justin introduced Matthew, first to a redheaded guy with a plethora of freckles that looked like you could play dot-to-dot on his face and never get bored.

"This is O'Brien. O'Brien, Matthew Paine, our resident physician afloat." O'Brien's blue eyes sparkled as he shook hands and his face didn't look much older than twelve to Matthew's mind.

"And this is Captain DeMarco. He'll be getting us safely to our final destination today," said Justin, mimicking a flight attendant as Matthew shook hands with him too.

"Which is really just safely back here," said DeMarco with a nod.

"And dealing with anything that happens in between," said Justin.

After a bit of technical discussion on navigation and logistics, Justin led Matthew back down to the parlor.

"When are we casting off? If that's the right term," said Matthew.

"Oh about," said Justin, looking at his watch. "Now."

Exactly three seconds after he'd spoken, Matthew heard at least one loud engine rev, though it was muffled inside of the yacht, and he felt a slight jolt and then vibration as he assumed that they had just left the dock.

"And you said this trip should be just a little over two hours."

"About two hours and twenty minutes, given the wind direction and speed. It should be a smooth trip, not too choppy," answered Justin. "We'll be tying up there just about sun up. So, you might as well settle in and enjoy the ride. There's wi-fi aboard if you want to get online. It's secure. Very secure," he added.

"If it were light out, I'd rather get out and walk around. But I don't think I can see much yet."

"Nope. Once we get off shore, you won't be able to see much at all. For now the shore lights reflecting on the bay should be a good view if you want to walk out and watch the departure."

"Sounds good," said Matthew. "Do you have an official job now?"

"Yes and no. I have some equipment calibration to finish up and then I'll have some free time until we make port. I'll need to be up on the bridge before we get within sight of the harbor there so that I look like the navigator that I'm supposed to be."

"I guess I'll go wander around out there and see the view as we're heading out."

"OK," said Justin, but his head was already back in his computer after he'd pulled three devices out of his bag and set them on the table in front of him.

Matthew wandered up on deck and to the stern as the ship had already turned, heading out to sea. Justin had been right, he thought. The lights from shore reflecting in the water were beautiful. He pulled his phone from his pocket, snapped a couple of pictures, and sent them to Cici. The view and the yacht would be romantic, he thought, under completely different circumstances. He shook his head, trying to clear his thoughts of his ex-girlfriend. This was a fact-finding mission primarily, but they had to be prepared to deal with whatever they found so it was far from a pleasure cruise.

After about five minutes, as the lights were disappearing rapidly behind him, he was turning to go back into the salon when he saw a message from Cici pop up, "*That's lovely. Where are you and why are you up and out on the water this early?*"

"*I'm the doctor afloat on a fact-finding mission. I'll probably be able to tell you where after we're back.*"

"*Wow! Promise me you'll be careful,*" she texted back. "*Honestly, I never thought I'd have to say that to YOU of all people! But promise me?*"

Matthew chuckled at that response. She had always told him that she loved how safe he was, how solid and secure and safe. Prior to a couple of months ago, he would have agreed with her but he understood why she couldn't say that so much anymore.

"*I'll do my best. I love you, Cici. I'll let you know when I'm back.*"

"*I love you too. And you all the way back in Peak can't come soon enough for me! Though that isn't completely safe these days either, is it?*"

He chuckled as he typed, "*Not entirely. But I'll be as careful as I can. Promise. I'm just a doctor, after all.*"

She had known that Justin was involved in her rescue from a crazy abductor a couple of months previously, but Matthew didn't share that Justin was involved now. He wasn't sure if that would make Cici's concern for him better or worse, but that was outweighed by the fact that neither was he certain if he was supposed to divulge to anyone that Justin was involved.

Matthew slipped back through the sliding door into the salon and slumped down into a leather couch. He was startled when he was awakened a couple of hours later by Justin telling him that they were nearing the port.

"Here, eat these," said Justin tossing two of the protein bars to Matthew and then handing him a water bottle."

"Yeah, I know, because you don't know when you'll have the chance to do it again," said Matthew as he sat up and looked around, surprised that he'd fallen asleep so easily after not having managed much of that the night before. The motion of the boat and the muted roar of the engine he credited with having lulled him to sleep. "At least I got the 'sleeping when I can' part right," he added with a grin.

He took his breakfast, such as it was, with him and wandered back onto the deck, munching as he went. Walking along a walkway with a railing down the port side of the yacht and up toward the bow, Matthew could see a glow on the distant horizon of the ocean. The sun wasn't up yet, but the sky was glowing a beautiful orange that spread across the reflecting sea like fire on the water. He took a few deep breaths of the fresh briny air and paused to appreciate the serene view before the hectic rush started around him on the yacht. The real deck hands were running about preparing to dock so Matthew, not wanting to appear as useless to anyone on shore as he felt in that moment, headed back into the salon and out of sight.

He knew that after they'd docked, Captain DeMarco and O'Brien would be shown around the facilities under the guise of evaluating them for future use. He and Justin wouldn't have an official role in that ruse but he wasn't sure if they'd be free to roam around or if they'd be confined to the yacht. It seemed to him that any actual deckhand would be curious about Freeport and would want to see the sights that Grand Bahama had to offer, so maybe it wouldn't seem odd at all if he wanted to disembark and look around a bit. At least he hoped that logic would pan out.

After the boat was secured, the roar of the engines died down considerably. Matthew could still hear a bit of engine rumble so perhaps they were still powering parts of the yacht, he thought. Justin reappeared from somewhere above and, much to Matthew's liking said, "OK, you want to go have a look around?"

"Yeah, I was hoping we'd be able to do that."

"It's kind of why we're here," he said jovially.

Matthew felt the gun holster under the side of his shirt and asked if they were taking those with them.

"Oh yeah," said Justin. "We're not going through customs or metal detectors."

"OK, where are we going?"

"I don't know yet exactly. Just keep a look out for anything that looks suspicious."

As they disembarked from the yacht, the sun had made it above the horizon and was blindingly reflecting off metal everywhere. There were several buildings with what looked to be tin roofs. Beyond those, Matthew could see rows upon rows of stacked shipping containers. They were the big corrugated metal sort that he'd seen on flat bed trailers behind eighteen-wheelers and trains. Some were newer and brighter than others, but they were each painted. Matthew noticed a few green and orange ones amidst the abundance of red and blue ones.

In some of the rows of containers that he was seeing beyond the buildings, they were stacked four and five high. The rows seemed endless and Matthew was fascinated with the sheer volume of them, wondering how many thousands of containers there were. Wandering past the office buildings, he pretended to stretch his legs and arms as if he were just getting rid of sea legs. He saw Justin respond to what must have been information in the earwig, muttering something in response that Matthew couldn't make out.

"Hey Matthew, they're going to Plan B to involve more of the staff here so they need me in the office for a few minutes," he said quietly. "You OK out here? Or do you want to get back on the boat?"

"I'm going to walk around and stretch my legs some," said Matthew loudly enough for any observers to hear him. "Is there more water beyond all of these containers?"

"Yeah, the nav shows canals coming in over there, and there," he said, pointing beyond the row of buildings on the right and to the far back of the huge lot of shipping containers.

"I wonder what the fishing is like over there. I'm going to go check it out," he called to Justin's retreating back, as Justin knew that he would.

Plan B Matthew knew was designed to involve more of the Freeport Shipping and Trading Company staff in the inspections if Plan A didn't pull enough of them into the office area and away from the rest of the facility. Apparently Plan A had not produced enough kowtowing on the part of the shipping company to accomplish that. Plan B meant that another of the guys that Matthew had met on the ship would disembark and pose as the owner of the yacht to personally review the facilities, the security, and the services available. Meanwhile, the alpha team would be looking around quite purposefully, some from above and some below the water.

Justin would be accompanying the guy posing as the owner of the craft to be consulted as the navigator so that he could easily be sent back to the ship under that pretense if some of the more advanced equipment was needed. Apparently, there was no hostility or Matthew too would have been recalled to the ship through Justin's earwig.

Matthew wandered down a pathway on gravel that appeared to be crushed oyster shells through the stacked containers which looked like buildings with narrow alleyway paths between them. As that thought struck him, he cringed just a bit recalling the alley in which so many horrid things had already happened back in Miami.

The maze of containers was in grid patterns of rows. First, he'd wander down a row heading straight out from the ship behind him, but then he'd encounter a wider row perpendicular to the ship behind him and the containers would run in rows that forced him to walk perpendicular to the ship before he could turn another corner and walk away from it again. Just as he thought he'd be lost in the maze of containers, he finally saw one last grid of rows in front of him that seemed to end in a wooded area. It was scrub wood and there was a gate and a pathway leading to a system of canals beyond.

As he was just about to open the gate, Matthew stopped and listened intently. He thought he heard a tapping sound. At first, he had thought it to be a woodpecker, which he wasn't sure there were any of out here. Then he thought it might be some other bird pecking. He then realized it wasn't that at all. The tapping he was hearing was rhythmic and sounded metallic, like metal on metal. As he listened, he realized that he was hearing three longer taps, three short quick taps, and then three longer taps again. And then it grew quiet. Knowledge of what that was froze him in his tracks.

Turning slowly, Matthew started to walk, stepping as lightly as he could manage on the crushed shells as he listened in the direction that he thought he'd heard the tapping coming from. He was walking back to the right, toward the far back corner of the huge lot of shipping containers. Wandering between the endless rows of containers, Matthew was wondering if he'd really heard the tapping at all or if he'd just imagined it because the back corner of the huge lot had become quiet.

He could hear the distant purr of motors and the clunk of metal near the front of the shipping yard where containers were being moved around and lifted onto and off of the waiting ships which were docked along the canal behind the office buildings. He had caught glimpses of the crane-like equipment moving containers around down the long wider rows of containers. He hadn't noticed it when they'd disembarked from the ship, but then the buildings were along that area on what he now realized must have been a wharf.

After another fifteen minutes of wandering around with the only sound he heard nearby being that of his own shoes crunching on the crushed shells, he suddenly heard it again. The sound was close by this time. Someone was indeed tapping out the dahs, dits, and dahs, an SOS distress signal.

Turning and running back the way he'd come and over two rows, he was closing in on the sound when it stopped again. Frustrated, he started tapping on the nearest container. Dit dit dit dit, quick pause, and then dit, quick pause and then dit, dah, dit, dit, quick pause and he repeated dit, dah, dit dit, dit, a final quick pause and then dah dah dah. After tapping out "hello," he paused, waiting and then he heard a responding tapping that sounded to be coming from the next row of containers over.

There was a high fence behind the row of containers he was on, so Matthew dashed back up the row he was on, turned the corner at the end of the row and then back down the row behind him. He realized that he must be on the back of the lot, the far southwestern corner of it. The last row of containers ran north to south, perpendicular to the entry aisle from the ship. These containers were stacked only two high and partially under the edge of the scruffy trees that grew behind the high fence line.

Unlike the brightly painted containers at the front of the lot, these looked older, rusted, and battered, like they'd been there awhile. Under the scruffy trees, they were probably in the shade during the afternoon hours but shade hadn't reached them yet because the sun was rising behind him as he stared at the container. Farther to his left, he heard the SOS tapping again and he zeroed in on the last container in the farthest southwestern corner of the lot.

He pulled out his cell phone to notify Justin but there were no bars. Instead his phone was endlessly searching for a signal and finding none. Was there really no signal to be had here or had someone jammed it he wondered. Frustrated, he stuffed his phone in his pocket and tapped back: dit, dah, dah, quick pause, dit, dit, dit, dit, quick pause dah, dah, dah, a longer pause and then dit, dah, quick pause, dit, dah, dit, a quick pause and then a dit tap. He waited a beat for a longer pause and then tapped dah, dit, dah, dah, a quick pause, and then dah, dah, dah, another quick pause and then dit, dit, dah. "Who are you," he'd asked in Morse Code.

When the tapping response came back, he froze in initial relief and then subsequent panic because he was alone with no earwig and no way to bring anyone quietly back to this corner of the container lot. What he'd heard gave him such a strong parental surge of energy that he hardly knew what to do with it all. He'd heard "Ariel Roberts" tapped back to him.

"Ariel?" he said softly in the general direction of what looked to be a vent in the top of the container. "Can you hear me?"

From inside he heard a whispered, "Shh, they're listening." Looking all around him for cameras but seeing none, he tapped back: dah, dah, dit, quick pause, dit, quick pause, dah, quick pause, dah, quick pause dit, dit, quick pause, dah, dit, quick pause and dah, dah, dit. The, he paused longer and added four dits, a quick pause, another dit, a quick pause, then dit, dah, dit, dit with one last quick pause before the final dit, dah, dah, dit.

Before he could make good on his promise to go get help, he was grabbed brusquely from behind as a large powerful hand was clamped over his mouth, and he was pulled backward quickly, crashing through the brush under the scruffy trees behind the container. As he was spun and slammed, not gently, with his back flush up against the back of the container. He turned to face his assailant and he found himself staring under a ball cap and into the intense blue eyes of Homicide Detective Warren Danbury.

Danbury loosened his grip on Matthew's arm, held a finger up to his lips, and motioned for Matthew to follow him. They zig-zagged through the weeds under the trees and slipped through an opening in the fence that Danbury pulled closed behind them. Down a rotting dock on the edge of the canal, they ran and darted behind an old wooden boat house that was barely still there. Crouching there,

Matthew heard the crunch of feet approaching on the shell gravel, two sets of them from what he could determine.

A very loud banging ensued, followed by a man's voice with some sort of accent that Matthew didn't recognize yelling, "Hey! What's going on in there? Who are you talking to?"

A second male voice, also heavily accented and belonging to someone who had obviously just circled the container, said, "I don't see anybody back there. The weeds are pressed down back there, though."

"Probably just wild animals, but let's check," said the first voice which was followed by a heavy metallic clanking, metal on metal, and then a loud wrenching noise, a squawking of rusted hinges protesting forced movement.

"Ow, it smells so bad in there," said the second voice, though it was muffled as if he'd covered his mouth and nose with something.

"What's going on in there? Who were you talking to?" demanded the first voice again. When there was no response he said, "Still not talking to me, huh? Have it your way."

The second voice said, "That one don't look too good."

"None of 'em look too good, but that ain't our problem. C'mon, let's get back to breakfast and the air conditioning. It's gonna be a hot one today."

Above the furious objections in his own head, Matthew heard the protest of ancient metal hinges followed by the clanging of heavy chains beating against metal, and then the retreat of feet on the crushed shells. As they walked away, the two guys were in conversation about something that was probably completely inane, thought Matthew angrily after overhearing the exchange.

"What are you doing here?" he and Danbury almost asked in unison as soon as the area was quiet again.

Matthew quickly filled Danbury in on how he'd come over by boat and who was there at the shipping yard at their disposal to help. Danbury told Matthew that he too had heard the tapping, though he wasn't certain that it was Ariel because he hadn't communicated with her directly yet. He had been working on a plan to get her out when

Matthew showed up.

"You can tell me how you got here later," said Matthew. "But there's no cell signal out here and I need to get back up there and get word to Justin that we've found her."

"In a shipping container," said Danbury simply. "I was checking it out in the alley. Then I saw two of Nelson's men. They were with a couple of thugs. I knew they were on the wrong side of this. Not undercover. I climbed in the container and hid. They moved it faster than I thought they would. I didn't want to be in it when they opened it. I got out when it was on a ship. I hid on the ship. It brought me here. And I've been looking around since. We need a strong pair of cutters to get through that," he said, changing the subject back to the urgent one at hand. "There's a padlock. On some solid old chain. That's holding the container closed."

"I've got to get back in there," Matthew said, looking around at the swampy area around the canal and the twelve-foot fence that wound its way alongside it for a distance of a couple of football fields. There had to be a break in it he knew because he had been about to go through a back gate off of the lot when he heard the tapping. Why couldn't he locate that gate from this angle, he wondered?

Part way down along the fence he noticed an outcropping of rock or broken cement that was stacked high against part of the fence that went out into the water.

"There's a gate. It opens out onto that private dock over there," said Danbury, "but the heaps of rubble there. They're on either side of the gate. Those would be treacherous to climb over. And there's a camera there. On this side. At the top of the fence."

"OK, I guess I risk going back in the way I came out."

"Yeah, that's all I've got. There are cameras everywhere. I don't know how they didn't see you."

"Me either, but let's hope that luck holds getting back in. Where will you be?"

"I'll wait behind the fence. Unless the tapping gets worse. She answered you, didn't she? Verbally."

"Yeah, in a whisper," but she was warning me that they were

listening.

"I heard you tap out that you were getting help."

"Yeah, right before you forcibly removed me from the end of the container," said Matthew, looking down and then brushing rust off the back of his shorts and dry fit shirt."

"Complain later. Let's move."

"I wasn't," started Matthew, but then realized that Danbury was already halfway back up the dock. On a second glance he wasn't sure how the thing was holding the weight of either one of them, much less both of them. He darted more quickly than he'd thought possible back along the edge of the rotting boards and into the relative safety of the weeds under the scrub trees.

"I'll be back," said Matthew to Danbury and then uttered under his breath as he'd heard his parents do on occasion, "Lord willing." And please be willing he thought as he slid the fencing aside and slipped through, closing it behind himself.

Opting to squeeze between the row of containers and the fence, stepping on whatever was down amongst the weeds underfoot that he was pretty sure he didn't want to know about, he moved behind the row of containers and emerged from the other end of them. He managed to keep from looking around and tried to keep his gaze down, nonchalantly, as he found the gate that he'd been about to go through to get out to the canal. He opened it and looked out, taking in the surroundings, and then quickly turned to make his way back the way he'd come.

That sun was quickly heating up the crushed shell walkways that he was traversing and he could feel the heat under his feet. He zigged and zagged his way back up to the row of what he assumed were office buildings, but saw nobody about outside of them. He made his way back to the yacht and climbed aboard the port side that was tied along the dock. He'd just stepped into the salon and closed the door to go in search of Justin or anyone else he could find when he heard the roar of an engine.

From the starboard side, he could see a speedboat tearing out of the port from somewhere to his right and bouncing precariously through the ocean waves, not slowing down because of them. There were three people on the speedboat. Matthew recognized one of them who was bound hand and foot and slumped sideways on a low seat as if not conscious. Dr. Rob was held up only by the guy beside him on the port side and the fiberglass wall of the boat on the starboard as the boat nearly went airborne over some of the waves.

27 ~ LAND, AIR, AND SEA

Opening the sliding doors on the starboard side of the ship, Matthew slipped through. He saw two of the dive team members in pursuit that he assumed to be part of the alpha team, although he really didn't know what that meant. Still clad in what he assumed were wet suits, they had lowered the jet ski lifts and, as soon as the jet skis hit the water, they wasted no time in chasing the fleeing boat.

Matthew's adrenaline was pumping but he had no current outlet for it. Was Justin still in with Captain DeMarco and O'Brien trying to be convinced of overwintering this behemoth of a boat? And where was everyone else?

Pulling out his phone again, Matthew saw that he had a connection on the boat and he pondered a moment before sending Justin a terse text that, if intercepted, would at least be cryptic enough to be confusing: "*Found mermaid.*" He went back inside long enough to grab his faux leather backpack containing his medical supplies and added three bottles of water, zipping them into a pocket on the outside. Bolt cutters, he thought, would there be such things on a yacht? If they were here, they'd maybe be in the engine compartment down below.

His thoughts were interrupted by what he thought sounded like a rapid backfire, and then two more bursts, from the watercraft that had just sped out of the port. The jet skis that were pursuing the speedboat wouldn't backfire, he realized. And neither, at least to the best of his knowledge, would a speedboat. Rushing back out to the rail of the yacht, he could see that the boat in the distance was bobbing across the water and still under full throttle, but it seemed out of control, like it was zagging at odd angles with the waves.

As he watched, the speedboat turned and was headed back toward the port, zigging and zagging and riding the waves it encountered perilously sideways but not slowing down. On either side of it pulled the two jet skis, both working to stay positioned alongside it. The guy on the jet ski to the port side of the boat managed to reach up and grab a gunnel rail. He held on, using the next bounce of the wave to hoist himself up over the rail and into the boat.

Matthew watched as the boat stopped, bobbling in the water, and the guy aboard handed a bundle, which he hoped was Dr. Rob, as carefully as he could in the waves to the guy on the other jet ski. As soon as the bundle was secure, the jet ski headed back in. The guy on the speedboat went back to the controls and spun the boat around, moving it toward his abandoned jet ski that Matthew had caught glimpses of bobbling between the waves. What happened next was like watching a train wreck that Matthew couldn't turn away from no matter how hard he might have tried.

The guy on the speedboat pulled up a cord from the jet ski and held onto it while he aimed the boat toward the end of the shore where there was what looked like the remains of an old dock and a jetty. In one smooth motion, as if he were a stunt man and had rehearsed it a hundred times, he jammed down the throttle on the speedboat and simultaneously flipped backward off the side of it. Matthew was torn between watching the boat careening toward the shore, the guy climbing back on the jet ski, and the approaching jet ski which he assumed carried Dr. Rob back to safety. Choosing the latter, Matthew grabbed his makeshift medical bag and ran to the stern of the yacht as the jet ski slid onto the lift.

Relieved to realize that the lift could be operated from beneath because he had no idea where the controls were on the yacht, Matthew watched as the jet ski with the diver holding Dr. Rob still slumped in front of him was rising up to him. He heard a crash and then what sounded like an explosion behind him, beyond the bow of the yacht on the point of the island but he didn't turn to look as he saw the second jet ski round the yacht and it too slid up onto an adjacent lift.

As the first lift came evenly alongside the stern of the yacht, Matthew helped the diver slide Dr. Rob onto the deck and started taking his vitals. He was thankful to find a pulse, though it was weak. Clearly the men on the speedboat were not planning to bring Dr. Rob back with them. Matthew thanked the diver for the rescue and he went to work on Dr. Rob.

Dr. Rob had all of the classic symptoms of drug overdose in addition to the weak pulse. He was still breathing, Matthew was happy to note, but his breaths were extremely shallow, ragged, and raspy. His face was clammy and pale and he had a blueish tint to his lips and fingernails. Matthew checked his pupils. In the shade of the yacht gunnel Dr. Rob's pupils should be small, but they were a mere pin prick.

Remembering the opioids that had been found on the overdose patients that were flooding the Emergency Departments the day before, Matthew reached for his backpack to retrieve the naloxone. He paused only a moment to think through what he needed to do. Knowing that naloxone is safe to administer because it has no effect on someone who doesn't have opioids in their system, he prayed as he worked that it would be what Dr. Rob needed and that he would be in time administering it.

Injecting the naloxone would mean uncapping the ends of the syringe, inserting the needle into the vial, filling it, and pushing the air out. He'd have to find the right spot on Dr. Rob's upper arm, thigh or buttocks to administer the shot and then recap the syringe. That would take longer, he thought, so he opted for the nasal injector.

Knowing that he'd only get one shot at dispensing the medication when he pushed the red button to eject the four milligrams of naloxone, he held the container carefully as he pulled the wrapping off of it. Tilting Dr. Rob's head back slightly, he inserted the tip of the dispenser into his nostril and pushed the red button until it clicked and the autoinjector did its job.

Matthew checked his watch, getting concerned, and began preparing a second dose. After nearly two minutes, Dr. Rob's breathing was better but he still wasn't responsive. Just as Matthew had pulled a syringe and vial out of his backpack, Dr. Rob tensed and said clearly, "My name is not O'Rourke!" before he slumped back to the deck of the yacht.

Startled by the sudden outburst, Matthew checked vitals again as Dr. Rob was finally beginning to stir on his own. Both his pulse and the color of his lips and fingernails were better, so he asked the diver who was still standing there, "Can you help me get him inside?"

The diver hoisted Dr. Rob, who was only slightly shorter than Matthew with the same broad shoulders and narrow hips, in his arms unaided and carried him into the salon as if he weighed nothing. Matthew guessed Dr. Rob to be nearly two hundred pounds, but he reminded himself to be impressed later.

The alpha team diver placed Dr. Rob gently on one of the leather sofas. "Prop him on his side," Matthew instructed as he followed. "Just in case." Only then did Matthew look up, as he was stepping into the salon of the yacht, to see the flames from the dock on the other side of the jetty. He could hear people shouting and a couple of men had either been on that side of the canal or had managed to cross it and were running toward the flames.

Returning his attention to his friend and mentor who had become his patient, Matthew knelt beside Dr. Rob. Checking his pulse, his coloring, and pinching the skin on the back of his hand, Matthew was happy to note some progress.

Dr. Rob opened his eyes and looked up at Matthew as he said, "Ariel?"

The diver, hovering over Dr. Rob on the other side, looked confused.

"We've found her. I was going to get her when we saw you being taken out to sea."

"Thank you," said Dr. Rob, trying to prop himself up on one elbow. "Is she OK?"

"I haven't seen her yet, but she was responsive less than thirty minutes ago," said Matthew, checking his watch again.

"Go get her, Matthew, please, go get my daughter," Dr. Rob begged weakly, his breath coming in gasps.

"OK, breathe as deeply as you can. Let's prop you up on some pillows. Can you drink some water? You're dehydrated." Matthew responded, as Dr. Rob nodded and the diver helpfully handed him two pillows and a bottle of water.

Matthew opened the water bottle and held it for Dr. Rob to drink as he explained, "It was a narcotic, a synthetic opioid, I think. You need to take it easy right now. I really shouldn't be leaving you at all but I'll put the water here within your reach. Drink that as you can. And I'll leave a second dose of naloxone, the nasal spray, just in case."

Turning to the diver, Matthew asked, "Are there any bolt cutters on board?"

"Bolt cutters? No, but how about a blow torch? Acetylene, so you can take it with you."

"That should work. Where is it?"

"I'll get it," he said as he headed for one of the doors at the stern end of the salon and disappeared down some stairs on the other side.

Matthew pulled more naloxone from his bag. Standing, he retrieved two water bottles from the wet bar, and stuffed it all into his pockets abandoning the bulky backpack. "OK," he said, "I think I have what I need to go get Ariel."

Just then the second diver appeared in the doorway. Matthew motioned him in and asked, "Do you have any medical training?"

"Army medic, another lifetime ago," the guy said. "Why, what do you need?"

"I don't know exactly yet," he said, pulling the guy out onto the walkway and sliding the door closed behind him. "But I was hoping you guys would come with me to go get at least one young woman who's been locked in one of these containers. I don't know for how long. And can we get a life flight in here? It sounded like there was more than one occupant of the container and I don't know how many or what sort of shape we'll find them in. But that boat blowing up was a great diversion. I don't know how you did that but nice job."

"Sure," said the guy as he stepped back into the salon and retrieved a SAT phone from behind the wet bar. As the second diver appeared with the blow torch, Matthew realized that he knew neither of them by name, but he'd seen what they were capable of. After looking in on Dr. Rob one last time, checking his pulse and his breathing and being marginally satisfied, he asked both of the divers, whose formal acquaintance he vowed to make later, if they'd come with him.

"Yeah, we'll gear up," said the taller one who had brought Dr. Rob back to the yacht and retrieved the torch.

"I've requested clearance to bring in at least one life flight to the island and told them we can land a chopper on the deck here," said the other diver, "Our teams will hold off any opposition to that." Both of them disappeared momentarily through one of the doors in the bow and quickly returned with shirts unbuttoned over their wetsuits; Matthew happily recognized the bulge under their arms.

Matthew partly led and partly pointed the way back down between the containers with his armed escorts, who had drawn weapons and were both crunching quickly through the crushed shells in water shoes, checking each corner before they turned it. Matthew recognized a Glock similar to his 19 and a Colt M4 carbine as they made their way through the maze of containers. Carrying his medical bag over his shoulder and the equipment and extra water bottles, Matthew had left his weapon holstered under his arm.

They saw no one, much to Matthew's relief, and he was sure that everyone else was dealing with the boat, the fire, and any occupants who might have still been in the boat. He hadn't seen what had happened to the two guys in the boat and he wasn't sure he wanted to know.

"This way," he said, making the last turn. As they made it there was gunfire ahead and all three of them ducked behind the container. Matthew was wondering if he could partially back track and come in from another direction to get to the far back container while the two divers had whoever was shooting at them busy. Deciding that was a bad idea, he watched as the taller guy was giving hand signals to the shorter one and he backtracked down the row but then turned the other way.

After a few minutes, Matthew heard "Clear!" from a few rows over and the guy in front of him stepped out, running along checking rows to the left after the taller guy had done so to the right.

"Clear!" he heard and then he dashed out, running fast in the gathering heat to the last container in the back corner.

"Danbury!" he yelled. "It's clear! We have help!" Over his shoulder, he said, "Big guy who looks like a misplaced Viking. He's with us."

Both nodded and Matthew called out to Ariel as he put the supplies down and fired up the blow torch. She didn't answer immediately, and when she did it was weak.

"Get back away from the door," he said. "It'll be hot." And it was. The heat was intense and he could feel the sweat pouring off his face by the time he'd cut through one of the links in the chain. The shorter guy reached in with a metal rod that he'd picked up from somewhere and knocked the chain, repeatedly, pulling and twisting on the hot metal with the rod until he had it separated and then unlooped from the handles on the outside of the container. He pried the doors open a crack with the bar.

Matthew carefully reached down lower and yanked to open the doors that were still screeching in protest. Danbury had materialized beside him and he helped to wrench them both open. What Matthew saw when the doors were open was both deeply disturbing and relieving at the same time. Ariel, her long hair matted and dirty, was propped up against the inside wall. She was in her underwear, either by choice because of the heat or for more nefarious reasons that Matthew didn't want to stop to contemplate.

He dashed in, scooped her up, and carried her into the edge of the tree cover. The taller diver pulled off his shirt, handing it to Matthew to put under Ariel before he joined Danbury and the other diver who rushed in and started pulling the other three women out of the container. From the smell of the container, at least one of them had not made it, Matthew knew, but he would let the sorrow over not being able to save them all wash over him later. For now he began with Ariel and the triage effort. She was severely dehydrated but still responsive as he held her head and tried to get her to take small sips of the water so that her body wouldn't reject it and throw it all back up again. Danbury took over that effort so that Matthew could check the others.

Another of the women was semi-responsive so he started the same process with her until the diver who said he'd been an army medic took over. A third young woman appeared to be in worse shape, her breathing swallow and her pulse weak.

"We can't get water in her this way, we need an IV drip," said

Matthew. The diver scooped her up and started to run with her back through the maze of containers. Matthew dreaded checking on the fourth woman because he already knew that she was the source of the stench. Her body was emaciated. Her eyes were frozen open staring, unseeingly, at the sky from where she'd been placed on her back on the ground. With a shudder Matthew gently closed her eyes and returned to the other two who were lying side-by-side. Ariel's head was in Danbury's lap and he was still giving her little bits of water and Matthew thought he'd never seen Danbury so intensely focused on gentleness and careful care. Another thing he'd contemplate later.

As he checked the woman beside Ariel, he said, "She's going into shock. Stop with the water. We need to get them both back to the yacht. He quickly splashed cold water on Ariel's face and neck to prevent her from shock. Danbury glanced over at the other woman. Matthew just shook his head.

Danbury gently lowered Ariel's head to the ground as he stood up. He bent over and scooped up the young woman who was going into shock into his arms and as he was sprinting off with her back to the yacht, Matthew called after him, "Cover her up with blankets when you get her there. Ask Dr. Rob what else she needs."

Another thing Matthew decided to remember to marvel over later was how these guys were both running at a full sprint in the intense heat carrying at least a hundred pounds. Matthew turned to Ariel and said, "OK, I know you can't walk, so I'm going to carry you."

As he knelt with his backpack already in place, he pulled her into a sitting position, leaning her up against him, while he put the shirt on her that she'd been lying on, buttoning it in a couple of places. This was Dr. Rob's daughter and she was stable enough that he could bring her back to her father covered, with that much dignity, and not be exposed to anyone else.

The other diver glanced over at the young woman who had perished in the container and said, with troubled eyes, "I've got her. You go ahead."

"Adrianna," said Ariel softly, on a quiet sob. "Her name is Adrianna. I think she's Polish."

"OK," the remaining diver answered quietly. "I'll bring Adrianna."

As Matthew scooped up Ariel, she tried to put her arms around his neck but they fell back across her chest as he looked down at her and said, "It's OK. I've got you. I'm not going to try to run with you, but I've got you."

As he started at a brisk walk back toward the yacht, Matthew could hear gunfire ahead as he carried Ariel back through the maze of containers, pausing to look before walking from one row to the next. He had almost reached the yacht when he saw first Danbury and then the other diver who had circled back for him open fire on some unseen foe behind the office buildings. The diver, who had apparently put Adrianna down somewhere behind him, sprinted forward and maneuvered into a spot where he too could see what was happening.

Then, Matthew saw Justin appear momentarily from behind the right side of the row of office buildings and throw something down to the left side. Whatever that something was, it exploded in a blinding flash just after the diver off to Matthew's right yelled, "Duck!"

Matthew turned backward, pushing Ariel up against the container and covering her with his body. "Are you OK?" he asked, just as the diver was yelling, "Run!"

He saw a slight nod from Ariel, and then he too took off at a sprint toward the waiting yacht. Through the dust he saw Justin dash out from behind the building with two other heavily armed men flanking him. They ran to the end of the building where Justin had just thrown the flash bomb and Matthew heard more shots fired.

Matthew ran across the opening on the crushed shells through the smoke and dust with Ariel, past Danbury and the taller diver who were protecting the yacht, up the gangplank, and through the sliding door into the salon. Dr. Rob was partially propped there on one of the leather sofas, and Matthew gently placed Ariel beside him, offering her more water, which she tentatively sipped as Dr. Rob wrapped his arms around her and sobbed openly.

Matthew stepped back, reveling in the fact that he had just run probably a hundred yards carrying a hundred pounds himself and he figured adrenaline could do amazing things, but that was nothing compared to the sight of a father and daughter reunited. Dr. Rob reached for the water bottle and took over offering Ariel small sips.

Apparently, thought Matthew, the doctor had taken over from the father, at least momentarily.

He checked the other two women, covering them both with the blankets that had made it as far as the couches they were on, but not as far as to be covering them before the shooting started. He assumed that Danbury and the taller diver had dashed out to protect the occupants of the yacht. He checked their vitals and both women were still breathing and had a pulse, though one was weaker than the other and her breathing more shallow.

He propped up their feet with more pillows and knew that monitoring them was the best that he could do until help arrived with the needed IV fluids. He heard a few more shots outside. Everything became eerily quiet until the taller diver strode back in, over to the wet bar, and pulled out the satellite phone. After he said a single word, he put it back again.

That single word, "Clear," which was followed by the sound of the chopper blades as it approached and then landed on the outside deck of the yacht were some of the happiest Matthew had heard. He dashed out to meet the paramedics, identified himself, and then identified the two girls who were the worst off.

After the first two women had been carried out and loaded, a paramedic stuck his head back in the salon and told Matthew and Dr. Rob that there was one more spot available on the chopper.

"But there's another one waiting to come in that can carry three more people," said the diver with the SAT phone. "They sent two, but we haven't suffered any injuries on our teams, so it's yours if you want it."

Dr. Rob looked up at Matthew and said, "She's stable and I'm not going to be separated from her again. Not ever if I can help it."

"OK," said Matthew, who went out on the deck to tell the waiting paramedic to go with the two patients already on board.

"Where to?" yelled the paramedic over the noise of the helicopter.

"Mount Hermon," yelled Matthew, remembering the helpful ED nurse, Judy Crew.

"OK," called the paramedic, ducking and climbing back on board.

The doors closed behind him.

Matthew's heart halfway sank as he watched the chopper clear the deck and then dart off and disappear quickly, heading west. After it was a speck on the horizon, Matthew could hear the welcome sound of more beating blades and he returned to the salon, asking the diver to help Dr. Rob out as he scooped up Ariel. Ducking under the blades, he didn't wait for the paramedics to come to him. He laid Ariel gently on a stretcher, identified himself, and started barking out orders for the IV drip that she so desperately needed. Matthew was usually very soft spoken, but in a medical crisis, he was also quite capable of taking charge to care for patients.

"That's all," yelled the diver as he approached with Dr. Rob's arm around his shoulder and handed him off to Matthew. That was welcome news, thought Matthew, that neither Justin nor any of his team had been injured in the shooting match. Nodding his thanks to the diver and realizing that he couldn't begin to thank him properly, Matthew put Dr. Rob's arm around his shoulder and walked him up into the chopper and over to the stretcher next to Ariel. He slid it over before locking it down, so that father and daughter were hand in hand, side by side.

Against Dr. Rob's weak objections, Matthew ordered an IV fluid drip for him too before settling into a jump seat beside them. The man was clearly dehydrated and the extra fluids would help fight off the after effects of the drugs.

"Where to?" the pilot asked Matthew.

Matthew glanced at Ariel for only a fraction of a second before he responded resolutely, "Grace Hospital, south of Miami. There's a helipad just beside the Emergency Department."

"Yeah, I know it. OK," said the pilot.

"I'll call it in," said the co-pilot as he flipped switches and pushed buttons overhead. The hatch door closed and the paramedics worked over their patients while the chopper lifted smoothly into the air and headed west.

28 ~ AFTERMATH

The helicopter arrived on the Miami shore at Grace hospital in only half hour or so by Matthew's estimation. He had finally relaxed, leaning back against the side of the chopper in a jump seat, allowing the paramedics to tend to Dr. Rob and Ariel, neither of whom were in imminent danger with the IV fluid drips doing their job now. Matthew knew that the adrenaline surge he'd felt earlier had entirely abated and left his body exhausted, but his mind was still racing with all that had happened since before sun up and everything he had yet to piece together.

Smiling at the two stretchers, Matthew was entirely thankful to have found both father and daughter in time and to reunite them. As the chopper touched down and the paramedics unlocked the stretchers, raising them and readying them to roll off, Matthew felt like he'd just come out of hand-to-hand combat battle as he rose, picked up his backpack, and steadied himself to exit the chopper with them. He followed the stretchers off the helicopter and into the Emergency Department entrance.

A different security guard than any he'd seen so far was at the desk as the double doors swung open in front of them and they made their way down the long corridor into the Emergency Department. Dr. Mayer stepped out from behind the main desk to check on the incoming patients. She looked momentarily confused and then the dawn of recognition must have struck as she realized who Dr. Rob and Matthew were and surmised who Ariel must be by association.

"You found her!" she said, pulling the charted notes that the paramedics had begun from the stretcher and checking them. "Vitals look good. Let's put her down there on the end to give her some privacy and we'll check her more thoroughly in just a minute. And him," she said indicating Dr. Rob, checking his chart, and looking confused. "Opioids?" she asked.

"Fentanyl, we think. He was drugged," supplied Matthew. "And nearly killed. Put him right beside her if you want to keep him on the gurney," he said to the paramedics as they pushed them both down the hallway to switch the patients to hospital gurneys and retrieve their stretchers.

"Taking over my ED, Dr. Paine?" she asked in amusement.

"Just that back corner. Thanks, Dr. Mayer. They've been through a lot," he added over his shoulder as he followed the stretchers and he saw a nurse heading their way, probably awaiting orders on what blood tests to run and what to look for.

Ariel was looking better after the first bag of fluids and she tried to prop up on one elbow to see her dad, so Matthew raised the head of the bed they'd just moved her into and did the same with Dr. Rob's so that they could talk.

"Thank you for finding me, Daddy. I told them you would."

"But I didn't," he responded. "Matthew did."

"You did most of the work yourself," Matthew deflected the praise back to Ariel. "That was smart thinking to tap out that SOS signal. How did you learn Morse Code?"

"Daddy taught me when he bought his first sailboat. That and how to tie all sorts of knots. I'd been tapping since the day before, hoping that someone would hear who knew what it was. I knew I couldn't scream or yell because the container was bugged and they'd just come and shoot me full of more drugs."

"Thank you both then," she conceded after a moment's hesitation. Then her features darkened and Matthew could see her face cloud over with concentration and concern for all of the unasked questions.

"Daddy," she said. "Gavin?"

"He's upstairs in the ICU. He's had a rough time but he's recovering. I'm assuming that's why Matthew told the pilot to bring us here," he turned to Matthew.

"It is. Gavin is conscious and recovering," affirmed Matthew, watching the relief spread across the pretty young face. It was what she'd been scared to ask, he realized. She was afraid to ask if Gavin had been killed or was still missing. They hadn't, he realized to his dismay, thought to give her that update.

"When can I see him?" she immediately wanted to know. "I need to see Gavin. And Lanie. Is she here?" As they shook their heads no, she asked "Is she OK? She must have been so worried too."

"You can go see Gavin when they release you but honestly, sweetheart, they're probably going to want to keep you at least overnight for observation. You're looking better now, but I think you had a closer call than you know. They'll want to run blood work and keep a watch on you for a while," said Dr. Rob.

"I'm feeling better. Can I at least see Lanie? She can come to me, right?"

"Tell you what," said Matthew. "As soon as they assign you a room, I'll go get her."

The nurse returned, jotting notes on the chart and explaining that Ariel needed more fluids. To restore her sodium and potassium levels, she explained, they'd be adding those electrolytes to the IV drip that the nurse began changing out as she spoke.

Dr. Rob and Matthew looked at each other and hid their smiles as both had already told Ariel the same thing, but the nurse obviously knew nothing of their occupations. After that next bag of fluids, Matthew was betting she'd feel much better, but he knew she'd need something a bit more nutritional too before she fully regained her strength.

"When was the last time you've eaten anything?" Matthew asked her.

"I don't know, a couple of days, I think," she said.

"Days?" asked the nurse, turning in alarm as she finished adjusting the machine that controlled the saline drip. "We'll get your blood work run and then get you some chicken broth. We'll start there," she said, rushing off to go put that plan in motion.

Matthew quietly slipped around Dr. Rob's bed, unlocking the wheel stops, and slid it over next to Ariel's. The nurses could come and go from the other side of her where the IV drip was, he thought, but Ariel needed her father right now and her father most assuredly needed to be close to her too.

"I'm going to go make some phone calls," said Matthew, and he slipped out quietly to ask the nurse to watch for signs of trauma, giving her a very quick summary of what Ariel had experienced. He still didn't know exactly what the young woman had been through, but he was certain that none of it was pleasant.

In the Emergency Department entrance, Matthew paced back and forth in the long room and called Lanie first. "I'm sure there are things she'll want you to bring her," Matthew told her after waiting for the initial jubilant shrieking to die down in his ear. "Probably clothes and a hairbrush and whatever else is part of her daily routine. She's going to need you now, Lanie. She's been through an ordeal. She and Dr. Rob both have."

Gayle Blevins was next on the call list. Matthew asked her to tell Gavin that Ariel was safe in the same hospital and she'd be up to see him as soon as she was released to do so.

He'd have loved to check in with his office but he knew his staff would ply him with questions, none of which he was prepared to answer yet, and he didn't want to interrupt their afternoon routines anyway. Instead he texted Leo to check on Max and was happy to hear that they were getting along well and Leo was still loving having him there.

Next he stepped outside to FaceTime Cici. It was evening in London, but not yet late and she answered after the second ring, "Matthew! I'm so happy to see you! Where are you? What happened? Are you safe? Did you find them? Are they OK?"

As she was exhausting the list of questions that she was plying him with all at once, he meandered out to the A-frame swing under the edge of the trees where Lanie and Dr. Rob had been sitting earlier and started to answer all of her questions, though guardedly because he wasn't yet sure what he was cleared to tell her. After many assurances that he'd continue to be careful and that he was headed home probably in a couple of days when Ariel and Dr. Rob could travel, they disconnected the call and Matthew felt a hollow feeling inside. He knew that he should feel relief and thankfulness, but something just felt empty.

He picked the phone back up and called his mom. That's what he was missing, he realized. He'd helped to reunite father and daughter and girlfriend and boyfriend soon too, but Cici was on the other side of the ocean he'd just been out on. His parents, his sister, and his little niece were over seven hundred miles away. But maybe he would make it home to spend Sunday afternoon with them in their usual family ritual of going out to lunch after church. Maybe, he thought hopefully.

He called his mom to thank her for the support and the prayers. Jackie answered and was elated to hear that all was well. She just said, "Thank God! I've been praying for you Matthew. We all have." She promised to tell his family the good news and to call Dr. Rob's mom to give her the update. They disconnected so that Matthew could get back to the list of things he still needed to attend to.

Tired of communicating in that moment, Matthew was wondering where Danbury and Justin were, if Justin was headed back to Miami and, if so when that would be. He knew that there must be a lot of loose ends to tie up and detangle as they sorted out who had done exactly what and with whom. He was happy to have escaped ahead of that process, but he was sure he'd be questioned and he wasn't excited about the possibility of having to testify.

Realizing that neither Ariel nor Dr. Rob had cell phones and that he was hungry, he went first in search of the café where he picked up a sandwich for himself and one for Dr. Rob along with two water bottles. Matthew hoped that father and daughter had savored their private time together for now, and he wandered around to the back corner of the ED where he found Ariel asleep, wrapped in Dr. Rob's arms with his head propped gently on the top of hers.

As Dr. Rob looked up over her head and smiled a tired but happy and satisfied smile, Matthew noticed their profiles for the first time. Their noses were shaped identically. Both had just the slightest upturn to the tip that gave them both a youthful look of surprise, and it enhanced Dr. Rob's boyish grin, which Matthew was thrilled to see again.

"We're going up to a room soon," whispered Dr. Rob, kissing Ariel gently on her still tangled and dirty hair. "Room 345. It's a larger corner so we can be together. They're not admitting me, but they'll let me stay."

"They're not admitting you?"

"No, they seem happy with my vitals. I guess the naloxone did the trick. Any idea why they snatched me? I mean, why me?"

"Not really," said Matthew, quietly. "They didn't say anything or ask you anything that gave you any idea?"

"I was drugged pretty quickly after I was forced into the car, so it's all hazy. They just kept telling me to stop with the aliases, that they knew who I was and what I'd done, and they kept calling me O'Rourke. That much, I clearly remember."

"Yeah, you said something about not being O'Rourke when you first came to. But that doesn't make any sense. O'Rourke was the guy who snatched you, so why would they call you by his name?"

"I wish I knew!" hissed Dr. Rob, still trying to whisper over Ariel's head.

"OK, you relax and rest up right now. I'm going to go get Lanie," said Matthew quietly, putting the sandwich and water bottle for Dr. Rob on the rolling tray table beside him. "She'll know what to pack for Ariel, but what do you want me to bring you? I'm going back to our hotel first because I really need a shower."

"Will they let you in my room?" asked Dr. Rob. "I don't have my key or my wallet or anything," he grimaced.

"They will," said Matthew resolutely and, in that moment he knew that he would be getting into Dr. Rob's room to bring him anything he needed, one way or another.

"I'll bring what you need and be back in a couple of hours," he said and slipped back out again.

From the Emergency Department, he ordered a Rydz car and stepped outside to eat his sandwich and down a water bottle, then waited impatiently for his ride to arrive. Logistically, the first thing he needed to do was to get Danbury's rented SUV from the street outside the alley. Other than Gayle's rental car, which he didn't want to commandeer, it was the only one they had. He'd pulled up the street address for the brasserie, gave that to the Rydz driver, and then settled in for the ride.

Lost in his own thoughts, he didn't fall asleep, but neither was he paying any attention to where they were going. He was startled as he realized that the guy driving the car could have taken him anywhere. As that unsettling thought flitted through his mind, he saw the brasserie just ahead and he had no idea how he'd gotten there.

Climbing out of the Rydz car with his backpack and checking to be sure he'd left nothing in the car, Matthew straightened up and glanced across the street to a sight he hadn't anticipated. Danbury was crossing the street from the waterfront farther south toward the SUV.

Matthew thanked the driver and quickly walked that way.

Turning, Danbury said, "Doc! It's good to see you here."

"You too," said Matthew. "I was just coming to get this. We're down to the one vehicle."

"What happened to the car?"

"Which one?" asked Matthew. "I went through two of them yesterday."

"What?" demanded Danbury. "What happened?"

"Where are you headed? I need to go back to the hotel to shower and pack a few things for Dr. Rob and then get Lanie and take her back to Grace Hospital."

"I was just going back to the hotel. For now same thing. I need a shower and a change of clothes. Badly. Then I need to get downtown. I reported the two cops who were down here," he said, motioning to the alleyway. "With the thugs. I didn't think they were undercover. They weren't. I went over Nelson's head to report it. He's not going to like that. I don't think he's involved. But I had to be certain. I couldn't take any chances."

"Could you drop me by the rental car agency near the Miami International Airport?" asked Matthew, realizing that was the first order of business since Danbury would need the SUV.

"Yeah, sure Doc."

"I need to get another car for a couple of days," said Matthew, climbing into the SUV. "It'll probably be a couple before Dr. Rob and Ariel are released for travel. And then I expect we'll have to arrange air transport for Gavin because I doubt that Ariel will leave him here and go home. And Dr. Rob won't leave her here to go home. You get the picture."

"Yeah, I get it."

"About those thugs you saw with Nelson's officers in the alley," Matthew began.

"Yeah?"

"Why didn't you tell me? Text me? Something? I thought they had you too. And then they forcibly took Dr. Rob at gun point. Until Justin showed up, I had no idea how to find any of you!"

"I thought you'd be safer that way, Doc. They'd obviously been bought off. I wasn't certain that they hadn't seen me. I didn't know how high their involvement went. Or what they'd do. I had hoped that they'd leave you alone. With me out of the picture."

"Safer? I've been nearly run off a bridge, shot at, and had Dr. Rob abducted right under my nose at gun point. How is that safer?"

"They tried to run you off a bridge? And shot at you?"

"All in one day! First, they tried to run Dr. Rob and me off the Brickell Avenue bridge and wrecked the first rental car we had. After that didn't work, they shot up the second rental car, I think as a distraction. If they'd wanted to kill us, I'm sure we'd both be dead. Then they took Dr. Rob at gun point, but I still have no idea why. He said they kept calling him O'Rourke, but Daniel O'Rourke was the one who took him!"

"I heard about Dr. Rob. After you were transported out. Nobody seems to know why. Why they took him. Except maybe it was mistaken identity. One theory is that they were after you."

"Me? Why me? Why would they be after either of us?"

"I don't know. I hope we'll find that out. Some people are being transported in the morning. From Freeport back here. Some are citizens of the Bahamas. And that's where it gets complicated. My guess? It'll be a while before it's all sorted out."

While they were en route, Matthew called the car rental agency and gave them what felt like everything but his shoe size in order to get a car reserved. Having covered that base, he relaxed for the rest of the ride and was just settling in when he got a text from Justin that read, *"Hey, you up for drinks tonight? At the hotel bar. Teddy's buying the first round."*

"Don't know about that. I'm tired. On the way back to Hialeah. Then I'll get Lanie. Then back to the hospital," Matthew texted back. He didn't bother to explain the steps in between or who Lanie was because Justin seemed to know everything about the trip to Miami and all of the people involved already.

"Bring Danbury," responded Justin.

"I'll ask. What time?"

"Back by 7. So, 7:30."

"OK, I'll try to stay awake that long."

"Hey, Danbury, you want to go have drinks with Justin's team tonight? He said to bring you. They're at a hotel just down from the alley where we just left."

"Are they back? I hitched a ride out. They were still sorting things when I left. I'm glad that paperwork isn't mine. Not this time at least."

"They should be back by seven. They're talking seven thirty or so and somebody named Teddy is buying the first round. Justin texted that like I should know who Teddy is."

"You don't?" asked Danbury. As Matthew shot him a rare look of extreme annoyance, Danbury said, "He's the taller guy in the wet suit."

"Oh," said Matthew. "The ex-Army medic. It was on my mental check list to ask their names. I'd like to thank them personally. Did you see how they rescued Dr. Rob?"

"I must have missed that," said Danbury, who had been at the back of the lot of containers at the time.

"They looked like stunt guys on the jet skis. If I hadn't seen it myself, I might not believe it."

"Huh," was all Danbury said in response.

"The drinks?"

"Yeah, if I'm done downtown in time. That's going to be a mess. Dirty cop is a serious accusation. And going over Nelson's head to report it. That's serious too."

"OK, well, you know where we'll be when."

*****

After picking up the rental car, Matthew parked it in the hotel lot and stopped by the front desk on the way in to tell them that he needed access to Dr. Rob's room. After explaining the situation three times to three different people, he was running out of patience and he was sure that it showed. Wearied of being reasonable, he'd told the third guy, who was apparently the senior manager, that the room adjoined his and he'd pick the lock if they didn't let him in.

The guy smirked at him and Matthew didn't understand why, until he explained, "There are no knobs with locks to pick on the insides of the doors, Sir."

Credit card, kick it in, dynamite, whatever, thought Matthew though he didn't say so aloud. He just knew that he was getting in that room one way or another to get Dr. Rob the things he needed.

"Wait," said Matthew, as his mind went back to that thought about the credit card. Dr. Rob didn't have one. His wallet and cell phone and everything he'd been carrying was missing, having been taken from him after he was abducted. "What I really need to do is to switch his bill to my credit card and just check him out entirely. His wallet is missing and he won't have the credit card that he used to hold the rooms with to pay for them anyway."

"That's highly unusual," said the manager, but Matthew figured this would be the point of capitulation because getting the bill for the room paid, one way or another would be the top priority. "But these are unusual circumstances, so I suppose we'll make an exception," the manager conceded.

Matthew handed over his credit card and they ran it for all three rooms, including Danbury's, that had previously been held under Dr. Rob's credit card. Apparently satisfied with that transaction, the manager then instructed the front desk clerk, the first person to whom

Matthew had explained the situation, to escort him up to Dr. Rob's room and log what was removed from it in case there was any issue later.

Turning toward the elevator after putting his credit card back in his wallet, Matthew was checking his watch and trying to determine if he'd have time to meet Justin for those drinks when the manager interrupted his thoughts, "Sir? Do you want your laundry? It's back from the cleaners," he said before Matthew had taken more than two steps away from the desk.

"Sure, that would be great," said Matthew, returning to the desk as the manager handed the package over to him.

The elevator ride was silent and the clerk merely said "Sir" as he opened the door to Dr. Rob's room with a key card and then stepped aside to allow Matthew to enter the room. After adding the toiletries from the bathroom to Dr. Rob's still packed suitcase and checking drawers and the night stand to be sure he hadn't missed anything, Matthew returned to his own room and showered hurriedly. Happily relinquishing the silky red boxers for his boxer briefs, he put on his own clean clothes, packed the laundry bag with Dr. Rob's necessities, then left to pick up Lanie.

As soon as he drove up, Lanie appeared on the upper balcony with a huge smile, carrying a duffle bag already packed. He slid out of the car to see if she needed help, but before he could get to the bottom of the steps, she'd bounded down them, dropped the bag at her feet, and hugged him excitedly.

"You found her and brought her back! Thank you!"

"I had a lot of help. She and Dr. Rob are both back safely."

"I can't wait to see her!" she exclaimed, snatching up the bag, throwing it in the backseat, and climbing into the passenger side before Matthew had taken the ten steps back to the car. She programmed the hospital address into her phone and told him the roads looked clear on the route they'd taken previously, and then proceeded to chatter incessantly all the way to the hospital, telling Matthew lots of anecdotes about childhood escapades with Ariel and Dr. Rob.

Matthew parked and walked in with Lanie. Together they found

Room 345. He felt almost the same thrill watching Lanie and Ariel embrace and cling to each other as he had when he'd handed Ariel to Dr. Rob. Almost, though nothing topped the father and daughter reunion. He quietly handed over the laundry bag containing the things he'd gathered to Dr. Rob and said, "I have the rest of your things in my room, so I can bring whatever else you need."

"This will be fine. Thank you, Matthew," said Dr. Rob after peering into the bag. The room was crowded, Matthew realized, as he noticed Gayle Blevins standing by the window looking out over the bay.

"Lanie," Matthew said, touching her on the shoulder, "I can come back and get you in a few hours but I'm going to get dinner and some drinks with the guys who got us out of Freeport. I can text when I'm on my way back."

"That's OK," said Lanie, wiping a tear from her cheek as she looked up at him and assured him that if there wasn't room for her to stay the night too she'd get a Rydz car back to Hialeah.

"Or you're welcome to stay with me," said Gayle, turning from the window. "I have an extra double bed in my room, if I go back to spend the night there. It's close by. You can have the room for the night if I don't."

That seemed to satisfy everyone so after he'd said his goodbyes for the evening and promised to be back in the morning, Matthew slipped out of the room and down the hallway. He checked his watch again and realized that with Miami traffic, he'd be a little late but he was hungry and for something other than a crepe.

Struggling to remember what the rental car looked like, he managed to locate it as he heard his stomach grumble in protest. Making his way back to the hotel where he'd spent the night before, Matthew easily found a spot to park much to his amazement. Friday nights must not be busy ones for the hotel, he thought in surprise. Finding the bar and grille area was easy enough because he could follow the noise, the sound of voices and laughter. As he walked in, Danbury, who had obviously managed to free himself up in time, waved him over.

"Silkies!" called out the guy that Matthew had now learned was named Teddy, but he wasn't sure who the guy was talking to except that he seemed to be holding a beer aloft in Matthew's direction.

29 ~ DETANGLING

"Silkies?" repeated Matthew, confused.

"Just go with it," said Danbury, who had appeared beside him. "It's a male bonding thing. Like a rite of passage. They've accepted you into their group. When they give you an embarrassing nickname."

"Embarrassing?" Matthew repeated under his breath, but Danbury had already moved back around the table. With an eyebrow raised, Matthew glanced at Justin and just laughed good naturedly.

"They had to come up with something for you," Justin said, shrugging. "I told them the story about the clean clothes that you found in the gift shop."

"Ah," said Matthew, catching the reference to the red silk boxers he'd worn that day. "I see."

"It could be worse. Believe me, it could always be worse!" said Justin. "Ask him why they call him Teddy. And you've met Rex too," he motioned at the other guy who'd been in the wet suit earlier that day.

"Get the man a beer!" said Teddy, holding his aloft again. "Any guy who can rescue a damsel in distress wearing red silk boxers deserves a drink!"

"Thanks, Teddy," said Matthew, blushing a bit despite himself because the whole bar and grille now knew that Matthew had been wearing red silk boxers and half of them turned to glance his way. The female half, though Matthew failed to notice that detail.

"And what I'd really like is a thick steak, medium rare, a loaded baked potato, and a side salad. You think I could find that on the menu here?"

Teddy, Danbury, and the guy whose name Matthew now knew was Rex all burst out laughing.

"Yeah, yeah, we know," said Justin. "We do that a lot."

"Let me guess," said Matthew as he understood what was so funny. "Justin just ordered the same thing?"

"I did," he said, clapping Matthew on the back. "It's not Derrick's back home, but it's pretty good. I missed lunch so mine is long gone." Justin settled back in at the high-top table and picked up his beer.

"OK, that'll work," said Matthew, waving to a server as he settled in at the large high-top table between Danbury and Justin as Teddy handed him a beer from the bar and joined them again.

After he'd placed his order, Matthew turned back to the group. "In all seriousness, I did want to thank you guys for going after that boat and bringing Dr. Rob back this morning. That looked like something out of a movie with stunt guys."

"Oh yeah, we're stunt guys, all right!" laughed Rex.

"They wish!" added Teddy, joining in the laughter.

These guys had obviously started their drinking process some time ago, Matthew surmised. Work hard, play hard, he thought, though he was hoping to get back to a serious conversation eventually because there were so many things he still wanted to know. He figured that Ariel had been snatched so quickly and forcefully because somebody on the dark web had ordered a petite redhead and Daniel O'Rourke had messed up twice and brought in women whose hair was only dyed red, and one of them bright stop-sign-red, at that.

He also figured that the easiest way to transport people, drugs, and weapons into or out of the United States was by private boat over to Freeport where questions weren't as frequently asked and customer service for yacht owners was key.

What he still wanted to know was why Sebastian had been shot, why Dr. Rob had been snatched, why he and Dr. Rob had been targeted at all, and if all of the players had been rounded up. If they had not, he very much wanted to know who was still at large. Also important on his list of questions was how the two women who were transported out of Freeport ahead of Ariel were recovering.

He tried, amidst the general revelry, to ask at least that last question and he learned that the two others were at Mt. Hermon Medical Center fighting for their lives and neither had bounced back quickly. There was still some question about who one of the women was. Both had been heavily drugged and both were, as he already knew, severely dehydrated. One had regained some semblance of consciousness but she was disoriented and couldn't answer basic questions, including her name. The other was still in the ICU.

That was all Matthew figured he'd learn for the moment and he settled in with his steak dinner and a tall glass of water before a second tankard of beer. He wanted to be sure he could still drive back to Hialeah. Justin it seemed had other ideas about how he'd spend his evening, Matthew thought. Justin didn't have to drive anywhere. The guy slept very little and was joining the others in drinking a lot. Matthew just marveled because he'd never been sure how his best friend managed any of that and still did the job he did, whatever that was exactly.

After another round of beer, Matthew was ready to call it a night. Justin said, "Hey man, you can bunk with me. Your Miami t-shirt is still up in the room."

"You don't' have a spare pair of the red silk boxers on you, do you, Silkies?" chimed in Teddy.

"No more silk boxers, no," said Matthew, taking the ribbing happily from one of the guys who'd rescued Dr. Rob from certain death. "But if you want some of your own, I can show you where to find them. They're right around the corner there," said Matthew, pointing, as they roared with laughter.

"Yeah," said Rex. "You should get you a pair of those. Then you can be a silk Teddy Bear!"

"Teddy Bear?" asked Matthew.

"That's where the nickname came from," said Rex. "I'll tell you the story but you have to stay and have another round."

Matthew put his hands up in mock surrender, "I'll stay if you'll answer a few more questions while you're at it," he said.

Danbury excused himself, begging off on the next round because he said he had to get up early in the morning and get back down to the precinct to complete more paperwork.

"So do we," said Rex. "But none of us is driving tonight," he added, putting his drink down a little harder than he'd apparently meant to as the beer sloshed out onto the table top.

"Good thing too," added Teddy and they all laughed, though Matthew was sure that the beer they'd already consumed made the timing of that gaff far funnier than it otherwise would have been.

As they were starting to tell Matthew about how Teddy had earned his nickname, Jett Johnson walked over to their table, "Mind if I join you?" he asked.

"FBI? Here? At this table?" joked Rex, albeit quietly to his credit, Matthew thought. "I don't know, man."

Justin slid out the chair that Danbury had vacated and Johnson sat down and hadn't managed to slide up to the table when Teddy raised his glass and much more loudly said, "Bring our friend here a beer!"

Johnson didn't decline, but Matthew saw an opportunity to learn something from the only person at the table who wasn't already at least tipsy. Justin had either consumed less or held it better because he joined the conversation with Johnson when Matthew started asking some of his questions.

"It's complicated," Johnson started off, looking to Justin for a nod of approval to share anything with Matthew.

"I guess it is one big tangle of confusion right now. Do you know what is known? There's obviously smuggling involved, and it was being run through the Bahamas from off shore here in Miami by boat, I'm assuming," said Matthew.

"Yeah, drugs coming in and weapons going out, a dangerous enough combination before you add in the people," confirmed Johnson. "Somehow their chain of handing off their goods got disrupted. Somebody in the middle messed up so that people met people who weren't supposed to know about each other. That's what got the guy you called Sebastian killed. That's not his real name and he wasn't an American either. But that's all I can share with you about that."

"Are all of the people involved in custody?" asked Matthew.

"That's some wishful thinking right there, my friend," said Johnson, taking a swig of the beer that had just been placed in front of him. "Not even close. We got most of two chains from what we think is about mid-level down. But that's not all of the supply or distribution chains that were operating, not nearly."

"What we did do," added Justin. "We did shut them down from operating through the Bahamas. They likely have other channels for the weapons and the drugs, but not the people. We closed the lid tightly on trafficking people, at least out of the United States."

"What do you mean, at least out of the United States?" asked Matthew, picking up on the nuance of what Justin had said.

"Potentially through some of the Caribbean islands, like Aruba where one of the other women was snatched, Americans could still be trafficked."

"One of the others we found in the container was an American who had been snatched while visiting Aruba?" asked Matthew.

"Right," said Justin. "We found identification for two women in one of the Freeport Shipping and Trading Company offices. One of those, we're not sure who it belongs to. It wasn't Ariel's or any of the others in that container. But the other, we're pretty sure it belongs to the woman in the ICU of Mount Hermon Medical Center."

"There might be more information coming," said Johnson. "We're getting computer files and boxes of records regarding the American dealings shipped to us from Freeport this week. The authorities there are overwhelmed and happy to hand those records over to us to work just as soon as they sort them all out. I think Justin left a couple of key resources behind to help with that effort."

"We did," agreed Justin. "After we broke up the ring in Freeport, the people there were all too happy to start talking and pointing fingers. They were just trying to make a living after hurricanes had destroyed much of the island and the tourist industry had tapered off.

That was their story. They claimed not to know a lot about what was going on, though they clammed up when we asked about the women in the container. They had to have known about them but chose to look the other way."

"Why did they take Dr. Rob?" asked Matthew.

"The guys who were taking him out on the boat from the port aren't here to answer that question," Justin said, gesturing at Teddy and Rex, who were laughing hysterically over something and not paying him any attention. "Speculation is that it was mistaken identity."

"Who did they think he was?" asked Matthew.

"More speculation? Daniel O'Rourke. They thought that either you or Dr. Rob had to be Daniel O'Rourke."

"Danny Boy?" asked Matthew, amazed. "He looks nothing like either of us. And he was the one who took Dr. Rob!"

"Those guys weren't Americans," said Justin. "They were Middle Eastern of some description, though we don't know exactly where they were from yet. I think they were the ones you described earlier as looking like the Blues Brothers. One was taller with a longer more angular face and the other shorter and chunkier with a rounder face. We've been told that they wore black, usually wore dark sunglasses, and often wore black hats."

"You're saying that to people of a totally different ethnic background, we all look alike?"

"Something like that," said Justin.

"But Daniel O'Rourke was the guy who took Dr. Rob at gunpoint and then I guess handed him off to them. How did they not know that he was the one they were looking for if he was working with them?"

"Like I said, it's all speculation at this point," said Justin.

"But think about it," said Johnson. "If he told them that he was somebody else and they didn't know differently and then he told them that one of you was him, how would they know if they'd never met him? He knew that and he used it to his advantage. He thought he'd stopped you from chasing him and them from chasing him, all at once."

"I guess that makes sense," said Matthew. "But wow, what a complete creep. What is O'Rourke wanted for in Nebraska and how did he get mixed up in this mess?"

"I can't discuss Nebraska except to say that it isn't related to this case," answered Johnson. "As for how he got mixed up in human trafficking, if you can find him ask him. We'd all like to know that."

"You haven't taken Danny Boy into custody?" asked Matthew incredulously.

"Nope," said Johnson.

"He's still MIA," said Justin.

"I had one last bit of information to track down that might lead me to *Playbuoy*, the yacht that he was traveling around in, but I hadn't made that contact yet. A sea captain who also might have been piloting the yacht at some point might know where it's usually docked. But your people talked to him, didn't they?"

"They did, but he had no information on O'Rourke, Rubio, or Danny Boy. He claimed to know no one by any of those names."

"*Playbuoy* has already been found in a slip at the Bayshore Marina at South Beach," said Johnson. "There was no sign of O'Rourke or any indication that he planned to return to the yacht. There was nothing personal aboard at all. It had been thoroughly sanitized. You might well have been the last person to see him, other than your colleague Dr. Rob who was apparently drugged up and then knocked out cold right after he was snatched, to see him," added Johnson.

"You've talked to Dr. Rob?" asked Matthew.

"Very briefly just before I got here," said Johnson. "I just came from the hospital. He could tell us a few things about his captors, including verifying that they weren't American. The language he overheard them speaking to each other, during the brief time that he was lucid between drug doses, wasn't one that he recognized."

"And his daughter," continued Johnson. "She was able to give us first names for the other three women in the container and verify that the one who is deceased was not an American and spoke limited English. They think that she was Polish and also snatched from one of the Caribbean islands. She was apparently the first one moved to the container, which explains why she was in the worst shape and didn't make it out alive."

"Adrianna," said Matthew quietly. "I think Ariel called her Adrianna." Johnson nodded in affirmation.

After a moment of contemplation and sadness, Matthew asked, "You said they were moved to the container?"

"From what we're able to piece together, the women weren't supposed to be in the container there at all," said Justin. "When the contact who was to pick them up didn't show up, somebody panicked and didn't know what to do with them. They were supposed to be picked up and taken to a hotel where they'd be cleaned up from the drugs and made up to be presentable. Then they'd be videotaped for the dark web buyers who would review the tapes and choose. There was still a market for them out there somewhere, and we think the people who dropped them off were trying desperately to find it to make the money they were promised by the people who didn't pick them up. Money from the sale of the women," he added with a sour look.

"Ah," said Matthew. "Their plan didn't initially include killing the women."

"We don't think so, no," said Johnson. "But I'm not sure about that because I was originally assigned to the drug and weapon operation. Those were moving around inside the country, coming in and going out, and we were trying to track that movement. That operation just crossed paths with the human trafficking and then we discovered that they were linked and all being shipped by some of the same people."

"Until it was disrupted," summarized Matthew.

"I'm not sure how it all happened yet, but I guess we'll figure it out. Eventually," said Johnson, and then asked Justin, "Where are you off to next?"

"I'll be up and out early in the morning, back to DC," Justin responded. "You can sleep in as long as you'd like," he added to Matthew. "Room checkout is automatic, so you can leave whenever you're ready."

Sipping the last of his beer, Justin set the glass mug down on the table. That motion apparently caught the attention of both Teddy and Rex, who declared that Justin needed another and set about providing a list of ridiculous reasons why they thought this was true, laughing hysterically at the reasons and effectively ending all serious conversation.

As Matthew pondered all that he'd learned, he decided that most of the tangle of confusion had been explained, at least all of it that was known and that he could know, and that left him with just a couple of things that he wanted to do before returning home to North Carolina.

30 ~ UNFINISHED BUSINESS

When Matthew awoke the next morning to the annoying noise of the alarm on his phone, Justin was, as he'd said, long gone. Matthew had a vague recollection of him stirring in the room sometime before it was light out but he'd mostly slept through it and easily sunk back into a deep sleep. He had never understood how Justin managed to be coherent so early in the morning and without coffee. In this case particularly after having stayed up so late the night before and having had more to drink than he himself had.

Coffee, Matthew thought, and that was the motivating force that caused him to prop up in bed and then pivot around to get his feet on the floor. His quick dry shirt, which he far preferred over the Miami shirt he'd slept in, he noted, had lived up to its name again and was dry on the back of the chair where he'd hung it after washing it and wringing it out in the sink late the night before. Technically early that morning, he corrected himself.

After a long hot shower, Matthew slipped his wallet and cell phone into his pockets and then picked up his backpack and stuffed in the Miami t-shirt, thinking he'd find someone who could use it, and left the room. He took the elevator down to the lobby where he found hot coffee, which he loaded with sugar and cream, and croissants, two of which he loaded with eggs, bacon, and a slice of cheese.

Matthew texted Lanie to learn that she had gone back to Hialeah. He kept his promise to go pick her up without telling her that he was much closer to the hospital and that Hialeah was very much out of his way. When he finally arrived there, some long time later in the heavy

Miami traffic, Lanie was waiting for him with more bags, though this time they were stuffed with shoes and clothing for Anna and Pedro. She sweetly asked if Matthew would take them to the children under the bridge because she wanted to go immediately to Ariel and spend the day with her.

"We started trying to detangle her hair last night so that she could take a shower and wash it," explained Lanie. "But I forgot her leave-in conditioner so we'll probably still have a little work to do on it today. She has such long thick hair!"

"OK, sure, we can do that. I want to see her and Gavin at the hospital this morning anyway, but I just have one errand to run first," he said.

"Oh," said Lanie, not hiding her disappointment well over the delay.

"But it's something I could really use your help with," he added.

"OK, sure," she said. "What do you need?"

"To find the smart phone store closest to the hospital down there. Or at least one on the way."

"Ohhhh," she said and brightened considerably at the prospect.

Lanie expertly guided him to the store and she was thrilled to help him pick out a phone and then a flashy case with a pop out holder on it for Ariel. "It's sort of like what she had before," she explained.

Matthew picked a sleek black one for Dr. Rob and explained the situation about the phones having been stolen or destroyed. He asked the store clerk to activate the new ones with the numbers that he and Lanie provided and deactivate the old ones.

"Hmm," said the clerk. "I can't really do that without the account owners' permission."

Matthew explained that the owners were currently hospitalized, after having been drugged, abducted, and nearly killed, and that they had no identification to be able to come into the store and prove their identities anyway.

"But they know the account information," said the clerk. "We can switch the phones over if they log into their account with that information but not without it. They'd have to log in and authorize it."

"I know the account information," Lanie pipped up. "Ariel is an administrator on their account. Can I do it?"

The young clerk screwed up her face, consulted a store manager, and then returned and agreed. Lanie happily typed the information into a tablet provided by the clerk, the phones were activated and the content from the original phones downloaded from where it had been backed up in the cloud. Matthew and Lanie tested both of them before leaving the store and Lanie was all smiles, thanking Matthew for thinking of and making that purchase.

Matthew fought the traffic through the remaining bit of the trip back to Grace Hospital, where he parked and they made their way back up to Room 345. As the hair detangling effort got underway, Matthew handed Dr. Rob his phone and explained that the content from his old one had been pulled down from the cloud and it was current from whenever the last time Dr. Rob had updated it.

"It updated automatically," said Dr. Rob, adding his profuse thanks and a promise to pay Matthew back for the phones, the hotel, the rental cars, and any other expenses he'd incurred on the trip down. "I owe you so much," he said, looking over at his daughter.

"No, you don't," said Matthew. "I know you. If this whole mess were reversed, you'd do it for me," and before Dr. Rob could argue further, he added, "I guess there are no other numbers that you need to schedule that helicopter then?"

"What helicopter?" asked Ariel, alarmed, apparently having overheard at least that bit of the conversation.

"Your dad's not leaving if you won't go home with him, and you're not leaving without Gavin going home with you, and he can't fly any other way yet," explained Matthew. "I figure your dad can make a few calls, maybe just one if Steven Garner wants us back there quickly, and he'll ask a few favors and get a Life Flight down here to take Gavin back to North Carolina."

Dr. Steven Garner, the senior-most partner in their family practice in Peak, had long been known for his connections. Dr. Rob had mentioned seeing that connectedness when he was traveling with Dr. Garner to conferences and said that Steven Garner was better connected in the medical field than anyone else he'd ever known. Dr.

Garner had chosen to practice medicine in Peak because he liked the small-town atmosphere to raise his family, not because he couldn't have moved anywhere he wanted to live and been invited into other practices with open arms.

"The best hospitals around are in the Raleigh area anyway," agreed Dr. Rob. "Duke is close."

"What about Gayle?" asked Ariel. "You'll need to consult her and she'll need a place to stay nearby. She can't commute from the mountains and it sounds like Gavin will be in hospital recovery for a while. Speaking of which, when can I go up to see him?"

"We'll figure that out," said Dr. Rob. "Maybe she can stay with your grandmother. I can call her and ask. Matthew's gotten word to her that we're OK, but I need to call her myself anyway now that I have a phone and I can. She's on the right side of Raleigh, a lot closer than Peak. But if it comes down to it, Gayle can stay with us. We'll just need to explain very thoroughly that I'm dating someone and it's purely a platonic arrangement. If she'll accept that and stop with the flirting, she can stay with us."

Dr. Rob was aware of it, thought Matthew, and then he added aloud, "I might have a few ideas on where she could stay too. But don't worry about it, we'll work that out. If it's OK with your dad, I'll go find a wheelchair and Lanie can take you up to see Gavin."

Dr. Rob nodded and Matthew slipped down to the nurses' station to make the request. He was met with a bit of resistance initially but then he explained that they'd have to sit on the young woman to keep her from going to find her boyfriend. If they'd rather she go in a wheelchair he told them, then they'd better find her one. The nurse nodded and said she'd have an aid bring one as soon as possible.

As he walked back into the room, Matthew overheard Lanie telling Ariel that Marianna Martinez, the site Director of the Hialeah and Little Havana Ministerios de Conexiones Saludables, was going to start working with the children under the bridge and she'd collected clothing and shoes for Anna and Pedro.

Ariel was clearly delighted with this news and Matthew used it as his excuse to slip out and do the last few things he wanted to before leaving Miami. "Lanie brought the bags with her and they're out in the car. I'm going to take them to Anna and Pedro next."

"When you're ready to book the flights, we can use my credit card," Matthew turned to Dr. Rob. "I know you'll have to have yours reissued and we flew down one-way. I'll check with Danbury and see if we can all go back together when you arrange the helo to take Gavin up."

"Thanks, Matthew, for everything."

"Sure. Just text me those arrangements and I'll check in with Danbury. I need to find him and talk to him today anyway. My parents might be able to house Gayle and they're in North Raleigh, much closer to Duke too. They've always welcomed people into their home, my friends and my sisters' friends, growing up, and anyone else who needed the temporary haven. Just let me know if your mom is up for it and I'll ask them."

As Matthew slipped out and headed for the elevator, Lanie passed him pushing Ariel down the hallway in a wheelchair. Both of them were beaming as they waved and thanked him again, but they didn't pause in their journey. Matthew thought about first love and Cici popped immediately into his mind. She hadn't FaceTimed him this morning and neither had he contacted her, he thought, vowing to fix that after he'd accomplished the final things he needed to do before leaving Miami. He could tell her at that point when he'd be returning home.

Finding his way out of the hospital and locating the rental car in the parking deck, Matthew wound his way back through the Miami traffic to Dock Side. He parked the car in the usual spot but realized, annoyed, that he had to register yet another vehicle as he pulled out his phone and pulled up the PayByPark app.

He planned to order a pizza and soft drinks and then ask for ice to take to Anna and Pedro when he took them the bags of clothing and shoes, so he pulled the bags and his medical backpack from the car, but he headed for Dock Side first. He entered through the main entrance, then turned to the right, skipped the bar area initially and headed for the food trucks to place the pizza order. After he'd ordered the pizza, he turned to see Courtney DeBerry, the bartender who had helped him find Danny Boy initially, standing at his end of the long bar with her back to the customers. She was motioning him over with one hand surreptitiously down in front of her while she held the finger of the other hand to her lips in warning.

When Matthew approached, she whispered, "Danny Boy is back. He's down at the other end of the bar, high as a kite on something and bragging about the women he's abducted and how his friends have police officers in their pockets and no one can touch him."

Matthew glanced carefully around her to see the other end of the bar, though he no longer needed her to point the guy out to him. He'd seen him up close and more personally than he'd have cared to very recently. The guy was brazen, Matthew thought, to show back up here like this, high or not, as if nothing had happened. But maybe from his perspective, nothing had. If he'd traded Dr. Rob off in his place, then he probably thought that the thugs he'd been working with presumed him to be dead.

"I just called your friend to tell him," she said quietly.

"My friend?"

"You know, the big guy. The one I knew was a cop from the other end of the bar, the guy who was in here the other night looking for him right before you found him. He left his card and asked me to call if I saw him, so I did."

"Ah, Danbury," said Matthew.

"Yeah, Warren Danbury," she answered. "That's the name on the card. I didn't get him, but I left him a voice message."

"Huh," said Matthew, wondering if Danbury was still in possession of his cell phone or if he'd ditched it and the message was just waiting out there in cyberspace somewhere. "Thanks Courtney. Can I leave this here for just a minute?" he asked indicating the bags and his backpack. As she nodded, he slid out of the backpack and put it all on the end of the bar.

"I appreciate it," he said quietly to her as he began to wander, trying to look nonchalant, down to the other end of the bar and up behind Daniel O'Rourke.

As Courtney had said, the guy was talking loudly to anyone who would listen and he was obviously strung out on something. Matthew lingered behind him to listen in briefly and, much to his disbelief and complete disgust, the guy was bragging about all of the women he'd seduced and about the friends he had inside the police force so that nobody could touch him for drugging and basically raping the women.

The anger that had been at a slow boil began to rise up in Matthew. Anger against this guy, the two he had overheard talking about the women in the container who "didn't look too good" not being "their problem," and the human trafficking operation in general. This guy in particular made Matthew's blood boil for taking both Ariel and Dr. Rob at gunpoint, apparently swapping Dr. Rob for himself and thinking that he was untouchable, the shape that Ariel had been in, the shape that Gavin was still in, the two other women who were currently fighting for their lives in the nearby hospital, the two who had been murdered. All of it came roiling to the surface as he tapped the guy, none too gently, on the shoulder.

Danny Boy turned to face Matthew's chest and then he looked up slowly into his face, which was most definitely an angry one. At first he looked confused but then as recognition dawned, his eyes bulged.

"I hear you've been talking about the friends you've made on the police force and the women that you've abducted down here. The three redheads, just for starters, two of whom have turned up dead," said Matthew, menacingly through clenched teeth, his hands also clenched into fists by his side. The fury that was boiling up through him was palpable. In that moment, he didn't care. His careful self-control was missing in action and in its place was an anger he'd rarely felt in his life, rage for the harm this one man had caused at least three women, the lives he'd wrecked in the process, and the audacity that he had to be bragging about all of it.

"Yeah," the guy said, looking a bit worried about having to explain it to Matthew. "I snatched all three. But I didn't kill them! I had no idea any of them would be killed when I handed them over!"

"What did you think was going to happen to these women when you took them and drugged them, O'Rourke?" demanded Matthew.

"I," stammered the man Matthew had come to know as Danny Boy but who looked yet more concerned that Matthew knew the name he'd gone by previously, whether his real name or not Matthew didn't know and he didn't really care. "I didn't know. I didn't really think about it," the guy stammered, looking truly alarmed now at Matthew towering over him.

"And you HAD friends on the police force. The dirty cops have been detained. They're currently under investigation," added Matthew.

As the color drained from the guy's face, Matthew could contain the anger no longer and he reached in and punched him, an uppercut to the gut that dropped the guy to his knees. What Matthew hadn't seen, just as he was letting Daniel O'Rourke drop to the cement flooring, was Danbury's approach from behind.

"I've got this," Danbury said quietly into Matthew's ear from behind. "And I saw nothing."

Kneeling down beside him, Danbury checked his pulse, pulled cuffs from his belt and cuffed the guys' hands behind his back. As the guy started to struggle, Matthew watched Danbury haul him to his feet and start to Mirandize him.

"Do you understand your rights as I have explained them to you?" he asked. Only after Danny Boy nodded in agreement did Danbury say loudly to the crowd that had gathered, "Nothing to see here, folks. Go back to your drinks."

"I'll need you to come down to the station. And make a sworn statement. About how you saw this guy abduct Dr. Richard Roberts. At gunpoint," he added to Matthew.

"I'd be happy to," said Matthew, as the anger abated. He knew he'd regret the violence he'd just perpetuated against another human being later. In that moment he felt that he'd begun the vindication process. For at least two lives lost, two more hanging in the balance, and multiple others that would be recovering from the trauma, potentially for many years to come.

"I'm not too welcome there at the moment," said Danbury, "but I'll face that to hand this guy over." Danbury said nothing further as he hauled Danny Boy, none too gently, out to his rented SUV that Matthew could see waiting at the curb directly outside the entrance.

Feeling his phone vibrate in his pocket, Matthew pulled it out to see a text from Dr. Rob telling him that Ariel would be released the next day, on Sunday, and that he had secured the Life Flight to get Gavin back home to North Carolina. His mom, he said, would be delighted to have a house guest and Gayle was on board with the whole plan.

"Hey Danbury," Matthew called, walking out to the street behind him. "Are you free to fly home tomorrow? We'll be life flighting Gavin back to North Carolina and the rest of us can fly home together if we can all get tickets."

"I'll be free," said Danbury. "I'm beyond ready. To get back to North Carolina."

"OK, I'll make the flight reservations and text you the details. I've got one last thing to do before I can meet you at the station and give that statement."

"Fair enough," said Danbury, as he got into the SUV and cranked it up.

Matthew turned back to Dock Side one last time, amazed that it hadn't even been a week since he'd first entered it and the whole nightmare had begun. The final thing he wanted to do was to deliver the pizza, two drinks, an icepack, and the clothes and shoes to Anna and Pedro.

As he approached the bar, he could see the incredulous look on Courtney's face as he asked if she had an icepack handy.

"For your hand?" she asked.

"My hand?"

"I saw you punch him," she said. "I've wanted to do that so many times. It was cathartic just to see you do it. I'll be sure that any video coverage of that gets mysteriously erased somehow."

"Thanks," he said, realizing that he'd momentarily forgotten there were cameras everywhere in this place and thinking that perhaps another less obvious method for taking the guy down would have been better. Maybe slipping his arm around the guy, as he'd seen him do to Dr. Rob, and grabbing him by the side of the neck, applying pressure to the carotid artery, enough to knock him out cold, but not enough to kill him. Maybe that would have been a better approach. He'd learned the technique as a teenager when he'd gotten his black belt in Tae Kwondo, but as a physician, he'd never thought he'd ever use it. And he probably wouldn't, he thought.

"No, not for my hand," he said to Courtney. "That guy was pure mush in the middle. I want the ice pack to take to Pedro."

"Oh," she laughed.

"Hey, do you speak Spanish?"

"Si," she said. "Hablo español con fluidez."

He wasn't sure what she'd said after the "si," but that was all that he'd really needed to know.

"When do you go on break again?"

Looking around, she said, "I don't have another one, but things are pretty quiet right now before the lunch rush. What do you need?"

"Someone to come and tell Anna and Pedro that they can trust Marianna Martinez, the director of a ministry in Hialeah and Little Havana who will be coming to work with them, checking on Pedro's foot, and providing a healthcare worker to remove his stitches in a couple of weeks if all is healing well."

"I can do that," she said. "Are you sure that's all you need?" she added, clearly flirting with him and, thanks to Danbury's girlfriend Penn back home in Peak pointing it out to him earlier, he recognized it now.

"It is," he said. "I'm heading home tomorrow. I just want to be sure that these children are taken care of and that they know it before I go."

"Oh," she said, clearly disappointed.

"If you can get the ice pack together, I'll go get the pizza and drinks that I ordered for them," he added, picking up the backpack. "These bags are for them too. Shoes and clothing and maybe a sheet or blanket or two," he said, realizing that he hadn't looked to see exactly what they contained.

"OK, sure," she said. "You know, I didn't like you much the first time I met you but you've grown on me. I'm sorry that you're leaving."

At this, he leaned over on the bar and smiled at her, his genuine warm smile. With an eyebrow raised said, "Just so you know, I don't usually go around punching people. In fact, outside of sparring in the Tae Kwondo classes I had as a kid, that was a first. OK, maybe a second," added Matthew ruefully remembering an encounter with a corrupt guy who claimed to be a lawyer and who had pulled a gun on Matthew and shot Penn the month before.

That encounter had not ended well for the lawyer and it had forced Matthew to do nearly the same thing to him. He really needed to step back from his role as a medical consultant for the Raleigh Police Department, he thought, at least for a little while. He definitely needed a break. He wasn't normally a violent person at all and he'd taken a Hippocratic Oath to do no harm. He'd have to deal with all of that later. He knew that he would.

"Noted," she said as she returned the smile and then turned to the ice machine to fix the requested ice pack.

OK, he thought, he was flirting with her just a little bit. Should he be concerned, he wondered? Was it just the after effects of the adrenaline that had been coursing through him about ten minutes previously? Matthew wasn't entirely certain as he walked back to the pizza vendor to collect his large cheese pizza and two Sprites, but it was irrelevant, he thought, because he was flying home the next day and he'd FaceTime Cici before he went to the police station to give his statement.

After collecting the pizza and drinks he and Courtney walked out of Dock Side and up the sidewalk together to deliver those, the bags of shoes and clothing, and the news that Anna and Pedro would be cared for after Matthew left.

They passed numerous people as they made their way to the far end of the rows of makeshift housing and reached the pod that Anna and Pedro occupied. Matthew saw Courtney start to say something but he held up his hand and said, "I've got this part."

Walking to the entrance of the pod, Matthew called out, "Pizza!"

As two dark heads popped out of the tent, Matthew said, "Hola, Anna. Hola Pedro."

After a meaningful nod to her, Courtney began translating the information about the clothing and shoes and that Marianna Martinez would be checking on Pedro's foot. Matthew knew that after a trip to the downtown police station to provide his statement about Daniel

O'Rourke, he would be finished with everything that he needed to do in Miami and he'd finally be heading to his solace in Peak, North Carolina. That couldn't come too soon, he thought.

EPILOGUE ~ THREE WEEKS LATER

Matthew was more content than he'd been in months as he backed his Corvette out of the garage of his condo on a bright sunny Monday morning in July. He'd moved back into his condo after the repairs were completed the weekend before.

Along with Max, Matthew was happily settling back into his quiet and peaceful life, having had more than enough excitement in Miami to last him for a while. In some ways it was as if they'd never left, though his great room was bare except for two folding chairs and a desk in the corner that hadn't been damaged by the fire from the Molotov cocktail that had been lobbed through his window a couple of months before.

Having tacked a blanket above the front windows, he was thankful that the smoke hadn't reached the back of his house because he'd managed to close off his bedroom. He still had blankets. He figured he'd eventually get around to buying furniture to replace the soft buttercream leather sofa, matching chair, ottoman, and area rug that had been destroyed along with his curtains.

Pausing momentarily on his way out of his neighborhood, he pulled alongside Mrs. Drewer, his neighbor who was out for her morning walk with her Pomeranian, Oscar. She had helped him throughout the restoration of his condominium and he thanked her, yet again, for all of it.

As he drove the short distance up Highway 20, across the railroad tracks, and into the downtown of Peak, it was as if he were seeing it through newly appreciative eyes. Miami could have been on a different planet as far removed as everything about it was from Peak. Never again would he complain about the traffic because the little town had grown and sprawled with new subdivisions and lots of people who had migrated down from northern states to work in the popular triangle area.

The new Physician's Assistant, Megan Sims, and her protégé, Sadie Peterson, the resident she'd brought with her, had proven to be worth their weight in gold as they'd been willing to step in more quickly than they'd planned and fill in for Matthew and Dr. Rob while they were away. The population of the little town had grown exponentially, Matthew thought, and hiring Megan and perhaps Sadie after her was a smart move on Dr. Garner's part.

After arriving back in Peak, Ariel had declared her intention to go to medical school and then apply to Doctors Without Borders. She was a tough young woman. He'd give her the credit due her – to have walked away unbroken from the ordeal she'd been put through with renewed determination to help people and to provide medical care for those most in need of it.

She was helping Gayle every evening with Gavin's care and rehabilitation as he was having to retrain his brain to walk and perform fine motor skills. Ariel had enough determination for both of them, Matthew had heard from Dr. Rob, so there was no quitting or giving up on Gavin's part. She simply wouldn't allow him to think about it as an option.

Ariel would be shadowing physicians at his practice for the rest of the summer during the daytime hours and, after spending the week with Megan Sims the week before, she would be joining Matthew on his rounds with his patients this week. He chuckled to himself as he remembered that the first patient of the day would be Mr. Waller, his geriatric patient who desperately needed hearing aids but who refused any such notion and vehemently denied any deficiency in his hearing.

Matthew parked the Corvette in his favorite spot in the corner of his office parking lot under the edge of trees that would provide afternoon shade, grabbed his satchel, and slid out of the car. Today in Peak, North Carolina, was supposed to be a scorcher for July.

He had to chuckle at that notion as he entered his office building through the back entrance. He figured it would always pale in comparison to the heat and humidity in Miami. The temperature range was the biggest difference in the two places. The daytime and nighttime temperature variability wasn't as disparate in Miami as it was most of the time in Peak. The cooler overnight lows in North Carolina made the mornings more bearable as the day hadn't heated up yet, he thought, as he let himself into his office.

Pulling his computer from his satchel and checking his schedule, stashing the satchel in his bottom desk drawer, and donning his lab coat, he stepped from his office into the hallway. There, he found Ariel already waiting for him. Her warm smile he knew was just for him as he'd gained the status of a family member and she thought of him as her long-lost uncle. Flattered by the family inclusion, he gave her a quick hug and said with a wink, "This morning, you're going to get a big dose of medical patience."

He quickly gave her the background on their first patient as they headed down the hallway. "We start the day with Mr. Waller," he told her. And then he added quietly. "As Gladys says, he's as deaf as a post and twice as stubborn." Gladys, his most trusted nurse, rarely minced words. "Dealing with the first patient today will be a bit of a shouting match. Mr. Waller is eighty-seven-years-old but insists that he does not need hearing aids. He comes in periodically with sinus issues but he refuses to have his hearing tested."

They greeted Gladys and Mr. Waller loudly as they entered the exam room and Matthew introduced Ariel. After he'd thoroughly examined the elder gentleman, he prescribed an antibiotic for the infection, which he clearly did have. Then Matthew asked if Mr. Waller had any questions about picking up or taking the medication. After the third attempt, Mr. Waller said, "Ain't this the one I've had for sinus infections before?"

"Yes," yelled Matthew. "It's the same one."

"Then I'm fine with it."

"OK, great. But, Mr. Waller, you've had a lot of sinus infections lately. I'd like you to come back for a recheck in two weeks when you've finished the antibiotic. I want to recheck you to be sure the infection has cleared up. And I want to check your hearing."

Clearly annoyed by this news, the older patient responded, "What for? There's nothing wrong with my rear. I've got sinus congestion."

Matthew admired both Gladys and Ariel, neither of whom laughed aloud at this. It was all that Matthew could do not to laugh aloud.

"No sir," Matthew yelled to him. "What I said was that I want to check your HEARING!"

"Oh," Mr. Waller said. "Well, I can save you the trouble. That works just fine!"

*****

Want more Matthew Paine mystery?

Everyone is dying to attend the Christmas gala given by Cici's prestigious law firm—the event of the season—until one of the hosts turns up that way. Dead, that is. When a doctor is urgently summoned, Matthew rushes to help. But he's too late to save the victim. Join Matthew as he tries to keep he and Cici alive for Christmas in <u>Christmas Punch</u>, next in the Matthew Paine Classic Mystery series.

Get the next book in the series

Get <u>Christmas Punch</u>, the fourth in the series, from your local bookstore or all major online retailers.

Start from the beginning

Download the short story prequel, *Pre Kill*, for free!

Get *Dead Spots*, the first in the Matthew Paine classic mystery series.

Be in the know!

<u>Join the author group</u> to get all the latest updates on new releases, events, giveaways, and more!

Acknowledgments

My most sincere thanks to Ken Dunning who provided a full description of how the abduction process works, and to Robert Johnston who graciously supplied the nautical information.

Also, my heartfelt thanks to Genie Clark and Dorothy Whitley, my fearless editors who take on the difficult job of keeping me straight. Bill Payne, my graphics guru, seems to be able to create anything I can dream up, so my most heartfelt thanks to him, too!

About the Author

Lee Clark is a coffeeholic and dark chocoholic who resides in North Carolina with spouse, two mostly grown children who are in and out, and a dwindling petting zoo of geriatric dogs and cats.

A North Carolina native, Clark is originally from Raleigh, with family roots in Virginia. Clark attended Campbell University, obtained a degree in journalism from East Carolina University, and then obtained a master's in technical communication from North Carolina State University. After working in the software technology industry for over twenty years, creating and building highly technical user information for software developers, Clark decided it was time to pursue a true passion: fiction writing.

Matthew Paine is a fictional character, though inspired by two very important men in the author's life, brother Sean and son Will. Both will see characteristics of themselves in the character and identify with some of Matthew's struggles.